A Dangerous Daughter

Based on a True Story

Dina Davis

Cover and book design by Evan Shapiro

Typeset by Green Avenue Design

Author photo by Arlo Davis Steinberg

ISBN: 978-0-6451758-1-3

Published by Cilento Publishing, Sydney, Australia
Member of the Small Press Network

This title has been published through the *Authors First* initiative,
an exclusive program run by Cilento Publishing for quality works
of literary fiction submitted by invitation.

A catalogue record for this
book is available from the
National Library of Australia

Disclaimer

This is a work of fiction. While *A Dangerous Daughter* is based on
the author's early life, names, characters, and incidents are either the
products of the author's imagination or used in a fictitious manner.

Praise for Capriccio: A Novel

Thomas Keneally, Booker Prize Winning author of 'Schindler's Ark'

I think this is a fine evocation with barely a false note. I was fascinated by this work and its crisp style. Let me reiterate: I believe you have an interesting and world-wide engaging book here. I think you'll ring a bell.

Garth, Alperstein, author of The Fourpenny Axe and a Snooker Cue (Ginninderra Press)

A sensuous and beautifully crafted story about three prominent poets. The author's writing ability does justice to the literary subjects. The characters are deftly drawn through skilful dialogue which offers profound psychological insight into their complex natures. The novel flows effortlessly and draws you on to the riveting end.

Eilat Negev and Yehuda Koren, authors of Lover of Unreason, the biography of Assia Gutmann Wevill

Just finished reading *Capriccio*. It was so heartbreaking to see Assia from a distance, through your eyes. The liberty you took from the documented facts was reasonable, and it was evidently a labour of love on your part. We congratulate you on getting to this end of the long, and no doubt sometimes frustrating journey.

Kaye Aldenhoven, Poet

Most relevant in Davis' novel is the randomness of fate, and the capriciousness of events. Themes of WW2, The Holocaust and anti-Semitism sustain the narrative. Emotional complexity is elegantly and empathetically developed by Davis, while she miraculously avoids mush. – *'Imprint' 2018, Journal of the NT Writers' Centre*

John S, Holocaust Survivor

My dad just finished *Capriccio*. He finished it in one night because he couldn't put it down. He said it had everything – jealousy, heartbreak, revenge, every emotion. He found it such a powerful book. The emotions are still with him– *Yvette, John's daughter*.

5 star review on Amazon

A gripping read. This beautifully written work covers so much ground: love, literature, abuse, religion, and the struggle for identity. I found it gripping and poignant, especially knowing the true stories of Sylvia Plath, Ted Hughes and Assia Wevill. –*Michaela, reader*

The author gratefully acknowledges the Gadigal people of the Eora Nation, and the Larrakia people, their elders past, present and emerging, upon whose land this novel was written.

Dedicated to my sisters, Dr Golda Lieberman and Norelle Robyn Ginges, (neither of whom are Laura), and to my children Justine Ruth, Joshua Saul and Anne Michaela.

Psychoanalysis is in essence a cure through love.

– Sigmund Freud in a letter to Carl Jung, 1906

CONTENTS

PART 1: RESCUED AND ABANDONED

1949 to 1954

One day, in retrospect, the years of struggle will strike you as the most beautiful.

– Freud, Sigmund in *The Letters of Sigmund Freud* ed. Ernst L Freud

1. BEFORE

It all starts with the gefilte fish.

'It's a witch's house,' Ivy whispers to Laura. They're standing with Mum and Daddy at the front door of a small house with a pointed roof. From inside the sound of footsteps is getting louder. The door opens and there stands Aunt Betsy, wearing a floral apron over her dress, and a string of pearls around her plump neck. She has a soft body, a round-cheeked face, and a faint moustache, clearly discernible under the light. Ivy nudges Laura, hoping she can see it too.

'Abe and Lily Morgenstern! At last – we're about to start. And I see you've brought the kiddies with you.'

A strong fishy aroma envelops them as soon as they step into the dimly lit hall. It wreaths up Ivy's nostrils from somewhere in the bowels of the house, like an evil ghost's breath. Ivy holds her breath so she won't smell it. Laura whimpers.

'Quiet, girls, and say *Good Yom Tov* to Aunt Betsy.' Daddy is using his visitor's voice. To Ivy's horror, Aunt Betsy leans down and envelops her in a fishy hug. The squeeze forces Ivy to let her breath out and the horrid smell in. When it is five-year-old Laura's turn to be squeezed, she wriggles away and clings to Mum's legs.

'So kind of you, Bess, to have us all to your *Seder*,' says Mum with a nervous smile. 'With my family far away in Perth, we'd have been all on our own. Here, I've bought my hazelnut cake. It's *kosher* for *Pesach* – I made it this morning.'

'Now Lily, you shouldn't have, you naughty girl. Come on in, all of you. The Jacobsens are here, and so are the Finkels. Their boy Simon is around Ivy's age – nine, isn't she?'

'No I'm not, I'm only eight. Won't be nine till the fifth of October.' *Why can't this not-really-relation talk to me, instead of to Mum and Daddy?*

'Is that so, little Miss? Well, that's even better. We might see a *shidduch* between young Simon and your Ivy one day.' Aunt Betsy winks at Daddy, and ignores Ivy. 'Cousin Ruth's been here all day helping. Come on, children, come and meet the other kiddies. Leah and Joe got a babysitter for their little ones – so considerate of them.'

Ivy detects nastiness in Aunt Betsy. Were she and Laura not supposed to come? Should her parents have got a babysitter? She glances up at Mum, and can tell from the way her lips are pressed together that she too had noticed Aunt Betsy's careless insult.

Down the dim hall they walk, the fishy smell getting stronger with every step. Ivy thinks she might throw up, and swallows hard to stop it. Laura runs ahead towards the chatter of children. Mum follows Ivy, giving her a slight push, and carrying the hazelnut cake with care. Daddy is unusually silent, but Ivy hears a great sigh from him, as they enter the crowded dining room. It is filled almost from corner to corner with a long table covered in a white lacy cloth. Silver candlesticks stand in the centre of the table, waiting for the candles to be lit. Guests, most of whom Ivy has never seen before, are already taking their seats.

After saying *Good Yom Tov* to all the cousins and aunts and uncles and the cousins' cousins, the four of them squeeze around the table. It turns out to be three tables put together to seat twenty people. Ivy finds herself next to her putative future husband Simon, who immediately sticks out his tongue at her. The room is full of chatter, until Aunt Betsy lights the candles. Because she is a widow and head of her household, she intones the familiar Hebrew blessing, *baruch atoh adonai eloheinu*.

Ivy is starving, despite the smell which lingers. She would have to put her hunger on hold; there's the long service to get through, with each person at the table taking a turn to read aloud from the brightly illustrated *Haggadah*. Ivy got the bit about the sea parting so that Moses could lead his people to freedom. *How ridiculous*, thinks Ivy, *as if the ocean would cut itself in half to let some Hebrew slaves through.*

Being the youngest of the gathering, it's Laura's task to ask the traditional four questions in Hebrew. What does the wise son say? What does the simple son say? Despite having practiced the ancient Hebrew rhyme for weeks, Laura freezes and starts to cry. Ivy wants to get the whole thing over with. She recites the questions for Laura in perfect Hebrew, while Mum shushes Laura. *Why is it only the sons who asked these questions? Did the ancient Israelites have no daughters?* she thinks. The service seems to take forever, like the forty days and nights the Israelites had to spend in the desert with nothing to eat but *matzo*. Ivy's stomach is rumbling, and Laura starts to grizzle, 'Mum, I'm hungry.'

'Shush, dear, it's rude to complain. Aunt Betsy's gone to so much trouble.' As if on cue, Aunt Betsy bustles in from the kitchen. Ivy saw her pulling in her round stomach so she could squeeze past the guests trapped at the table. Small noises of protest come from Ivy's mother as she tries to get out of her chair, saying, 'I'm coming to help you, Betsy, let me dish out the soup.'

Mum flays about, stuck between Daddy on one side and Uncle Myer's thick thigh on the other. There is no room to move. Daddy is busy talking to a lady with very red lipstick who keeps laughing at his jokes, and Uncle Myer is lifting a forkful of chopped liver to his mouth. Neither shift their chairs for Mum. Ivy sees her mother's cheeks go pink, standing there helplessly as cousin Ruth brings bowl after bowl of steaming chicken soup to each guest. Ivy looks suspiciously at the dumpling floating in the greasy liquid, and decides not to eat it.

'Not as good as yours,' she hears Daddy whisper into Mum's ear. Mum looks like she's trying not to smile.

With an air of triumph, Aunt Betsy places a dish of whitish grey balls nestled in a jelly-like substance in the middle of the long table. Ivy holds her nose against the same smell that had accosted them at the front door. That night she learns how to hide the gefilte fish under a mound of red cabbage, so it would look like she'd eaten it all. It is a skill that will stand her in good stead in the future.

*

There is no greater crime in a Jewish family than not eating. Food is love. Food is sacrifice. And food is also a bargaining point. Right from infancy the Jewish child is told 'Eat!' for nothing would make a mother happier than to see the child of her belly grow strong and fat, a testament to her maternal success. Written in glowing red and gold letters on the stained glass of the synagogue window are the words: *A Woman of Worth is Beyond Rubies.* A mother's worth is measured in the bounty of her table, the increasing girth of her husband, and the rosy cheeks of her plump children.

From birth, Ivy has been a bitter disappointment to her mother. Not only was she scrawny and sallow as an infant, but also she refused to suck on the proffered breast, turning her head away in disgust. At six weeks she almost died in the great February heatwave, and they had to force water into her wailing mouth. At twelve months Ivy weighed the same as a six-month-old baby. It was enough to drive her mother to a nervous breakdown. And it did. Lily went to a sanitorium for her nerves, and Ivy was put into a special home for wayward babies.

Three years later Laura was born, and everything changed. At four years old, Ivy was pale and skinny, the runt of the litter. Laura was a chocolate box baby: rosy and chubby. She was hale and hearty from the moment of her birth. Laura sucked at her mother's breast enthusiastically, fulfilling something in Lily that Ivy could not. To both parents' delight, Laura's appetite is voracious. By the time Ivy is eight and Laura five, the girls are not very different in size. Laura has grown tall and strong, while Ivy stays small for her age. It makes her feel ashamed. Ivy fears she isn't Daddy's favourite any more.

Laura has glossy dark curls and deep brown eyes. Ivy's eyes are neither blue nor green, changing colour according to her moods, or the weather. 'Hazel' her mother calls them, but to Ivy that sounds wishy-washy. She wills them to turn blue, and to stay that way.

'Why can't you eat all your vegetables like Laura? Don't you want to grow big and strong?' Daddy says, frowning at Ivy while they have tea at the kitchen table. Mum says hardly anything, her gaze fixed with pleasure on her youngest daughter's fast emptying plate. Ivy tries to be a good eater like her sister, but her throat closes tight after a few mouthfuls of the hearty meals her mother cooks.

Mum makes crimson borscht, noodles with cream cheese, and on special occasions potato latkes and blintzes filled with cherry jam. Ivy likes the blintzes, the finely made pancakes enclosing a filling of cream cheese or cherry jam, but their appearance is a rare treat. Gradually the Viennese dishes her mum learned from her own mother give way to 'meat and three veg' in an effort to fit in with Australian suburbia. Ivy remains a picky eater while Laura gobbles up everything in front of her.

Even before The Voice begins to control her, Ivy feels afraid of the ooziness, stickiness, and formlessness of food. The thought of chewed morsels making their way from mouth to throat to stomach, and out again the other end, disgusts her. How could such revolting stuff transform inside her body into the cells that make her grow? Does she even want to grow?

*

Not long after the night of the gefilte fish, Ivy, Laura and Daddy are sitting at the breakfast table. Mum is standing at the kitchen bench, her hands busy buttering toast.

'Mum, please can I have my toast with the butter not soaked in?' Ivy asks every morning. The thought of slimy butter melting into toast revolts her. She's relieved they don't have to eat *matzo* any more, now that the Passover week is over.

Daddy's reading the paper, rustling the big pages in front of him. Ivy senses him go still. There is a chill in the air. He makes a sound like a choke, or a sob. She sees his face change into an angry mask.

'My God,' he says. His voice sounds weird.

'What is it, Abe?' Mum calls from the kitchen counter, butter knife mid-air.

'Take Laura out of the room. Now.'

'No, I don't want to! I'm staying here!' Laura's round face crumples as she's bundled out of the kitchen by her mother, kicking her stocky legs.

'Ivy, stay here. You're old enough now to understand,' Daddy says. 'I want you to see this.' His voice is low and shaking.

Ivy stands behind her father. The newspaper in front of him looks to her like a pattern of black and white dots. The double page starts to form into a grainy photograph. As she stares, shapes materialise into a pile of human skeletons, sprawled all over each other, some with mouths open as if frozen in horror, some face down on top of other bodies. What shocks Ivy most is their sticks of legs and arms, bones barely covered by skin stretched taut to breaking, skulls showing through shorn heads. It's hard to see which are men and which women, except for shrunken empty breasts on some and ugly dangly things between legs on others.

Daddy's mouth is grim, his eyes hard. 'You see what the Nazis did? I want you to remember this always, to know that these corpses are our people. The Nazis, those *momsas*, murdered them. Children too.' He is pointing at the grey and white picture, jabbing his finger at tiny dead bodies.

'But – why? Why would anyone want to kill children?'

'You want to know why? Because they were like you, Ivy, you and Laura, your mother and me. Do you realise this could have happened to us? If my parents hadn't left Europe, if you'd been born over there, instead of in this godforsaken country, we'd all have been murdered. Do you realise now what it means to be Jewish?'

He reaches out his hand and pulls Ivy so close to him she can smell his sweat. 'Look, and remember.'

Ivy doesn't want to look. She can't understand why her father would want her to see such a horrific scene. He holds her wrist so tightly it hurts. She sees tears in his eyes, and feels terror like a ball of fire in her stomach. She runs to the bathroom. The hot ball in her stomach rises to her throat, and she vomits violently into the ceramic bowl of the toilet.

2. IRINA

Ivy is practising her scales on the piano when she hears the doorbell ring. Mum, with her apron still on, opens the door to their visitors: a man about Ivy's father's age, but not as tall, and a small pretty woman wearing a close-fitting hat and a shabby gabardine coat. Standing behind them is a girl who looks a bit older than Ivy. She's tall and slender, with long shiny plaits and her mother's pretty face.

Mum speaks half in German, half in English. 'Lena! Oscar! *Ich heisse* Lily. *Bitte kommen* – out of the cold – *komm essen.*'

The girl stands staring at Ivy, who's left the piano and is standing behind her mother. The man steps forward, and reaches for Mum's hand. To Ivy's embarrassment, instead of shaking it, he raises it to his lips and very gently kisses it. Ivy shudders when he turns his attention to her. To her relief there is no hand kiss, only a beaming smile.

'This is my daughter, Irina,' the man says, resting his hands on the girl's shoulder. 'You must be Ivy. Abe has told me about you, he is very proud. And of your little sister too.' He has a strong accent and smells of cologne. His English is slow and careful. He puts his arm around his wife. 'You can call us Aunty Lena and Uncle Oscar.'

Ivy is not sure how to respond. She decides to try her school German. '*Willkommen. Wie heiss* – um – *heissen Sie?*'

The girl called Irina answers. 'How do you do,' she says carefully, as if she's rehearsed the greeting. Ivy realises she's made a mistake using German when it's probably a language the visitors want to forget. She smiles at Irina.

'Go on with your practice, Ivy, play that Chopin you learned last week,' her father says. Ivy wants to hide from so many eyes. The Chopin prelude is new, and difficult. Her hands are sweaty and shaky at the thought of playing in front of new people. She looks at Daddy.

'May we perhaps hear you play later?' says Aunty Lena. She has a strong accent, and her English is strangely formal. 'I remember how my students would perform much better when they are relaxing.' Ivy is inordinately grateful. She's sure this lovely woman, smelling of perfume and cigarettes, has read her mind.

'Yes, later,' says Mum. 'First we must eat.'

Laura runs into the dining room at the mention of food. She seems to have a radar, especially for the *kugelhöpf,* oozing with chocolate. Mum slices it into generous portions.

'This is Laura, our baby,' says Mum, as Laura plonks herself into the chair nearest the cake, and stretches out a plump hand.

'I see,' says the lady. 'May I ask, if you please, why you did give – gave – your two daughters such English names?'

Mum moves the cake out of Laura's reach. 'Not yet, pet, it's visitors first.' She turns to her visitor. 'Laura's second name is Elisheva, after my mother, may God rest her soul. Ivy's middle name is Aviva. We didn't want to give our children Hebrew first names after what happened to our people in the War, may God rest their poor souls. Even here, it could happen again.'

Ivy is still smarting from the feeling of being on show, and of disappointing Daddy. She half hears the adults, Oscar and Lena's accented speech, her mother's softer one, her father saying little. The visitors take their seats at the table. Visitors first, and ladies before gentlemen, these are the rules in the Morgenstern home. Laura, being family and youngest, is served last. She squeezes in next to Mum.

'Can't I have any cake yet?' she whines.

'As you can see, Laura enjoys her food, not like Ivy here, she eats like a bird,' Mum says, as she places a slice of *kugelhöpf* on everyone's plate. In a few seconds there are chocolate swirls decorating Laura's face, like the face painting she got for her fifth birthday.

Ivy is sitting opposite Irina. She's fascinated by this shy girl, with her old-fashioned clothes and quiet manner. She likes the sparkle in Irina's blue eyes, and the way a few curls escape from her shiny brown plaits.

'*Nu?* tell us, how are you settling in here?' Mum asks Aunt Lena.

'I was English teacher in Austria,' Aunt Lena replies, 'I try here to get same work, but it is not easy.'

'No indeed,' Oscar says. 'We must try to not speak in Yiddish, even here in this free country. We do not trust nobody – anybody. Of course we do exactly trust you, dear Abe and Lily.'

'It must have been unbearable for you.' Daddy sounds bitter. 'We can hardly believe the things we read in the papers, yet more and more people are arriving with shocking stories. It's unthinkable what those *momsas* did. Even little children were bashed to death in front of their parents. It's unthinkable.'

Abe's voice is breaking, his eyes wet. There's a charged silence around the table. Ivy sees again the newspaper, the twisted bodies piled in jagged layers, limbs splayed in contorted shapes. She hears his voice again. *You must never forget this.* The cake on Ivy's plate stays untouched.

Daddy has told Ivy that the whole of Irina's family was murdered by the Nazis. Because Irina has no grandparents, aunts, or cousins, and is quiet and pretty, Ivy wants very much to be her friend. Catching the girl's eye, Ivy suspects she feels the same, wanting to escape the adults. She addresses Irina for the first time.

'Do you like reading? I could show you my books.'

Before Irina can answer, Uncle Oscar says in a booming voice, 'My Irina's a sportswoman, so crazy she is on horses! As soon as we did come to this new country, so big, so empty, we promised Irina that here she will have a horse of her own. We're going to a special riding school on Thursday, where she can practice, and maybe, who knows, find a horse for her own.'

Irina jumps up from the table and hugs her father, planting a kiss on his whiskery cheek. There's a twinkle in his eye. The whole table draws a collective breath of relief at the change of subject. Ivy stands up and beckons to Irina, who smiles back. Ivy notices a dimple, like a secret comma, on Irina's pale cheek.

The girls walk single-file down the hall to Ivy's bedroom. They stop for a moment in the doorway. The gauze curtain at the window moves in the gentle breeze. A shiny white desk and matching bookshelves stand by a single bed with a puffy blue quilt.

'Ach, is so – so beautiful! The bed where you do sleep, and the – how you call it? Eiderdown?' Irina's blue eyes are wide with wonder.

'Do you know, that's a German word? I think it means duck feathers. I'm going to call it that from now on, instead of that boring word "quilt". Come, sit here,' Ivy pats the space beside her on the bed. 'I have a good idea. Why don't you help me with my German, and I can help you with English? Not that you need much help, though. But wouldn't it be fun?'

'I would love very much to do that,' Irina says, hugging Ivy. A stray curl brushes Ivy's cheek.

'We can use my German-English dictionary. Look, here are the books I told you about,' says Ivy, springing up from the bed and going to the bookshelves with their rows of volumes, some squeezed tightly together, others lying horizontally where there was no space on the shelf.

'So many you do have! And see – is here one in German!'

'Yes, that's *Das Wunderkind*, our German reader from last term. You can borrow it, if you like. We can talk about it next time you come to visit.'

'Really? So kind you are! *Danke schön!*' Irina takes the book from Ivy's hands and smooths its cover with reverence.

'I realised something,' Ivy says. 'Our names both start with 'I', so we're meant to be friends. And see? We even look a bit alike.' The girls stand together and stare into the oval mirror above Ivy's dressing table. 'Except for your blue eyes and my hazel ones, we could be sisters. We both have curly hair, except yours is golden brown, and mine's auburn. I wish it was as long as yours.' They make faces at each other in the mirror.

Irina laughs. 'One day, can we go to a beach together? I never did see a real beach in my country.'

'Of course we can! It'll be the school holidays soon. Let's go ask your parents.' They run down the hall.

'You must join us next Friday night for *shabbat,*' they hear Ivy's father saying. The two girls hug each other again.

*

The following Friday, Ivy wakes with a feeling that something is wrong. She can't shake it off through the day, not even in her favourite German lesson. At home that afternoon she helps set the table for *shabbat*. Mum tells her to use the good silver cutlery, and the crystal glasses they keep for best; she always makes everything perfect for visitors. The shiny *challah* with its twisted surface sits on a breadboard edged with silver.

Ivy's been thinking of Irina during the week, wondering how her riding adventure went, and planning a day on the beach during the school holidays. She pictures the two of them with their heads together, poring over her dictionary, learning new words from each other.

Mum sets the decanter of kosher wine on the white embroidered tablecloth. It's one of the few possessions that survived from the old country when Mum's parents arrived on a boat from Vienna before the war, penniless and stateless. The silver candlesticks gleam in the dying afternoon light. Ivy hears Daddy's key in the door. He ushers in a wintry gust, chilling the cosy warmth in the house. Laura and Ivy run to greet him. Ivy's first to bury her face in his greatcoat, with its smell of tobacco and cologne. He digs into his pocket, and pulls out two chocolate bars.

'*Shabbos* presents! But you can't eat them till after dinner.' 'Did you bring one for Irina too?' asks Ivy. 'H'mm, let me see … I must have forgotten,' Daddy says, his face serious.

He shrugs out of his coat, and hangs it on the hatstand by the front door.

'Here it is! I found it!' Laura laughs, as she draws a third bar of chocolate from the coat's deep pocket.

*

It is already dark by the time Mum checks the oven for the hundredth time. 'The chicken will be too dry if we don't eat soon, and the *kugel's* getting too brown. I wonder what's keeping them?' To Ivy she sounds unusually irritated.

'Let's not worry,' Daddy replies. He sounds tired. 'They have a long way to come without a car.'

'But Abe, why didn't you pick them up? They could be lost, or...' Mum stares at Daddy, her eyes wide with worry.

'They wanted to be independent,' he says. 'There's a bus to Castleton from the migrant camp. They could've missed it. I wouldn't have thought they'd be this late. Very late. I'll go for a drive to see if I can spot them.'

Ivy's sense of foreboding from that morning returns.

'Should I at least light the candles? It's after sunset,' Mum says, her face creased into her annoyed expression. The phone rings in the hallway. Ivy's stomach tightens.

'Ah, that'll be them. I'll get it,' Daddy says.

Laura starts whining, 'I'm hungry! Mum, can I have some *challah*?'

'Soon, dear. They'll be here soon, and then we can all eat.' Mum pats Laura on her shoulder. Ivy kicks Laura under the table.

Laura yelps. 'Mum, Ivy's kicking me! Make her stop!' For once Mum ignores her youngest daughter. She has a distant, listening look on her face.

Ivy creeps into the hall, straining to hear Daddy, trying to catch a word. He speaks more softly than usual. It's taking an awfully long time for the call to end. At last she hears Dad's footsteps. He's walking back very slowly.

'It was Oscar,' Daddy says. His face has gone grey. 'There's been an accident. It's Irina.'

'What? What accident? Where are they?' Mum whispers.

'At the hospital. Irina's in the operating theatre. She took a fall from that damned horse yesterday. It's bad.'

'But – Irina will be all right, won't she?' Ivy can't quite grasp Daddy's words.

'Dear God, I hope so. She has a serious head injury.'

Ivy can see Irina's face as if she were right there, remembering how her eyes shone with excitement at the promise of a horse ride. 'But – Irina's a good rider. Isn't she? Why would she fall?'

'It happens to the best of riders, Ivy. I think we should light the candles and start our dinner. We'll say a special prayer for Irina.'

'Shouldn't we go to the hospital?' Mum asks.

'I already offered. No visitors, and they want to deal with this on their own. No, we'll have dinner. They obviously won't be joining us.'

It is a subdued meal, except for Laura chattering away about how her best friend at school had pulled her hair, and how now she isn't her best friend any more. Ivy can't force a morsel down. She hears a voice in her head. It whispers, 'you can't eat at a time like this.' She stares at her plate of chicken and *kugel* and knows she must obey.

When the phone rings again, everyone freezes. Dad takes the call. There's a silence. It seems to Ivy he's taking hours, not minutes, coming back to the table. Dad looks at Mum, and shakes his head.

'No, it can't be,' Mum says, staring at him, white-faced. 'Prepare yourself, Lily. They're coming over here now. They have no one else.'

'What's happened?' asks Ivy, although she already knows.

Daddy puts his arms around Ivy. 'It's Irina, poor little Irina. She – she never woke up from the operation.'

Mum starts crying.

Laura stops eating, her eyes wide, looking from one parent to the other.

Daddy's voice breaks. 'As if they haven't suffered enough.'

Ivy pulls away from Daddy, staring at him in disbelief.

'You mean – Irina's dead?'

Daddy doesn't answer. He sits down hard, and puts his head in his hands. After a long wait, silent except for Mum's crying, there's the jarring sound of the doorbell. Dad gets up slowly, goes to the door. Ivy follows. She sees Oscar first. His usually dapper hair is awry, his eyes red. She notices his white shirt is stained, and ripped down the front. He falls forward onto Abe's shoulder, sobbing.

Lena walks straight past the embracing men. Her makeup is intact, her dark hair still coiled in a perfect French roll. But her eyes are blank, her face suddenly old. Her skirt looks wrinkled as if she's slept in it, and her white silk blouse is escaping from the waistband. Mum holds out her arms to Lena, but she stares past Mum and stretches out her hand towards Ivy, as if to grab her, a look of such longing and pain on her face that Ivy wants to embrace her. Mum pulls Ivy back from the beseeching hands, and stands in front of her, shielding her daughter from Lena's touch. It's the first time Ivy realises her mother must really love her. Lena stumbles forward, arms outstretched. Mum catches her as she falls.

Ivy runs away from the horror, flings herself onto her bed, burying her face into the blue eiderdown where only a few days ago, she and Irina had embraced. She takes her German-English dictionary from the bookshelf and throws it with all her might across the room.

It is at that moment Ivy decides to stop eating, as a way of honouring Irina, and in solidarity with the children killed in the war, whose pictures had been cruelly displayed to her in the newspaper. If her plan works, she will soon join Irina. They would be friends again. Ivy stops crying and lies still, staring into the darkness where Irina's face smiles down at her.

3. THE SKIN DOCTOR

Every day and every night Ivy thinks about Irina. How could God let such a thing happen to a little girl with so much life unlived? Sometimes Ivy wants to die too, partly from curiosity. Would she see Irina again? And meet her grandparents who died in the Holocaust?

Over the months of summer Ivy goes to the beach every day, turning red and later brown in the sun's angry rays. She tries to read, lying on her tummy in the sand, but the thrill of words on the page has palled. Wherever she goes there's a shadow out of reach, the faint figure of a girl with long plaits appearing and disappearing. *Irina would have loved these waves, this sun, the book I'm trying to read.*

If it weren't for Joel next door, Ivy would have stayed in bed all day, trying to sleep her sadness away. They are best friends, she and Joel. He is older than her, with a big open face and a shock of blue-black hair. She can tell Joel things she would never tell Mum, Daddy or Laura. Sometimes he comes to the beach with her, riding far out on the waves on his surfboard while she watches with pride and envy from the shore. Ivy thinks perhaps she loves Joel, but isn't sure if the flip she feels in her stomach is love.

At twelve and a half, Ivy has grown a little taller. On her chest are two hard little lumps where her breasts are starting to grow. She tries to ignore them, and wears a singlet a size too small, to squash the lumps flat. To make things worse, Ivy's body is changing at an alarming rate. She's still skinny (*petite*, her mother says fondly), but now hairs are sprouting under her arms and between her legs. It's all so revolting.

Instinctively, Ivy knows Daddy won't lie down with her at night if her breasts get bigger. She remembers the first words of Peter Pan, one of her favourite books when she was little. It begins: *All children, except one, grow up.* She wishes she could be that one child. Ivy doesn't want to grow up, or out, or through the ghastly Looking Glass called *puberty.* The very word sounds disgusting.

Occasionally she hears a Voice in her head, the same voice that had spoken the night Irina died. *If you stop eating, you'll stop growing, and those lumps on your chest will disappear.* Often she skips lunch, or takes only an apple to the beach.

*

'What's that on her face?' Daddy says one morning, staring at Ivy's forehead with a frown.

'I don't know, Dear. It's probably a pimple,' Mum answers without looking at him.

'Well, get rid of it.' Daddy stands up from the breakfast table and lights his first cigarette of the day, pushing his plate of congealed egg on toast away.

Ivy and Mum go to the bathroom. Mum puts pink smelly stuff on Ivy's forehead, with bits of cotton wool. The trouble is, there's not one pimple, but several, more sprouting every day. Mum squeezes them with a cold metal instrument that has a hole in the top for the pus to ooze through. No matter how much squeezing and how much pus is exuded, more and more pimples come, some starting as little black spots called blackheads. Mum squeezes those too.

When more and more pimples appear day by day, Mum makes an appointment with a dermatologist. *Whatever it costs,* Daddy says, *we can't have her out in public looking like that.* Ivy feels ashamed, as if she's willed the pustules to bloom on her face, planted by her like seeds under the ground. Perhaps the doctor would apply a magic ointment, like weed killer on the garden, and make her face clean again.

In the doctor's surgery, Ivy can smell Dr Harris's breakfast as he peers at Ivy's face through a light taped to his forehead. He's close enough for her to see oil seeping from his pores, and small black hairs sprouting from his nostrils. He puts on giant glasses like telescopes, and examines every inch of her face. When he brings his jowly face close to hers, Ivy can smell his skin; it has an unpleasant odour, like that given off by beef stock simmering on the kitchen stove. A smell that Ivy's sure could only come from a man.

'It's a bad case of adolescent acne,' Dr Harris says as he pulls his big face away from Ivy's, and turns to speak to her mother. 'Haven't seen one this severe for quite a few years. Probably hormones, but she'll need to change her diet, as well as continuing the daily treatment with the lotion I'll prescribe.'

'Oh,' Mum says with a quaver in her voice. 'She's never been a good eater. Right from a baby, we've had trouble with her. Even then, she wouldn't feed properly. I don't like the idea of restricting her food. But of course, Doctor, you know best.'

Ivy's heard all this before, all her life in fact. *Shut up*, she wants to say to her mother. *You're making it worse.*

'Now then, Mrs Morgenstern, it's not about quantity, but the type of food she eats. You need to understand that your daughter must avoid certain foods which aggravate acne. Now, young lady,' Dr Harris brings his face close to hers again, the smell of old egg unmistakable now, 'I want you to cut out all fatty foods such as cheese, eggs, and, I'm afraid,' here he gives her mother a little wink, 'ice cream and sweets. I'll write out a diet for you. Basically, you're to have fruit for breakfast, and perhaps some toast, no butter, remember. And for lunch a sandwich of wholemeal bread, with salad. No butter of course. For dinner grilled meat or fish, plenty of steamed vegetables. Oh, and I want you to drink plenty of water.'

'Yes, Doctor.' Mum's face is alight with purpose. 'Of course we can do that, can't we, Ivy?'

Ivy is silent, thinking how well these instructions will please The Voice, the one that's helping her stop growing. *Good*, it says, *you can easily stop eating all those things and more besides.*

'How long will the diet take to work?' Ivy says, trying not to breathe in Dr Harris's foul breath.

'That depends on you, young lady. We'll see if you can stick to it. Come back and see me in three months. My secretary will make you another appointment.'

'Thank you so much, Doctor,' Mum says, as she follows the doctor out.

Ivy pokes her tongue out at Dr Harris behind his back.

From then on, breakfast is toast with no butter, and lunch is brown bread sandwiches with lettuce and tomato. Most of them end up in the bin in the school playground. Only meat and plain vegetables for dinner. Nothing that could add its evil oils to the excrescences on Ivy's face.

*

Ivy's lying on her side, reading *Bleak House*, a gift from Daddy for her twelfth birthday. It's part of a set, each volume bound in maroon leather, with its title stamped in gold letters on the cover and down the spine. Ivy loves each precious volume and has read them all more than once. Her favourite is *David Copperfield* which she suspects is based on the author's own life.

She sits up, surprised, when instead of Daddy, Mum comes into her bedroom with a thin booklet in her hand. Ivy's eyes go to the title, *Growing up for Girls*. She shudders, knowing what's coming. She keeps her place in *Bleak House* with her bookmark.

Mum's face is slightly flushed, and her lips are pressed together, as if she's embarrassed. She sits down on the edge of Ivy's bed.

'I've brought you this pamphlet to read, dear. Now that you're growing up, there are some things you'll need to know. It's all quite straightforward, things that happen to every girl.'

A corner of a page in the thin booklet, about half way through, is turned down, breaking Ivy's rule that only bookmarks should mark one's place.

'You mustn't read past this page, Ivy dear. Not till one day when you're a little older. Read to here, then you can ask me questions if you like.' Mum's mouth twitches a little. Ivy knows exactly what the forbidden pages are about, having read extensively on the subject of sex and reproduction in the library. There'll be diagrams of a woman's insides, and a man's disgusting appendage hanging between his legs, and rude pictures of his thing no longer hanging but sticking out (*the man's penis fills with blood to make it hard*) and of him putting it inside the woman. Ivy thinks how dreadfully painful that must be, and determines it will never happen to her.

*

The day the blood comes Ivy's caught unaware, a sudden shock of brownish red staining her white interlock pants. Time for the buckles and pads her mother had shown her a few months before, after that excruciating non-talk, warning Ivy of what is to come. Ivy decided that if she could stop it happening, she would. But the dreaded thing called 'periods' or 'monthlies' is here, undeniably, as more blood seeps onto her pants, and her stomach twinges low down. She hates the whole business, and the smell too, a gamey smell as if she's turned into an animal. She wonders what the blood tastes like but doesn't dare try.

Mum's given Ivy a tight harness attached to this bulky white thing called a pad that goes between her legs. It's attached to the harness by safety pins, and is to be disposed of in the bathroom bin, not, Mum says firmly, down the toilet. Ivy can't tell Mum how scared she is, how she'd give anything for it not to happen.

The worst part of it is when Mum gets on the phone, ringing her friends to herald the big news. Ivy hears her say to Cousin Ruth, with a note of pride in her voice, 'It's happened to Ivy at last. I can't quite believe it. My little girl's a woman now, all grown up.'

Soon after that Ivy decides to stop eating altogether. The Voice is getting louder and more insistent. *You can do it, ignore the hunger, food will only make you grow,* it says. Ivy doesn't dare tell anyone about The Voice, lest they think her mad. She thinks of the story in the Torah of how Abraham fasted for forty days and forty nights to purify his soul. When she'd heard this story, called *The Revelation of Abraham,* at Sunday School, it struck two chords in her: first that her own father's name is Abraham (Abe for short), and second that a human being had managed to stop eating for forty days and forty nights, and had lived to a ripe old age.

Ivy knows these stories are symbolic but she likes to believe this one is true. The story has it that an angel came down from Heaven in a cloud of glory, so stunning that Abraham fell like a stone at the angel's feet. Angels didn't need to fast because they never ate. They were so pure that they were neither male nor female; sexless, innocent yet powerful, loved by God, dwelling in paradise. To be an angel must be the highest form of life. Perhaps, Ivy thinks, if she fasts for forty days and forty nights she too will attain purity and turn into an angel.

Ivy feels in control of her life at last. Clean and strong. All she wants is to lose her body, to remain pure and unsullied by blood and excrescences. A spirit of happiness fills her, better than all the food in the world.

At breakfast she says, 'Half a slice thanks Mum, and no butter, remember what the doctor said?'

'Of course, dear. It's good that you're following Dr Harris's advice. We'll have your skin cleared up in no time.'

Ivy stares at the triangle of toast on her plate already growing cold. Her mouth waters. She jumps up from the table, runs to her bedroom.

'Sorry, Mum, I forgot my Latin reader. Be back in a minute.'

A moment later she's out the door, swinging her schoolbag, before Mum can stop her.

*

Ivy lies rigid in her bed. Her stomach feels hard, frighteningly full. At dinner that night Mum served crumbed lamb cutlets, everyone's favourite. Ivy's mouth waters at the memory, but a wave of guilt washes over her and she wants to vomit. But she can't, she won't. To Ivy vomiting is a revolting act, a complete loss of control. She will never do it on purpose.

The cutlets are tender and sweet. There are two on her plate, nestled on a bed of mashed potato, with tender green peas on the side. Everyone has the same except for Abe, whose plate holds three cutlets and, along with mashed potatoes, his favourite pickled cucumber instead of peas. Ivy finishes her meal more quickly than usual. Before she can stop yourself, she blurts out, 'Can I have another cutlet?'

Daddy and Mum look at each other with surprise. Is this their daughter, their faces seem to say, the one who is picky, who refuses the healthy food her mother makes? Ivy asking for more? Their world was turned upside down.

There's a shocked silence, broken by Daddy. 'Feed a cold and starve a fever, that's what they say. She might be sickening for something.' He looks closely at Ivy's face, feels her forehead with his big warm hand. 'Is your throat sore, Ivy?'

It isn't, but Ivy nods, eyeing the third cutlet on Daddy's plate.

'Give the child another chop, Lily, what are you waiting for?' The Voice starts to remonstrate but Ivy's hunger is louder.

Mum's mouth twitches in a smile, as she dishes out the last cutlet onto Ivy's empty plate. Ivy feels a small shock of self-congratulation. For once, The Voice has quietened. The corpses from Dad's photo aren't staring at her any more, telling her to be a skeleton like them, to become a creature of death. Only then will Daddy truly love her, more than Laura, more than Mum.

Later, lying in bed, feeling the extra cutlet stuck in her belly, wishing she could un-eat it, Ivy breaks into a cold sweat. She can feel the food she allowed into her stomach swelling inside her. The pressure of her belly squeezing against her lungs makes it impossible to breathe. She begins to pant, the wheeze of asthma almost choking her.

'Help! I need help!' It's clear she's going to die, and she doesn't want to die any more. 'I will never do it again, never!' she whispers, trying to placate The Voice which has come back louder than ever. *How could you, you greedy pig. What would Irina say if she could see you now?*

A shadowy outline appears in the doorway.

'Ivy, what is it, is it your asthma? Sit up and I'll get you another pillow.'

'Get a doctor, quick,' Ivy gasps. 'I feel sick. I'm going to die!'

'Don't talk that way, Ivy. Of course you won't die. Not after you were such a good girl tonight eating all your dinner. You even had a second helping!'

A red haze envelops her. Between chokes she screams so loudly her head is about to burst.

'Ring Dr Killen,' is the last thing she hears someone say, before everything goes black.

*

Ivy falls into a dream in which everything in her life is upside down and inside out. She sees her German teacher Miss Trent plain as day, only she's become an old woman. She must be at least sixty yet she looks the same: golden hair, blue eyes, slightly crooked front teeth. Ivy hears her beautiful voice, deep as the ocean, saying something witty. Ivy is hiding at the back of the classroom when Miss Trent speaks. 'Welcome back, Ivy. I thought you were dead, after all these years.'

Ivy wakes to muffled conversation outside her bedroom door, men's voices, one her father's, the other deeper, more gravelly. *Must be Dr Killen's,* she figures, smiling to herself because Daddy calls him Dr Kill 'em for a joke, not to his face of course. She catches a few words: 'nervous disposition', 'highly strung'. Her ears strain for more. It all floods back, the terror, the dreadful feeling in her stomach, the pressure there. How she wanted to cut it open, to get the food out.

'You'll need to watch this girl carefully,' she hears Dr Killen say softly. 'I've given her an injection to calm her down. Check on her food intake. She's seriously underweight. But the main problem seems to be' – she hears an apologetic cough – 'psychological'.'

'A moment, doctor.' Now it's Daddy's voice, smooth and steady. 'With all due respect, I'll have you know my daughter's highly intelligent, top of second year high school in German and Latin. There nothing wrong with her mind, she's sensitive, that's all.'

'If you say so, Mr Morgenstern. But I strongly recommend you consult a specialist. I can refer you to a woman psychologist, who specialises in –

er – this sort of thing. She's especially good with children. Quite frankly, we medical men don't have an answer for this type of problem.'

Ivy sits up in bed. She listens for her father's voice, but both voices get fainter as footsteps recede down the hall. It must be quite late. There's no light from Laura's room opposite. After many long minutes, she hears the front door open, then close softly again. Mum comes tip-toeing into Ivy's room.

'I'm not asleep. I know Dr Killen's been. Mum, what's wrong with me? What did he say? Am I going to die, like Irina?'

'Don't be silly, dear. Of course you're not going to die. You need to eat up, like a good girl, and stop making us all worried. There's nothing wrong with you that a healthy diet won't fix. Now you get off to sleep. You've got to get up for school in the morning.'

Ivy feels her mother's cool lips on her forehead, a kiss scented with lavender and carrying with it a faint apology. An excuse, perhaps, for not loving her enough to tell her the truth. Or for not loving her, full stop.

4. WINCHESTER HOSPITAL

Ivy has learned her lesson. She will never give into hunger again. The Voice becomes her constant companion, drowning out everything else. *Remember what happens when you disobey me*, it says, when Ivy eyes a cream bun in the school canteen. She eats it with her eyes while her mouth fills with saliva. Her bones start to stick out everywhere. The hard wooden chairs at school cut into her fleshless bum. Even German lessons with her beloved Miss Trent float over her head, and this time her marks are mediocre.

Her mother comes into the bathroom unannounced one morning. Ivy is standing naked in front of the bathroom mirror. The bony plates of her face are covered with tightly stretched skin, skin that is still scarred with teenage acne. She looks like a walking skull with smallpox. Mum halts at the sight of Ivy's bony back, the blades of her shoulders sticking out like little wings. It is the first time she's seen Ivy's naked body for months, because it is usually covered by her heavy school uniform, navy serge with big pleats all the way down, with a white long sleeved shirt which hides the long hairs growing on her arms.

'She's skin and bone, Abe,' Mum says. 'I can count every rib.'

Ivy curses herself for not locking the bathroom door. She doesn't want anyone seeing her body, especially not her mother. Mum is the one person she can't bear to hurt, and now Ivy's very existence is threatening to send Mum into another breakdown. She hears tears start in her mother's voice. Ivy sits on the cold edge of the bath not daring to come out. She hears Mum start to scream and sob. 'Abe, we've got to do something. I can't take this any more. What if she dies?'

Now Ivy hears Daddy's voice, gravelly and thick. 'We'll have to send her to Sydney for that drastic treatment after all. It's the last thing I ever

thought would happen to our family, our daughter in a lunatic asylum.'
Ivy just catches his last few words, muffled over Mum's sobbing. 'No-one
must know about this, my dear, not even Laura. It's just between us.
But what choice do we have?' Through a crack in the slightly open door
Ivy can see her parents locked together, Daddy's arms around Mum's
shaking shoulders.

*What's going to happen to me? Where will they send me? Don't they know
nothing will stop The Voice?*

*

Dressed in her plain white cotton gown, the same as all the other
patients wear, Ivy wanders through the hospital grounds. The gardens
are deserted. Flower beds stand in geometrical patterns, their colours in
stark contrast to the brown brick wall and black iron gates.

Ivy has to get out of here. If all attempts to escape fail, she must think
of another way. *Use your brains, that's if you'll have any left after this*, The
Voice whispers, the same Voice that says *Food is Poison*.

She stands at the great iron gates, pulling at the bars with thin hands,
striving to reach the heavy bolt locking her from the world outside, a
world where people wear bright clothes and hurry down the street in
leather shoes, clop-clopping along to their work or homes or schools.
Ivy longs to join them, to squeeze herself through the narrow gaps
between the bars.

A voice behind her makes her jump.

'Come on now, it's time for your treatment. A fine thing it'd be if
Doctor's kept waiting.' Nurse Watson pulls Ivy away, prising her fingers
from the bars, and half pushes her towards the hospital building. 'Get
a move on, slow coach. No wonder your parents put you here.' She half
leads, half pushes Ivy back to the ward.

Ivy hears her own breath rasping in her chest as she climbs onto
her hard bed.

'I didn't know you were asthmatic,' Nurse Watson says, rubbing
something cold and wet on Ivy's skinny arm inside Ivy's elbow.

'I didn't tell you I was,' Ivy retorted, rudeness her only weapon.

'Ah, I can always tell from a person's voice. There's a lot of it where I hail from, back in the Old Country.'

Ivy hears Nurse Watson's broad vowels. She wants to ask her about England, but when she opens her mouth and moves her lips, there's no sound. She feels her legs go wobbly, like jelly, and a soft wandering dream starting. Her eyes grow heavy. Nurse Watson has slipped a needle into the cold spot on Ivy's arm while they were talking, yet Ivy hasn't felt a thing. *Too late now*, is her last thought, as she drifts into oblivion.

*

A man in a dull green apron arrives in the ward. Ivy and the other patients stiffen, each one fearing it might be her turn. This morning, the man comes straight to Ivy's bed. Her heart thumps through her bony chest. She knows 'treatment' is a euphemism for 'torture'.

He rolls her onto a trolley. It's cold and hard. Instinctively, she struggles against the broad leather belts pinning her down. She's strapped to the trolley like a piece of luggage. Under the thin sheet she feels rubber, its smell in her nostrils sending a sharp signal of fear. She's trundled along the corridor by the man in green who she can't see because he's behind her. They reach the thick opaque double doors that open as the trolley touches them. Ivy knows without knowing that this is the entrance to Hell.

Three other patients are lined up, strapped to their trolleys. Ivy sees the one nearest her, a middle-aged woman with grey frizzy hair, babbling about getting the police. She sees her go suddenly still as a doctor in a white coat approaches. He's wearing a stethoscope around his thick neck, and round horn-rimmed spectacles on his fleshy nose.

'Now, Mrs Lacey, we're going to make you better. This won't hurt a bit, it'll be like going to sleep.'

Ivy feels a surge of fear.

The woman looks up at him, terrified. He puts something hard and transparent into the woman's mouth and covers her eyes with a piece of green cloth. She starts to struggle. The doctor places two white pads on either side of her forehead. He gives a signal to someone behind him, lifting his hand in a kind of salute. The woman's body convulses, her limbs jerk, her jaw clamps rigid in a ghastly grin as her head rolls from side to side, eyes almost popping out of their sockets.

Ivy watches the woman's flailing body. Her mouth goes dry, her heart bangs in her chest. She tries to heave herself out of the leather straps, with all her failing strength. At that moment the doctor approaches and stands over her, looking down at her, unsmiling.

'Now, who've we got here? You must be one of the youngest I've seen. Come on now, be a brave girl.' He smiles a mouth-only smile, while his eyes remain hard. For a moment Ivy's sure he means to kill her, like the children in those camps were killed in the war. She knows she's being punished for the sin of not eating, a sin that she's powerless to stop.

'Your parents have agreed to this treatment, and have signed all the papers. It'll make you better, and you'll be able to eat again. I must also warn you that it may affect your memory, but only temporarily, as far as we know. Do you understand?'

Ivy stares at the doctor. Her lips move yet no sound comes out. She wants to plead with him, to promise she'll be good if he lets her go. But he's busy pressing wet pads to her temples and pushing a mouth guard between her teeth. There's a rumbling noise in her ears like distant thunder, and a burning pain behind her eyes as her teeth clamp down. Then a white blinding light. Then blackness.

*

Ivy's eyes feel as if they will burst from her head. They open slowly, to strange surroundings. She wonders how long she's been asleep. Where is she? Who are those women, lying on their beds, or sitting in chairs, with vacant stares on their faces? Does she know them? Perhaps this is some sort of camp, like the one long ago she'd been to with her school. Only these people are grown-ups.

Each time she wakes from the drugged after-sleep, it takes her longer and longer to remember her own name. Ivy knows her brains are being fried. It exhausts her to try to remember where she is, and who she is. She sinks onto the pillow and closes her eyes. When she opens them, a boy is sitting by the bed, looking at her. He seems vaguely familiar. He's smiling.

'Hello you. What have you been up to, giving us all a scare, eh? '

Ivy has no idea what he means. She feels curious, and calm. Her head swims with the effort of remembering.

'You tell me, and we'll both know.' The words that come from her throat are harsh and rasping, as if she's been screaming.

'Who are you, anyway?' she manages to ask.

The boy stares at her with a puzzled look.

'It's me, Joel, from next door. I'm your best friend, remember?' The boy's voice sounds wobbly.

'How old are you?' Ivy asks, feeling a stab of pity for him.

'I'm fifteen, you duffer. In third year at Boys' High. Remember how you helped me with my German homework?'

Ivy doesn't know what he's talking about.

A woman in a white dress approaches Ivy's bed. She sets down a tray of food on a moveable table and wheels it to Ivy.

'Here's your lunch, darl.' She smiles. 'Are you going to eat it all up, like a good girl?' The woman in white looks at Joel, and whispers something to him. Joel stands up, glancing back at Ivy. She catches a quick wink from him as they walk away.

Ivy stares at the tray. On it there's a round white plate, and on the plate there are two slices of something brown, covered in a slimy sauce, two white domes of something soft, some slender green shoots, and a few orange coloured discs. The colours are vivid and pleasing. Her stomach rumbles and her mouth waters. She takes a forkful of the white stuff, stopping with it halfway to her mouth.

She remembers something, a warning, a danger. *Don't put that in your mouth*, the thought bubble in her head says. *But I'm starving*, she answers. *YOU CAN'T EAT IT,* The Voice says in loud letters. She looks up to see Joel has come back in and is sitting beside her. He looks sad, as if he is trying not to cry.

'Oh good, you're back,' she says. 'I need you to help me eat this. Can you pull the curtains please?' He does as she asks.

'Ivy, listen. That nurse said the only way you'll get out of here is if you start to eat again.'

'You sure Ivy's really my name?

'Course it is. Come on, try to remember. Hurry up and get out of here, so we can go to the beach again and talk like we used to, about books and things. You have to eat, even if you pretend. It's the only way they'll let you out.'

'Please help me this time, so they'll think I'm better. If you don't, they might kill me.'

Joel shrugs, and picks up the fork from Ivy's plate. He starts shovelling the white stuff into his mouth, talking all the time. He spears the green and orange things onto the fork and eats them too. He looks at the brown lump with sauce spilling over it.

'Looks like meat loaf. Don't know what's in it, but it's sure not kosher, as my Dad would say.'

'Thank goodness you've come. I can't remember anything, like where I live when I'm not in this awful place. Do I have sisters or brothers?' She stares into Joel's face as if the answers might be written there.

'Geez, Ivy, how can you not remember Laura? Your little sister? Are you having me on?'

'I have a sister?' Ivy doesn't know whether to believe him.

'Sure. Can't get over how Laura's grown. You better start eating, or she'll soon be taller than you.'

'How old is she?' Ivy says suspiciously.

'She's younger than you, by about three years I think. You're thirteen, aren't you? I guess she'd be around ten, but she could pass for fifteen. Don't you want to see her?'

'Doctor says my family's not allowed to visit, but I can see friends as long as they don't "upset" me, whatever that means. Whereabouts do I live?'

'In Wave Street, right near Summer Beach. The beach we've been going to together for the last three years. Don't tell me you've forgotten that too.'

Ivy searches her scrambled mind for the words "Wave" and "Summer". All she finds is a whiteness, blank as milk.

'Never heard of Wave Street, or Summer Beach. Can you bring me a picture of my house? And my sister?' She's already forgotten the name, something starting with 'L' or 'P'.

'Sure. Good excuse to try out my new box brownie. Got it from Josie for my fifteenth birthday.'

'Is Josie your girlfriend?'

'Na, just a friend who happens to be a girl.'

Ivy's empty stomach flutters with something more painful than hunger. She struggles to understand. What have they done to her in this dreadful place? Her memories have been wiped like the blackboard duster wipes the white words from the board. At least she remembers that. She'll have to get out of here before they kill her mind completely. But to get out, she has to eat. Or be seen to be eating. Joel's helped her this time, but what about the next meal, and the next?

'Can you come again tomorrow?'

*

The next day Joel does come back, and nearly every day after that. Ivy looks forward to seeing him as if to a party or a holiday. The whole world is brighter with Joel sitting beside her, always with a smile or a joke. She knows now he's her best friend, that she can tell him anything.

As soon as bits of memory float back, Ivy writes down whatever shreds remain in her brain. She keeps a secret notebook under her pillow. Soon she has quite a collection of memories, starting with her own name, although she wouldn't mind if it wasn't Ivy. It's such a plain name, with clinging connotations, the complete opposite of her yearning to be free. Perhaps she should take this opportunity to change her name, maybe to Imogen, Cordelia, Ophelia or Juliet, names that come from somewhere in the recesses of her mind. Such romantic, pretty names. She must have read them once, before the electric shocks wiped her memory.

*

The only good thing about treatment day is that there's no breakfast for the victims, no porridge forced into her mouth. On other mornings Nurse Watson is supposed to watch Ivy eat the bowl of the gluey mess. The porridge sticks in her throat. Nurse Watson looks bored.

'Come on, I'm not going to stand her all day while you play with your food,' she says. Whenever the nurse glances at the watch pinned to her starched white uniform, right where her breast pokes the material to a point, Ivy secretes a gob of porridge deep inside her cheek. She holds it there until Nurse Watson takes the half empty bowl away. Ivy spits the porridge into a large handkerchief she keeps under her pillow, trying not to gag.

Joel and Ivy are clever about the food. Sometimes Joel puts it into a lunchbox he brings with him in his satchel. Other times he wolfs down Ivy's lunch while Nurse Watson leaves the room for a moment.

In her secret book Ivy writes the names of people and places she's forgotten, as soon as Joel mentions them. She uses the back of the book for Latin declensions and French vocabulary.

'Will you look after this for me when you come next time? If Nurse Watson finds it she's sure to throw it out, or even sneak a look at my memories. She wouldn't understand half of it anyway, cos it's full of Latin and French.'

'Course I'll look after it. Guard it like my life. Latin, eh? You're such a little swot – bet you'll beat everyone in the exams.'

'Don't be silly, you know you're much cleverer than me. I'm only a girl, after all. Mum says there's no point in all these books and study.'

'Only a girl, eh? Well guess what, Ivy Morgenstern, I reckon you could do anything you want. And I for one am glad you're a girl.' He gives her his crooked grin, and her heart flips over.

5. RESCUED

Days turn into weeks. Ivy has been in Winchester for two long months. Every morning she finds a way to empty her porridge bowl, sometimes being forced to swallow a gob of it, if a nurse is watching. If she takes too long chewing, the nurse shrugs and hurries off to attend another patient.

Lunch times are harder, when Ivy is confronted with a large plate of meat, a baked potato and some ghastly green vegetables, usually soggy cabbage or mushy cauliflower. She prays for Joel to come, but now the school holidays are over he can only visit at weekends.

Dinner is hardest of all, when the dreaded Nurse Watson comes on duty for the night shift. Ivy fears Nurse Watson is the one who will find her out. She and the nurse dislike each other. When the dinner trolley comes around, Ivy makes sure she has one of Daddy's large handkerchiefs under her pillow, into which she spits mouthfuls of half-masticated food while pretending to cough. Whenever Nurse Watson turns her back, Ivy scoops a chunk of potato or a wedge of meat into the hanky. She always leaves the greens on the plate, because everyone knows children hate vegetables. Otherwise it might look too good to be true.

Twice a week the man in green comes to her with his trolley, and twice a week she watches other bodies convulse, their silent mouths twisted in pain, until it is her turn to have the wet pads pressed to her temples. Mercifully she forgets everything after the doctor lifts his hand, signalling a switch to be thrown. She knows with growing horror that surges of deadly electricity will burn into her brain, destroying more and more memories.

Ivy keeps working harder than ever at her lists of words, in Latin, French and German. She can only concentrate for five minutes at a time, before an enormous weariness overcomes her, and her eyes grow heavy.

The new notebook under her pillow, which Joel has brought to replace the one she'd given him, is almost full. She keeps its scribbled pages well away from the handkerchief soiled with spat out food.

She wonders whether Joel is her boyfriend. Have they ever kissed? Her cheeks burn at the thought. He is always very careful with her. One time he squeezes her hand, which makes Ivy's stomach quiver. Anyway, thirteen is much too young to have a boyfriend, isn't it? She only knows his visit is the highlight of her day, and he is her trusted accomplice in this dangerous game.

Ivy's own family stay well away. At the beginning, when she woke calling for Daddy in her sleep, she couldn't believe he wasn't coming to save her. 'Where's my Mum?' she asked the doctor when he first told her she'd be having shock treatment. How could Mum and Daddy let such a horrific thing happen to her?

'It's better for everyone if you don't see your parents while you're here.' Dr Henderson peers at her over his glasses. 'You must concentrate on getting better and eating up, like a good girl.'

'But why? Why can't they come?' Ivy stares belligerently at the doctor. 'They're probably paying a fortune for this place, so at least they should be allowed to see me. And I'll get better quicker if I can see Daddy and Mum.' *A difficult child. Always gave her mother grief. Her poor parents.* The words drifted through her head from somewhere long ago.

'Now, now, you'd better calm down, unless you want one of my special injections.' Ivy shudders, feeling again the slow ebbing of her senses, the hours of dullness that an injection would mean. Dr Henderson is threatening her, and she is no match for this monster in a white coat who is frying her brains.

One day a man in a suit and tie comes with Dr Henderson on his morning rounds.

'Hello young Ivy, this is Professor Palmer. He's a special doctor for the mind.'

'How are we today, young lady?' the professor says in an oily voice. Ivy looks around for the 'we' but there is no other young lady to be seen.

'I hear you may be leaving us soon. There are many other sick patients who need a bed here, you see. Now, how do you feel about that?'

'Please, please, let me go home. I promise I'll be good, and eat everything, if I could only be with Daddy and Mum again.' Ivy feels her eyes getting wet with hope and dread at the same time. She knows she won't, can't, eat at home, even if it means coming back to this place. Ivy knows it's wrong not to eat. She tries to make herself, but the fear of food is too strong. It's beyond her control.

'Very well. But tell me, don't you have a sister? Do you remember her name?' The professor is writing quickly with a silver pen in a small notebook he drew from his top coat pocket.

'Of course I do. Her name's Laura, and she's three years younger than me, which makes her ten.' She silently thanks Joel for the memories he's restored to her.

'Very good! Now tell me, what day is it today?'

Ivy has no idea. She knows it isn't a weekend because Joel hasn't come. She takes a wild guess. 'It's Wednesday, isn't it? Although every day's the same here.'

Professor Palmer smiles, and whispers something to Dr Henderson. Has she failed the test?

'Almost right, young lady. It's actually Tuesday, but you're only a day out. As far as I'm concerned, you're ready to leave, providing you come back to see me once a week. Dr Henderson here is very pleased with your progress. I must say he's done an excellent job,' the professor touches the doctor's shoulder, 'and he tells me you're starting to eat again and gaining strength. We're going to let you go, to see how you fare in the big world outside. But not to your family, not yet. They've arranged for a relative to call for you this coming Friday. Remember you are still a very sick girl, and you'll need to be quite well before you go home.'

'Can I go back to school?'

'Not quite yet,' Dr Henderson says. 'We'll be keeping an eye on you, and making sure your progress continues. You'll be staying with your relative, a distant cousin, with a child, I believe. We don't want you upsetting anyone, especially the little one. Otherwise we'll be having them here too for treatments.'

Is that a joke? Is he a Nazi, disguised as a doctor, planning to wipe her and her relatives out with his electric torture?

*

When Ivy is let out, it is in a wheelchair, as if she were a cripple. Every time she tries to stand her knees buckle and she sinks to the ground. Her brain won't control her limbs, so that when she tries to walk, her legs wobble like that drunk man she saw once in the street.

A woman with dark hair, a pointed nose, and a determined expression, comes to collect her. She is vaguely familiar. Ivy knows she likes her, but wonders who she is.

'I'm Esther, your mother's cousin,' the woman announces, in answer to Ivy's unspoken question. Esther wheels her to a waiting black car, and helps her from the wheelchair into the back seat, which smells strongly of leather. There is a little girl already inside, who looks about five.

'This is Sarah,' says the lady called Esther. The child shrinks away from Ivy. 'Say hello to your cousin, Shooshie.'

'No, don't want to!' Sarah screams. 'She's a witch!'

Ivy shrinks back into herself. Is she so frightening to a small child, with her stick-like legs and shrivelled arms? Heaven only knows what her face looks like. They weren't allowed mirrors, scissors or combs in Winchester.

'Now,' Esther says, 'we're going to see the Queen! She's only in Strathfield for one day, so you're very lucky to be allowed out today.'

'What Queen?' Ivy asks. She racks her tender brain. Little Sarah, forgetting her fear, started singing, *'We're off to see the Queen, we are, the wonderful Queen of the Weld,'* to the tune of The *Wonderful Wizard of Oz.* A memory rushes in of going with Daddy when she was four, to see the film about a girl called Dorothy and her strange friends. The magic of it, and the image of Dorothy's sparkling red shoes on the yellow brick path is tucked into a corner of her brain.

'Queen Elisabeth is not the Queen of the world, Shooshie. She's the Queen of England and the whole British Commonwealth. Poor girl lost her father, the King, you see, and now she's on the throne. Only twenty-six. So young.'

Driving through the streets Ivy feels a tremor of excitement. There are bright banners on lamp poles, and people lining the footpaths waving flags. The air of eager expectation thrills her.

'We have a special disabled permit to come to the oval, because of your wheelchair. You've done us a favour, you see, dear.'

They drive up to barrier where a policeman checks Esther's papers, nods, and lets them through. They enter a big space where people crowd around the edges. Some have brought blankets and thermos flasks. It is like a fairy tale.

'They've been here all night,' Esther says. 'See how lucky we are?'

Sarah sidles up to Ivy, and peers closely at her. 'I'm glad you're here now,' she says, 'cos you make us get in quicker. But you still look like the Wicked Witch of the East.'

'Well, soon I'll look like Glinda, the good witch, who's beautiful. You'll see.' Ivy's smiling at the little girl with honey blonde curls and large brown eyes, behind small pink-framed spectacles.

'Let's get you out of your magic chariot.' Esther helps Ivy to her feet, supporting her by putting a strong arm through hers.

Yes, thought Ivy. *I do like this lady.*

*

It doesn't take long for Ivy to feel part of the sprawling messy semi-detached cottage, far enough away from seaside Castleton to be in another country. Aunt Esther (*Call me Esther, dear*) is so kind, and Sarah so adorable, that Ivy stops longing for her own family. The only person she misses a little is Joel.

'How come you call Sarah Shooshie?' Ivy asks Esther.

'Her Hebrew name is Shoshanna, but I call her Shooshie for short. Her father, God rest his soul, wanted to call her Susan because it's safer, but that's such an ordinary name.'

'Can I call her Shooshie too? It's suits her more than Sarah.'

'Of course you can, dear. Do you have a Hebrew name, Ivy?'

'It's Aviva, which means Spring. I like it much better than Ivy. When I grow up I'm going to change my name to Aviva.'

'That's a beautiful name, dear. Would you like me to call you Aviva while you're staying with us?'

'Oh! Would you really?' Ivy throws her bony arms around Esther. She can't believe a grown-up can understand her so well, without the usual judging and reprimands. When Ivy asked Mum to call her Aviva, Mum replied, 'Don't be silly. We called you Ivy because it's a perfectly good name, and will never single you out. Hebrew names are only for when you die, or get married.'

Little by little more memories return, but they are mostly from long ago before Ivy started school. There is a great hole in her mind when she tries to think about what happened before Winchester, and how she ended up there. Because no one is forcing her to eat, she is able to eat a little more, and grows stronger. She soon stops using the wheelchair.

Esther works in a dress shop, which she calls a 'boutique'. Daddy calls it *Esther's shmutters*, which Ivy thinks sounds rude.

'We're all in the rag trade, what else is there for people like us?' is one of Daddy's constant refrains. Ivy supposes he means that poor Jewish people back in London couldn't enter a profession. All that was left for Abe, and for 'people like us', was to open a shop and be a pretend tailor with a tape measure around his neck. He tells his customers he sews every stitch of their three piece suits with his own hands. *Made on the knee,* a sign says in his tailor's shop in the main street of Castleton. Nothing could be further from the truth, but customers liked to think Abe Morgenstern is the real thing, a Jew plying his trade by hand. Little do they know Abe is an artist, and a frustrated intellectual, forced into business to give his daughters the education he'd never had. Daddy has no head for business, Ivy's heard him say; that's why Mum has to help with "the books". How would Abe support his girls, give them opportunities he'd never had, unless the business made a profit?

One wintry night, Esther comes in from work laden with shopping bags. As she drops them on the floor and stoops to pick up Shooshie, she says 'I got a call from your father today, Ivylie – I mean Aviva.'

Ivy fells a pang of envy. Why didn't Daddy ring her instead of Esther? He only rings Ivy on a Friday night to say Good Shabbos, crack a few jokes and pretend everything is 'normal', whatever normal means.

'What did he say?'

'It's good news Ivy. He said it's time for you to go home.'

'Don't go! I want Ivy stay!' Shooshie cries, hanging on to Ivy's bony legs. With her face screwed up and tears spurting from her eyes, Shooshie looks like a baby monkey. Ivy feels terror at the thought of leaving the sanctuary of Esther's warm loving home. She feels like crying too.

'Quiet, little one, stop your *qvetching*. Ivy – I mean Aviva – will come and visit often, you'll see. Why don't you get your pencil box and do a special drawing for Ivy to take home with her? But first – see what I've brought for you, Ivylie, from the boutique. It's a one-off, too small to fit anyone but you.'

From a bag stamped with *Paris Down Under,* Esther draws a heavy garment. It is a coat, full-length, with a smart stand-up collar, square tortoise-shell buttons down the middle, and a nipped-in waist. What Ivy loves is the colour: an earthy red, much like the one called 'burnt sienna' in her paintbox. It is vivid yet subdued. The coat is lined in ruby-red silk, and has deep pockets to keep her hands warm.

'It's last season's, left over from the stocktake, and straight away I thought, perfect for Ivy! Let's see if it fits.' Esther holds up the coat.

'For me? Really? Oh – Aunt Esther – I mean, Esther – I love it!' Ivy says, slipping her arms into the wide sleeves, and giving a little shudder of pleasure as she wraps the coat's folds around her. It is much too big. The sleeves are too long and the hem nearly touches the ground, but Ivy feels warm and safe.

'Hmm, I can take the hem up a few inches, and it might be OK over your winter clothes.' Esther holds her head on one side, pursing her lips as she calculates the length. Ivy hugs Esther, squeezing her aunt's generous breasts almost flat, and leaning into her powdery perfumed neck. 'Thank you, it's beautiful! I don't care at all if it's too big.'

'Nothing that a belt won't fix,' Esther extricates herself from Ivy's embrace. 'I'll shorten the hem for you before you leave. It won't take long.' Esther whips the coat off Ivy and disappears into her sewing room.

'Size extra-extra-small, and still too big for the poor girl,' Ivy hears Esther mutter over the rumble of the sewing machine, as her foot goes up and down on the treadle.

The sound reminds Ivy of the old Singer in the back room of Paris Down Under, where she's spent many happy hours minding Shooshie while Esther serves her customers, most of them ladies of a certain age with heavy accents. She loves the smell of the fabrics, woodiness and camphor overlaid with a faint scent of perfume. In a few moments the machine stops, and Esther comes towards her.

'Here, try it on, dear.' Reverently, Ivy slides her arms into the silk-lined sleeves and settles the coat onto her shoulders.

'It's perfect! I never want to take it off.' She hugs her aunt again. Esther holds Ivy close, much closer than her mother ever has.

'I'll miss you, Aviva, and so will my Shooshie.'

The little girl holds up her drawing, a stick figure with a giant head and big round eyes. Ivy sees she's drawn a red coat on the androgynous body.

'That's so clever, Shooshie. Look, you've even given me my new coat. Thank you, darling.' Ivy bends to kiss her cousin, wishing she had the strength to pick her up and hold her. A far cry, she thinks, from that first day when Shooshie shrank from her.

'Ivy will come back to visit us often, won't you my dear?'

Ivy whispers 'Yes' into the soft crease of Esther's neck, knowing that she won't see her or Shooshie again, at least not for a very long time.

6. THE RED COAT

Since leaving Esther's and arriving home, time doesn't work in the same way as before. A minute seems to take an hour and an hour a minute. Ivy isn't quite sure if it's morning or afternoon. Try as she might, she can't remember when she last washed her hair, or what she ate yesterday.

Ivy is allowed back into her old school, despite the months of hospitalisation which have left her weak and struggling with memory loss. She is eager to face the challenge of schoolwork again. Her parents encourage her to return, fearing their eldest daughter will 'get behind' and spoil her emerging record of academic excellence.

When her father drops Ivy off at the school gates on a rainy day, she is shivering with fear inside her Aunt Esther's magic coat. Inside it, Ivy feels safe. Its scarlet fabric swamps her shrunken body, which is as well, since she'll have to face curious eyes. At least no one will see the long fine hairs that cover her arms, or notice the sharpness of her bones at knee and elbow. Ivy looks around her at the strange faces, buildings that she's never seen before. Although she has, of course she must have, now she's in her second year of high school.

'Come on Ivy, we're going in,' a voice above her says, making her jump. Someone takes her hand. She looks up to see a tall thin girl with frizzy fair hair. The girl leads Ivy across the asphalt into the dank corridor where leather satchels hang on giant hooks. There's a smell of mould and wet raincoats.

'You can hang that coat up on the hook next to mine,' the girl says.

'No, thanks. I'll keep it on. It's too cold in here.' Ivy stares at the girl as she speaks, trying to remember who she is.

'What's happened to you? How come you don't know me?' The girl's blinking tears away. 'We're best friends, how could you forget?' the girl says, staring at Ivy with wet eyes.

Ivy looks hard at the girl, trying to imprint her face in her mind. It takes a huge effort to scroll through what's left of her memory.

'It's me, Meg! You must remember. I've slept over at your place lots of times. We do Latin together, and you beat me in the exam last year.'

Meg, Ivy says to herself, over and over. Should she pretend to remember, if only to save this girl's feelings? 'Hello, Meg. I'll try to remember but it might take me a while. I'm sorry for forgetting. I've probably forgotten all my Latin too. You see, when I was in the hospital I kind of lost my memory.'

'Really? How terrible for you! I can't imagine what that must be like. Especially to forget your best friend.'

'The doctors told me some of my memory should come back.' Ivy wants to explain, but she can't find the words. She wishes she could go home.

'Don't worry, I'll help you remember.' Meg takes Ivy by the hand and leads her to a group of girls chatting excitedly in the corridor. 'Hi, everyone,' she announces, 'you might think this strange, but I'm going to introduce you all to Ivy here, even though you already know her. See, when she got sick she lost her memory. We all have to help her to remember things. So – Ivy, this is Claire, Julie, Libby and Fay. Once we get inside you'll hear their names a lot,' Meg says, 'cos they're the ones who get their names called out for talking in class.'

'Says you, Margaret Bennett. You can talk, stuck-up thing with your airs and graces,' says Julie with mock affront. 'Anyway, welcome back Ivy. What was wrong with you? Besides getting skinny, of course. Why did you lose your memory?'

The others girls encircle Ivy, staring at her, waiting for an answer. 'Why are you allowed to wear that overcoat at school? It's not part of our uniform, and anyway, it looks silly,' says Libby, coming closer to Ivy and fingering the rich red material of her coat.

'My father wrote a note to the Headmistress asking to let me wear it in class. It's because I feel cold all the time. And no one knows what's wrong with me, but now I've got a thing called amnesia, like when someone gets hit on the head and loses their memory.' She backs away from Libby's curious hand and wishes again that she could go home, end this inquisition.

The group breaks up. The girls move away like a flock of birds. Ivy hears one whisper 'that Jewish girl' and 'weird'. She turns to Meg and examines her face. 'I think I do remember you somehow, especially your eyebrows – they're thick, just like Frida Kahlo's.'

'Who's she? Did you meet her in the hospital?'

'No! She's a wonderful artist, from Mexico. It's strange the things I remember when I've forgotten all the other things. Anyway, her eyebrows are so thick they meet in the middle. And she has a moustache. But guess what? Those things make her beautiful.'

Meg throws her arms around Ivy. 'You're still the same Ivy,' Meg whispers, her lips lightly brushing Ivy's ear. 'You always did come out with these obscure facts. Can I give you some advice? Ignore the others if they stare at you. And for heaven's sake, take off that coat before we go into class. It's much too big for you anyway.'

'I know, but it keeps me warm. And I feel kind of safe in it. Who cares what the others think – I've been through worse than being teased and stared at.'

'Gosh Ivy – I can see that. Even your face has shrunk. Just looking at you makes me want to cry.'

Inside the classroom, Ivy feels eyes boring into her back as she slips behind her desk. Miss Jamison, the history teacher, is a square-shaped woman with a ruddy face, and thin grey hair showing bits of pink scalp. Occasionally the teacher scratches at her chin and neck, as if it helps her think. She is in full flight about how Australia became one nation. "Federation" is the new word in Ivy's growing vocabulary.

Ivy observes everything around her as if it were a film, or a performance put on for her benefit. She can't follow the lesson, feeling only the nagging emptiness of her stomach, and her relief at this emptiness. Soon she'll be back home, and her mother will be there, with the freshly squeezed orange juice.

At last the bell rings, signalling the end of the period. Miss Jamison picks up her books in her sturdy arms, and the girls all stand.

'Good afternoon, Miss Jamison!' they chant in unison, faces bright. Ivy chants with them, picking up the exact beat, laughing silently at how ludicrous this charade is. As the girls file out, suppressing giggles and whispers, Meg takes Ivy's hand. She looks up and sees Meg smiling at her, her eyes bright under bushy eyebrows.

At lunch time, Ivy throws her mother's sandwiches into the yawning mouth of the playground bin, making sure no one sees her. She feels a pang of guilt, quickly replaced by relief, as if saved from putting poison into her mouth. The carefully cut and peeled apple pieces, however, she does eat, slowly sucking the juice from every segment. They won't make her fat, she hopes, and the sweet juice soothes the constant griping of her empty stomach.

'It's German next period,' Meg says. She nudges Ivy, widens her eyes at her, and grins. 'Your favourite subject.'

'Why's it my favourite subject?' Ivy feels an uneasy stirring in her stomach.

'You'll see. It's because of Miss Trent. She's your crush, just like Mrs Halliday for Latin's mine. That's why I'm always top in Latin and you're top in German.'

'No it's not, I'm probably good at German 'cos my parents talk Yiddish at home. It's almost the same as German. They don't know I can understand them, but I always do.'

Ivy, Meg and six other girls whose names Ivy still can't remember, file into a small room. It's more like an office than a classroom. The eight of them sit around a big oak table instead of at desks. There are covert glances at Ivy, still wearing her rust red coat, and a ripple of whispers as she takes the only empty seat, near the head of the table. She's aware of a bristling in the air, breaths held in anticipation.

A flood of memory threatens to drown Ivy. She remembers every detail of Miss Trent's face: her wide sea-blue eyes, her *retroussé* nose, her full lips, lightly lipsticked, parting over slightly crooked, perfectly white, teeth. With awful clarity she recalls the shine of pure gold from Miss Trent's hair, curling recklessly around her face, stray strands reflected in the translucence of her skin.

Ivy catches a faint spicy smell, as a young woman carrying a pile of exercise books enters the room. She is exactly as Ivy remembers, only more real. The girls' voices fade like a wave receding. Miss Trent's voice, deep and rich, sends another jolt of recognition through Ivy's body. She shivers slightly, and huddles deeper into her coat.

The young teacher flashes a smile at everyone, and the room seems to light up. She takes each girl into her gaze, one at a time yet all together. She seems to freeze when her eyes fall on Ivy. The few seconds' silence seems like an hour.

'Why, Ivy my dear, you're back with us at last! We've all missed you, haven't we girls?'

There's a general muttering of assent around the table. Ivy's face grows hot. She's aware of Meg across the table, trying to catch her eye. Ivy almost faints from the heady smell of Miss Trent's perfume. She watches the way her lips move, loves how her teeth are slightly askew, the two front ones fluted like a butterfly's wings.

'*Guten morgen, Mädchen.* We'll continue with our reading of *Buddenbrooks* in a moment. But first, here are your assignments from last term, long overdue I'm afraid. Ivy Morgenstern, once again you've topped the class with a mark of 90.'

Meg opens her eyes wide at Ivy across the table, as if to say, *See? I told you.* Ivy looks away. Her skin quickens under her layers of clothes, as if she's coming back to life. She knows it's somehow shameful to be entranced by Miss Trent. What is this feeling? It's not as visceral as when she's near Joel, that almost painful stirring deep inside. Looking at Miss Trent, hearing her voice, makes Ivy feel hopeful, whole, as if she's found something she lost long ago.

A bell signals the end of the lesson, making Ivy jump as if woken from a dream. The girls stand as one, gathering books, spilling out into the corridor, chattering like birds released from their cage.

Ivy is the last to leave. A soft touch on her shoulder stops her.

'Are you well now, Ivy? I know how worried your father's been.'

There it was again, the eternal concern for her parents' suffering, as if they were the afflicted ones.

Ivy manages to whisper, 'Yes thank you, Miss Trent,' not looking at her teacher's face. She almost runs down the corridor to catch up with Meg.

'See, what did I tell you?' Meg whispers. 'I knew your memory wouldn't let you down where Miss Trent's concerned.'

'But I don't remember properly, like what happened before. Tell me everything. Please, you must.'

'You've got an enormous crush on Blaise Trent, that's all.'

'What d'you mean, "crush"?'

'It means we're kind of in love with them, and we follow them round, even on weekends.'

'You mean I'm a lesbian?'

'Course not, silly, it's just a crush. All the top girls have them. It makes you work harder. Anyway, just wait till you meet my Mrs Halliday again.'

'Why is she called "Mrs" when the other teachers are all called "Miss"?'.

'Her husband was killed in the war. There's a general rule that teachers aren't allowed to work once they're married but Mrs Halliday was allowed to have her old job back,' Meg continues, 'because of the war and everything.'

'That's stupid. All that knowledge they can pass on, going to waste.'

'Well, it's the system. You can't argue with it.'

Oh yes you can, thinks Ivy. *Just like I fooled those stupid doctors at the hospital. If I'd let that system have its way with me, I'd be a complete vegetable by now, instead of getting bits of my brain back here in the real world.*

'It's nothing like that with Miss Trent. I don't want to be with her, I want to *be* her. To be grown up, and free, like her.'

Meg nodded, her face serious. 'I know. That's exactly how I feel about Mrs Halliday.'

By the end of the day Ivy's almost fainting with weakness. She still has her coat on, comforting her with the thought of Aunt Esther's kindness. She tries to lift her satchel from the hook in the corridor. It slips from her hand and drops to the floor.

'Come on, I'll walk you home. Meg picks up Ivy's satchel. The girls start along the footpath, Ivy staggering a little. 'It's only two blocks. Let's take it slowly.'

Nothing moves in the quiet afternoon air, except for the trees lining the street, their leaves shaking gently in the cool breeze. They reach Ivy's house. The house stands silent, its windows blank eyes, giving nothing away.

'I have to go – um – Meg. Mum will be waiting for me.' Ivy hurries up the side path.

'See you tomorrow then. Don't worry, the other girls will soon come around.'

But Ivy is already past the oleander bush, the one that taps on her window at night. Once, when she was younger, the dark pink blossoms turned into old-fashioned ladies wearing big pink hats, nodding and bowing to her through the window, beckoning her to come outside with them. It was both scary and exciting. She didn't dare leave her bed in case they turned into witches and spirited her away, but she remains forever curious.

*

Every day now since Ivy got back to this place she calls home, but which is as foreign to her as a hotel, the afternoon glass of orange juice is all that sustains her, both physically and emotionally. Like the milk she'd refused as an infant, the juice comes from her mother, from her hands, if not from her breast. Now Ivy craves the golden liquid. To her it's the draught of life, but only if it comes from her mother.

Ivy's been told again and again how she'd almost been the death of Mum. All Ivy's fault, like everything else. *A criminal waste, selfish, spoilt, wicked child, attention seeking, needs a good slap,* say the aunts and uncles. *Ignore her, pretend it doesn't matter, she'll come around when hunger gets the better of her,* say the doctors and the rabbi.

Going down the path to the back door, she finds it unlocked, which is unusual. Her throat's parched. She can't wait to see her mother's hand with its strong fingers holding out the glass with its sunshiny juice. It's the proof that Mum loves her still, in spite of everything.

In the kitchen Ivy drops her school bag onto the laminex table. 'Mum, I'm home!' The silence in the quivering air is as loud as a siren. She waits, hardly breathing. Slowly she walks down the hall, past the empty bedrooms. Laura must be at her piano lesson. She looks into her parents' bedroom at the end of the hall. The bed with its dusty pink satin spread is neat as a pin. The pillows with their matching ironed pillowslips are prettily plumped. In the light breeze, the white marquisette curtains covering pale cream venetian blinds shift slightly. Her mother's nowhere to be seen.

'Mum!' Ivy calls again more urgently, feeling tears prick her eyes. Her mother was always there for her, after school. She runs back down the hall, her heart banging in her chest. In the kitchen she looks around wildly, at the perfectly clear benches on either side of the stainless steel sink. She looks in the cupboard underneath, as if she might find her mother hiding there.

The refrigerator stands white and massive, its impassive face daring Ivy to open it. She wrenches the door open. There, on the middle shelf, in front of the stewed fruit, and the eggs in the white bowl, stands a small glass of freshly squeezed orange juice. It stares malevolently at her.

Ivy slams the fridge shut. Something's terribly wrong. Her legs start to shake. Mum never leaves the house in the afternoons, and what about the unlocked door? Maybe Mum had fainted like that other time, and had to go to hospital for her injection. But why no note, why no neighbour to explain? She must've been kidnapped!

'Help!' screams Ivy. She runs outside. She can't stop herself from screaming. 'Someone's taken my Mum!'

She dashes down the side path, into the silent street, her eyes darting from side to side. Screams come from her throat, one loud wail after another. She crosses the street. A car screeches to a stop in front of her. A man with an angry mouth glares through the windscreen.

'You stupid kid, watch where you're going!'

She keeps running, keeps screaming, running, until there, in the distance, she sees a small figure walking unsteadily towards her. She recognises the slightly sideways gait. As the vision approaches, Ivy sees a small pink hat perched on top of dark curls, her mother's curls. The matching gloves, hat and shoes, are all the same dusty pink as her mother's bedspread. Ivy stops screaming. She runs up to her mother, almost knocking her over.

'Mum! Mum, where were you? I thought – I was scared – '

Ivy bursts into sobs, snot and tears running down her pockmarked face. The more she tries to stop, the more she chokes, weeping uncontrollably. Her mother stands there, looking over her shoulder, her ivory skin turning a blotchy pink.

'Stop it, Ivy, for heaven's sake. What will people think? I've been to town, that's all. Your father had a problem with the books, so I had to hurry in to the shop.'

A curtain twitches in the house opposite the spot where Ivy and her mother are standing.

'See over there, that'll be Mrs Ward having a good look, the old busybody,' Mum says, a fake smile on her face. 'For heaven's sake, Ivy, why are you carrying on? I left the door open for you, and your juice in the fridge in case I was held up.'

'But I want you to give it to me, or else it's no good,' Ivy says, through her sobs.

'Give it to you? What – the orange juice? Couldn't you have waited? I don't understand you, Ivy.'

'*You* have to give it to me or I can't drink it, don't you see?'

'What on earth do you mean? What difference does it make whether I give it to you or you help yourself? You're acting like a baby.'

Ivy wants to tell Mum how it makes her feel safe, and loved, if she gets the orange juice from her, but she can't find the words. She wants to tell her it's like a rule, which must not be broken. She starts to cry again, tears running unchecked down her cheeks.

'Be quiet – now it's Mrs Chapman staring at us through her window, nosy old thing. Let's walk on quietly like nothing's happened,' Mum says, still smiling inanely.

'But something has happened! I thought you'd been kidnapped!'

'For goodness' sake, lower your voice! Can't I go downtown without worrying about a grown girl? When I was your age, I was cooking dinner for my whole family, cleaning and washing, with my poor Mumma always sick.'

They've reached the front gate of their neat, gabled house. Ivy's mother takes the key from her handbag and opens the front door, although the back door's still open.

'Quick, get inside before anyone sees the state you're in. You'll drive everyone crazy if this goes on. I'm ringing your father straight away.'

Once inside, Ivy sinks down onto the carpet in the hall, shaking all over. She hears her mother speak into the new cream phone.

'Abe,' she says, 'I can't go on it like this. We have to do something about Ivy before I go mad.'

Her father's voice floats through the receiver. Ivy can't catch the words, but takes comfort from the familiar tone, the clipped English vowels. Daddy would make everything all right.

After dinner Daddy comes into Ivy's bedroom. She's deep in one of her favourite books, *Anne of Avonlea*. The red-haired teenager, like herself, is something of an outcast. Tonight Daddy sits on the bed and puts an arm around her. She feels the tension in him, and a tremor of fear runs through her.

'Ivylie, your mother and I have something to tell you.' Ivy stiffens. His voice is too serious. 'We're terribly worried seeing you like this, hardly any better after all that expensive treatment. And I have to say your behaviour this afternoon was a poor example to set for Laura. It's getting too hard for your mother to cope, she needs a break from all this too. We've decided it would be a good idea for you to have a little holiday.'

Ivy can't think for a minute. Is she being banished again? Is 'holiday' another word for 'hospital' and its horrors?

'Uncle Sid and Aunt Sonia in Perth have invited you and me to stay with them for a week or so,' Daddy continues, still with that tight, formal tone.

'But I've only just started back at school, and made friends with Meg again. What will Laura do without me? And I don't want to go away from home again.'

'I know, I know, *schönele*.' Daddy's voice softens a little. 'But it will only for be for a little while. And I'll be coming with you, Ivylie. It will be an adventure.'

'A little while? How long? How can you leave the Business? I don't believe you.' Ivy's mind is reeling. Why on earth would they send her away when she's starting to get better? She tries to hold the tears back.

'About a week or two. Jack from the agency will look after the shop, and your mother will keep an eye on things. It will be good for you, Ivy. And it's about time you got to know your mother's family in Perth. You have aunts and uncles to meet, and cousins too.'

'I don't want to meet them. I want to stay here and be with you and Mum and Laura. I don't need a holiday. Please, please, don't make me!' The tears won't wait any longer. They burst from her eyes. Daddy stiffens again, and speaks in that un-Daddy tone, like a school teacher.

'Our minds are made up, Ivy. It's time you thought of others besides yourself. Now stop crying, and think how lucky you are to be having a holiday. Let's say your *shema*, and I'll lie down with you till you go to sleep.'

7. THE HOLIDAY

Flying over clouds that look like peaks of snowy white meringues, Ivy thinks of Mum dropping little white balls of egg white and sugar onto the oven tray. Her mouth waters, tasting again their sweetness, seeing the meringues tinged golden brown, still chewy on the inside, crumbly outside. *There I go, thinking about food again.*

The aeroplane smells of leather and disinfectant. It is exciting and frightening to be up in the air in a metal machine. The air hostess is dressed in a navy-blue suit with gold buttons down the front. Her bottle-blonde hair is done up in a French roll, although why it's called French, Ivy can't imagine. The hostess brings a tray of food with clever little compartments for each item.

'My tummy's hurting, so I better not eat that. Safer that way in case I throw up.' Daddy sighs, and gets that black look on his face, the look he gets when he argues with Mum.

'Try a little bit, Ivy. Remember, you've had no breakfast.'

'I was much too excited to eat this morning. Besides, I read that it's best to start a plane trip with an empty stomach, in case you get airsick. That's what these brown paper bags are for.'

Her strategy works. Daddy stops looking at the untasted food on her tray. He takes the bread roll from its specially recessed slot, biting into it with hard chews, as if he's angry with it. Ivy moves closer to him, and rests her head on his arm. Why is he silent, not even arguing? He takes the packet of cigarettes from his trouser pocket, then digs deeper, searching for matches. Frowning, he lifts his hand and beckons the air hostess. The nicotine stain on his forefinger reminds Ivy of mornings at the breakfast table, when he used to stab the air to make his point. It is so much part of Daddy, that finger. The hostess sashays down the aisle, a fixed smile on her lipsticked mouth.

'I wonder, would you have a match, my dear?' Daddy uses the silky tone, like when he talks to Ivy's teachers, or Mum's lady friends.

'One moment, Sir.' The hostess glides back up the aisle. Ivy sees her father's eyes behind their horn-rimmed spectacles follow her retreating backside. She walks back to him, holding a silver lighter. Leaning over him, she touches the lighter to his cigarette. She is looking straight into Daddy's eyes. Ivy can smell her scent; it's sickeningly sweet, and makes her shrink back into her seat. Daddy bends forward, his hand almost brushing the tips of her manicured fingers.

'Allow me,' he says in his faint London accent, gently taking the lighter from the hostess, snapping it open, all the while looking into her eyes. The red-gold flame flares between them in the second before he touches it to the tip of his cigarette. 'Thank you, my dear.' Daddy's voice is smooth as honey.

Ivy notices a flush creeping up the hostess's neck as she straightens, the smile fixed on her face again.

'My pleasure, Sir.'

*

Ivy has fallen asleep on Daddy's shoulder. In Ivy's dream she's back in Winchester. A woman is jerking like a puppet on haywire strings. Ivy forces herself awake before it's her turn. She shakes her head to get the ghastly dream out of her head.

There's a sudden jolt, and a baby's wail reminds Ivy she's up in the air, and the plane is moving downwards.

'What's happening?' she asks Daddy, stiffening with fright.

'The plane has to refuel in Adelaide, ready for the next flight to Perth.'

'Can we get off in Adelaide?' She wants to get out of this space that confines her, like the straps on the hospital trolley.

'We'll have an hour at the airport, time to get a bite to eat, something better than this aeroplane slop. You must be hungry by now.'

Of course she's hungry. Starving to death. She's perfected the art of not eating, obeying The Voice in her head. It is far stronger than the gnawing emptiness of her belly.

'I'm OK, I'll wait till my tummy settles.' She stretches her cramped legs as best she can. Even the soft leather seat hurts her bony backside. Daddy pats her hand, not looking at her. His expression is sad and angry at the same time. She knows what he's thinking, and wants more than anything to make him smile, and laugh with her again.

*

Adelaide airport was a desolate place, with no food on offer except ham sandwiches or sausage rolls. 'Not kosher,' Daddy grumbled. Ivy was relieved she had a good excuse to refuse the food.

Back on the plane, night is falling. Ivy has no desire for sleep. She takes her Latin homework from the schoolbag she's allowed to keep with her. She mustn't let Meg beat her in Latin next term. The regular rhythm of parsing and conjugating quietens The Voice.

'Listen to me, *Ivylie*,' Daddy says. 'When we get to Perth, I want you to make a good impression on your Uncle Sid and Aunt Sonia. Don't hide away with your books all the time, they won't like that. And remember the names of your cousins, Alex and Deborah.'

Daddy only calls her *Ivylie* when there is something serious to say. Ivy closes her Latin textbook with a sigh, the comforting words *amo, amas, amat* fading from her sight.

'How old are my cousins?'

'I wouldn't know, *schönele*; it's your mother who keeps track of these things. Younger than you, all of them, I'd say. The little one's only a baby.'

*

The first thing Ivy notices when they land in Perth is the space. It's as if the city were an empty house waiting to be furnished. Through the taxi's window she sees a straggle of houses with flat roofs, squatting like

55

mushrooms higgledy-piggledy in a field. Not like the crowded streets of Castleton back home.

Daddy, sitting close beside her on the sticky leather seat of the taxicab, lights another cigarette. Ivy breathes in the acrid smoke, grateful for its familiar smell. Neither of them speaks, exhausted by the long flight. Ivy's starting to feel really queasy now, her stomach clenching as much in fear as in hunger. She's managed to eat nothing so far except for the barley sugar sweet she was given to suck by the flirty hostess.

The taxi pulls up outside a large sprawling house, with a red light illuminating a sign over the front porch: *Dr S Bronsky, General Practitioner. Hours: 8am to 1pm Monday to Friday, 3pm to 7pm Monday to Thursday.* There's a phone number underneath the times, and a note in small writing: *House Calls Available After Hours.*

Ivy's impressed, and so is her father, who points at the sign and says to the taxi-driver, a young man hardly out of his teens: 'My brother-in-law, you know. Put himself through medicine by working in a fruit shop. You have to give him credit...'

'Dr Bronsky's a household word 'round here, mate. He brought me and my brother into the world, and saw my grandma out of it. Wouldn't go to anyone else.'

Ivy sees Daddy's smile of satisfaction, as he hands the boy a crisp pound note.

'Keep the change, Son,' he says. The boy looks wide-eyed at the money in his hand and quickly pockets it. He springs from the cab to open the boot. At that moment Ivy notices Daddy's brought only a small pigskin bag, not the big suitcase that was on top of the hall cupboard back home. *Of course, only enough for a week, thank goodness.*

Ivy's own suitcase is new, containing more books, as well as the clothes Mum has helped her pack. Far too many for a week. Winter ones as well as summer, *because the weather's changeable in Perth, Ivy. You might need your jumpers, as well as some summer frocks, and I've packed one good skirt to wear on Friday nights, and a good outfit for Schule. It's too big for you now, but we're not wasting money on new clothes. Please God you'll fill out again soon, so these'll fit you again.*

It's still early morning, the air fresh and crisp, as Ivy and Daddy stand on the front porch of a rambling brick house, waiting for an answer to Daddy's firm knock. The silence hangs between them. After several long minutes, a tall thin woman with red hair arranged in carefully crimped waves, opens the heavy front door.

'Doctor's not open yet,' she says crossly.

'That's all right, young lady,' says Daddy. 'I'm Sid's brother-in-law, and this is my daughter, Ivy. You can call me Abe. And what might your name be, pretty girl like you, eh?'

Ivy notices two red patches flaring on the girl's cheeks and stares in fascination as they spread, until the girl's whole face is a blotchy crimson.

'Oh, sorry Mister. Me name's Daphne. I'm Dr Bronsky's secretary. I s'pose you better come in then. This door's only for patients, so's you know. Family comes in round the side.'

They follow Daphne into a dark room set about with several high-backed chairs. There's a small table in the middle, piled with magazines, some tattered, their once bright covers dull.

'The waiting room,' Daphne announces with a degree of pride. She uses a key from the bunch at her waist to open a door leading into another dimly lit room. Inside is a sofa covered in purplish brocade, and several easy chairs.

'Sit y'selves down,' says Daphne. 'I'll get Mrs Bronsky.'

'Can I read those magazines, Miss Daphne?'

'It's just Daphne to you, young lady. Course you can, they're a bit old, but. I'll be bringing some new ones when me mum's finished with them.'

Ivy perches on the edge of a large chair, its seat sagging sadly. She thinks it might not bear even her weight. She takes a *Women's Weekly* and turns its yellowing pages. It's full of advertisements for shiny refrigerators, like the one back home that replaced the old ice chest. Daddy sits across from her on the sofa, his long trousered legs crossed. He appraises the room with a look of disapproval.

'Not what you're used to at home, eh? Needs a good coat of paint and some new furniture, I'd say.'

They sit in silence in the cold air of the lounge room. Ivy feels someone watching her. Turning, she sees a little boy of about seven, his dark eyes staring at her under floppy brown hair.

'Hello, you must be Alexander,' she says, relieved to see a sign of life in this silent house. 'I'm your cousin Ivy from Castleton.'

The little boy smiles, and she sees a gap where his front tooth should be. He's wearing pyjamas with toy cars printed on them. 'It's Alex for short,' he lisps. After a moment's hesitation, he runs off.

A bronchial cough sounds from the hallway, and a short round woman, her housecoat flapping open, rushes into the room. 'Abe!' she cries with a phlegmy sound. 'You're here already? Such *nachas*!'

'Wonderful to see you, Sonia. Lily sends her love, of course,' Daddy says, embracing his sister-in-law. 'We are both so grateful to you and Sid.' He grasps Sonia's chubby hands. Ivy wonders what Daddy's grateful for. Is it the offer of a lift not taken? A seat on a lumpy sofa?

'It's the least we can do, we're family after all. But tell me, how did you get here? Don't tell me you *schlepped* all the way from the airport on the bus?' Sonia prattles on, her voice rising with each question. Ivy detects a faint foreign accent. 'Sid would have picked you up, if he didn't have patients to see. Morning surgery, afternoon surgery, up to his ears in the paperwork.'

'Nonsense, we wouldn't dream of putting Sid to trouble, not after all you're doing. You mustn't worry yourself, Sonia. You have enough to do feeding your own brood. Ivy can look after herself, and be a help to you, too.' Daddy's smile is starting to look fixed.

'A help? She looks like she can't lift an envelope. Come here, girlie, let me look at you.'

Ivy stands up and faces her aunt. Face to face, she sees darting black eyes, sharp cheekbones and flared nostrils. They make Ivy think there must be a bad smell, and maybe it's coming from her body? Unwashed after the long journey? But when Aunt Sonia draws breath to talk, her nostrils stay wide.

'So this is your Ivy? *Oy gewalt*, now I see what you mean in your letters. All skin and bone, she is. Ha! Wait for Sonia's special *cholent* and cheesecake. I'll soon fatten her up.'

Ivy stares back at her aunt. Her fists clench inside the long sleeves of her cardigan, which she's pulled down to warm her hands. Words come to her before she can stop them. 'You're not my aunt really, only by marriage, and that doesn't count.'

Ivy glimpses the shadow of a smile behind Daddy's moustache. He gives her a gentle push towards Sonia. 'Ivy! Apologise immediately!'

Aunt Sonia's shiny black eyes fill with tears. She squares her shoulders and comes closer, so close Ivy can smell stale onions on her aunt's morning breath. 'You ungrateful girl! Spoilt is what you are. I've known you since you were a baby, and what a drama that was. You refused even your mother's milk, put poor Lily in a sanitorium.'

'Now now, Sonia. Best not to stir up old memories,' Daddy says, suddenly stern.

Aunt Sonia ignores him. 'My Sid was there with Lily when you came into the world, did you know that? We're your family and I'm your aunt. Don't you forget it. Look at you, girl!' Sonia's voice becomes shrill. 'How could you do such a thing to your parents? There'll be no such nonsense in this house.' She turns her back with a 'humph', tossing her head and muttering under her breath. 'Come, I'll show you your rooms,' she calls over her shoulder.

They walk from the lounge room into a short hallway. There are some yellowing photographs in frames along the wall. Ivy recognises a drawing of her grandmother, sitting on an old-fashioned sofa, her short grey hair framing a care-worn face, round spectacles on her bulbous nose. It was a print of the portrait Daddy had done of Lily's mother before she died. *My Buba must have been Uncle Sid's mother too, as well as my mother's mother*, she realises. The connection makes her feel less afraid.

The hallway leads to a large kitchen, which to Ivy's relief is bright with morning sun. *Thank goodness not every room in this house is dull and dingy.* There's a rectangular table pushed against the wall, with two windows above it, their frilly curtains tied back to reveal a well-kept kitchen garden. An old-fashioned oven with the familiar kookaburra emblem on its door stands against the far wall. The floor is laid out in mustard-coloured linoleum squares. *Such a horrid colour, like vomit.* The only other furniture in the kitchen, besides the four chairs around the table, is a large pantry cupboard, its doors made of wire mesh.

Two small rooms lead off the kitchen. On the left is a scullery, where a sink and draining board stand under a window. Ivy glimpses a large white ice chest. To the right there's a small room, not much bigger than a cupboard, containing a narrow single bed with a floral bedspread thrown over it.

'That'll be Ivy's room,' Aunt Sonia says, standing back to let her guests get a better view. 'It was our maid's room, but the blasted girl's gone walkabout again. Can't trust these abos, y'know. We give them a decent home, teach them some manners, feed them, and like as not they take off, with no rhyme nor reason. Molly went walkabout, as they call it, without never a by-your-leave. Well, it can be Ivy's room now.'

'But – look here,' Daddy says, 'this can't be a bedroom. It's much too small. Where will she put her books?' He stops suddenly and exchanges a secret look with Sonia.

Ivy can't quite work it out. Does that secret look mean that the grownups are plotting something behind her back?

'It's all right Daddy,' she says quickly, 'I love this room, it's really cute and old-fashioned. It'll be like when we went camping that time, when Laura and I had our own little tent. After all, it's only for a few days, like you said.' Ivy's heart leaps at the thought of sleeping in this tiny room, all to herself.

'What's that she says? A few days?' Aunt Sonia's mouth stays open, showing small, sharp, teeth. 'I thought …' Daddy gives a short cough and Sonia stops, catching his eye, and closes her mouth. There's an awkward silence. Ivy feels a tremor of fear. *'Nu*, what am I thinking?' Aunt Sonia, shrugs her plump shoulders. 'Letting you stand here with nothing to eat. Let's all have a cup of tea.'

Ivy hears the sharp thump of water hitting the bottom of the kettle. She steps inside the maid's room and drops her bag onto the bed. Her father follows her. He speaks to her softly, but his eyes are flashing behind his glasses. 'How could you say you love this *verschtinkene* room? After your beautiful big room at home? We've given you everything, spared no expense.'

'You said I should be polite, didn't you? I'm just doing as I'm told,' Ivy replies, straight-faced. Her father turns on his heel. Ivy follows him into the kitchen, her heart heavy with guilt and confusion. Why does it matter which room she has for such a short visit?

A small girl runs into the kitchen. She has thick dark hair standing up over her head in unruly tufts, and holds a brush in her hand. Her large brown eyes regard Ivy and Daddy solemnly. Aunt Sonia comes out of the scullery holding the kettle, heavy with water, deposits it on the stove and lights the gas.

'Debbie!' she says, seeing her daughter standing half-dressed in the middle of the kitchen, 'Mummy can't do your hair now, darling. Daphne will help you dress today. Now, be a good girl and say hello to your Uncle Abe and cousin Ivy.'

The child stares open-mouthed at Ivy. 'Why's she so skinny?'

Aunt Sonia hugs Debbie, and calls, 'Daphne! Hurry up, it's getting late.' Daphne looms in the doorway, and grabs Debbie by her arm. 'Come and get ready for kindy, you little scallywag,' she says in her broad Australian accent.

'No! I want Mum to do my hair!' screams Debbie, her little face turning a puce colour, angry tears welling in her eyes.

'Come here, *bubele*,' Aunt Sonia sighs, plonking her broad backside into the nearest chair, and settles Debbie on her lap. She expertly brushes at the knots from Debbie's thick fair hair. 'I shouldn't give in to her, but it's easier this way. Please, make yourself comfortable, take a seat. Ivy, can you make the tea?'

Ivy's never been allowed to enter the hallowed realm of her mother's kitchen. They had a daily help back in Castleton, who did all the heavy cleaning. Mum did all the rest, like tea-making. She shrugs. 'No, I can't.'

Aunt Sonia stops brushing Debbie's hair. 'I didn't mean *can* you, as if you don't know how, you silly girl. Must be my bad English. I'm asking you to get the pot, put the tea leaves in, and pour the boiling water over. You can do that, can't you?'

'Sonia, don't worry yourself on our account, Ivy and I ate on the plane. We'll have tea later, you have your hands full now,' Daddy says.

Ivy goes to the stove, turns the gas off under the whistling kettle, and looks around for a teapot. There's a big brown china pot, its sides bulbous and shiny, sitting close to the range. There's a caddy nearby, with the word *TEA* inscribed in green letters on its cream enamel surface. Ivy lifts the lid and scoops one spoon into the pot.

'Wait!' calls Aunt Sonia, pushing Debbie off her lap, 'Didn't your mother teach you anything? Don't you know you have to warm the pot first? And it's one spoon for each person, and one for the pot.' She takes the caddy from Ivy's hands and drops four generous scoops of leaves into the waiting teapot, shaking her head all the while.

8. ABANDONED

Waking in the tiny room, Ivy struggles to remember where she is. Gradually, the mists of sleep clear, and she sees her own bony shape under the patchwork quilt. She remembers this is Uncle Sid's house, and she's in the little maid's room that disgusts Daddy. Through the closed door she hears voices, and recognises Aunt Sonia's faint accent and throaty tone. The other broad Aussie voice must belong to the secretary, Daphne.

'When I *has* a cuppa tea, I *has* a cuppa tea, like me mother always says. Strong, like, with three sugars and no milk. So thick y'can stand a spoon up in it. *That*'s proper tea.'

Ivy listens for her father's voice; maybe he's not awake yet, seeing this is a holiday. It's early, only six-thirty according to the wrist watch she never takes off, except in the bath. It'd been a present from Mum and Daddy for her tenth birthday. There's a photo of her holding her wrist to her ear, listening to the ticking of her brand new watch. That was Before, when she still wore her hair in plaits, when she still had her child's body, clean and straight, when she was a Good Girl.

Ivy reaches for her diary on the floor near the bed, and starts to write carefully with her special blue fountain pen. The diary is her best friend, the one she can trust with her secrets. It comes everywhere with her. She wants to save everything that happens on this holiday, so she'll always remember it.

*

Met uncle Sid yesterday. He's not like Daddy, much quieter, not as tall, no glasses, or moustache. I liked him straight away. Funny to think he's Mum's brother, and was once a little boy. I wonder if they played together, or if they were too far apart? I got through yesterday with two cups of sugarless and milkless tea, a piece of pineapple, and one square of my secret chocolate bar. Never mind, I'll be home in a week, and all this will be like a nightmare, soon forgotten.

There's a knock at the door, and a voice calling. Ivy quickly hides her diary under her pillow.

'Miss Ivy? You're wanted in the kitchen.' It's Daphne's voice, too strident this early in the morning. Ivy swings her legs to the floor, searching for the blue felt slippers that should be there. She remembers she hasn't unpacked. Why bother, for such a short stay? Barefoot in her pink interlock nightie, she pads into the kitchen.

'Sit down, Ivy,' says Aunt Sonia. 'I need to tell you something.' Her aunt is tightly packed into a floral dressing gown, her large bust rising before her as if she's a carved goddess on the prow of a ship. Her glance slips sideways. She looks pleased, as if she has a secret she's bursting to share.

Alarm sets Ivy's heart beating wildly.

'Where's Daddy?' She looks around the kitchen as if he might materialise, sitting in a chair at the table in his business suit, having his first cigarette of the day, like he did every morning at home.

'Your father's had to leave, Ivy. He'll be on the plane back to Castleton by now.' Aunt Sonia hands Ivy an envelope. She recognises Daddy's curly handwriting, with her name scrolled across the envelope.

'No, he can't be!' Everything goes black for a few seconds. She feels her eyes fill with tears of shock.

'You'll be staying with us now, child, for as long as it takes you to come to your senses, get over this foolish fad of yours.'

'No!' Ivy sobs as the tears course down her cheeks. 'I'm going home too! I'm not staying here.'

'You poor kid,' says Daphne. She stands up and hugs Ivy, who pushes her away. Stumbling into her bedroom, Ivy bangs the door shut, not caring about the noise, hating everybody. Sitting on her bed, she tears open the envelope.

My dearest Ivy,

It breaks my heart to leave you like this, but you'll soon see it's for the best. Your mother and I want only to have our old Ivy back. That's why I've brought you to Perth, so your Uncle Sid can look after you, and help you get better. It's been too much for your poor mother to see you like this, getting thinner day by day, when there seems nothing she can do about it. Please be a good girl, and help your Aunt Sonia as much as you can. Your mother and Laura are already missing you, but not as much as I am. I'll write to you often. Please write back, and let me know if there's anything you need.

You'll never know how much I love you,

Daddy

Ivy starts to retch, but only a thin trickle of green bile comes up.

*

The rest of the day passes like a nightmare. Ivy stays in her bedroom, speaking to no one. She hears Alex and Debbie go off to school and kindy, their voices ringing in the morning air as they call goodbye. *Lucky things, to have a mother and father to say goodbye to.* How could Daddy leave her here, dump her like a piece of rubbish? He only pretends to love her, she knows that now. Unless – there's been a mistake. Or Aunt Sonia's lying. *I wouldn't put it past her,* Ivy thinks.

By afternoon the house is quiet. The plate of cheese sandwiches lies untouched on Ivy's bedside table, where Daphne has silently placed them. Uncle Sid's gone on his house calls, and Aunt Sonia's driven to the grocery store down the road, she guesses. Ivy heard her tell Daphne to do the ironing while she's gone. This is her chance.

Ivy's knees creak as she uncurls from her narrow bed and stands up, still in her night clothes. She tiptoes through the kitchen and down the hall to the surgery. Her feet in their thick bed socks make no sound. The surgery's empty as she knew it would be. She breathes in the faint smell of disinfectant, eyeing the jar of brightly colored jelly beans hungrily. She used to like the black ones best, with their strong taste of licorice. *Don't you dare*, says The Voice, as saliva rushes into her mouth.

The black telephone sits solidly on Uncle Sid's enormous desk, its surface covered with a stack of medical journals, blank notepaper, a black fountain pen and a jar of blue ink. There's a big white blotter sitting square in the middle, its corners covered in dark brown leather. Ivy's hands shake as she lifts the receiver from its cradle. She takes a deep breath and dials zero. The line buzzes as it connects.

'Number please,' says a woman's voice.

'Please get me Castleton in NSW, under A. Morgenstern.'

She knew the number off by heart once, long ago, before the shock treatment. There's crackling on the line.

'Sorry Miss, there's two numbers under that name. What's the address?'

Ivy thinks for a long time, hearing the operator breathe impatiently. Joel's words back in Winchester come back to her through broken memories.

'It might be Wave Street.'

There's a buzzing sound, and the relentless sound of a phone ringing and ringing, until Ivy could bear it no more. Tears of frustration roll down her face as she bangs the receiver down.

'Hello, what's this?'

Ivy turns to find herself face to face with Uncle Sid.

'I'm – I'm sorry, I'm sorry. I have to talk to Daddy. He's not answering.'

'That's because he's probably still in the air, Ivy. Now what's all this about? You should know you can't use the surgery phone. It uses a special line for patients only.'

'I don't believe Daddy's gone. He wouldn't leave me here, by myself.' Her tears turned into sobs.

'Now, now. You're not by yourself. I'm here, and so is your Aunt Sonia, and Daphne, and Alex and Debbie. We all want to help you, Ivy, but first you must help yourself.' Uncle Sid holds out the jar. 'Here. Have a jellybean.' He twisted the metal lid off and shook the contents, holding the jar out. The colours danced before her eyes. A black one was right on top. Ivy's mouth watered.

'I – I can't,' she whispers. *Don't you dare take it,* says The Voice

*

Back in her room, Ivy lies face down on her bed, her father's letter fallen to the floor. She stretches out her hand and picks it up. She wants to destroy it, burn it, but something stronger than anger stops her. That would be like burning Daddy, wouldn't it? She sits up, wipes her eyes with the back of her hand, and reaches for her diary.

I hate him, I hate him, I hate him! she writes. Her silver propelling pencil stabs at the paper, tearing it. *How dare he do this to me? It's all lies when he says he loves me, and that we're going on a holiday. Some holiday! I should've known when he only brought the pigskin bag that he was lying, telling me we'd be away for two weeks. Now I'll miss the beginning of third term, and fall behind in German and Latin, to say nothing of Maths and Science. I have to get out of here, any way I can, and I will! Like I got out of Winchester, by pretending. I'll have to trick my way out. And what about Mum? She must have known. Maybe she's glad to be rid of me. And what will Laura do without me, when the other kids bully her at school, calling her little Bett-Bett?*

Ivy's writing is getting more and more out of control, the letters large and loopy, not like her neat handwriting that Daddy had admired. *I'll have to write to him.* She carefully tears a blank page from her diary and begins, trying to stop her hand shaking.

'Dear Daddy,

I can't believe you left me alone here! How could you do such a thing? I got such a shock when I woke up this morning and you weren't there. I guess you had to get back for the business, otherwise we'd all starve! (joke). Only it wasn't fair to tell me we'd be having a holiday here together. I'm not a child any more, you know. I can handle the truth.

Did you leave me here because I don't eat enough, and it makes Mum nervy? I'm trying really hard, please believe me. I ate a good breakfast this morning; hot buttered toast and tea with milk. I even managed a boiled egg. It must be the different air here in the West, because I'm hungry all the time! The lies pour out of Ivy like the tears of her desperation.

Aunt Sonia is very busy, and I don't want to put her to extra trouble. She already has Alex and Debbie to look after. Besides, I don't need looking after now I'm nearly fourteen. It's interesting to meet my cousins, but they're much younger than me, and they'll be going to school or kindy every day. Uncle Sid is frightfully busy, and I'm sure I'll hardly see him. You can't imagine how much I already miss Laura, after only two days!

Please, please, Daddy, can you come and get me soon (like tomorrow?) I can't stay here more than another week, or else I'll miss the start of Term 4. You want me to come top in Latin again, don't you? Please, please, come. I promise I'll be good if only I can come home.

Give my love to Mum and Laura,

Your loving daughter

Ivy.

PART 2: EROS AND THANATOS

1955 to 1957

Someone finally believed me, and more importantly, someone finally knew—and could name—what was happening to my body.

– Fiona Wright, *This Woman is Hysterical.*

9. FRENCH TOAST

In the weeks and months that follow her father's departure, letters to and from Castleton are lifelines to the world Ivy has left behind. From Daddy come reassurances that all will be well, and that her removal from the family is for the best. The phrase 'for your own good' sets Ivy's teeth on edge. How can something as cruel, as alienating as exile from one's family, be good?

Occasionally Meg sends a letter about what's happening at school. When she writes that Miss Trent's got engaged to a handsome ex-serviceman, Ivy feels a pang of jealousy, hating herself for it. She doesn't answer Meg for weeks, not wanting to be reminded any more of all that's lost to her.

Although Ivy begs to go to school in Perth, Uncle Sid says she is not well enough. If she can eat more, he says, it might be possible. Meanwhile, he arranges free correspondence lessons in English, Maths and Latin so that Ivy won't fall too far behind. But it's not the same, sitting alone in the dark dining room with books and papers spread on the table, as being in a class, listening to Miss Trent or Miss Jamison, talking with Meg and helping each other to unravel a difficult sum or translation.

Every Friday Ivy is allowed a call home, reverse charges of course. It always starts with "Good Shabbos" from her father. She does not hear much from her mother, no doubt because of Mum's nervous breakdown caused by Ivy's not eating. Ivy always feels a stab of sorrow when reminded of what she's apparently done to her mother. She's most comforted by Laura's light lisping voice, telling her every detail about a book she's reading or a new dress she covets.

It is only to Laura that Ivy writes freely, of her own secret fears and hopes. To Joel, Ivy writes of how different Perth is to Castleton, even having different names for things, like "bathers" for swimming costumes. She is careful also to focus her words on him, rather than on herself, hoping he will see her as necessary in his life.

Aunt Sonia treats Ivy half as a servant, half as a challenge to be conquered. She seems determined to turn Ivy into a "normal" girl competent in the domestic arts which, she constantly reminds Ivy, are sadly lacking due to her indulgent upbringing. Alex and Debbie mostly ignore her, although Alex allows her to read to him sometimes. Only Uncle Sid, busy as he is, spares Ivy an occasional kind word or glance.

*

One of Ivy's jobs is to collect the mail from the metal letterbox on the front fence. Amongst the bills and medical journals Ivy brings to the surgery she sees a letter with Daddy's familiar curly writing. It's addressed to her. She quickly puts it in the pocket of her pinafore, her heart skipping a beat in a moment of joy. As she deposits the mail on Uncle Sid's desk, her eye falls on her father's handwriting again. It's an opened letter, a cheque attached to it with a silver paper clip. Ivy doesn't hesitate.

'Dear Sid,' she reads,

'Lil and I were beside ourselves when we got your letter. You say Ivy's not getting any better – in fact in your medical opinion she's worse. We're distraught. After the psychiatrist assured us that the shock treatment had worked, and she would grow out of it, we were sure we were doing the right thing sending her to you. It was partly, of course, to do with Lil's nerves; she simply couldn't take any more. And we thought a break from the family, a whole new environment, would help Ivy snap out of whatever's wrong with her.

Thanks for finding out about Dr de Berg. I've never heard of a psycho-analyst, but if as you say she specialises in children, and trained with the great Anna Freud, we may as well give her a try. What have we got to lose, after all? I'll do anything to make our Ivy better. The rabbi says to have faith, but it seems prayers aren't enough.

Please go ahead and make the appointment. From what you told me about the fees, this isn't going to come cheap. I've enclosed an extra cheque covering the first three months' treatment, in addition to the usual.

Once again, we can't thank you and Sonia enough for taking care of our precious girl. She had such promise, a top student, and now look at her. It's breaking our hearts, let me tell you,
Yours truly,

Abe.

*

Ivy watches Aunt Sonia dip each slice of thick white bread into a bowl of beaten egg, and lift it, dripping, into a pan of sizzling butter.

'Don't just stand there gawking, girl. Make yourself useful, go fetch the serving plate to drain on. And get down the golden syrup from the pantry. You can wash up after as well. There'll be no shirking in this house.' Ivy does as she's told, storing Aunt Sonia's words to add to her complaints in her next letter home.

A piece of French toast squats on Ivy's plate winking at her, daring her to eat it. Her mouth waters as she cuts it into small squares. Debbie stars whining, and throwing her food onto the floor.

Sonia turns to Sid, as he comes in from the surgery. 'See? What did I tell you? Look at Debbie. She's not eating! playing with her food.' Now Debbie is pushing her cut up bits of bread, carrot and apple into a little mound on her plate, like a sand castle.

Uncle Sid's eating very fast and slurping hot tea, as if he wants to get the meal over with. In between bites he loosens his tie. 'Debbie, show Dadda how you can make that castle on your plate disappear into your mouth.' Debbie chuckles and pushes a stick of carrot up her nose.

'I said into your mouth!' shouts Uncle Sid. Aunt Sonia glares at him.

'Can I have golden syrup on my bread?' pipes up Alex.

'It's called French toast, Alex, though why it's French I've no idea,' says Uncle Sid as he passes the syrup jar to his son. 'Not too much, now; sugar is bad for you.'

Ivy silently thanks Alex for his deft change of subject. She puts a square of bread into her mouth, and chews it for a long time, taking care not to swallow. Her eyes linger on Alex's plate; she loves golden syrup, and her mouth fills with saliva so that she almost swallows the sweet morsel. *Get rid of it!* The Voice says loudly. She runs to the bathroom and spits the liquefied bread into the toilet. When she comes back, Uncle Sid and Aunt Sonia are shouting at each other. Ivy hovers in the doorway out of their sight. She hears every word.

'She's copying that girl, see? Do something, Sid. Do you want our little girl to be all skin and bones like your crazy niece here? You never should've agreed to take her. More than three months she's been here, and she's as impossible as ever. She can't sit at the table with us if this is how it's going to be.'

Uncle Sid's face reddens and his neck seems to swell above his collar. 'We'll have no more discussion about Lil's daughter not eating with us. She's my flesh and blood, and I've promised Lil and Abe we'll take care of her as best we can. After all they've done for us it's the least we can do.'

'You want me to put the food in front of her so she can spit it? Are you crazy too? Must run in your family.'

Ivy slips back into her seat beside Alex. Aunt Sonia gets up, lifts Debbie from her chair, and takes her to the kitchen. Alex looks from his father to Ivy. To her surprise, his small hand reaches for hers under the table.

After that night, Aunt Sonia feeds Debbie separately in the kitchen. Ivy feels a weight of guilt that the family is split because of her, because of The Voice, which she can't control. Each meal is torture. She uses every ruse in her bag of tricks, chewing one mouthful for ages, taking care to cut up the food on her plate slowly and methodically. She hides chunks of meat under a mound of mashed potato. None of this fools Uncle Sid, she's sure, but he says nothing. Alex and Ivy pull faces at each other, and make each other laugh. But inside, Ivy's screaming *make this stop, make The Voice go away!*

One night after another meal of French toast (it's served often because Alex loves it, and it's cheap), Ivy takes the plates and cutlery to the scullery. Before she can stop herself, she lifts a knife still smeared with golden syrup and licks it. She does the same with all the other knives. It's as if her hand is detached from her body, its volition even stronger than The Voice shouting in her head.

Later Ivy feels the need to confess, to be absolved for such a shameful act. 'I've done something terrible,' she tells Uncle Sid, who's still at the table, reading the evening paper.

'What's this terrible thing you've done? Tried to burn the house down?'

'No, it's worse. I – I licked a knife with golden syrup on it.' She doesn't dare say she licked not just one, but every knife.

Uncle Sid's mouth twitches for a moment. Is he going to laugh or cry? He doesn't speak for a long minute, then says, 'I wouldn't describe licking a knife as a terrible thing. Why did you do it?'

'I was hungry, and now I feel bad and disgusting,' Ivy says, relieved to speak the truth, and grateful that Uncle Sid hasn't been as hard on her as she's been on herself.

'That was pretty silly of you, Ivy, and dangerous too. Besides, you could get germs off a knife that someone else used. In your weakened state, even a cold could make you seriously ill. Maybe even kill you. If you don't start eating soon, I can't help you. In fact, you may not survive.'

For the first time Ivy feels death waiting in the shadows, tempting her, claiming her, and she is afraid. Surely she can't die from not eating. She remembers Irina, dead at twelve. Does she want to join her? But what if there's no afterlife, heaven, or hell? Whatever happens, she is slave to The Voice, even if it wants to kill her.

10. CRIMES AND MISDEMEANOURS

'Set the table, Ivy. Tea's early tonight. Hurry up, won't you, girl. Don't forget, you're babysitting tonight while Sid and I go square-dancing,' Aunt Sonia says, dishing out mashed potato and lamb chops. 'And mind you don't go upsetting our Debbie tonight. We don't want her copying your tricks, she's picky enough with her food as it is. Anyways, it's about time you did more round here, so's me and Sid can get a bit of time to ourselves.' Aunt Sonia's spiky teeth look sharper than usual.

Good, I'll be glad to have a bit of time (bitter time) without you breathing down my neck, Ivy thinks. 'Sure, Aunt Sonia,' she says, perfectly polite as usual. 'What time's lights out?'

'Same as always, you should know by now. It's eight o'clock for Alex and seven for Debbie. Alex has a glass of milk last thing, then we let him read for half an hour.'

'I'll read to Debbie, shall I? She loves *The Magic Pudding* by Norman Lindsay. We started reading it last week.' Ivy always includes the author's name when she mentions any book. To her it's more important than the book's title.

'As long as she gets to sleep. She's been coming into our bed again last few nights. Must be something, or someone, upsetting the poor *bubele.* Wonder what? Or who?' Sonia narrows her eyes to slits.

Ivy doesn't bother to reply. She takes a handful of cutlery from the kitchen drawer. Knives and forks for Sid, Sonia, Alex, and herself, and a baby bowl and spoon for Deb. *I'd never do anything to hurt Debbie. Could it really be my fault she's a fussy eater?*

Ivy can't help staring at her aunt and uncle as they leave that night. Uncle Sid's transformed from the dignified family doctor into a cowboy from the Wild West: wide trousers and a bright checked shirt, finished with a red and white scarf tied rakishly around his neck. Aunt Sonia's wearing a brightly coloured skirt that swirls when she moves, and a lacy white top with a plunging neckline, showing most of her ample breasts. *Disgusting*, thinks Ivy.

Aunt Sonia and Uncle Sid have never left her in charge before. It makes her feel strong, as if she were really a good person. Perhaps Aunt Sonia doesn't hate her after all. She remembers the French toast and the dreadful, unspeakable act she'd performed, licking the knives until they shone like new. Shame floods her again.

Ivy finishes the washing up quickly, and goes to check on the children, first to Debbie in her room just off the main bedroom. She's brought the book Debbie loves, but the little girl's fallen asleep already, curled up in her cot. It makes Ivy smile to see her little bottom stuck in the air. Ivy thinks Debbie should have a proper bed, now she's four. The cot's much too small for her. She pulls a blanket over Debbie's small pink feet, careful not to wake her.

Alex is already in bed, looking at illustrations in an oversized book with a picture of a train on its cover. He's lying down, the book propped on his chest, when Ivy brings him his milk. He drops the book and sits up.

'I don't much feel like my milk tonight. When will Mum be home?'

'Not till after you're asleep. Meanwhile you've got me.'

'But you're too skinny. How can you save us, if there's a fire or a robber or something?'

'First of all, I'm stronger than I look. I'd ring the fire brigade straight away, or the police if there was a robber. The firemen would come with ladders and hoses, and save all of us. Of course, I'd lift Debbie from her cot before I made the calls. Second of all, I'd grab a handful of ginger biscuits and fill our pockets with them, in case we got hungry.' Alex sits up, staring at Ivy with wide, frightened eyes.

'Will you be my girlfriend when I grow up?'

'Of course, I will. I can be your girlfriend now, if you like.'

'Really? Does that mean we have to kiss and stuff?'

'Not necessarily. We can be sort of best friends, and see how we feel later, when you're quite grown up.'

'Anyway, I'm going to marry Mum when I'm big. I've promised her.'

'We can still be best friends. Now, lights out, or you'll be all droopy at school tomorrow.'

'I've got a pain in my tummy. I want M-mum!' Alex's eyes fill with tears. His bottom lip trembles.

'What would Mum do if she were here?'

'She'd make my pain go away.'

'It's all right. I know a magic spell for sore tummies. Can I show you?'

'S'pose so.' Alex looks at Ivy curiously. Ivy pushes up her sleeves and lays her right hand lightly on Alex's abdomen.

'Abracadabradiggerredo, tummy ache, tummy ache, go away, do.'

Ivy moves her hand in a circular motion around Alex's navel while intoning the magic spell over and over.

'There. You'll be better now. Just close your eyes and keep on saying the spell till you fall asleep.' Alex lies perfectly still, his eyes closed. As Ivy tiptoes to the door his eyes fly open again.

'Can you leave the door open, and the hall light on?'

'Sure. I'll leave the bathroom light on too.'

When Uncle Sid and Aunt Sonia came home, Ivy is curled up like a cat on the old sofa, lost in her book. The sound of the key in the lock and their laughing voices bring her back to the moment. They don't greet her, but go straight to check on the children, as if they expect them to be harmed, spirited away, or worse.

An eerie silence floats towards Ivy, followed by her aunt, who stands in front of her, hands on her hips. Her nostrils flare.

'You filthy girl. Leaving that mess for me to clean up.'

Ivy stares at Sonia. Her heart slowly freezes.

'What mess? Where?'

'You know where. It's them laxatives I seen you take, don't think I don't know.'

'What? I don't know what you're talking about.'

'Is that so? Just you come with me, and I'll show you what I'm talking about.'

In the bathroom, the white paint and tiles around the lavatory bowl are spattered with brown runny faeces. Inside the toilet bowl, more of the foul stuff floats.

Ivy gags and puts her hand over her nose and mouth, to stop the stench hitting her nostrils. She shakes her head and stares denial at aunt Sonia, who's rolling up her sleeves.

'Couldn't even bother to clean it up, could you? Go fetch me a bucket of water and the disinfectant from the laundry. Get a move on.'

'No! I didn't do this.' *Always getting the blame just because I'm different.* Ivy's anger rises in her throat like vomit. She confronts Aunt Sonia, and in a clear voice says firmly, 'I'm not cleaning this up. I told you, it's nothing to do with me. I do enough of the dirty work around here and I'm not touching that filthy mess.'

'Think yourself too high and mighty to clean up your own shit? That figures, the way you was brought up never to do a tap of work. Your stupid mother made you into a princess, no good for anything.'

'How dare you call my mother stupid! She's got twice the brains you've got.' Ivy's hands are shaking, with the joy of telling Aunt Sonia off, as well as with an exhilarating fury.

Aunt Sonia stands still, speechless, glaring at her, her mouth hanging open. 'Sid! Come here,' she calls, never letting her eyes leave Ivy's face. Suddenly those eyes shift focus and she is staring beyond Ivy, at a figure standing in the bathroom doorway.

'Mum, it wasn't Ivy's fault. It was me. I had a bad pain in my tummy, and then that happened. I wanted you to see.'

'What are you saying, Alex, lovey? Don't worry, Mum is home, you don't have to pretend. Of course it was Ivy's fault.'

Uncle Sid, his checked shirt half unbuttoned showing his sweaty torso, appears in the doorway. 'What on earth's going on? Everything looks fine. Debbie's fast asleep.'

'It's not Debbie. It's your niece. She shat all over the toilet and won't admit to it. Now Alex is trying to cover for her.'

'Alex, what happened?'

'I felt sick and the pooh came out too fast. I didn't know what to do.'

'It's OK, you go straight back to bed and I'll be there in a minute.'

Alex starts to cry. 'But it wasn't Ivy's fault!'

'Of course it wasn't,' says Uncle Sid. 'You're a brave boy for telling the truth. Have you been sneaking those liquorice lollies again?'

'No! I promise!' Alex sobs. Aunt Sonia just stands there with her mouth open.

'Sonia, please apologise to Ivy.'

'What? Do my ears hear right? Why should I apologise to that lazy lump? She didn't even clean up her own mess.'

'Because you blamed her, Sonia, and it clearly wasn't her fault.'

Tears prick at Ivy's eyes, as soon as she hears Uncle Sid say the words *it clearly wasn't her fault*. She slips away down the hall before they can see her cry. Back in her maid's room, she flings herself face down on the narrow bed. She's half sobbing, half smiling. In the distance she can hear her aunt and uncle shouting at the top of their voices.

*

That night Ivy hears a rustling outside her bedroom window. Probably a possum, or maybe a rat, she thinks with a shudder. Or one of those birds that come in the night to dig up the garden. There's a rhythm to the rustling, like breath, or the sea: in, out, pause, in, out, pause. Rather than a creature of the night, could it be a human animal? She freezes, lying very still, and listens.

There's been a man prowling about in the suburbs of Perth. The newspapers are full of his dreadful deeds: abductions, rapes and murders. The police haven't caught him yet. They've urged all girls and women to stay inside at night, and never to walk home after sunset. Ivy's taken little notice of the increasingly scary stories, sometimes wondering if they're made up by an ambitious journalist who wants to be a real writer, like she does. But what if it's all true, and she's about to be his next victim? *Ridiculous*, Ivy tells herself, *what would he want with the likes of me, half-dead already?*

She shakes herself, kneels up on the bed, and peers through the window. The sky has that eerie light that happens just before sunrise. As her vision sharpens, she sees two large black eyes looking back at her through the window pane. She stifles a scream and bangs the window shut, twisting the lock. There's a soft tap, tap, on the glass.

Something about those eyes impels Ivy to look again. Curiosity overcomes her fear. This time she sees that the eyes are set into a dark brown face, the face of a young girl. Her skin is smooth and shining, her hair twisted into a thousand dark curls that escape from beneath a white cap. The cap of a nurse, or a maid.

Is it an angel or a devil? Am I having one of my visions, like when the oleander blossoms became fancy hats on ladies' heads? Pulling on her thick winter dressing gown Ivy creeps out of bed and through the back door which leads to the outhouse. The morning sky is streaked with crimson, like a child's finger painting.

There is no one there. Yet Ivy still has the feeling of a presence in the air, something alarming yet benign. Looking around once more, she shakes herself as if to free her mind from an encroaching vision, and creeps back to bed.

As her eyes start to close Ivy's sees the face again, clearer this time. It belongs to a young girl of fourteen or fifteen. Her eyes gleam in a shining dark-skinned face. Ivy knows that this girl-child is more terrified of her than she herself is of this apparition.

'My name is Lowanna. I been gone long time. But I left something in this room. My room.'

Ivy tries to speak but not even a whisper emerges. She wants to ask this vision to help her. She wants to tell Lowanna that she can have her room back, of course she can. *Then there'll be nowhere for me to stay in this alien place so I'll just have to go home.* But the dream fades just as Ivy finds her voice and hears herself calling out.

'Help me! I don't belong here. Yes, yes, it is your room. Come back, help me escape so you can stay!'

A light goes on in the house. Aunt Sonia stands in the doorway, outlined by the glare from the kitchen.

'What's going on? I heard voices. Are you all right?' Sonia's eyes are puffy with sleep. She tightens the belt of her dressing gown. 'Well?'

'It was nothing, Aunt Sonia. I had a bad dream, that's all. And I need to go to the loo in a hurry.'

'Told you not to take them laxatives, you silly girl. It's talking in your sleep now, is it? Anyways, Sid's been called out to Mrs Hall's baby, otherwise I wouldn't be awake. We'll have to cancel morning surgery.'

'I'll write a notice to put up outside, if you like,' Ivy says, grateful that the task of the moment had turned her aunt's mind from suspicion to action.

Back in her room she pulls a blank page from her Latin workbook, and in her best block printing writes: *Morning Surgery Cancelled for Today.* All the time she is writing the dark girl's face stays in her mind, looking at her with beseeching eyes.

11. MUTINY ISLAND

Since spying her father's letter to Uncle Sid, Ivy waits for the axe to fall. There's to be more treatment, the letter said. More invasion of her mind and body, more people trying to change her. Why couldn't these adults consult her instead of each other? She lives in fear every day and every night of being locked up again in a place like Winchester. All she wants is to be left alone with her imperfect self, and with The Voice that both protects and threatens her.

She remembers the letter from Daddy she tucked in her pinafore pocket. It is full of the usual platitudes: *We all miss you very much, and pray you will be home with us soon. Rabbi Schein said a special brocha for you in Schule last Shabbos. Everyone in Castleton asks after you, and sends their love.* Ivy wonders if that includes Joel. He's never actually said he loves her, but his letters are full of concern, and she detects a warmth in them that's more than friendship. Why would he write to her as often as he does, if he doesn't love her?

*

Ivy's dreaming of big chunks of chocolate cake and bowls of rainbow ice cream, when a child's voice wakes her, just before she takes a forbidden bite of cake.

'Wake up, Ivy! It's my birthday, and we're going to the island! Hurry up! We mustn't miss the boat.' Alex pulls her blanket off as she struggles to open her eyes. She looks into Alex's round brown ones. Dear Alex. Over the last six months he's treated her like a normal human being, without pity, blame or disgust. He seems to see past her skeletal frame and gaunt face. She feels as close to loving him as her shrinking heart allows.

'I'm coming, just let me get dressed. Oh, and happy birthday! I got you a present.'

'Bring it with you,' Alex calls, as he scampers off.

The whole family assemble on the pier waiting for the 12 o'clock ferry. It's a hot day in early February. Everyone but Ivy's wearing shorts and sandals. She's dressed in navy slacks to hide her sticks of legs, and a viyella blouse under a plain blue jumper

'I can see the ferry! Quick, it's almost here,' calls Aunt Miriam. She's Ivy's youngest aunt, sister to Mum and Uncle Sid, only ten years older than Ivy herself. 'Come on – don't forget the hamper– there's something special in there!' They walk in single file along the wooden plank and onto the ferry that goes twice a day to Mutiny Island. Every few seconds Alex glances over his shoulder, as if to check that she's following.

It's a short, choppy trip from the mainland to the island. As soon as they're on the big old ferry, Debbie's face turns a yellowish-green colour. Aunt Sonia sees what's about to happen, scoops her daughter up and out onto the deck where the child spews copiously onto Aunt Sonia's new shoes. *Ugh,* says Ivy to herself.

*

The house on Mutiny Island has been in the Bronsky family for decades. It's a rambling weatherboard place, with wide wooden verandahs on three sides. It's right on the water, with views across to the mainland. The windows of the main room open to the sea. There are several moth-eaten sofas, throw-outs from the families' various homes. It's the sort of house where no one stands on ceremony.

Aunty Miriam tells them how young folk used to get up to all sorts of unmentionable things on the island. Ivy suspects Aunty Miriam got into mischief herself when she was younger. Now she has to be respectable, befitting her status as a nice Jewish girl who's engaged to a nice Jewish boy. Her fiancé, Sheldon, is still overseas with his Army unit on a special mission, although the war's been over for years.

Ivy loves going to Mutiny Island for holidays or birthdays. Even Aunt Sonia relaxes here, kicking off her shoes and stockings, and from the look of her rounded stomach, even her step-ins. Uncle Sid looks completely different from his stern workaday self, wearing khaki shorts and leather sandals, with a brightly coloured shirt, giving him a carefree tropical air.

Ivy sinks onto the verandah, letting the cool sea breeze run its fingers through her hair. She's chosen a shadowed corner where she can see the waves, but hopes no one can see her. She can hear the children's voices high with excitement.

'Mum, where's my bavers?' Debbie's hopping from one foot to the other with impatience.

'Wait, *bubele*. Mummy's still unpacking, give me two minutes to get my breath.' There's a smile in Aunt Sonia's voice, a gentleness that Ivy's rarely seen.

'Coming for a swim, Ivy?' Alex is jumping up and down, eagerness in every fibre of his body.

'Not just now, love, I like it here. You go ahead. But first – here's your present.' Ivy reaches into her shoulder bag and pulls out a bright orange beach towel, trimmed with thick white fringes. 'Happy birthday,' she says as she hands it to him. His eyes widen with pleasure, and he flings the towel over his bare shoulders.

'Just what I wanted! It really is, I'm not just being polite,' he smiles at her, his crooked front tooth gleaming.

'I know you're not, silly – when've you ever been polite? Go on, catch up with the others.'

'Come on everyone, race you to the first breaker,' Alex calls as he scampers down the rickety wooden steps to the beach. Aunty Miriam as chaperone follows more sedately, svelte in her pretty floral one-piece. The three of them run across the gravel road and onto the sand, hopping as the heat hits the soles of their bare feet.

The beach is only a few metres from the house. Ivy can hear the children's splashes and faint shouts through a daze of half dream, half thought. She wishes she could sink into those waves and disappear. Will she ever be able to swim again? She remembers winning swimming races at school, the joy of it. How she longs to jump into the translucent green water, immersing herself in it, salt and spray washing her pain away. Instead she lets the warmth of the old wooden boards sink into her, soothing the constant cold from her bones.

Even in this relaxed place, Ivy knows she mustn't reveal her ravaged body. Aunt Sonia's told Ivy she's not allowed to wear bathers, not with her bones sticking out like that, frightening the children. She's wearing loose slacks and a long-sleeved jumper at Aunt Sonia's insistence. 'No one wants to see the state of you, girl, with those skinny legs of yours, and your hairy arms. Don't you go spoiling Alex's party, drawing attention to yourself.'

At the other end of the wide verandah, Aunt Sonia sits in a wicker chair fanning herself with a Women's Weekly. Uncle Sid opens his shirt collar and kicks off his shoes. Ivy's glad to see his collar and tie aren't choking him, as they seem to when he's in doctor garb.

'We don't need another *meshuggene* in the family.' It's Aunt Sonia, speaking loudly enough for Ivy to hear every word. She can't decipher Uncle Sid's answer, but knows he'll be defending her. 'That girl, she'll end up like your poor sister, Bella, with her nerves,' Sonia continues. 'Bella doesn't get Reuben's dinner on the table till after nine o'clock. I tell you, she burns the chops and serves up the veggies all mushy. No wonder Reuben's got an ulcer. That niece of yours, she'll end up like Bella, you'll see. You say it's a sickness the girl's got, but I tell you, she's spoilt rotten ... '

Ivy tries to shut out her aunt's voice as it drones on, intercepted with weak protests from Uncle Sid. He's been kind to her, but he's no match for Aunt Sonia. Yesterday he'd taken her aside, and explained that she'd be starting a new kind of treatment with a woman doctor, and that her first appointment was in a week's time. Ivy's scared of what this might mean; more damage to her brain? Why couldn't everyone just leave her alone to do The Voice's bidding? Only then she'd be safe. Her fear of the unknown is even worse than the hunger that somehow thrilled her as much as it tortured her.

Drowsing in the warmth, she comforts herself with thoughts of Joel, and his latest letter to her in halting German. She longs for three words: '*Ich liebe dich*', but they never come. Joel's letters are like school compositions, describing the books he's reading, or his young brother's latest exploits. He wrote this one to practice his German, she suspects. Her own letters to him are about her dreams for the future, and how she wants to be an authoress one day. Last month she enclosed a short story she'd written, about a man and a woman from the stone age, a weird story drawn entirely from her feverish imagination. Joel's the only one she's shown it to. When his next letter bears no mention of her story, Ivy's filled with bitter disappointment. Unwritten is her biggest dream, of sharing her life with Joel, when one day she'll be healed, and this nightmare over.

Sounds come from kitchen, the clank of metal, and the dull beat of a wooden spoon against a bowl. Ivy's mouth waters as the image of a cake comes unbidden to her mind: a cake for Alexander's eighth birthday. She imagines the cake's sweet vanilla flavour – or will it be the dark wicked taste of chocolate? Will there be cream, luscious white clouds melting in her mouth? And icing, pure sugar, so intensely sweet, so forbidden? Images of all the cakes from her birthdays colour Ivy's half dreams. She remembers the sponge cake when she turned seven. It was decorated with bright green frogs. When she and Laura greedily took bites of the frogs, expecting sweetness, they spat out the bitter marzipan, crying with disappointment. On her eighth birthday there was an ice cream cake, packed in dry ice so that it wouldn't melt. Ivy remembers not liking the cold hard texture, wishing it were spongy chocolate cake instead.

'Where's Ivy?' she hears Uncle Sid say. He sounds lazy, different to his busy doctor self.

'Gone off on her own as usual,' Aunt Sonia snaps back with an audible sniff. Ivy shuts her ears, and curls up into a tighter ball on the edge of the verandah. Her stomach aches with emptiness.

Children's voices wake her. They're running back from the beach, flinging down sandy towels, shouting to each other. Alex shakes drops of cold water onto Ivy's face, and runs away laughing.

She blinks them away and sits up. 'Hey, watch out, you scallywag, if it wasn't your birthday I'd be after you!'

Alex runs off, wet hair flopping into his eyes.

The smell of vanilla drifts through the kitchen window. Aunty Miriam's high sweet voice floats through the air. She's singing, "It's a Long Way to Tipperary". The war songs are still popular; Ivy guesses they remind Miriam of Sheldon, her fiancé who is far, far away. The screen door opens, its hinges squeaking as Miriam nudges it with her elbow. In her hands she carries a platter bearing a two-tier cake. It has a thick layer of soft white cream in its middle. On its blue iced surface is written *Happy Birthday Alex*. The icing is not quite set, dripping down the sides of the slightly lopsided cake. Ivy's mouth waters.

'Did anyone remember candles?' Miriam asks, setting the platter down on the worn table, its wood warped and stained.

'Do you think I'd forget the candles on my own boy's birthday?' Aunt Sonia grins. She takes a packet of tiny coloured candles from her striped beach bag. She carefully places eight candles, each a different colour, around the cake's perimeter

'Come on everyone!' Uncle Sid's voice booms. 'Time to blow out the candles!'

Alex comes bounding up to the table, still wearing his bathers, Ivy's towel draped over his shoulders. They all crowd around him, singing Happy Birthday. Little Debbie lisps the words along with the others as Alex takes a deep breath and blows out all eight candles in one go. Everyone claps and cheers. Alex stands proudly, knife poised over the cake.

'Don't touch the bottom or you'll have to kiss a girl!' Aunty Miriam calls, as she hands Alex the big silver knife, handle first. With a theatrical flourish he slices into the cake, careful to avoid touching the words expertly piped onto the icing. The knife stops just in time.

'I didn't touch the bottom! But if I had, I know who I'd kiss,' he says, grinning at Ivy. Her heart skips a beat with love for this little cousin, the only one who seems to see some good in her.

On the scarred wooden table, Aunt Sonia puts a plate of fairy bread, its hundreds and thousands twinkling in the sun, and a dish of fresh scones laden with strawberry jam and lashings of cream. Aunty Miriam adds her specialty of bright green and red jellies, set in scooped out orange skins, and cut into quarters.

'Tuck in everybody, there's plenty for all, and we don't want to cart it all back on the ferry,' says Uncle Sid, helping himself to a fluffy scone, ignoring the cream on the end of his nose and the strawberry jam turning his moustache scarlet. Debbie shrieks with laughter, pointing at her father.

'Daddy looks like a clown!' she calls, as she crams a second slice of fairy bread into her mouth.

Ivy stares at the festive spread, swallowing saliva as she fights the hunger in her belly. She takes a scone and pushes it around on her plate with a fork. Aunty Miriam cuts the cake into generous wedges and passes them around on paper plates.

'Here you are love, have a taste,' she says to Ivy. Her pretty young face is flushed from the heat, as she holds the plate out.

'I can't,' she whispers. Aunty Miriam looks confused.

'What do you mean, lovey? Don't you like cake?'

'I love cake, but – but I'm not allowed to eat it.'

She feels sorry for Aunty Miriam, wishing she could take away the disappointment on her face. 'It looks delicious though,' she says, her eyes fixed on the blue icing, golden crumbs escaping onto the white plate. She imagines licking her finger and pressing it into those crumbs, every one of them, and putting her finger into her mouth.

Aunty Miriam stands there, holding the plate. She shakes her head, tears forming in her eyes.

'It's just not fair. Not fair at all. Can't a little girl have a piece of cake, at her own cousin's birthday party?' Aunty Miriam disappears through the screen door. It bangs behind her with an angry sound. 'No cake for Ivy,' she says to Aunt Sonia. There's a little catch in her voice as if she's stopping a sob.

Ivy stays where she is, quite still. Where are the words of anger, reproach, she's come to expect? Maybe, just maybe, young Aunty Miriam understands.

Ivy hears Aunt Sonia snort, and mutter, 'Could've told you – what did you expect? The girl's crazy.'

12. DR B

When Ivy leaves for her first meeting with the dreaded psychoanalyst, it's an abnormally hot day in early April. In the fierce Western Australian sun, sweat runs down her shrivelled legs as she waits for the bus. When it comes, she summons all her strength to pull her frail body up by the thick metal handrail. The driver averts his eyes as she hands over the damp copper coins. There's a vacant seat near the front of the bus. She sinks down into it gratefully, staring straight ahead.

Ivy knows she resembles a giant stick insect wearing its skeleton outside its body. Her arms are covered with long fine hairs, and her legs, just visible below the hem of her long cotton skirt, are nothing but sticks. Passengers turn their heads away quickly, and avoid looking again. She looks more like a woman of seventy than a girl of fourteen. Would anyone have stood for her, had the bus been full?

As the sweat dries on her limbs, Ivy feels cold, in spite of the warm day. Coldness is as constant and gnawing as the hunger always with her. She climbs off the bus, her legs shaky, knowing the eyes of silent passengers are boring into her back. She feels the driver's impatience as he idles the engine, keen to be rid of her and off again.

She walks half a block across the fresh green grass of King's Park to the small elegant cottage that has a sign on a shining gold plate. *Dr Elisabeth De Berg, Psychoanalyst, specialising in children.* The last three words are in smaller print. The house is a thirties-style cottage, brick with a verandah. Its entrance is cool and dark.

Twisting the doorbell with clammy fingers, Ivy stands still, hardly breathing, until she hears the faint echo of bells, and soft footsteps approaching from somewhere inside the house. Her heart beats harder as the steps get louder, and there, opening the door, is the doctor herself:

tall, stately, her dark blonde hair swept up from her face. She silently ushers Ivy inside. In the hallway the air changes immediately. It is cool, with a faint smell of old books, and something else sweet and spicy. Ivy follows the doctor into the consulting room. It is nothing like Uncle Sid's surgery. Dimly lit, it has elegant furniture: a couch covered in a rich brocade against one wall, and a high-backed armchair positioned behind it. Mahogany bookshelves crammed with many volumes stand against the opposite wall. In this inner sanctum, all is as quiet and holy as a church or a synagogue.

'Welcome, Miss Morgenstern,' says the tall blonde woman, smiling. She is not beautiful like Miss Trent, but handsome, with what Ivy thinks of as a noble face. This doctor is nothing like Ivy expected. She had pictured an older lady wearing horn – rimmed spectacles, with grey hair drawn into a tight bun. Instead of a white coat, Dr de Berg wears an elegant flared skirt with a matching jacket. Some of the dread leaves Ivy's body. She realises she's been holding her breath in fear, and lets out an audible sigh of relief.

'May I call you Ivy?' Dr de Berg gestures to the couch with a smooth white hand. Ivy nods, and sits herself down on the very edge, afraid that a procedure will follow, maybe a needle in her arm or worse, a metal clamp to her head. 'You may lie down and make yourself comfortable while I explain how we will work together.'

Ivy gingerly stretches her shaky body full length onto the brocade couch. Dr de Berg sits behind Ivy's head, in an upholstered upright chair, which Ivy glimpses as she lies down. With a sigh, she lets herself sink onto the couch, feeling the pain leave her aching legs. She feels somehow foolish, as if she's been caught in an intimate act. Here, in this new space, she gives in to the weakness in her body. She can almost forget the griping of her stomach as she feels her tight muscles relax.

'While you are here, nothing you say will go beyond this room,' says Dr de Berg from behind her head. 'The most important part of this treatment is for you to tell me whatever comes into your head, even if it seems silly. I will sit here and listen, without interrupting. In this way we can both observe your thoughts, and try to understand what is troubling you.'

'You mean there'll be no needles or anything? All I have to do is talk?'

'That's right. A lay term for psychoanalysis is "the talking cure". Have you heard of it?'

'No. Uncle Sid just told me this is a new form of treatment for people with a mental illness. Does coming here mean I've gone mad?'

'We don't use that word here, Ivy. Nor words like 'crazy' or 'normal'. Rather, our task is to explore the workings of your mind, in order to confront the cause of your suffering.' There's a pause, while Ivy takes in the softly spoken words. She feels tears gathering, amazed that instead of blame, there is an acknowledgement of her pain.

'Through your dreams and fantasies we delve into a part of the mind that is usually hidden from us. You may start to talk whenever you're ready. But remember, we have a strict time limit of fifty minutes for each session.'

For a long time Ivy says nothing. It is peaceful lying there, as if all the pressure inside her head has magically lifted. She fancies the spicy smell in the room is Dr de Berg's perfume. *This is certainly better than having my brains fried,* she thinks. At the same time she feels a little resentful, wondering why she has to do all the work in this strange treatment. The silence in the room stretches until it becomes a presence, and a rebuke.

At last the doctor speaks. Ivy expects a reprimand, but Dr de Berg's voice is gentle. 'What are your thoughts? Perhaps you can remember a dream to tell me?'

Ivy speaks in a whisper, befitting the sanctity of this space. Wanting now to please this woman, who she calls "Dr B" in her mind, she recalls the dream that troubled her some nights ago.

'I've called this dream *The Night Before the Dead Walk.* I like to give all my dreams titles, like they're stories I've written. Maybe I'll write them all down one day, when I become an author.'

In the dream my mother is sitting at a small café table. She looks different somehow, her hair blue black like it used to be before she got grey strands in it. Everyone says she went grey because of me – sorry, that's not part of the dream.'

'You can say whatever comes into your head,' Dr B says. 'It's called free association, and it means holding nothing back, whether it's a dream, or your thoughts that arise from it. Please go on.'

*

'My mother's skin is flawless. Not like mine, dry and itchy, full of scars from acne. I think Mum is younger in my dream, way before she had me. Her eyelashes are thick with mascara, and she wears blue eye makeup. Daddy would say she has ointment on her eyes, like he says about film stars who wear creamy blue or green eye shadow. She looks nothing like the mother I said goodbye to, before I got sent here. Her lips are shaped into a crimson cupid's bow. In real life she wears pale lipstick, and never eye makeup. I go up to her and say, "Is it really you?" She doesn't answer, so I get down on my knees before her, and say, "It's me, it's Ivy, I'm your child." Her skin is alabaster white. I kneel before her. I want her to kiss me or hug me, but she just sits there. "It's me, your daughter," I tell her. But my Mum's not moving. She has a glassy look in her eyes. She is looking beyond me at something in the distance.'

In another part of this dream,' Ivy continues, inventing as she goes along, 'Dr Henderson from Winchester appears. "Your brain is missing," he says. "You're going to need more treatment." I was more surprised than scared. How could I live without a brain? Maybe The Voice would stop if I didn't have a brain.'

*

It is the first time Ivy has mentioned The Voice. She's been careful to avoid it, mainly because she doesn't want to make it real.

'What voice?' Dr B asks.

'It's a Voice in my head. It tells me I must not eat. It wants me to die, and I'm afraid of it but I still have to do whatever it tells me to.' Ivy stops. She's said enough. What if Dr B is in league with Dr Henderson, and reports Ivy to the authorities for being crazy?

Dr B doesn't pursue The Voice story. Instead she asks, 'Why do you think you called your dream *The Night Before the Dead Walk?*'

'I've no idea. The title just came to me.'

'It's the things that come to us for no reason that are telling us a truth about ourselves, often a truth we don't want to face. These thoughts, and our dreams, come from the same place. We call it our Unconscious.'

'Does Unconscious mean the same as when you faint or have an anaesthetic?'

'Not in this case. It refers to a great part of our mind that's hidden from us, yet it can have a powerful influence over our lives. It was first described by Professor Sigmund Freud.' Dr B's voice from behind Ivy's head sounds as if she were miles away, instead of in this very room.

'Who is he? I've never heard of him,' Ivy says, curious to know more.

'He is, or was, the man who dared to challenge the accepted views about mental illness, in the late nineteenth century. He is known as the father of Psychoanalysis. His theories have profoundly changed the way we think about not only the mind, but art, music, and literature.'

Ivy's silent for a long minute, then asks, 'Will you tell me more about Freud next time?'

'Of course. I see you are keen to learn, and I like your curiosity. Of course I will tell you more as we go along. Understanding Freud's ideas can only help us in the fight to free you of your troubles.' Another long pause. Ivy hears the minutes ticking away from the clock on the mantelpiece.

Dr B's voice breaks the silence. 'Perhaps the dream about your mother reveals your fear that she might die?'

Ivy doesn't answer. Now Dr B is putting words into her mouth. She recalls how white Mum's face was in her dream, deathly white.

'And no doubt your dream also reveals your wish for your mother to love you, both physically and emotionally,' continues Dr B. This is easier territory for Ivy to enter. Love is easier to talk about than death.

'When I was little I think she did love me,' Ivy responds. 'But now I'm a danger to her, I make her ill with her nerves. I want to get better, then maybe she'll love me again. Can we fight The Voice?'

'Of course, if you are prepared to fight it with me.'

'I'm frightened of It. The Voice is trying to kill me. That's why It's telling me to stop eating.'

'Ivy, we have a great deal of work to do, and I need you to trust me. Together we can be stronger than your Voice. Our journey will be painful sometimes, yet through seeking truth we can fight your demons together.'

Ivy looks forward to her next session with Dr B. She is strict but reassuring, and treats Ivy as an intelligent fellow human, instead of as an afflicted malcontent, to be pitied or shunned. This time she determines to trust the doctor more with one of her earliest memories, which has never left her, even after her brain was electrocuted.

*

'When I turned eight I started at a new school. It had a uniform, which I never had to wear at my other school. Mum always bought things too big for me, and it swamped me. I clearly remember my tummy being in a knot of fear, right where the belt of my uniform was too tight. Laura had just turned five, and it was her first day of school.

When we got to the school I saw straight away that none of the other girls were wearing a uniform. They'd come in their day dresses, mostly of faded floral material, and some weren't even wearing shoes. My own shoes were brand new black lace-ups, polished to a shine the night before, and so were Laura's. I felt betrayed by Mum, and ashamed for having new clothes when the others didn't.

At lunch time I wanted to make friends with the other kids. They ignored me, and wouldn't let me join in their game of hopscotch. I looked for Laura and saw she was playing skippy with some other new kids and looked quite happy. I wanted to get away but there was nowhere to run.

The boys in the playground looked big and rough. They seemed like angry dogs ready to bite me. The two biggest boys forced me to the ground. I struggled, twisting this way and that to get away. Brown eyes, pickle pies, blue eyes beauty, they chanted together, over and over. I tried to tell them my eyes were hazel, not brown. Ants crawled up my legs. Someone ripped off my belt, and you know what? I was glad, because I'd look more like the others. The boys punched me and kicked me, chanting, "Dirty Jew, dirty Jew. Your father's a dirty Jew."

All of a sudden I saw Laura running towards the scrum. Her face was red with fury, and before I could call out to her to run away, I saw her sturdy little leg kick one of the boys on top of me with the full force of her shiny new shoe. To this day I want to cry when I remember how my sister tried to protect me. I miss Laura so much.'

'I was pinned underneath the two boys. A big girl broke through the scrum and pulled them off me. She must have been nine or ten. I thought she'd come to save me. I was wrong. She kneeled on top of me with her face so close to mine that her thick yellow plaits tickled my face.

"Give me your ring," the girl said. Or snarled really. She yanked me to my feet and pushed me against the playground fence. Warped grey wood sent splinters into my bare legs. The big girl twisted my wrist; it felt like burning. I let her take my ring just to get away from the pain. She waltzed off with my ring squeezed onto the tip of her little finger. It was much too small for her of course. The mob followed her, shouting, "Brown eyes, pickle pies. Your father's a dirty Jew."

I thought of how Daddy had slipped that ring onto my finger, and how it had glittered in the sun. It had my initials entwined on it, I.A.M, for Ivy Aviva Morgenstern. I stood alone in the middle of the playground, biting my lip to stop myself crying. A voice a long way above my head said, "Where's your lunch? Go and eat it like the others, before the bell goes."

It was our teacher, who I'd only just met. I think her name was Miss Fitzsimmons. She had very black hair rolled in a thin sausage around her head, and a bright red mouth, pulled into a thin line. Her eyes drilled into me. "What's wrong? Lost our tongue, have we? My word, don't we look a sight. You're that Jewish girl, aren't you? You people all think yourselves better than us decent folk. Now go and wash yourself and get your lunch like the others."

Perhaps being Jewish meant wearing clean socks and new shoes to school. I knew it had something to do with lighting the candles on Friday nights, and eating sweet challah, and maybe it was about having egg sandwiches cut in neat squares in a little silver box, instead of bread and meat wrapped in newspaper like the other kids had. It definitely meant being different. I wished that day I wasn't Jewish, and I've often wished it since.'

*

'That's a shocking story.' Dr B spoke gently. 'It obviously traumatised you, judging from the physical sensations still imprinted on your memory.'

'I told my parents I'd lost my ring, but they didn't believe me. They went to the school and complained that it'd been stolen. I was allowed to stay home for a few weeks till all my bruises had healed. When I went back to school, I insisted on wearing a play dress and sandals. To my surprise quite a few of the girls started to wear a uniform even if it was a hand-me-down from their big sisters. Some even wore shoes. It was like they were accepting me. I never wore my uniform again—it was all torn anyway—but I still always felt different.'

'How do you feel now about being Jewish?'

'I like some of the rituals, and I quite like being part of such an ancient culture.'

'Good. We can talk more about this next week, if you wish. Perhaps in our next session you might tell me more about your mother, and why you feel she may not love you.'

Ivy struggles to stand up from the couch. She can see Dr B faintly in the dim light, holding a small book in her hand. 'Here, my dear. This gives an outline of Psychoanalysis in Freud's own words. You can keep it – I have other copies. Read it and we can talk about it at our next session.' She leads the way to the front door.

As Ivy leaves she feels she's been banished from Paradise.

13. THE EGO AND THE ID

An Outline of Psychoanalysis. Sigmund Freud, Vienna, Ivy reads, *We are lived by unknown and uncontrollable forces.* Freud wrote those words long ago as part of a book called *The Ego and the Id.* The words resonate with her. Unknown? Uncontrollable? Exactly like her Voice, a force that wants her to die, stronger than the part of her that wants to live. How can mere words and telling her dreams save her life? She feels the old terror that death is stalking her, and that The Voice will win in the end.

Ivy reads on, feeling that she's been let into a secret society. *The Ego is not Master in its Own House,* is the title of the first chapter. She learns that the Ego is not the thing people mean when they say someone has a big ego, and think themselves high and mighty. Rather, it's the most evolved part of a person's mind, or psyche, as Freud calls it. The other parts, the Id and the Superego, are often hidden from ourselves. Ivy recognises in the Superego something akin to The Voice, that criticises and controls her, and makes her feel guilty if she doesn't obey it. She supposes another word for the Superego is her conscience, or perhaps The Voice.

It's hard for Ivy to take all this in. Her head is reeling with new words, new concepts, yet they speak to her as if she's always known them. The following week, back in the consulting room, Ivy speaks slowly and carefully, embellishing her memories with touches of drama for Dr B's entertainment. She has spent some time preparing her story of Maisie and Mr Butler.

*

'I remember one day when Mum sacked the cleaner who'd shouted at me, and I felt proud, and not a scrap guilty for Maisie losing her job. I was about three, hiding under the table where I could play with

my imaginary friend,' she began. 'He was called Mr Butler. Under the dining room table I saw the bristles of a broom pushing towards me. They were like the bristles of Mr Butler's peppery moustache and the thick hairs of his bushy black eyebrows. Mr Butler came with me everywhere. He knew the answers to all my questions, and never scolded or laughed at me. I knew no one else could see him but me.

"Get out of here, you skinny brat!" I heard a woman shouting, and straight away Mr Butler disappeared. Maisie's upside-down face was peering at me, and her hand was lifting the hanging folds of Mum's lace tablecloth. "How can I clean this blasted place with you always in the way?" She was pushing at my bare legs with the tickly bristles. I thought if I closed my eyes she wouldn't see me. It's strange what children believe. Of course she didn't disappear, just went on shouting. "I said scram. You deaf or something? Spoiled brat, that's what you are. Need a good spanking on your skinny bum."

I slid across the carpet and wriggled out from under it. I stuck my tongue out at Maisie and ran to find Mum. I looked in the kitchen. It was cold and empty, with a sharp smell, like cough medicine, from whatever Maisie used to clean the lino floor. Mum was in the laundry, turning the handle of the wringer, squeezing soapy garments between its twin rollers. One by one the clothes dropped from the wringer into the tub of cold water in the laundry trough.

I stood in front of Mum and tugged at her apron. "Mum, Maisie pushed me with the big broom." The wringer stopped mid-turn. Mum said something like "What do you mean? Is this another made-up story?"

"No!" I tried hard to make Mum believe me. "Maisie hurt my leg and said scram. And she said 'bum'." Mum slowly dried her hands and stood up straight. I can see her now, with her face slightly red, and her damp hair falling over her forehead in wayward curls. (Don't you just love that word, wayward, Doctor?)

"That does it!" Mum said. Her lips were pressed together in a thin line. I followed her into the dining room. Maisie was running a carpet

sweeper over the floral carpet, humming to herself. She looked up when she saw Mum standing in front of her, with her hands on her hips.

"Nearly done here, Missus," Maisie said. "I'll be off in a tic."

"Get out and don't come back," Mum said. "You're fired. No one speaks to my daughter like that." I couldn't believe my ears. My heart swelled. Mum wanted to protect me, like I was precious to her. Maisie's eyes went wide. She seemed to freeze on the spot.

"I wants me wages then," I remember her saying. "And that kid's not normal, if you ask me. Always talkin' to folk who ain't there." She held out her hand for the money.

"You can call around tomorrow for whatever I owe you. Now please go."

Maisie picked up her string bag from the doorknob and walked out, glaring at Mum. I had a feeling of triumph, and also one of fear. What if when Maisie came back she tried to hurt me? But I realised Mum wouldn't let her. It was such a good feeling.'

Ivy stops, fearing she might have sent Dr B to sleep.

There is a long silence from behind Ivy's head. Dr B speaks at last. 'Thank you for bringing that memory to life, Ivy. I can see why it's stayed with you. Do you remember anything else about your mother?'

Ivy uses her imagination to embellish a faint memory.

'Later that same day, Mum had a visitor. A man dressed like a soldier stood in the doorway. He was so tall he had to duck his head when he came inside. "Ivy dear, this is Uncle Dave. Or Digger for short," Mum said. Her voice was shaking a bit. The mother I knew was changing. She had a silly smile on her face when she looked at the visitor. "Digger" is such a silly name. It sounds like a name for a dog.

The man squatted down to my level. I was not quite three, remember. "My, you're as pretty as your mother, and that's saying something.

How would you like a special treat?" He reached into the top pocket of his jacket and pulled out a small packet wrapped in silver paper, and pulled out a pale green stick. "Have you ever tasted real chewing gum? It's all the way from America. Don't be scared now; it tastes real nice, like a mintie. Do you have them here? You can chew it, but make sure you, don't swallow it."

"Oh no, she's too young for that, only two and a half," Mum said. "I'm scared she could choke on it." I was glad to see she was being my proper Mum again.

Digger stood up. "How about some for your lovely mother, then?" He held out the stick of gum to Mum. I thought he was standing much too close to her. Mum just stood there, saying nothing. She was looking up at Digger, and her eyes were shining. He came closer, and put the gum right into Mum's mouth. I remember it made me feel all shivery, like now. I probably started to cry. Mum bent down and picked me up. I didn't like to see her mouth chewing. It was not like Mum at all. "Come on, darling. We'll go and play with the doll's house." Over Mum's shoulder, I stuck my tongue out at Digger. He grinned back at me.'

That night, when Daddy came home from work, he scooped me up in his arms and kissed my cheek, tickling it with his moustache. He turned to Mum and gave her a quick kiss, well a peck really, shrugging out of his overcoat at the same time. Mum said nothing about the visitor. But she told him straight away about Maisie. "I had to fire her," she said, "for talking to our daughter like that."

"Quite right," I remember Daddy saying. "We'll have to find you someone else. I won't have you doing all the housework with no help." I wondered if Daddy would be angry if he knew about Digger. But surely he'd be pleased to see Mum looking happy for once, all her jitteriness and frowning gone. If Daddy loved Mum he'd be happy too. I looked up at Mum's shining face and decided not to tell about the visitor, although I still wonder what Mum and Digger were talking

about all the time I'd been bathing and dressing my dolly. Leonie, her name was.'

*

Ivy draws a deep breath, exhausted from so much talking. She thinks she's getting quite good at this free association. There is no response for a long time from behind her head. At last Dr B speaks softly.

'Very good, Ivy. You have an excellent memory, considering what happened to your brain last year.'

'I don't know if I'm remembering or not. I'm saying what's in my head, like you said to. And I make a lot up when I can't remember. I'm sorry.' Has she disappointed Dr B, who is nearly her friend? Shame floods her.

'It doesn't matter at all whether what you tell me is a memory or a made-up story, it all comes from the same place. Why do you think this memory is important to you?'

'Because it's a time when I knew Mum really did love me, and protect me. Also that there's more to my mother than being an obedient housewife.'

'I see. And perhaps you see too, that being ill may be a way to get back her love and protection?'

Ivy feels hot and cold with anger. 'I told you, I'm not ill on purpose. Everyone thinks I'm starving for attention – literally – but it's The Voice forcing me not to eat. I'm not doing anything to hurt my mother, or anyone else in my family. Now you think I'm bad too, just like all the others.' Tears burst from her eyes. She brushes them away with quick angry movements.

'You are telling yourself these things, Ivy, and projecting those thoughts onto me. Projection is a natural process in psychoanalysis, and one which we both need to be aware of. I am simply trying to help you confront your own fears, rather than to pass judgement. Our work here is to delve into your Unconscious for the secrets it's hidden from you.

We are making good progress. It will not always be easy, yet by searching your psyche through memories and dreams, you will begin to heal.'

*

After the session with Dr B Ivy feels restless, empty. In King's park opposite the doctor's cottage there's emerald green grass underfoot, and native plants all around her. Below, the Swan River winds its blue ribbon around the city. The air's fragrant with flowers. Ivy sees a rotunda, round like a birthday cake, perched on the highest point of the park. She feels the familiar urge to move her body, to burn off the meagre amount of food she's eaten that day. *You need to walk more, you lazy girl,* says The Voice. Ivy runs up the steep hill, her legs straining with every step.

14. BIG BREASTS AND LATIN

Dear Daddy, Mum and Laura,

How I miss you all! You've no idea how hard it is being so far away, in a place where no one cares about me. Aunt Sonia expects me to earn my keep. I have to wash the greasy dishes in the scullery off the kitchen after tea every night. I take out rubbish to the outside bin, and bring in the mail. I like this last job best, because it means I have to go into Uncle Sid's surgery to give him his letters and magazines. I have to wait outside until the patient with him leaves, then I knock on his door.

This family's very different to ours. The Bronskys don't do Friday nights, with the candles and the challah (is that the right spelling?) I never thought I'd miss our Shabbos dinners, yet it's like something's missing from the week when there isn't a time for the whole family around the shabbos table. Please don't think I'm getting all religious though. I still find it hard to believe in God, specially because He or She let all those innocent children die in the war. And why wouldn't He or She make me better if He or She is supposed to be so merciful? (I see no reason why God shouldn't be a woman, although then we'd have to say Goddess which is rather a mouthful, like "thank Goddess" or "Goddess-fearing" or I wish to Goddess that … etc.) I must be very wicked indeed to be punished like this, if there's a God/dess who expects atonement for sins like on Yom Kippur. Well, I'm fasting enough for one hundred Yom Kippurs but it's not making any difference. That's why I doubt there's a God at all.

Aunt Sonia says I've been spoilt rotten, and she's going to toughen me up, seeing as she can't seem to fatten me up. Anyway, she's a hopeless cook, not like Mum. Instead of Mum's sponges and famous hot dishes we get tomatoes on toast and bought biscuits.

Laura, I can't believe you're nearly twelve already! Wish I'd been there for your party, it sounds such fun. Who did you invite? Have you got any special friends at school? Not counting Nina from down the road of course – I know you'll always be friends with her. Tell me, what books are you reading now? Is Biggles still your favourite? Now you're older, you might like to borrow some from my bookshelf. I highly recommend everything by Dickens especially Great Expectations, my favourite. Also you'd like the book called Heidi about the little Swiss girl (I can't remember who wrote it.) Please remember to give my love to Joel, and tell him he owes me a letter!

Do you still play 'In the Snow'? It must be no fun at all to play it by yourself, because who would you throw the pillows on? And what would you hide under the eiderdown when there's no one to guess what it is? Anyway, please, please, write back to me very soon. I'm starved for news from home.

That's all for now. Sorry this turned out to be such a long letter. I have much more to say, but will keep it till next time.

Your loving daughter and sister,
Ivy

PS I'm enclosing a photo that Alex took with the new camera he got for Christmas. It's of me and Debbie in the back garden. Isn't she cute?

*

When she's not going backwards and forwards to her sessions with Dr B, Ivy spends her time either walking at the insistence of The Voice or poring over books from the Correspondence School of WA. She's struggling to keep up with fourth year Maths, Science and Geography. On the other hand, the English, French, Latin and German lessons are too easy, leaving Ivy feeling bored and frustrated.

Ivy's sitting at the dining room table in Uncle Sid's house. Her Latin lessons are spread out in front of her. The room is dim and musty, rarely used for dining. Sometimes Aunt Sonia holds card nights in it, when she serves tea in floral cups and saucers, and sandwiches with the crusts cut off.

Aunt Sonia sits beside her, frizzy hair bristling, hands red and chafed. 'When I was your age,' she begins, 'would you believe I was quite pretty, though I say so myself? I had a boyfriend, and went to dances. Then I met my Sid.' Her small eyes take on a dreamy look. 'And I knew he was the only one for me.' She straightens her shoulders. Her eyes lose their softness, turning hard as she focuses on Ivy.

'Just look at you! Sitting here with that *meshuggene* homework, getting you nowhere. You look like a skeleton, a *nebbisch*. Yellow skin, hairy arms, all skin and bone. Men like plump women, like me, someone they can hold onto. They especially like a girl with big breasts,' Aunt Sonia says, puffing her bosom out. Ivy notices there is no division there, and wonders if her aunt has just one huge breast. 'No boy will ever ask you out. If you eat more and put on some weight, you'll see, you could be quite attractive. Why don't you fix yourself up, wear a little lipstick, brush your hair now and then?'

'Why don't you just leave me alone? I'm trying to finish my Latin, to get it off to the post before Friday. The Correspondence School takes off marks for lateness.' Ivy's eyes smart. It's true her breasts are still little buds. She hasn't had a period since that very first one, a fact that gives her some satisfaction. *Who'd want that embarrassing blood on your pants every month, and the pain in your tummy, and the fat pad chafing between your legs?*

'Latin *Schmatin*! What good will it do you, you stupid girl. It won't get you a husband, that's for sure. You'll be an old maid with your useless books, and only a cat for company. And don't you dare talk to your aunt that way.'

'I'm not stupid.' Ivy's eyes filled with angry tears. 'I'll have you know I topped the whole year in Latin back home. I can't afford to get behind any more, just because you won't let me go to school.'

'School! Look at you! A feather would knock you down in the playground. You'd be a laughing stock and so would we. Think of your family, you selfish girl.' Aunt Sonia's face was vivid with anger, her nostrils flaring wider than ever. 'By the way, we want you to catch the bus further down the road, so the neighbours don't see you. What will patients think when they see the doctor's niece all sick and skinny? Your uncle has his reputation to keep up, you know. We don't want people to think Dr Bronsky can't look after his own family.'

Ivy's head is pounding, her stomach twisting with hunger. All she wants is for Aunt Sonia to go away and let her disappear into her declensions and translations, to take her mind off the aching emptiness in her body.

'Pull yourself together, my girl, and think of your poor mother's suffering, the worry you put on her. You'll be the death of Lily, mark my words. How could you treat your family this way? It's your father's fault, he always did spoil you.'

'Don't you dare talk about Daddy like that! I can tell you hate him.'

'To tell the truth if you want to know, I never liked him with his stuck-up airs, thinking he's better than us, looking down his nose just because we never had any money in the old days.' Sonia puts both hands on the table and hauls herself up. Ivy sees weariness in her sharp face. 'Well, there you are. I promised Sid I'd have a heart-to-heart with you. What more can I say?'

'Nothing. You can tell Uncle Sid I don't care about being pretty and having big breasts, and anyway I detest boys.'

Aunt Sonia gives a deep sigh, and shrugs her plump shoulders. 'I can't sit around here talking all day, I've got too much to do before the kiddies come home from school.'

*

The Voice will never let Ivy miss her walk, rain, hail or shine. The need to move all the time is compelling, and her daily walks relieve her incessant restlessness. She sets off around the block, then branches out to the edge of the bushland that lines the road.

Outside the weather's warm. Ivy quickens her pace, ignoring the hollow in the pit of her stomach, the painful griping. It hurts, yet she welcomes the ache as an assurance from her body that she's doing The Voice's bidding. The hungrier she gets, the happier she feels. But tonight, just tonight, she'll allow herself a bite of the chocolate bar hidden in the bottom drawer of her bedside table. It's what gets her through the long day, the thought of the sweet reward melting in her mouth, letting her fall asleep in spite of her hunger.

*

The ghost girl Lowanna appears to Ivy just as she switches off her light. This time Ivy's not afraid of the apparation. *Perhaps she's come to help me get out of here.* Ivy has an urge to reach out and touch her, but as she does her hand moves through empty air.

Ivy thinks she sees the ghost's hand point towards the bedside table just before the vision of Lowanna dissolves. She pulls open both drawers and empties the contents onto her bed. Her father's letters, her diary and fountain pen, and the photo of herself and Laura taken before she got ill, lie in a pile on the bed. Ivy lifts the paper lining the narrow drawer. She feels something hard and round.

It's a bracelet of tiny beads strung together with strands of what looks like human hair, in hues of orange, deep gold, brown and red. All the colours of the earth. Ivy gives a small cry of surprise. Could this be what the dream girl was looking for?

Ivy hears footsteps coming towards the kitchen. She switches off the bedside lamp and springs back under the covers.

A light goes on in the kitchen. Without knocking, a hand opens Ivy's door.

'I heard a noise. Did you have another one of them nightmares?' Aunt Sonia peers suspiciously around the small room. 'I'm telling you, it's because there's nothing in that belly of yours. That'd be enough to give anyone nightmares.' Ivy opens one eye from her pretend sleep. She keeps her hand, still clutching the bracelet, well under the covers.

'Um – I must have called out in my sleep. I was having a bad dream, about a huge eight-legged, a tarantula it was, all hairy. Thank goodness you woke me!' Ivy can never say the actual word spider, so great is her fear of all arachnids.

'No, missy, it's you who woke me with them bad dreams of yours. I hope your fancy lady doctor can make you stop this night talking. It's the least she can do, taking your father's money and making no difference that I can see. Now I'm awake I'll have to have a biscuit or two, it's the only way I'll get back to sleep. Thanks to you I'll be getting too fat to fit into my square dance skirt, tight as it is already.'

Ivy feels a stab of pity for Aunt Sonia. Maybe she has a punishing Voice too, only she can't obey it when she's tempted to eat a forbidden biscuit.

'Sorry I woke you. I hope you can get back to sleep,' Ivy says in a fake sleepy voice.

'Humph,' says Aunt Sonia. She pulls Ivy's door shut. 'Mind you don't do it again.' A mild retort, Ivy thinks with relief, expecting far worse. There's the sound of a tin being opened in the kitchen and the loud crunch of a biscuit being bitten in two. Ivy's mouth waters and her stomach grumbles.

'Lowanna, are you still there?' she whispers. Silence. Then she hears the whispered words *You must want to get better with all your heart*. Ivy leans over and peers under the bed. But the spirit girl has disappeared, like a magic trick that clowns perform at the circus. Ivy's still clutching the bracelet, warm with its secret life. Instinctively she slips it onto her wrist where it fits perfectly. *I know you will protect me*, Ivy whispers. *I will wear you always.*

15. FIFTEEN

As winter turns to spring, and the days lengthen, Ivy is terrified that she is going to die. She imagines her mother and father and sister, even Aunt Sonia, weeping over her dead body. At last, and at least, she'll be loved, but what's the point when she won't be there to bask in the warmth of their affection?

A parcel arrives from Castleton, just in time for Ivy's fifteenth birthday. In it are three frocks: one in lemon and white checked gingham with short sleeves and a nipped in waist, another in blue floral with puffed sleeves and a wide satin sash, and lastly a plain cotton shift buttoning down the front, in a blue-green colour called aqua, according to the label. Ivy loves this colour of the sea with its Latin name for water. She guesses this will be her everyday frock. The blue one could be for a party, not that Ivy ever goes to parties. She likes the lemon gingham one best and decides to wear it straight away.

The box is so big, Ivy almost misses the letter tucked into the folds of tissue paper around the clothes. It's in a pink envelope, with her name on it in Mum's handwriting, which Ivy's only seen on shopping lists and in recipes before. She picks it up and sniffs at it. It's Mum's perfume all right, that smell of roses that straight away takes Ivy home. The very first letter she's had from Mum in over a year. Ivy wants to cry for a second, then presses her lips together. *Remember, Mum doesn't want you, you make her sick, she's sent you away to a place where no one loves you. Why would you ever want to go home?*

She tears open the rose-scented envelope.

Dear Ivy,

Happy Birthday darling. I can't quite believe you're fifteen already. Is it really that long since I lay on that hospital bed, waiting for you to arrive? You were my first baby, remember, and I was very scared. They gave me gas to breathe in for the pain, which was excruciating. But it was all worth it, to at last hold my first baby in my arms. I wasn't to know all those years ago what troubles this baby would bring to me.

I hope you like these frocks, Ivy dear. I can't imagine how tall you are by now, so I've made sure they all have wide hems so that you or Sonia can let them down as you grow.

We all miss you very much, especially poor Laura. She cries herself to sleep nearly every night. Perhaps you could write her a special letter? She loved the last one so much that she slept with it under her pillow.

Ivy, I hope you're being a good help to your Aunt Sonia, it must be awfully hard for her with her own two little ones, and now you as well. Can you be sure to always clear the table after meals, and help in any way you can in the kitchen? We can never thank Sid and Sonia enough for taking you in, knowing how ill you are. Please give them my love, and a big hug for dear Sid. How is my clever brother? We are all extremely proud that he became a doctor against all odds.

Well, I must close now. I hope you like the frocks, it took me ages to pick them. I thought you could wear the lemon gingham to Schule. It would look quite pretty with a white hat and gloves. I'm enclosing a five pound note so you can buy these for yourself. Maybe you could ask Sid or Sonia to take a photo of you all dressed up for Schule.

Now I really must go. Laura will be home from school soon, and there's the dinner to cook. Happy birthday again, my grown-up girl. I hope soon you will be all better and come home to us.

With much love,

Mum xx

Ivy folds the letter back into its envelope, and carefully puts it, together with the five pound note, into the top drawer of her bedside table. *What makes Mum think Aunt Sonia or Uncle Sid would want to take a photo of me? They think I'm a freak. Anyway, Laura told me Daddy tore up the photo of me and Debbie. Whatever Mum says, I'm going to wear the lemon frock any time I like. Can't wait for Dr B to see it. I'll definitely wear it tomorrow for our next session.*

Aunt Sonia hovers in the doorway of Ivy's room, which is so close to the kitchen that it's almost part of it. She glances at the clothes spilling their colours out of the box. 'Huh! might as well show me. What did Lil send you this time?'

Ivy hesitates, steeling herself for a rebuke, although she's done nothing wrong. One by one she holds up each article for inspection. Aunt Sonia scrutinises them, and sniffs loudly.

'Think yourself lucky, young lady,' Aunt Sonia says, when she sees the spoils. 'Where you'll wear them fancy frocks I'm sure I don't know, seeing as you never go anywhere except on those crazy walks of yours.' She sniffs, and for a moment Ivy thinks she looks envious. 'Now clear out of the kitchen. I've got a special cake to make for someone's birthday.'

It is the closest Aunt Sonia has come to wishing Ivy a happy fifteenth birthday, and gives Ivy quite a shock. *A cake! For me! I'll have to force myself to eat a little bit. Surely The Voice will let me, today of all days.*

Ivy hangs the lemon frock on the back of her bedroom door. She folds the other two back into the box and shoves it under her bed. Outside the weather's warming up, as it always does on Ivy's birthday. There's wisteria out in the next door garden. Ivy smiles to herself, that even here that gorgeous deep blue vine blooms without fail in early October. Other than the Spring weather and the wisteria, it doesn't feel like her birthday at all.

*

Ivy crosses the park to Dr B's house. She notices the bushes of Geraldton wax in full bloom, and feels almost happy. Perhaps they are blooming for her, especially for her birthday. She reaches the threshold of the house with the gold sign outside, and feels her heart give a little jump of pleasure when Dr B opens the door to her.

This room is where Ivy feels loved. Waves of love wash over her. She wishes Dr B were her mother. In spite of her gift and letter, Mum always gives Ivy the sense that she's disappointed in her. Dr B's aura is full of trust and kindness, as if she can see the good in Ivy when no one else can. Ivy loves the sound of her voice, mellow with a rich lilting accent. Its warmth envelops her, so that some of the ice in her heart melts each time she hears it.

Lying stretched out on the brocade couch, Ivy smooths out the creases in her new frock, hoping Dr B will notice it. Her gaze falls on the painting on the opposite wall, as it always does. It isn't an actual painting, Ivy realises, but a sketch of a very old man with an expression both sad and wise. His hooded eyes look into the future, perhaps not his but the world's. Ivy loves that drawing. She knows every strand in the man's long wavy beard, white like the hair on his head which cascades down to his shoulders.

'Who is the man in that picture?' Ivy asks at last. 'Who drew it?' She waited for an answer, thinking all the time that Daddy could have drawn that picture, with the same minute detail of skin and eye.

'The artist was a very great man. His name was Leonardo da Vinci and he drew that picture 500 years ago. He called it "Portrait of an Elderly Man." Scholars think it's a self-portrait. Tell me, Ivy, what does it make you think of?'

'It's like a drawing my father did, of an old rabbi, with long white wavy hair and beard just like the one here. Only this man in this painting – his eyes are different to that rabbi's. They're sad because perhaps they can see visions of war and murder.

'I see,' Dr B says, as if a disembodied voice were floating above Ivy. 'Can you tell me more about your father?'

Ivy decides not to tell Dr B everything. She goes on, 'When I was little, Daddy used to draw pictures of fairies and elves, kings and queens. That's when he loved me, before I got sick and made him angry.'

Ivy is silent for a long time. She doesn't feel like sharing any more thoughts. She realises she's getting into dangerous waters, and feels afraid, although she doesn't know why. Yet she wants to please Dr B. She switches to a safer subject.

'Mum wrote me a letter, with some presents she sent for my birthday. This new frock is one of them.' She looks down at the crisp material, its yellow and white checks like sunshine against the dark couch.

'I've been admiring it,' said Dr B.

A pause while Ivy imagines her mother's face. 'Mum has a kiss curl that always falls onto her forehead. It reminds me of a question mark on a white sheet of paper, because her skin is very pale. Everyone says she's beautiful, but to me she's just Mum. When I was little she loved me, specially if anyone was mean to me like Maisie was. But after Laura was born, she didn't love me as much.'

'Why do you say that, Ivy?'

'Because Laura is prettier than me. She looks like Mum with her deep-set eyes and dark curly hair. She eats all her food and even asks for more. Only her skin is very brown, unlike Mum's or Dad's. When she started school the kids teased her. They called her Bett-Bett, like the little Aboriginal girl in *We of the Never-Never*. I wanted to hit those kids, but they were much bigger than me. I told them to shut up or I'd tell the teacher how rude and mean they were. It would never work of course. The teacher didn't care anyway, and the other kids knew that.' Ivy hesitates, wondering if it's safe to go on. Dr B waits silently behind her.

'I sometimes think there's another reason Mum loves Laura more than me. Maybe Laura's only my half-sister,' Ivy blurts out. It's a relief to give words to the vague suspicions she's had for so long. 'Maybe Digger – Uncle Dave – is really her father. He was always hanging around Mum, even after Laura was born.' Ivy waits for a shocked response from Dr B.

'There are many reasons why you might think that. Whether or not it's true, wouldn't that mean that you are closer to your father than Laura is? In fact that you're his only child?'

Ivy tries to think. Her mind goes fuzzy, whether from hunger or a recognition of something she hardly knows. 'But Daddy loves Laura, and he always has. He must love her more than he's ever loved me, seeing she hasn't upset the whole family.'

'Perhaps deep down you wish you were your father's only child, to have him all to yourself. It's what Freud would call a phantasy. Like a dream, it's a wish-fulfilment.'

'You mean from my Unconscious? Like Freud writes about in *The Interpretation of Dreams*?'

'I mean that many of our deepest impulses are hidden from our conscious mind. It's here, through analysis, that we can recognise them, and see more clearly what might be making us ill, or sad.'

'Is my Voice from that part of my mind too?'

'Anything that comes without you willing it is from your Unconscious.'

Ivy thinks for a few minutes. She remembers the words from the booklet by Freud that Dr B lent her.

'I think The Voice is my Superego. It wants to punish me for being bad.'

'How are you bad, Ivy?'

'I'm still alive when so many children just like me and Laura perished in the war. My mother nearly died because of me. I have to make up for it all somehow.'

'Why do you think you have to make up for the atrocities of the war? Rather than take on such a burden, can you see it was external forces at work? Where you were born, for example. Your inability to thrive as an infant. I'd like you to think about these things to see if you can make sense of them. You see, it takes a long time before we can conquer the destructive forces in the Unconscious. This is the first step.'

A mélange of thoughts swirls around in Ivy's head, too many ideas to contain. It is almost a relief when the session ends, and she doesn't have to free associate any more.

'We have achieved a great deal today, Ivy. And we've come to the end of our session. We'll have to finish for today.'

Dr B stands up. Ivy sees she is holding out a small package. 'Happy Birthday for yesterday, Ivy. Fifteen is a big milestone.'

Speechless, Ivy unwraps the white tissue paper. Inside is a pale blue scarf, with a fine thread of white weaving through its fabric. Silk, Ivy guesses, because of the way it slips through her fingers.

'Thank you,' she whispers. 'It's beautiful.'

16. THE BLUE SCARF

'Take that ridiculous *schmutter* off!' Aunt Sonia says the same thing every time she sets eyes on Ivy's scarf. 'It does nothing for your neck, scrawny as it is. Boys like a plump neck and a glimpse of bosom. Don't you want to be pretty? At your age I…'

Ivy's already out the door. She can't bear to hear again Aunt Sonia's long diatribe about how, at only fifteen, she met Sid at a dance in the Town Hall, and he fell for her hook, line and sinker. What if she hadn't worn that blue polka dot dress with the low neck, showing her cleavage? Maybe he'd have been swept off by a prettier girl with even bouncier breasts, and she and Uncle Sid wouldn't have got married, and Alex and baby Deborah wouldn't have been born, and there'd be two less people in the world, and wouldn't that be a dreadful shame?

Ivy touches the scarf loosely knotted around her neck. Its square shape allows for several variations: she can fold it into a triangle and knot it, kerchief style, around her neck. Or else it can serve as a head covering, over her unwashed hair, tied either at the nape or under her chin, which makes her resemble one of her Russian peasant ancestors. Its ostensible purpose is to conceal the bony outgrowths of collarbones almost bursting through her skin, and to keep her exposed neck warm. Its real purpose is to protect her from all evil.

Ivy wears it every single day to keep her close to Dr B. She's never washed it, fearing it might disintegrate, or lose the touch of Dr B's hand. It is her talisman, the one piece of protection in her life.

*

'Am I mad? Like, really crazy? Please tell me the truth, doctor.' Ivy thinks about her mother's 'nerves' and wonders if that was a euphemism for madness. She remembers Aunt Sonia's scornful comments about her sister-in-law who 'couldn't cope.' Is she cursed with a hereditary insanity?

'Can madness be passed on through my ancestors, like red hair or being left-handed?' Ivy asks Dr B.

'What makes you think so?' asks Dr B.

Ivy loves the way no question or comment ruffles the doctor's calm, steady presence. 'Well, for a start it's my Voice. That couldn't be normal.'

'When you say you "hear" this Voice, do you actually hear a sound?'

'Not really. It's more like a thought that just pops into my head every time I want to eat anything.'

'We've already understood that this Voice is really part of you. Another word for it could be your Superego, which all humans have in their psyche, according to Freud. Perhaps this part of your mind has simply grown too strong for you to banish without help. Recognising the true nature of your Voice is an important step towards overcoming it.'

'You mean I'm not losing my mind? Besides the bit that was lost already by the shock treatment?'

'I understand why you might think so, but I assure you that you have a good and strong mind, and in my experience you don't display any symptoms of psychosis, which is another name for madness. If indeed I detected psychosis, I would not be able to treat you, and you wouldn't be able to understand the complexities of your mind as well as you obviously do.'

'What about the stories I make up? And how I once saw real fairies when nobody else could?'

'Why not tell me about it,' says Dr B.

*

I was four or five; I know I hadn't started school yet because I used to play make – believe to amuse myself at home while Mum was busy with baby Laura. But I know this wasn't make-believe. I was in our back garden when I saw it, plain as day. The light around me turned golden, and there in front of me a beautiful creature appeared. She was tiny, about half my size. She had hair of spun gold, and transparent wings spread out like those of a beautiful butterfly. Her clothes were sheer gossamer in all the colours of the rainbow. I stood before her, speechless. I'm telling you, she was real. I could have put out my hand and touched her. To my amazement, this exquisite creature held out her rainbow skirt and curtseyed to me.

Because I wanted to be sure she was real, I felt the need to tell the whole world. I asked the fairy to please wait for me and ran inside the back door, calling my mother. She was feeding the baby, and said in a bored way, "Yes, dear," when I told her there was a real fairy in our garden. But she wouldn't come outside with me to see for herself. I ran next door to Mrs Chegwyn's who had no children and sometimes looked after me.

'Quick, quick, you have to come now to see my fairy!' I remember jumping up and down, and pulling her by the hand; she must have dropped several stitches from her knitting. Dear Mrs Chegwyn. She always believed me, and made me feel she was a true friend. Anyway, when we reached the back garden, I was utterly amazed. There was not one, but five fairies, all as real as the first one, curtseying to me all in a row. They held their skirts out so prettily and bowed very low, as if I were a queen. I bowed back to be polite.

'See? Look, there are five fairies now! Aren't they magical!' I said to Mrs Chegwyn. I looked up at her and could see straight away that she wasn't looking properly. Her eyes were not focused where my fairies were curtseying, but way beyond them.

"Yes, I can see the fairies, Ivy. They are very beautiful." I loved Mrs Chegwyn after that, because she understood me.

Another time the oleander blossoms outside my bedroom window came to life. The dark pink flowers became turbans nodding on the heads of pretty ladies, just like in a story book I'd read when I was much younger. I had the same feeling of amazement as when I'd seen the fairies, as if I couldn't believe what I was seeing. I smiled and waved at the nodding ladies as I knelt at my bedroom window. Their turbaned heads bobbed in the morning breeze. I've never told anyone about the oleander, lest people thought me mad.'

*

Ivy could have gone on remembering or inventing, she hardly knew which. But the visions of the fairies and the oleander ladies were so real in her mind, that it was a relief to finally share them with someone who would not judge her.

'I believe you were very lucky to have such visions as a child,' Dr B said at last. 'This memory shows that you are gifted with a vivid imagination, one which, if you put it to good use, could lead you to an enriched life. I do not doubt you truly saw these things, which manifested out of your creativity. This certainly doesn't mean you are insane.'

'Do you think one day I could become an authoress? I've never told anyone that it's my ambition, ever since the day everyone laughed out loud when it was my turn to stand up in front of the class and finish the sentence "When I grow up I want to be…". The right answer seemed to be "a nurse" or "a teacher". One girl even said she wanted to be a film star, and nobody laughed at her. But as soon as I said the word "authoress" even the teacher laughed.'

'Perhaps if you'd said 'writer' they would have understood you better. People often laugh at people or words that are different, unexpected. In fact the laughter can cover fear of the unknown, rather than show ridicule. When you understand the way the mind works it's easier to forgive. Of course at the age of seven or eight you were too young to see that their teasing might cover confusion.'

Ivy relaxes, as she takes in the doctor's words, and realises she can let the feeling of shame and secrecy go, not only about her wish to be a writer, but also about her illness. Her mind feels lighter, free to pursue her dreams and fantasies. Her illness no longer feels like a wicked deed of her own volition, but a puzzle her Unconscious is trying to solve.

'Tell me more about your father,' says Dr B from behind Ivy's head.

*

'With other people, Daddy was always jovial – the life of the party, everyone said. But at home he had his black moods, when he'd push away the plate of food Mum had cooked for him and go into the living room to smoke one cigarette after another. "I should never have left England," he'd say grimly, as he left the table. Which I took to mean that he wished he'd never met Mum and married her and had me and Laura. So that meant he wished we'd never been born.

When Daddy was in a good mood, he could make us all laugh with his jokes, and his funny acts. He would imitate the accent of the Hungarian lady who sold him pickled cucumbers; he loved them, and maybe her as well, so much so that he'd drive for an hour to her little cottage. I remember those cucumbers were big and green and pickled in brine, and he always said they tasted just like the ones his mother used to make, back in England.

My grandmother was forced to marry my grandfather who had fled Russia with his first wife during the pogroms, a time when Jews were robbed of their property, tortured and even killed. She never spoke Russian, only Yiddish. In those days Jews were second-class citizens in Russia, you see, not entitled to speak the national language. They were persecuted and despised for no reason except that they were Jewish. My grandfather settled in the East End of London in England. When his first wife died having their fourth child, he sent for his wife's younger sister, who became my grandmother. That was the tradition amongst orthodox Jews. My grandfather died just before my father's Bar Mitzvah, leaving my grandmother with twelve children to look after. I can only imagine how terrible it must have been for her, a stranger in a strange land, far away from her family. Just like I am now. Except at least I speak the same language.

Daddy used to do beautiful drawings of me and Laura. They were life-like sketches, every hair on my head carefully drawn. He was really an artist, you see, not a business man at all. But he had to make money for us to live on, and had to give up his art, except for those drawings.

He used to tell us how he'd won a scholarship to the Slade School of Art back in England, and how he wasn't allowed take it up. His family was very poor, so he had to leave school early and go to work. Whenever he was drawing me, he seemed to be in another world. He would look at me with the eye of an artist, not like a father. He seemed proud, as if he believed I was his creation – well of course I am, in a way. I knew that I must never disappoint him if he were to be as proud of me as he was then. Sometimes, when I was younger, he would stroke my face softly; that is until my skin erupted just before I turned thirteen. He was angry then; angry with me, angry with Mum, angry with the world. He wanted me to be perfect, you see, so that he could draw me without any blemishes.

When I stopped eating, everyone was mean to me back home, and told me I was naughty for upsetting my parents, and Laura. "Why are you doing this to them?" my Aunty Bella would ask. "I'm not doing anything to them," I wanted to say. "Something's doing it to me." But I knew no one would ever understand.'

'At night before I went to sleep, Daddy always came in to say goodnight to us, ever since I was really little. When I got older I had a room of my own. At first I missed Laura, but after a while I liked being able to read as long as I liked. I had a torch under my pillow, letting me read far into the night and nobody would know. One night I was scared for some reason – maybe from reading the story of Oliver Twist, poor little boy – and I asked Daddy to stay till I fell asleep. He lay down next to me.'

Dr B's voice seems to come from far away. 'Can you remember how old you were then?'

'I think about eleven or twelve.' Ivy remembers her father's long lean body lying next to her on the pink chenille bedspread, the rough gabardine of his suit rubbing against her arm.

'Whenever I couldn't sleep, which was most nights, Daddy would come and lie down with me until I closed my eyes. After that he lay down with me every night, even when I wasn't scared. I would fall asleep breathing in the smell of his shirt, and the smoky tang of his hair as he lay with his back turned to me. Soon I couldn't go to sleep at all unless he was there. After he showed me the picture of the corpses in the paper, I was scared every night.'

'The last night Daddy lay beside me he was restless. He mumbled into the pillow so I could hardly hear him, "I can't do this any more, Ivy. You're getting too old now for me to lie down with you." I felt his body stiffening as he said it. Shock went through me at the thought that I was too old to be loved. I hated myself for growing up, and getting bigger. My body was changing against my will. Bits of ugly hair appeared under my arms, and down there – you know. I wanted to stop it happening.

'If I listened to The Voice telling me to stop eating, perhaps I'd magically get to be younger and littler, like Alice in Wonderland when she ate the special cake – or was it when she drank from that bottle labelled "drink me"? I decided that somehow, I would stop growing, become small again, and then Daddy would love me like before, and help me fall asleep.'

*

Ivy falls silent, wishing Dr B would say something, to tell her if she is on the right track. But Ivy suspects there is no right track where she's concerned.

'What you say about your father's behaviour concerns me, Ivy. It's important that you tell me the truth. Did he ever touch you or hurt you in any way?'

'Whatever do you mean?' Ivy replies. Her whole body went cold. 'Daddy would never hurt me. He loves me.'

'Do you realise it's unusual for a father to lie down with his daughter when she's reached the age of twelve?'

'What does that matter?' Ivy retorts. *This doctor's stupid after all,* she thinks. *I knew I shouldn't tell her everything.* 'Daddy used to lie down with me because I asked him to, so I'd be able to go to sleep.'

'Perhaps, Ivy, it's your love for your father that's created these memories and fears. We need to understand that it is natural for a girl to seek her father's affection. It is not at all your fault that he chose to comfort you in that way.'

Ivy wants to stop this painful digging into her most private thoughts, but at the same time feels relief at letting them out of her head and into the hallowed air around Dr B. She rushes on, 'We used to joke about Daddy's "girlfriends". Women seemed to fall in love with him all the time. Poor Mum; she had to treat it all like a joke too. "*Who is he among us who has not sinned?*" It says that in the Bible somewhere, most likely in the New Testament which is all about turning the other cheek. The Jewish God is less forgiving. *If thine eye offends thee, pluck it out.* My father quoted it to me once, when he was disgusted with me for shaming the family. Well, he did pluck me out, didn't he? And deposited me here as far away as possible from home.'

Another silence. With relief, Ivy sees the clock's hands moving towards the hour, when the fifty minutes would be up. Dr B is very strict that they never go over that time.

'Anyway, it didn't work, did it? Not eating to stay small, I mean. And now I only feel safe when I'm hungry and know I'm shrinking. Daddy doesn't want me in his life any more, else why would he just dump me here, with Aunt Sonia making me wash and clean, telling me how ugly I am? I hate it here.'

'I can imagine how painful that can be, feeling such a great distance between you, your mother and father, and your sister, while you are so very ill,' said Dr B. 'We must work together against this illness, so that you can soon go back to your family.'

'I don't know if I want to any more.' Ivy is surprised at the words coming from her mouth.

17. SATURDAY

It's a more cheerful atmosphere in the Bronsky home on weekends. Alex and Debbie are free to play in the back garden, taking turns on the swing, and hiding in their cubby. Aunt Sonia has a late breakfast, and Uncle Sid joins her, unless he has an emergency house call. Ivy leaves just as they sit down together, successfully avoiding breakfast herself.

One Saturday Ivy takes the bus across the city to the *Schule* in Mount Scopus. Even the bus driver seems in a jolly mood. Ivy supposes it's because he's looking forward to a day off on Sunday, when no buses run in Perth. She imagines what people are thinking, making up stories in her head about the other passengers. It's to distract her from The Voice telling her *you're fat and greedy inside, no one could ever love you.*

As she's promised her mother, she wears the lemon gingham dress under her red woollen cardigan, with white gloves and a hat that Aunt Stella has lent her. Because she looks presentable although skeletal, she's allowed to wait at the bus stop closest to the house. She has a faint hope that by following her family's blind attachment to prayer, a miracle might occur, and she won't die after all.

Arriving at the old stone building of the *Schule*, the only synagogue in Perth, Ivy's surrounded by peace. Even The Voice is stilled in the cool, silent air. It's not piety that drives her to this place, but a sense of curiosity.

Upstairs in the women's gallery she studies the stained glass windows, the filtered light from bright colours washing over the heads of men below, turning floating dust motes to rose, blue, or green. The black Hebrew letters stand stark against the pastel panes. Opposite her is a stained-glass window with an inscription in red and gold Hebrew letters, and underneath the translation: *A Woman of Worth is Beyond Rubies.*

There they are again, the words she remembers from home, words which always anger her. She supposes 'a woman of worth' is one who cooks and cleans and has people over for meals, like Aunt Betsy did when she invited the entire extended family for the Passover meal, the *Seder*. Ivy wrinkles her nose at the memory of the gefilte fish. She determines never to be a Woman of Worth. She can't imagine being a woman at all. Her only period was over two years ago, and her breasts are shrunken. Will she be stuck forever in this in-between state, neither child nor adult? She keeps her eyes on the prayer book, and feels invisible.

Instead of following the service in the *Siddur*, Ivy turns to *The Ethics of the Fathers* in an alternate prayer book, sitting on the ledge in front of her. She's fascinated by the ancient sages' ruminations on the trivia of life, such as when it's essential to wash certain parts of the body, and why it's a health risk to eat pork and seafood. 'Thou shalt not boil a calf in its mother's milk' is written on the English side of the prayer book. It's meant to explain why Mum never puts cheese or butter on the table when she serves meat or chicken, but Ivy's not convinced. What harm would it do to eat meat and milk together in this day and age, when no one would cook a baby cow in milk from its mother?

She's chosen a seat well away from the cluster of women and children who mostly ignore her after a few curious glances. Dressed in their best, with stockings and gloves, matching handbags and shoes, they chatter together like birds at dawn. It's a pleasant background to Ivy's thoughts, rather like the droning of crickets.

Ivy looks down at the men sitting or standing in the pews below. Some rock back and forth on their heels, muttering prayers or silently praying. *Davening*, her father calls it. They wear silky white *tallises*, fringed and bordered in blue, over their padded shoulders. Small black *yalmukas* perch on their heads. Occasionally one of the men looks up and puts his fingers to his mouth, in a 'shush' gesture, to silence his wife, mother, or sister-in law. It's to no avail; after a few seconds of abashed silence, the murmuring is back again.

Many of the men look old, with lined faces and heavy jowls. Except for one, a boy with thick fair hair and blue eyes. She catches him looking up at her, before turning away. It gives her a small thrill, to be looked at instead of shunned. *Why would anyone want to look at me? I look like the Straw Man from the Wizard of Oz, only with less stuffing.*

After the Sabbath Service Ivy tries to sneak away from prying eyes. Too late. At the Schule's exit, a plump, smiling lady puts out a hand to touch hers. '*Shabbat Shalom.* We haven't met before. I'm Mrs Levy, the Rabbi's wife. People here call me the *rabbitzin* – it means the same thing. How should I call you? Do you have family here?'

Ivy swallows, wanting to run away from such probing questions, feeling forced to answer this imposing woman.

'Um – I'm Ivy, Ivy Morgenstern.'

'Ah! You must be related to the Sol Morgensterns from Scarborough. How's poor Sol since his heart attack? I heard he's home from hospital, thanks to God.'

'No – my father's family's not here. I live with my uncle, Dr Bronsky.'

'Not Sid Bronsky! You don't say. Such a fine man he is, and what a doctor! He'll come to the house, rain, hail or shine. Half our community goes to him. In fact, I'm sure he's been looking after poor Sol. Are you sure you're not related to the Morgensterns?'

'Quite sure. Excuse me, I have to go now.'

Mrs Levy seems not to hear her. 'I thought perhaps you'd like to meet some other young people? Our Schule runs a youth group, boys and girls around your own age.'

'Uh – no thanks, I've got too much schoolwork to catch up on.' A stupid excuse, she knows, but can't think of another.

'Forget schoolwork! A pretty young girl like you should be having a good time at weekends. Let me introduce you to Simon, our group's leader.'

Ivy blushes at the 'pretty', thinks it a cruel joke. She looks up to see the fair-haired boy standing behind Mrs Levy, looking as trapped as Ivy feels.

'This is my boy, Simon. Darling, this is Ivy, she's new here. Why don't you invite her along to next weekend's excursion?'

'But, Mum…'

'Now, Simon, be a gentleman. Ivy's new to our community. She needs to meet people her own age.'

'No, really, Mrs Levy, I can't come next weekend. I have to babysit.'

'Nonsense! I'll talk to Sonia. Surely she can spare you for one weekend. Although I do like to see Sid and Sonia have a night off, they're both so hardworking. It's lucky to have you, that they are.'

Simon's shuffling his feet, his face blank, eyes not meeting Ivy's. She notices how his tawny hair's so thick it won't lie flat.

'Give Ivy that pamphlet, dear, with the information about the excursion in January.'

Simon pulls a piece of paper from the pocket of his jacket and hands it to Ivy, still not looking at her. She wishes the ground would swallow her up. Her mouth goes dry. All she wants is to get away.

'Thanks – I have to go now.' She almost runs down the white stone steps into the street, stuffing the paper into her pocket as she goes.

*

It's only a few blocks from the Schule to Aunty Rosa's house. She is her mother's and Uncle Sid's older sister, yet she rarely visits the Bronsky house. The few times Ivy has met her at a family birthday or Jewish holiday, she is struck by how different Aunty Rosa seems from her siblings. She never stands on ceremony or gossips about other family members, and lived her own life without pandering to convention. She seems more free than Ivy's other aunts, not caring as much for What People Think. Aunt Rosa has told Ivy on the few occasions they've met that she's welcome any time, and had finally set a date.

Weakness and hunger slow Ivy's steps. The wooden gate's stiff when Ivy tries to open it. She doesn't have the strength to push its rusty latch. As if by telepathy, Aunty Rosa appears, opening the gate as wide as her arms, spread out in greeting. She hugs Ivy close, without the slightest shudder when she feels the sharpness of her bones.

'Come in, darling! Sally's here too, she's dying to meet you.'

Ivy follows her aunt down the long hall, its walls lined with books and paintings. A tall woman with flaming red hair comes towards her, smiling. Ivy's drawn to her wide green eyes, shining with an inner light.

'This is your cousin Ivy, Sally love,' Aunty Rosa says. 'She's staying with Uncle Sid and Aunt Sonia. Ivy, this is my Sally'

As if in answer to Ivy's unspoken question, Aunty Rosa says, 'Sally's been in hospital, haven't you love? But she's much better now.'

'Hello,' says Ivy. Sally says nothing, just looks at Ivy with those transparent eyes.

'Sit down, girls. I've made us a buffet lunch. Help yourself, eat as much or as little as you like. Tuck in, no need to wait for anybody.' There is no pressure on Ivy to eat, or to do anything else she didn't want to do. Instinctively, Ivy knows that Aunty Rosa understands.

Sally sits down at the kitchen table and starts piling her plate up with food. There's a sliced German sausage called *würst,* pickled cucumbers, olives, and a wedge of cheddar cheese. Ivy sees that Aunty Rosa obviously doesn't keep kosher, putting meat and cheese on the table together, and likes her all the more. She feels at home here, and wishes she could live with this Aunty instead of Aunt Sonia.

'Mum, where's Nealie?' Sally says, her mouth half full and open.

'Remember, I told you, love. Your brother's off on National Service, doing his bit for the country. Like your Dad did in the War.'

Sally's eyes fill with tears while she continues chewing. She gives a big swallow and whimpers, 'I want Nealie, I want Nealie.'

'It's all right, Sally. Nealie will be coming home for Rosh Hashonah. That's only seven sleeps away.'

Ivy puts a slice of challah on her plate, pretending to pick at it. No one says, 'Is that all you're having? Or, 'Take some more.' Or, 'Waste not, want not'. No one pushes the butter towards her.

Sally starts singing with her mouth full, her voice thick and juicy. 'Ivy, Ivykin, why oh why are you so thin?'

'That's a sweet song, Sally love. It's not from your Voices again, is it?' Aunty Rosa looks at Sally with a worried frown. Sally shakes her head, long hair swinging, and keeps on eating with gusto.

I like this new cousin, Ivy thinks. *She hears Voices too. Perhaps we're a bit the same and we've both inherited the madness thing.*

*

When Ivy gets back to uncle Sid's, a scrap of paper falls out of her pocket as she hangs up her best dress, much creased from all the sitting in Schule and at Aunty Rosa's house. She sees it's a typed note: *Please join the PJY (Perth Jewish Youth) on the last Sunday in September for the PJY annual excursion. Meet at the Schule at 8am where a bus driven by our caretaker, Mr Wolff, will take you all to a surprise destination. Mr Wolff will also act as chaperone.*

Ivy screws the note up to throw in the rubbish bin later. How can she contemplate meeting other people her age who would most likely make fun of her? From what she could see at the Schule, the teenage girls were all tall and well-built, with an air of confident privilege. The boys were nondescript, except for Simon, who stood out because of his awkwardness and his shock of tawny hair.

'Of course we can spare her from next weekend, Esmé.' Aunt Sonia had said on the phone to Mrs Levy, the *rebbitzin*. Her over-polite accent grated on Ivy's ears. 'What was the girl thinking, that we keep her a prisoner here? Believe me, Esmé, it's a handful she is. It's for Sid's sake I put up with her, with her crazy ways. Refuses to eat, and now my little Debbie's copying her. I'm beside myself with worry.'

Ivy, eavesdropping in the dining room, wishes she could hear Mrs Levy's response. 'Yes, of course I'll tell her,' said Aunt Sonia into the mouthpiece. 'It's so kind you are, Esmé, but you don't have my aggravation every minute of the day.'

Ivy stops listening, feeling sick to her stomach with dread. She can't think of any way out except to feign sickness on the day. She wouldn't have to pretend very hard, but dreads attracting even more negative attention from Aunt Sonia. Ivy picks up the ball of paper and smoothes it out.

18. AN EXCURSION

'This ice-cream's been lurking in the freezer for ages. It'll be pretty polio by now. Sorry, guys and gals. Throw?'

The girl holding out the ice-cream for inspection, the self-appointed leader of PJY, is called Jasmine. How can she joke about polio, the disease that's crippling children everywhere? Ivy feels an instant dislike. Jasmine is a template for the other girls, who look like a different species to Ivy. Exuding rude health, they burst out of shorts or bathers, their golden flesh displayed freely.

Ivy notices how Jasmine assumes authority because they are in her parents' holiday house. This girl has a way of flaunting her breasts and hips as she speaks, showing her curves to best advantage, which Ivy thinks is disgusting. Jasmine sniffs the ice-cream, and shrugs her brown shoulders. 'I guess we'll be having lunch without dessert.'

Simon snatches the tub, holding it high above his head. 'Right, who says we ditch it?' He's grinning at Jasmine who pouts back at him, their eyes locked. Those two appear to be the unspoken leaders in this group of gangly boys and nubile girls. Everyone except Ivy is in their thrall.

He must be her boyfriend, Ivy thinks, a little disappointed yet relieved. *Stupid to imagine he might even look at me.* Ivy had seen his embarrassment when his busybody mother forced him to give Ivy the invitation to this 'surprise destination.' She'd imagined a beautiful piece of bushland, not this house, all glass and expensive-looking furniture. It adds to Ivy's feeling of being in the wrong place at the wrong time.

'Hey, you can't leave the ice-cream there, the oldies'll have a fit,' says Jasmine, pushing past Simon, making sure her bare arm grazes his. She grabs the tub from the bin, and empties the glutinous white stuff down the kitchen sink.

'No oldies here,' says Jasmine. 'I've paid old Wolffie to leave us alone, and come back for us tomorrow.' Ivy catches a look between Simon and Jasmine.

Rachel, a tall girl in a blue one-piece costume, smiles at Ivy. Rachel's the only one not wearing a two-piece. The other three girls, Sharon, Audrey and Jasmine, wear miniscule shreds of material only just covering their breasts, their buttocks barely covered by the tight shorts matching their tiny tops. How can they manage all that surplus flesh?, Ivy wonders. She looks down at the plaid skirt covering her bony knees, and is glad of her cream viyella blouse with its long sleeves. Although it's a warm day, her body's like ice underneath the clothes that protect and disguise her.

'Let's go down to the beach. Lunch can wait. I'm not hungry anyway,' Rachel says. No one answers, as if they're all waiting for the go-ahead from Jasmine.

'Yes, let's – the water looks so enticing,' Ivy says, smiling back at Rachel. There's an awkward silence. Rachel looks at Ivy curiously. 'What's your name again?

'It's Ivy. Ivy Morgenstern.'

'Where are your bathers? Why're you dressed like that?'

'Bet she's got her visitors,' Sharon sniggers. Ivy supposes 'visitors' was yet another euphemism for periods.

'It's called menstruation, if you want to know, and no, I'm not bleeding from my uterus at the moment.'

'Christ,' says Barry, a skinny boy with ginger hair and freckles. He elbows the boy next to him, who snorts, 'She's off her rocker.' The others stare at her from a huddle of exclusion. She knows her body looks like a grasshopper's, all sharp angles, and hard hairy skin.

'Hey, Ivy here says 'yes' to the beach. Who else is coming?' Rachel calls in a loud voice, ignoring the stares and nudges from the others. 'I can lend you some shorts,' she says softly to Ivy.

'No, it's OK, I'm not keen on swimming,' Ivy says. What a lie, she thinks, remembering how she'd won every swimming race at school, before the darkness and the hunger robbed her of her strength. 'Don't do us any favours,' mutters David, the boy who'd snorted.

'Lay off the kid,' Adam, the quietest and smallest boy says, pushing up his wire-rimmed spectacles, which are always slipping down his snub nose.

'You all go ahead. Simon and I will catch you up later,' Jasmine says.

Ivy sees the look that passes between Simon and Jasmine, and feels a flash of envy. She doesn't know what the look means, except that it's an intimacy she can't share.

Sharon, the girl with glossy golden brown hair and two mounds of creamy flesh emerging from her brief costume top, grins and looks at the others. 'Let's leave them to it. We all know what you two'll get up to,' she says with a smirk, looking around for affirmation. There's an uncomfortable shuffling, and a few giggles. Again, Ivy is confused but doesn't dare show her ignorance.

The four girls and three boys climb down the narrow rocky path winding through the bush to the beach. Ferns brush at Ivy's legs as she breathes in the salty fishy smell of the sea. Nostalgia for home swamps her. She catches her breath at the sight of pure white sand stretching forever, leading down to shimmering green water, occasional white caps breaking the sunlit surface. The water looks irresistible, but she doesn't dare throw off her clothes, exposing her shrunken body to malevolent stares.

The boys whoop and shout, throwing down towels, kicking off sandals, and running straight into the surf. She sees their hairless chests above thin woollen swimming trunks, reaching almost to their knees. They plunge into the waves head first, racing each other past the breakers. Barry and David surge ahead, while Adam follows in their wake. In her mind Ivy is swimming with them, imagining every stroke slicing through the translucent water.

Rachel, Sharon, and Audrey stretch out on their towels, like patients waiting to be anaesthetised, faces turned up to the blazing sun, eyes half-closed.

'Who's got the coconut oil?' Sharon murmurs dreamily.

'Me, seeing I need to tan the most.' Audrey, her pale skin already turning pink, turns over onto her stomach, and reaches into a striped beach bag.

'Hand it over, Audrey,' Sharon says. 'Maybe Ivy can do the honours, seeing she obviously doesn't want a tan, not with all those ridiculous clothes on.' Sharon stretches out a lazy hand, her eyes almost closed. Ivy ignores her.

'Hey, Ivy, can you do my back?' Rachel sits up and takes the bottle from Audrey. 'I'm trying to get my shoulders brown, but all they do is peel.'

Ivy takes the bottle from Rachel and pours a little fragrant oil into the palm of her hand. She spreads it on to Rachel's back, over shoulder blades sticking up like little wings. Rachel's different to the other girls, less fleshy. She moves the straps of her simple one-piece, so that Ivy can rub the oil into her skin.

'Don't want strap marks, do I? Thanks, Ive – can I call you that? Hey, why don't you at least take off your blouse? You must be boiling.'

'I don't feel the heat,' Ivy answers, enjoying the feel of Rachel's smooth skin under her hand. She thinks of Laura. It seems a lifetime ago that she and her sister had sunbaked together on the golden beaches of home. Taking off her shoes and socks, she sinks her toes into the warm white sand.

'Hi guys!'

Ivy's surprised to see Simon jump down from the track above, landing on the sand in front of her. At the same time, David emerges from the waves, shaking water off his sinewy body. Simon glances at David and winks. Without a word, David sprints off, up the track to the house. Ivy watches Simon run straight into the surf.

Sharon, who's been gazing out to sea at the boys catching waves, jumps up. 'I'm going in.' She runs down to the edge of the water, letting its ripples tease her feet and ankles. To Ivy she looks like a cut-out doll, her shape cleanly outlined against the sand and sky. Sharon takes faltering steps into the sea giving little shivers and yelps, then is submerged under the swell of an inrushing wave.

Adam and Barry are beyond the breakers, further out than Simon. Sharon starts to swim towards them, diving under the crests of foam. Ivy looks away, sick with envy. She'd rather be back at Uncle Sid's, at the place she can never call home, but where she doesn't have to make such an effort to be 'normal'.

When Ivy looks up again, she notices something dark grey breaking the surface of the sea. Instantly she recognises the triangular shape, the way it slices through the water. She leaps up.

'SHARK!' Ivy screams, running toward the water, arms waving. Her feet sting on the hot sand. 'Get out! Quick!' The boys are too far out to hear her. 'Help!' Ivy screams with all the breath she can muster. Audrey and Rachel are standing up too, hands shading their eyes, scanning the horizon.

Ivy runs to the edge of the water, her skirt clinging to her legs, and stumbles under a wave. She sees Sharon's head appear above the surf for a moment, then go under. She drags herself up, yelling 'Shark!' again. There's no thought in her head, only an instinct to get Sharon and the others to come out of the water. Sharon goes under again. The grey fin has disappeared. Was it a figment of her imagination?

Barry is swimming towards Ivy, dragging Sharon by her armpits, backstroking with one arm and kicking violently. 'Out of the way, you idiot!' he shouts as Ivy is dragged under by another huge wave. Memories of her days surfing in Castleton, when she was a champion swimmer, come back to Ivy. She lets her body go limp, waits for the next wave, submits to its force, and is delivered onto the sand. For a moment everything goes black.

When Ivy comes to, she's weak and giddy. She can't remember anything. Barry is pressing on Sharon's back, pumping up and down with his hands crossed over each other, his elbows straight. Sharon coughs, and a mixture of vomit and seawater spurts from her mouth.

'Thank God,' says Barry. Simon comes running out of the water towards them.

'Is she OK?' Simon's panting, bending over and clutching his knees. The others stand staring, shock stiffening their faces.

'It was close,' Barry says, straightening up and helping Sharon to her feet. She's still coughing. Rachel runs to her with a towel, and wraps it around Sharon's shaking body.

Something at the back of Ivy's mind sends a signal of alarm. She sits up, soaked and shivering, hardly breathing. Now she remembers. She's seen two boys come out of the water. Three had gone in.

'Where's Adam?' All eyes turn towards her. No one speaks. 'Quick! Get him out!' she cries, wiping salty water from her stinging eyes. Simon starts racing towards the surf. The others wait, still and silent.

'Look!' shouts Audrey. She's pointing at a tiny speck way down the beach. She runs towards it. Ivy strains her eyes to see Simon carrying something heavy.

'No, please no,' Rachel whispers. Audrey lopes back as if in slow motion. Ivy can see the horror in her eyes, and fears the worst has happened. Simon follows. On his back he carries Adam, piggy-back style. Adam's head is lolling. Blood is gushing onto the sand.

'It's Adam,' Audrey's panting, crying, snot mixing with tears running down her face. Simon's holding Adam in his arms. Blood's pouring from a huge gash on his left leg. Rachel and Sharon scream.

'Don't just stand there blubbering.' Barry glares angrily at the girls, before he doubles up and vomits onto the sand. Simon ties a towel around Adam's thigh in an attempt to stanch the jets of blood spurting from the hole gouged in it.

'Someone get to a phone and call an ambulance,' Simon cries, tears merging with the salt spray running down his face. No one moves.

'I'll go,' says Ivy. She's weighed down by her sodden clothes. With an enormous effort she gets to her feet and runs as fast as she can through prickly bushes to the holiday house. Bursting in, she hears groaning and sighing. Jasmine and David are writhing on the floor, their legs entwined.

They are naked. Ivy stops in the doorway, horrified. Weird sounds, like moaning, escape Jasmine's lips, while Barry pumps away on top of her. *What are they doing? Is he hurting her? Is this the sexual intercourse everyone talks about, but no one really does? And what about Simon? Isn't he Jasmine's boyfriend?* It's all too horrifying and confusing for Ivy to compute. A dim memory of seeing her parents once intertwined like Jasmine and David leaps towards her. She brushes it away, remembering why she's here.

'Hell, it's the weirdo,' Jasmine shrieks, extricating herself from underneath a red-faced David. Ignoring them, Ivy runs to the kitchen where she sees a telephone squatting on the sideboard. Ivy's heard Uncle Sid call for an ambulance many times, and she's no stranger to the routine. She dials zero to get to an operator.

'Quickly! I need to be put through to the ambulance service!' Ivy screams to the maddeningly cool, calm and collected woman who finally answers. After an interminable minute, she hears a gruff man's voice. 'Ambulance here. State your name and location.'

'Ivy Morgenstern. Caves Beach. There's been a shark attack.'

'Keep calm, young lady. What's the street address?'

She calls into the living room, 'What's this address?'

'What the hell,' she hears David curse.

'It's 12 Rathbone Street.' Jasmine comes into the kitchen, unashamedly naked. 'What on earth's going on?'

Ivy ignores her and repeats the address into the phone. 'But go straight to the beach. Shark attack victim, teenage boy. If you don't hurry he'll bleed to death.'

There's a maddening pause before Ivy hears a man's voice crackling over the phone. 'On our way. Stay with the injured boy. Tie something tight around his injury, a towel, anything you can find. Don't try to lift him.'

Ivy feels drained. Her legs give way, and she sinks onto the kitchen's cold lino, her wet skin sending shivers through her body.

Jasmine, pulling on her swimming costume in a vain attempt at modesty, stares down at Ivy. 'I said, what's going on?'

'It's Adam. Ring his parents, tell them there's been an accident, and an ambulance is on its way. I have to go back to the beach.'

'What? Who d'you think you are, you twerp, telling me what to do in my own house?'

'Get out of my way. Adam could die. Anyway it's your parents' house, not yours.' Ivy stands up shakily and pushes past an open-mouthed Jasmine. A siren sounds in the distance. Finding the last of her strength from some hidden source, she limps as fast as she can back to the beach.

*

The ambulance men are there before her. The men are lifting Adam's limp body onto a stretcher, the others crowding around him. An oxygen mask is clamped over his face. As he disappears into the ambulance Ivy feels her legs give way again. Faces peer down at her.

'Look how skinny she is! Who'd have thought she'd have it in her?' says Audrey. 'Thinks she can swim, dressed like that? What a freak!' Voices merge into a chorus of disagreements buzzing round Ivy like a horde of flies.

'Shut up, all of you. If it weren't for Ivy, Sharon might've drowned,' Rachel says, helping Ivy to slowly sit up. 'We should be thanking Ivy for trying to save us.' Rachel's voice rises over the others, who fall silent. She puts a protective arm around Ivy's shoulders. The warmth of Rachel's skin, the gentle pressure of her arm, are like a balm to Ivy's exhausted body and mind. *Maybe I've made a friend today,* she thinks through a haze of relief.

Simon's squatting on the sand, his head in his hands. He stands up, walks over to the group. 'Thank you, Ivy. You've helped to save one life today. Let's pray you've saved two.' In his hand he's holding Adam's wire-rimmed glasses, staring at them as if he can't remember how they got there.

19. TARANTULA

Ivy chides herself for missing several sessions with Dr B since she's become too weak to make the journey. As soon as she feels a little stronger, she takes the bus to Dr B's house. Her legs buckle as she crosses the park. Inside at last, Ivy falls onto the couch as if into a mother's arms.

'Ivy, you are clearly unwell,' says Dr B, alarm in her normally calm voice. 'I am not sure we should continue our sessions while you are so weak.'

'Please don't let's stop. I promise I'll be better, it's just today. I'm a bit shaky. And I've brought you a dream that's been haunting me.'

'Very well. Let us continue – for today. I will take advice from your uncle as to your fitness to continue.'

*

I'm in bed with the light on. I see a huge furry tarantula on the light switch. The light goes out. I scream, "Daddy! Uncle Sid! Alex!" Not Mum, she'd be too scared. In my dream cousin Alex brings a torch. Next thing the creature's on the floor, looking even bigger than when it hung on the wall. The thickness and fur of its eight limbs spread out terrify me. I race down the dark hall and out onto the verandah, fumble for a light switch among the many buttons set in bakelite squares. Every other light but the verandah one goes on. I feel shivers of revulsion each time I touch a switch, as if it was Dr Henderson's button, pressed to wipe my memory and make me convulse. Or in case another eight-legged creature or a relative of the first one is lurking behind the switch.

On the dark verandah I stand outside and breathe in clean night air. A group of pudgy schoolgirls walks past the house. They fling taunts:

"There she is, the freak. Look at her ugly mug. Thinks herself better than us just cause the doc's her uncle. Look at her skinny legs, and hairy too. Who does she think she is?" And so on. I stay still and quiet and stare them down and they go away, marching in cohort, chanting their evil curses all the way down the street. When they finally disappear from sight like a cloud of mosquitos, they lose the power to bite.

I go back inside to my little room to finish packing for a journey. It's Friday night, already eight o'clock, and no shabbos dinner. There is a commotion in the kitchen. I hear a thud. Have they caught the eight-legged creature? I imagine Alex holding up its crumpled body by one hairy leg.

Venturing down the hall I see that nobody moves. Uncle Sid is collapsed on the floor, eyes rolling, clutching his diaphragm, struggling to speak through choked breath. "Get an ambulance," I call out, but there's only me, released from the catatonia of horror. I go to the phone on the kitchen wall, now illuminated by a camping light. I dial the operator: "Send an ambulance for Dr Bronsky. It's urgent." I give the address. I run to clear the hallway of toys, schoolbags flung down, sundry objects including piles of my packing. I'm trying to escape. Aunt Sonia will be angry and I feel angry with her for being angry with me.'

*

From behind Ivy's head come golden words from Dr B.

'There are some powerful images in this dream or fantasy – it makes no difference which. I'd like you to think about what the spider image means to you. It can have more than one meaning, as can your dream.'

Ivy shuddered at the very word *spider* which she's unable to utter. 'It's something I'm terrified of, something that wants to kill me. I'm calling for help like I always am, in my mind.'

'What do you think that 'something' might be?

Ivy thinks for a moment. 'The Voice. It wants me to die, and it terrifies me, yet I'm powerless to fight it on my own. But a strange thing happened after the excursion in the holidays. The Voice disappeared for a while.'

'Tell me about it.'

'The girls on the excursion were like the girls in my dream, only not as nasty. I've told you before how a boy was attacked by a shark, and one of the girls almost drowned, and how apparently I helped to save them both, though I can still hardly believe it. It must be true, because Simon Levy sent me a bunch of flowers, believe it or not.

'That's wonderful, Ivy. You see, there is great strength within you. Often those who know true suffering are less afraid of disasters in reality, because they are well practiced in confronting horrors. But tell me, what happened to The Voice?'

'First of all, there was no time for us to eat at the beach house, because the accident happened at lunch time. That meant I wasn't confronted with food, and The Voice was silent. But I noticed that when I thought about eating after the ambulance came, I gave myself permission, instead of being told by The Voice to starve. I ate a sandwich – well, a quarter of a sandwich – and didn't punish myself afterwards.'

'You see Ivy, it was your Ego, that is your true self, who was in charge during the emergency. It overcame your Superego, The Voice, and supported your natural instinct to eat, your Id. Our work here is helping to heal your psyche. I'm proud of you, both for your courage in the part you played in the rescue, and for the insights you've absorbed through our sessions. We will build on this inner strength as we work towards recovery. We must strengthen your healthy side, and silence the negative thoughts. It will take time, but you have the knowledge and power to believe in yourself.'

Ivy's cheeks are wet with tears. This is why she must continue her analysis. She drinks in the doctor's words. 'Does the dream about Uncle Sid mean I want him to die? Isn't that what Freud would say, that a dream is wish-fulfilment? He must be wrong in this case. I would hate anything to happen to Uncle Sid. He's been very kind to me lately.'

'Dreams have many layers, Ivy. This one could be masking a fear rather than a wish. There is always more than one interpretation to our dreams. Perhaps you were re-enacting your call to the ambulance at the weekend, and were rescuing your Uncle in your dream, just as you helped to rescue your friends.'

'They're not my friends. I'm too different from them, and they don't like me. I'll probably never see any of them again.'

'What part of your mind is telling you this? You've shown by your actions at the weekend that you have great courage, and a strong Ego.'

'Do you think I'll ever get better, and be like those other girls on the excursion?'

'You are already getting better in your mind, Ivy. But I'm concerned to see how fragile you've become, and even with the strongest Ego your body is a material being, subject to the laws of nature. To survive you must give it the nutrients it is crying out for.' As if grasping for a life line, Ivy wills herself to fight The Voice.

*

Back at Uncle Sid's house, Ivy gathers her strength for her afternoon walk. Every step is like swimming through treacle. Her breath is jagged, hurting her chest. She makes it as far as a gum tree and sinks down under its shade. In spite of conquering her nausea Ivy feels her life is running out. She's feared death before, but it's never seemed real to her. Today her body tells her there is little strength left to go on living. She puts her head between her legs and sobs.

She lifts her head and looks at the red tipped leaves of the giant gum tree quivering in the autumn breeze. She sees the sky, blue as the sea, looking down at her through little puffs of snowy clouds. 'Please help me,' she whispers to the sky, not knowing who she's addressing, whether it's the universe or the God she doesn't quite believe in.

Ivy staggers from the pain in her legs and back, yet her heart fills with hope as she makes her way back to the place she doesn't call home. *You must want to get better with all your heart*, the ghost-girl Lowanna had whispered in Ivy's dreams. And at this moment, she does.

20. AN APPLE A DAY

Soon Ivy can't sit in a chair without pain when her protruding bones almost pierce her skin. She is living on a cup of black tea and a sliver of toast in the morning, an apple in the afternoon, and a square of chocolate last thing at night. She has stopped feeling hungry; instead a euphoria takes hold of her as her body shrinks.

In desperation she asks uncle Sid, 'Can I come with you when you go on your calls? I won't be any trouble, I promise. Maybe I can even help you.' Ivy knows she is safe with her uncle; being with him quietens her underlying fear of dying.

Uncle Sid's having a rare few moments of relaxation between surgeries when Ivy makes her plea. Looking up from his newspaper, he stares at Ivy. 'Good idea. We'll start on Monday. It'll be better for you than those walks of yours.'

An apple a day keeps the doctor away keeps going through her head like a nursery refrain. Without appetite, Ivy forces herself to bite through the skin of an apple, which she keeps eating in tiny bites all day, until its flesh is as wilted as her own. She sneaks one or two apples whenever Aunt Sonia isn't looking, and hides them under her bed, along with her emergency block of chocolate.

*

Esmé Levy calls unexpectedly on Aunt Sonia just when Ivy hopes everyone's forgotten about her heroics at the excursion. From her hiding place in the hall outside the dining room, she eavesdrops on their conversation.

'You should be proud of that girl of yours,' Mrs Levy says. 'Pity she's such a *nebbish*, looking like a gust of wind would blow her over. It's brains she has, but she won't win any beauty prizes.'

'Don't talk about my niece that way.' Ivy can't believe her ears. 'You wait till she gets better before you say anything about her looks,' continues Aunt Sonia. 'She's smart and plucky, as well you know, after what's she did for that poor boy.'

'Oh of course, my dear, of course. I wonder, would she be well enough to come to us for Shabbat dinner on Friday?'

'I'll have to ask Sid about that. Now, would you like a cup of tea and some of the caramel slice I made yesterday?'

Ivy creeps back to her room to reflect on the conversation. *Aunt Sonia actually stood up for me! She's not so bad underneath it all. Maybe she even loves me a bit. But I hope Uncle Sid says I can't go to the Levys' for shabbos.*

To Ivy's dismay, Uncle Sid agrees to the dinner at the Levys'. The day looms nearer, and with it Ivy's terror of revealing herself as a freak, an embarrassment. She tries to stretch her stomach by flooding it with water. On Friday she goes for an extra long walk in the vain hope it will stimulate her appetite.

Uncle Sid drives Ivy to the Levys' that evening, while on his after-hours house calls. Ivy dresses carefully, in the blue floral dress her mother had sent for her birthday, now hanging looser on her frame. Uncle Sid is silent on the drive, his forehead creased. She wants to hug him when he stops to let her out, but doesn't dare. He'll feel her bones sticking out, and worry about her even more.

The Levys' house is in one of Perth's elegant suburbs. Like the others in the street, it has a lush front garden with neatly trimmed shrubs, and a path leading to grand columns flanking a wide verandah. Ivy takes a deep breath as she stands on the threshold, her finger on the shiny gold doorbell. The door opens immediately. Mrs Levy, her broad face flushed, spreads her arms wide in welcome.

'Come in, darling! What a lovely dress! How pretty you look this evening!'

What a brazen lie, thinks Ivy. 'Thank you for inviting me,' she manages, following Mrs Levy down a richly carpeted hall to the dining room. As soon as she sees the snowy white cloth on the long table, the gleaming silver candlesticks, the shiny *challah,* she is back home. How long has it been since she's had a real *shabbat* dinner? Her heart almost stops with the pain of remembering. Are her mother, father and sister sitting at a table just like this one back in Castleton?

'Do sit down, dear. Simon won't be long, he's just finishing off his homework. It's the Leaving Certificate this year, and the poor boy's up all night studying.'

Rabbi Levy takes a seat at the head of the table. 'Hello, you must be Ivy, the girl of the moment. I've noticed you often at Schule at the morning service. You're becoming quite a regular. Tell me, are your family religious?'

'My family back home are. My Mum tries to keep kosher and we always have Friday nights. My father's President of the congregation in Castleton.'

'Really!' Rabbi Levy's gingery eyebrows shoot up over his rimless spectacles. 'And your family here in Perth?'

Ivy feels under interrogation. She doesn't want to tell tales. 'They are religious in their own way,' she says.

'I'm intrigued. I have the greatest respect for Sid Bronsky, wonderful doctor, but I almost never see him in Schule.'

Ivy is quick to defend her uncle. 'He's too busy delivering babies and saving lives.'

'You're a spirited girl, I see, even though there's nothing of you. Loyal too, I like that. Simon's told us all about you. I'm Ivan, so our names are almost the same, eh?'

Ivy warms to this man, with his thinning hair, sharp nose, and bright blue eyes. Like Simon's eyes, she can't help noticing. 'Thanks, Rabbi Levy.' She manages a half smile.

'Call me Ivan for heaven's sake! We don't stand on ceremony in this house. Ah – here's the boy himself.'

Ivy's aware of her face growing hot, and fears it's gone bright red. Simon saunters into the dining room still reading a book, his thatch of blond hair floppier than usual so that it almost hides his eyes.

'Hi,' he says as he pulls out a chair letting his long legs spread to the side. Ivy's heart gives a little bounce when she sees he is wearing spectacles with wire rims, much like the ones Adam had almost lost, along with his life. Ivy has a sudden memory of that day on the beach, and of Simon, almost weeping, holding the broken spectacles.

'Hi,' Ivy whispers back, knowing her voice would tremble if she speaks louder. She can think of nothing else to say for a long minute, then remembers. 'Thanks for the flowers. They're beautiful.'

'What flowers?' Simon looks up from his book in genuine surprise.

'Darling, I told you,' Simon's mother says. 'We need to thank Ivy properly for all she's done, so I organised flowers to come from you as a gesture of gratitude. Now put that book away, and we'll light the candles.' Simon shrugs, closes his book, and glances at Ivy. His eyes are blank, and he quickly looks away.

Ivy is slightly disappointed. *Not that I'd want him to look at me the disgusting way he looks at Jasmine.*

Esmé Levy covers her head with a white lacy scarf, closes her eyes, and intones the blessing, before lighting each candle. Ivan Levy pours a little kosher wine into a silver goblet and passes it around. The challah is broken into chunks, and a piece given to each of them. The blessings for wine and bread accompany these ritual offerings, which Ivy is achingly familiar with. Her throat swells. She can barely add *Amen* to the blessings.

The first course is chicken soup with matzo balls. Ivy can manage the liquid, but almost chokes on the tiny bite of fluffy white ball dotted with flecks of matzo meal. Her face goes hot and sweat breaks out on her forehead as she coughs, covering her mouth.

'Are you all right, dear?' asks Mrs Levy, ladle poised half way between the pot and Simon's plate, which she's already refilling. Ivy's cringing with embarrassment. What will Simon think of her?

'Sorry,' Ivy says, attempting a smile. 'It went down the wrong way.'

When the plate of roast chicken and *kugel* is placed before her, Ivy makes a valiant effort, hiding uneaten portions under a slice of challah. It is the first proper meal she's attempted in years.

*

Back home Ivy's stomach feels enormous, a balloon stretched to its limit. It is visibly swollen. Like the survivors of concentration camps, Ivy's stomach threatens to burst when she first puts real food into it. Like them, she vomits her first meal.

Uncle Sid comes into her room to check on her, wearing his stethoscope around his neck, every bit the professional physician. The warmth in his voice and the concern in his eyes betrays him. 'Just lie very still, Ivy. The sickness will settle if you move as little as possible. How many times have you been sick?'

'Vomit, you mean? Can't remember. At least four or five times. It all came up, everything I made myself eat.'

'Listen Ivy, your stomach's shrunk. It's not ready to hold much yet. If you want to get better you must start small, and increase gradually. What did you eat yesterday?'

'At the Levys' house, Simon's mum cooked roast chicken and potato *kugel*. I made myself eat a whole chicken leg, except for the bone of course. It felt ghastly, like I was eating dirt with stones in it. But I told myself I had to swallow, because I don't want to die. I tried hard not to spit it all out, truly I did.' Ivy stops as a wave of nausea sweeps over her. She swallows bile, and forces herself to continue. 'I ate the chicken and it sat in my stomach like a brick. It hurt terribly. The pain got so bad, I thought I was going to die. I started to shake. I went hot and cold, and my mouth filled with spit. My stomach heaved into my mouth. I just made it to the outside loo in time.' Ivy's eyes stay dry. She falls back against the pillow, exhausted.

'You poor kid.' Uncle Sid has abandoned his show of neutrality, and looks like he might cry himself. He squeezes her shoulder. 'It was brave of you to try so hard. But you don't have to do it all at once, Ivy. You should stay resting this morning until the nausea settles. I'd recommend starting with some weak tea, no milk, and a little sugar. Later, a slice of dry toast. No butter or anything fatty yet.'

Ivy lies in her narrow bed in the maid's room, willing herself not to throw up again. Gradually the churning of her stomach subsides. When she wakes next morning, Ivy feels a little better. She throws away the two rotten apples hidden under her bed, somehow knowing that one or even two apples a day will never keep the doctor away.

21. THANATOS

Over the next few weeks Ivy succumbs to weakness and exhaustion, so much so that she's had to miss some sessions with Dr B. Her whole body aches, her head pounds, and her breath struggles to reach her lungs. She's stopped feeling hunger weeks ago. Inside her stomach is shrinking. On the outside, her belly is distended so that when she catches sight of herself in the mirror she sees a grossly misshapen creature, an alien, with eyes staring from a shell of bone.

For some weeks after her sixteenth birthday, Ivy begins to feel a strange resignation, as if she's giving in to the inevitable. Her efforts to force food down had resulted in more involuntary vomiting. She was too weak now to attend her sessions with Dr B. Without her support Ivy fears she has no ally against The Voice. Knowing it comes from her own mind, her Superego, gives her strength, but without her analyst's words of hope she feels only despair.

'Either you'll have to go to hospital to be tube-fed, or you'll have to start eating. That is, if you don't want to die just yet. Sixteen's a bit young, don't you think?' Uncle Sid's brow is creased with worry lines, as he wraps a wide band made of rubber around Ivy's upper arm. It goes around three times, instead of once like in a normal person, he tells her with a frown.

'Your pulse is so slow it's almost disappeared. And your blood pressure has taken a dive. From a medical point of view,' Uncle Sid continues, 'your organs – heart, lungs, liver and so on – are soon going to fail. With no nourishment you'll either have a heart attack, or maybe a stroke. In any case, I'd give it a couple of months. Ivy, you're killing yourself. Do you really want to die?'

Ivy stares at uncle Sid as he hands her a death sentence. Useless telling him it's not her, Ivy, but The Voice who wants her to die.

He would never understand. She feels a great yawning hole inside herself, and the constant twisting of her stomach.

'Ivy, think of your poor parents, and your little sister. What have they done to deserve this?'

Always, think of your parents, your family. As if they are the ones trapped in this hell, fighting to stay alive, hearing The Voice that wants to kill me.

Ivy stares at the jar of jellybeans holding down a pile of mail on Uncle Sid's desk.

'Would you like one?' Uncle Sid says, suddenly kinder.

Ivy's mouth begins to water. *Disgusting, I'm disgusting.*

'I would like one, but I can't. The Voice won't let me.'

'What voice?'

'The Voice that tells me not to eat,' she whispers.

'What nonsense is this? I don't understand you. How can you deliberately stop yourself from eating when you know what's at stake?'

'It's not on purpose. The Voice stops me. I don't understand either.'

'Then I'm sorry, Ivy.' Uncle Sid stands up. He shakes his head as if in disbelief. Ivy's surprised to see his eyes are wet.

'Now off you go, I have patients waiting, people with real illnesses that I can treat. At least think about what I said. I will have no choice but to admit you to hospital if you can't see sense.'

Ivy rises stiffly, shivering although the surgery is warm. The spasms of her stomach, the empty ache, are no match for The Voice. *You don't deserve to live, just like he says. You're wicked and ungrateful. Too late to make amends now.*

*

Ivy stares at her lesson book through a haze. Lines of Latin poetry run together in a way they're not supposed to. All sense, all rhythm, all the beauty of the language disappears. Her hands shake as she turns the page. Her eyes are burning, her breath hurting. She feels her life running out. She is helpless.

Without being able to read and write, why would she want to stay alive? She can barely hold her pen when she tries to write in her diary. It's the place where Ivy lets The Voice out of her head and onto the page. When It gets angry, words like 'shit' and 'bugger' appear on the page in fat black letters, in a hand not like her own. Words eject from her pen like excrement. Often the page is torn, when the fury of Ivy's pen pierces the paper.

Ivy's fighting The Voice now, fighting for dear life, fearing every day it will become louder and more insistent than ever. She's been terrified ever since Uncle Sid told her she has only two more months to live. That's if she continues like this, he told her, eating nothing by day, and an apple at night, ignoring the hunger that ravages her body.

She doesn't want to die. Freud calls the death wish Thanatos; it's an impulse towards destruction that resides in the psyche, and which healthy people keep under control. Ivy's will to survive is no match for The Voice, its work almost done. Yet a force inside her, greater than despair, more urgent than hunger, is fighting the death-wish. It is Eros, the life force, that is the most powerful instinct in humans. That is, if they're normal human beings, which Ivy knows she is not.

*

Uncle Sid calls Ivy into his surgery again, after the last of his morning patients have left. He has a medical journal open on the ink-stained blotter with the leather corners. Ivy stares at it, wondering if he has more bad news. *Please not the tube-feeding, I'd rather die.* She rubs out the last few words from her mind.

'Sit down, Ivy.' His voice is gentler than usual, and he's looking at her not in anger or frustration, but with real concern. She sits in the patient chair opposite him, grateful for its soft padding against her sharp sitting bones. She feels like a genuine patient.

'I have something important to tell you.'

She can feel her heart beating through the wool of her jumper. It frightens her as much as the serious tone of Uncle Sid's voice.

'I'd like to read you something. It's about you.'

How could it be about her? She reads the name of the journal upside down from where she sits: *The Lancet, London 1956*. She's never been to London where her father was born, although she'd very much like to go there one day. *If I live long enough.*

Uncle Sid begins to read from the tightly typed words before him. "The patient, a seventeen-year-old girl, was eventually diagnosed with *anorexia nervosa,* a crippling disease of the mind and body. It has the highest mortality rate of any mental illness. The symptoms are self-starvation, amenorrhoea, and excessive movement, leading to a state of emaciation. The patient has no control over the illness, the cause of which is unknown."

Ivy says the words to herself: *anorexia* might mean a lack of something, from the prefix 'an', and *nervosa* was easy to translate from Latin – to do with 'nerves'. Are they the same nerves her mother suffers with? Maybe, just maybe, all this is not entirely her fault. It might be a family disease, something she's inherited with her mother's milk.

'What does that long word *amenor-something* mean?' she asks Uncle Sid.

'It means not having your monthly periods for a long time, which is exactly what's happening to you. Ivy, do you realise what this means? We have a diagnosis, a name for what's wrong with you. Now that we know it's real, it exists, it has a name, we can fight it together.' He looks jubilant, as if she's turned into a different person, one with credentials rather than a pitiable wreck of a girl.

'It says here that *Anorexia,* from the Greek word loss of appetite, is an emotional disorder characterised by refusing to eat,' Uncle Sid continues. 'Sir William Gull MD, the Royal Physician, first described and named this disease way back in 1873. At first he thought the young women who were brought to him in an emaciated state were suffering from tuberculosis, or "the wasting disease" as it was known then. But he found no such physical ailment in these patients, only symptoms of advanced starvation and an incessant restlessness. *It seemed hardly possible that a body so wasted could undergo the efforts of physical exercise it was put through*, Sir William wrote of one patient. Ivy, do you realise what this means? Your refusal to eat, your insistence on walking till you drop, are all documented here. We have a name for what's wrong with you!' Uncle Sid's eyes are shining with the joy of discovery.

Ivy doesn't know what to think. Should she be proud that a girl on the other side of the world is suffering like she is? She wonders if the girl in London has a Voice in her head too. Is it really necessary to have a label for her sickness in order to be believed? She looks around the surgery at the heavy dark furniture, the grey metal filing cabinet bulging with patients' records, breathing the slightly antiseptic air.

'Can you tell me what happened to the girl in that article who you say is like me? What was her name? Did she die?'

'I can't tell you her name, because of patient confidentiality. But I can tell you she's very much alive, in fact she's training to be a doctor.'

Ivy finds this hard to believe. A girl as sick as she is, able to study Medicine? 'How—how did she get better? Was she force-fed with a tube stuck down her throat?' Ivy can think of nothing worse, except vomiting, like she had after dinner at the Levys'.

'No, she wasn't force-fed. The treatment was simply for her to begin eating—slowly at first. Little by little she regained some weight, and with it her health and strength returned. These days there is more awareness of anorexia, at least in Europe. There are special programs there where the whole family undergoes counselling together, and supports the patient. Sadly these modern ideas haven't reached these shores yet.'

Ivy thinks for a moment, remembering some words from the article. 'Does this mean I'm still going to die?'

'Why would you think that?'

'Because the article says this anorexia thing is fatal.'

'No, no, Ivy. It *can* be fatal, more than other – er – mental illnesses. But now we know what it is, the next step is to find the proper treatment. We've found out just in time, from the looks of you. You have a very rare disease, and there's no cure except your own willpower. I'm sorry you've had to go through this alone, but we didn't know, you see. We didn't understand that your illness is not your fault.'

Through Ivy's tears the jar of shiny jelly beans squatting on the blotter, red and green and black, were a broken rainbow. 'Will you tell Aunt Sonia that?'

'Of course. But first I'm going to wire Abe and Lily to tell them their daughter is fighting a real illness, and that she's one of the bravest people I know.'

Ivy does nothing to stop the tears escaping down her cheeks. She cannot believe that she's to be forgiven, pardoned, loved even. 'Can I read the article?' she manages to blurt out.

'It's full of technical language and medical terms you won't understand. The important facts are that the only thing that will save you now is exactly what Sir William Gull prescribed nearly one hundred years ago: complete bed rest, warmth, and a steady supply of small nourishing meals every two hours.'

'But I can't! I need to walk every day!'

'Nonsense. Your body needs complete rest if it's to recover. And we have to keep you warm, so your hands won't be blue with cold like they are now. You do want to get better, don't you?'

'All I know is I don't want to die. I'll try, Uncle Sid, I really will. But it might be too hard for me to start eating, and stop walking.'

'It won't be easy for you, but you'll have our support – mine, Aunt Sonia's, and the rest of the family's. You've shown us you've got the strength to do whatever it takes. Think of this as another challenge, except this time it's yourself you'll be rescuing.'

'Will you tell Dr de Berg? She can help too.'

Uncle Sid gave his nervous cough. 'Quite honestly, Ivy, I don't think that woman's doing you any good at all. She has no medical qualifications, and we in the profession know very little about this new treatment called psychoanalysis. There is no evidence in the literature that it works. Dr de Berg's costing your father a great deal of money, you know. If she was worth her salt she should've been onto this herself. Anorexia nervosa's in her field, after all.'

'But – Uncle Sid, she does help me, I always feel better after our session. Please don't tell Dad to stop my treatment.' *I can't do this without her,* Ivy thinks, bereft at the prospect of no more sessions with the wise and kind doctor. She touches her blue scarf, her touchstone.

'We'll see. Don't worry about Dr de Berg now, just concentrate on getting better. Like I said, you must start small at first, then gradually build up. Remember, your tummy's forgotten how to cope with anything but a tiny amount of food. And Ivy – I'm proud of you. We can fight this strange illness together, now that we know what it is.'

Anorexia nervosa, Ivy whispers to herself, in bed later that night. Now she has a real illness, like measles or polio.

*

It is unbelievable what a difference a name makes. At last Ivy has a credential to prove to the world she's not a malingerer. Aunt Sonia immediately sets about making jellies, junkets, and custards for Ivy's new regime. Alex, without any prompting from his parents, offers to swap rooms with Ivy.

'You can sleep in my bed, Ivy, and I can sleep in yours. That way you'll be warmer 'cos the sun comes in all day. And you won't have noise from the kitchen to keep you awake. It'll be good for me too, so's I can get up early and not be late for school any more.'

'Are you sure, dearest Alex? What about your bookshelves? And Tigger?' She hugs her cousin, knowing to refuse such an offer might hurt him, and loving him all the more.

'I'll take my books with me, so's you have room for yours. And I don't need Tigger in my bed any more. I'm not a baby,' Alex says.

'Of course you're not – you're almost grown up. You'll be Bar Mitzvah'd when you turn thirteen, and overnight you'll turn from a boy to a man.'

Alex looks alarmed at this. 'Not sure I want to do that. Will it hurt?'

'Course not, silly. It's just a tradition. You don't have to do it if you don't want. Anyway, it's still years off.'

Ivy brings her books and diary, her precious letters and pens, and piles them on the empty bookshelf Alex has left for her. As soon as she's set up in the freshly made bed, the sheets and pillowslips smelling of lavender, and the sun streaming in to warm her body, she feels like a queen. In the blink of an eye she falls into a deep sleep, and doesn't wake until Daphne appears with a tray on which is a small bowl of jelly and custard.

'Mrs Bronsky's gone to pick up the kids. She wanted to bring you this herself, only she didn't want to wake you.'

Ivy looks at the quivering red and yellow concoction, and her gorge rises. She gags when she tries to swallow a spoonful. The Voice makes a feeble effort to stop the food going into her mouth, let alone into her stomach. *'Shut up'*, she tells it. Now that she knows, thanks to Professor Freud and Dr B, that The Voice is part of herself, she is learning to control it. She manages to get two spoonfuls down.

Alex tiptoes in as soon as he's home from school. 'D'you like being in my room?' he asks, pride in his face.

'I love it. How do you like it in my room?'

'It's a bit small but I'll get used to it. Actually I might just take Tigger there to keep me company. I can tell he's missing me already.' Alex hugs his stuffed toy to his chest as he leaves the room. Ivy smiles to herself. He's still a baby after all.

The days pass slowly. Uncle Sid calls in to check on her every day after his morning surgery. He takes her temperature, measures her blood pressure, and listens to her heart through his stethoscope. 'Good,' he says when the rubber cuff takes two and a half turns around her arm instead of three, evidence that Aunt Sonia's nursery dishes are having the right effect. The Voice has been silent for days.

The hardest thing is not walking in the bush, breathing the clean air. Her legs twitch and jerk with the impulse to get up and move. The best thing is seeing Aunt Sonia's face without its stony, critical expression. Instead there's concern, kindness, and an occasional pat on Ivy's shoulder as if to say, 'I believe you now.' Ivy still fights the nausea day after day, meal after meal, and is proud when she keeps the food down.

Now that she's officially ill, Ivy receives letters and cards from friends she never knew she had. The Levys send flowers again, this time without pretending they're from Simon. Rachel writes long letters about what she's doing at school, and how Adam's recovering. She visits one day, and Ivy is delighted to talk with her about favourite books, and who has a boyfriend, like normal teenagers.

Daphne brings her a mid-morning snack of a sliced peeled pear. It is sweet and juicy and at last slips down easily. Along with the fruit she hands Ivy a letter. Ivy's heart jumps when the she sees the sender's address on the back of the blue airletter:

Joel Hammerstein, 30 Wave St., Castleton, NSW.

She tears open the airletter and devours every word:

Dear Ivy,

I hear you've been in the wars again. Your Dad told me you've got a rare disease with a fancy name, and you nearly died. Don't you dare ever die, Ivy. You wouldn't do that to me, would you? Who'd I have to practice German with, and to write letters to? And maybe one day when you're better, to hold hands with, and so on? (I won't go into details).

Anyway all seems well at No. 32, now they know you're getting the right treatment. Is it very beastly living so far from home, away from the beach like you told me in your last letter? And having to look after little kids must be a drag. All the more reason for you to get better fast, and come home to civilisation.

I got a credit in German in my half-term exam, and a distinction (!) in Science. Bet I would've got one in German too if you'd been here to practice with. Looks like I'll be going down to Sydney Uni next year if I score high enough in the Leaving. Wish me luck, I'll need it!

Talking of exams, I'd better get back to swotting for Monday's Maths test. Can you send me a photo? I almost forget what you look like, it's such ages since I saw you.

Laura's turning into a real doll, now she's thirteen. You won't recognise her. She misses you a lot, and so do I.

Write soon,

Joel x

Ivy sinks back into the plumped pillows, closes her eyes, and holds Joel's letter over her heart. *Maybe he really does love me. Holding my hand and so on. He wouldn't say that if he didn't want to be my boyfriend, would he? And what about the kiss at the end?* Ivy's imagining what a real kiss would feel like, and hardly hears Debbie when she tiptoes into the room, holding a sheet of paper.

'I drawed this speshal picture for you at school, and Miss Butler said I can take it home.' Debbie holds up the paper in front of Ivy. It's a drawing of a girl, wearing a triangular skirt decorated with flowers in red, purple and orange. The girl's blouse is coloured orange. Her face is drawn in pale yellow, and her eyes are two round blue circles. Red swirls of hair on either side of the face complete the picture. In shaky letters below the drawing, Debbie has written: *Deer Eyevy, Get Betar Soon.*

'Darling Debbie, it's absolutely beautiful! What an amazing artist you are! Who is your picture of?'

Debbie smiles, showing a gap where two of her front teeth have fallen out. 'It's a pitcher of you of course. See your red hair?'

'It's wonderful! And I've always wanted blue eyes! Can I give you a hug?'

'S'pose so.' Debbie cautiously approaches the bed, first placing her drawing carefully on the counterpane. She wraps her chubby arms around Ivy's neck and nestles her face in the hollow there. With the soft, warm little body pressed to hers, Ivy feels a surge of love for her tiny cousin.

'Thank you, darling Debbie,' she whispers. Buoyed by Joel's letter and Debbie's drawing, Ivy feels a lightness of spirit and a whisper of joy.

22. EROS

During the months of rest and recovery, Ivy's grown stronger. Her arms and legs have a little more flesh on them, and her face, when she looks in the mirror, looks less like a skull.

Gradually Ivy's strength returns. As soon as she can stand up, Ivy thinks about school. When she feels a little better, Ivy drags the Perth phone book from its place under the hall table. Her weak hands can hardly hold the heavy volume. She almost drops it. Turning to the section under 'Schools', she runs her fingers down the tiny print until it reaches the Modern School where her friend Rachel goes. Determined to do this on her own rather than involve Uncle Sid, who's too busy, or Aunt Sonia, who won't approve (*what good is book learning to a girl, it'll turn the boys off, you should be working like me when I was your age*) she sends for an application form, fills in details which might have been best left unwritten, and posts the form off with hope in her heart.

Ivy can't wait to resume her sessions with Dr B, which she's sorely missed during the painful period of battling to stay alive, when all her energy had to go into healing her body. Day after day Ivy fights The Voice, and mostly conquers it. She hears Dr B's words in her head, encouraging her, believing in her, and they give her the strength to slowly begin eating more.

'It's quite pretty you're getting, Miss Ivy, now you has more flesh in them cheeks of yours,' Daphne says as Ivy prepares for her first visit back to Dr B since her diagnosis. Uncle Sid insists on driving her, as if she is precious cargo, too fragile for anything as dangerous as a bus.

'I don't want you catching anything off passengers,' he says as he drives through the quiet afternoon streets. 'I've had a chat with Dr de Berg to make sure she understands everything. You're lucky Abe's agreeing to let you continue –for now.'

Ivy smiles to herself.

*

Ivy is lying back on the brocade couch, smoothing down the skirt of her lemon frock, now a touch tight for her. She's surprised when Dr B speaks first. After all these months Ivy is used to beginning each session herself, sometimes lying in silence for long minutes while she gathers her thoughts.

'I'm very proud of you, and happy to see your health returning.' The doctor's voice shakes a little. *Is she crying? Surely not.*

'I suspected anorexia nervosa from the start, and was about to contact your uncle when he telephoned me with the news. Only a medical doctor can make the diagnosis, although it's a disease of the mind as well as the body. We know very little of it here in Australia, and I thank my colleagues overseas for alerting me.' There was a silence behind Ivy's head, as if the doctor needed to collect herself. Ivy felt the need to fill it.

'I didn't want to die,' she said, 'but Uncle Sid told me I had only two months left. Instead of The Voice, I heard your voice, and it gave me the strength to fight my Superego until The Voice lost its power. It's still there, probably always will be, but I'm not afraid of it any more. You've helped to save my life.'

'It's you, Ivy, who've chosen life over death. I've only been a guide to show you the inner workings of your mind. And we must continue our work. Tell me, what would you like to talk about today?'

Ivy answers instantly. 'I want to go back to school. And I want to go to school in Perth next year, so that I can keep on seeing you.'

'That will depend on your parents agreeing to extend the analysis, of course, but I believe we have more healing to do before you can be truly cured and ready to take on school again.'

'I've missed too much learning, yet I'm scared of facing school again.'

'What are you afraid of?'

'Being bullied. Being laughed at. Like I was before.'

Ivy remembers her very first day of school, when she was bashed by other children simply because she was Jewish.

'I'm sure you'll be more than a match for anyone foolish enough to attack you for your religion, or for any other reason.'

A silence. Ivy lets her mind roam free.

'Freud himself was Jewish, wasn't he?'

'Indeed he was, although not observant.'

'To me Judaism is a culture rather than a religion. It's the closeness of family, the food we eat, the festivals we keep. I don't like how rigid some of the rituals in the name of religion are. Some of the strict rules forbidding certain foods don't make any sense. I suspect that's why The Voice had such a hold over me, because I grew up with restrictions. But I see now that I don't have to obey The Voice, any more than I have to separate milk from meat, like it says in the Talmud.'

'A useful insight. Does it feel liberating to have vanquished The Voice?'

'Oh, it's not gone forever. It's lurking in the background, if you know what I mean. I know if I drop my guard it could come back.'

'Perhaps it might, but you are well-armed with your new understanding. The Voice is part of Freud's Unconscious, which is always with us. But you are learning how to manage the forces within your psyche that are destructive. I believe this knowledge will stay with you throughout the challenges ahead.'

Ivy thinks about this. Will she always be strong enough to quell the death wish, without Dr B's constant reinforcement?

*

In Schule the following Saturday Ivy sits in the women's section. This time she is not alone. Rachel sits next to her, but neither are following the prayer book.

'*Shush,*' whisper voices from the gossiping women behind her, whenever they hear a giggle or exclamation.

'The only reason I came today was to see you,' says Ivy as quietly as she can. 'Thanks for your lovely letters, they really cheered me up while I had to stay in bed. It was dreadfully boring.'

'Is it true you're going to school next year?' Rachel whispers, shrugging Ivy's thanks away. 'Why can't you come to the Modern School where Jasmine and I go? I'm sure you're bright enough; it's selective, you see, but you'd easily get in.'

'To be honest, I've applied there. I'm still waiting for answer. But Rachel, I'm nearly seventeen and I've missed three years of school already. I'd have to go back to third year with all the fourteen-year-olds. I couldn't bear it.'

'I see what you mean. I'd hate that too. But how are you going to catch up?'

'With a lot of swotting, I expect. And maybe you can help me with the Maths – I'm hopeless at it.'

'Of course I can. You can come over to my place at weekends and I'll show you what you missed in fourth year.'

Everyone around them suddenly stood up with much scrambling and putting down of handbags from the gallery of women above. Rachel and Ivy get to their feet and pretend to join in the Hebrew song that heralds the end of the Sabbath service. Ivy moves her mouth pretending to know the words; a few come back to her from her times back home in the Castleton Schule with her family. She squeezes Rachel's hand beside her.

On the way out the girls have to shake hands with Rabbi Levy, who gives them a stern look. 'Ah, Rachel, you've graced us with your presence this morning. And Ivy, it's good to see you again, looking so well.'

'Thanks, Rabbi.' Ivy stops herself from saying 'Thanks, Ivan', remembering the painful *shabbat* dinner she'd sat through at the Levys'.

Passing through the gates of the synagogue, Ivy hears a voice close by. 'My word, you *have* improved.' It's Simon, speaking almost under his breath so that only she can hear him. Ivy's face gets hot, and she curses herself for blushing. Her stomach does a somersault when she looks up and sees the admiration in his eyes. Too amazed to answer, Ivy nods slightly and links arms with Rachel.

23. ELISABETH

When her application to the Modern School is refused, '*Unfortunately you are beyond the age range for fifth year, and have missed too much school,*' Ivy is disappointed but not surprised. She has more luck with the technical college Uncle Sid recommends; she applies to do a one year matriculation course, and is accepted.

Hightown Tech is a school for misfits like me, she thinks, *people who are somehow flawed.* Ivy chides herself for being prejudiced, and thinking herself any better than the ex-prisoners, returned servicemen, disgraced girls who'd had babies, and 'mature-age' students. The latter is a new phrase, which refers to men or women who've realised late in life that they'd missed out on an education. Then there would be those, like Ivy, who have been forced by illness to give up school.

*

It makes Ivy feel quite grown-up to be in the company of adults who, like her, have had their education interrupted. There are lots of men in khaki uniforms who had been snatched away by the war, and only now realise that they couldn't fight forever. A piece of paper with a qualification would be the passport to a new, and possibly boring, life. On the whole Ivy likes these ex-servicemen, out of their depth just as she is, battle-scarred like her. They are awkward around some of the other students, as if embarrassed by their very presence amongst women, young and old, and men in civvies.

Every morning Ivy chooses one of the new summer frocks her mother sent when news of her recovery brought joy, and many such gifts from home. The new clothes are still size double extra small, but fit her newly rounded shape better. She packs a sandwich and an orange for lunch, promising herself she'll eat it all. The Voice tries to scold her, telling her she's being greedy, and will be sorry. *An apple a day is all you're allowed*, it says. Ivy drowns The Voice as she chews slowly and deliberately at lunchtime. *I will never go back to an apple a day*, she shoots back.

At lunchtime Ivy joins a group of other girls, uninvited. Their leader is a tall girl called Elisabeth. She has shiny brown hair and a face that would be pretty if she didn't scowl so much. Her left leg, on which she wears an iron brace, is shrunken and twisted.

'Polio,' Elisabeth says dramatically, 'has ruined my life for ever. I'm only here so's I can get into University and study Medicine. I'm determined to find a cure for this foul sickness.' She sits with a proud bearing, her full skirt covering the leg brace. Her very posture says she is better than all of them, and gives not a fig for what anyone else thinks. Yet the girls have clearly designated her their leader. She fixes Ivy with a stare that radiates hostility to anyone who is sound of limb. 'So what's your story?'

'I couldn't go to school for the last three years, because I have – had – a thing called anorexia nervosa.'

'What on earth's that? A fancy name for being a spoiled brat?'

The other girls titter on cue, not looking at Ivy, but gazing up at their idol, Elisabeth.

Ivy stares straight back at Elisabeth, not smiling. 'Actually anorexia is a rare illness, and it means that you can't eat because of something that happens in your brain.'

'Your brain, eh? Well now, let's see if you can keep up the pace here, because I'm telling you, whatever your name is, we're here to do two whole years of school in less than one. What makes you think you can do it?'

*

The English teacher, a tired, grey-haired woman, distributes students' assignments by tossing the papers onto their desks with something like aggression.

'Ivy Morgan', she says as she tosses Ivy her paper, 'stand up and read your piece to the class.' Everyone turns and looks at Ivy.

'My name's Morgenstern, not Morgan,' Ivy retorts. 'And if you don't mind I'd rather not read my story aloud. What's wrong with it, anyway?'

There's a ripple of amusement through the class. Even the soldiers look up, shaken out of their boredom. Ivy remains sitting.

'Very well, Miss Morgan-something, if you deign not to read it, I will do it for you.'

Ivy wants to dematerialise, to float away, be anywhere but here. Through the beat of her heart in her ears she hears Miss McKenna intoning the words she, Ivy, had written in a hurry the week before. Gradually she's aware of a silence from the others in the class as they stop sniggering and look to be listening intently.

Ivy's story is a far-fetched fantasy, an attempt to write a thousand words on any topic. Most students have written on topics like 'My Goal in Life' or 'What I did in the War.' Ivy has written about a stone age couple, a man and a woman, and their discovery of plants that can heal their sick child. Somehow the words had poured out, and she'd found it hard to stop at the word limit.

'This is what you should all be aiming for,' says Miss McKenna into the stillness in the room. 'Something that will grab the reader's attention, that's an original idea, and that flows without all the grammatical errors most of you need to unlearn.'

At lunchtime the next day Ivy decides to join the lunch crowd in the leafy grounds of the college. Elisabeth is holding court as always.

'Never thought she had it in her.' Elisabeth's words float towards Ivy as she approaches. 'You'd never know, looking at that skinny kid, that she'd be capable of…'

'Shh,' says Alice, one of Elisabeth's disciples.

Ivy sits down on the grass and takes out her vegemite sandwich. The girls nudge each other, exchanging looks and sneaky smiles.

'I heard what you said,' Ivy says calmly, looking straight at Elisabeth, 'and I take it as a compliment, if not to me, then to my writing. I'm happy to help any of you with English if you like.' She doesn't take her eyes off Elisabeth for an instant.

There's a stunned silence, until Alice deftly changes the subject. 'Hey, did anyone notice old Mr Rhinehart eyeing off Susan's boobs? Disgusting, eh? She does ask for it though, sitting in the front row in that tight sweater.'

'I wouldn't mind old Rhiny looking at me that way,' says a girl Ivy doesn't know. She has glossy brown hair pulled back in pony tail, and a pert nose. 'He could be quite a dish if he shaved off that awful moustache and ditched those thick glasses of his. Reminds me a bit of Gregory Peck.'

'Shut up, all of you,' Elisabeth says, tucking her brace further under her skirt. 'It's sickening to talk about Rhiny or anyone else that way. If he took advantage of any of you, guess who'd get the blame? Not him, I bet.'

The group falls silent again, but Ivy can hear the words no one dares to say hanging in the air: would anyone look at Elisabeth that way with hidden desire? Or Ivy, for that matter?

*

Ever since she's taunted Ivy for her skinny arms and memory lapses, Elisabeth has been Ivy's bête noir. Last week she said, in front of the whole English class, 'Ivy didn't really write that story. No way.' There was a bitter edge to her voice.

Writing is fast becoming Ivy's release, not by pouring her anger into her diary, but by crafting her words carefully, choosing those which will have impact on her imagined readers. In spare periods she goes to an empty classroom she's discovered. It's the perfect place to write without distraction.

Settled at her desk, her note book open at an empty page, Ivy revels in her solitude. She stiffens when she hears uneven footsteps approaching. Elisabeth Coleman limps through the study room door. Ivy looks up and half smiles, expecting the worst.

Elisabeth stands in front of Ivy, balancing on her good leg. 'I want you to read a story I wrote, before I show it to anyone else.'

'Oh, I see, so now you want help from the skinny girl who doesn't have it in her?' Ivy says before she can stop herself. Elisabeth has the grace to blush.

Ivy looks at Elisabeth's open exercise book thrust in front of her, wishing its owner would go away and leave her in peace. All down the margin of the composition, their English teacher has written comments in scarlet ink, such as: 'lacks cohesion', 'barely legible', 'not logical.' The teacher's writing is tiny and neat like her narrow mind, Ivy thinks.

Ivy recognises immediately that Elisabeth's writing is special, ignoring the few spelling mistakes. She checks for words that are boring or clichéd. Instead she finds the language rhythmical, and the story fascinating.

It is about a boy called Nigel, who'd been born with female sex organs inside him. He hated being a boy, right from when he could talk. At two years old, he wanted to wear lacy dresses, not the boxer shorts and striped tops his mother dressed him in. When his big sister Penny got a tea set and a new nightgown for her fifth birthday, Nigel grabbed the pink plastic teapot and ran to fill it with water. He tried on the nightie, which was much too big for him. Penny smacked Nigel's hand away from the tiny pink teacup, and laughed at him getting all tangled in the long nightie. The story ends with Nigel changing his name to Nigella.

Ivy wonders if Elisabeth's story is based on her own life. Was she born a boy, and had she changed her name from Edward to Elisabeth? That wouldn't explain her shrivelled left leg, but might be a reason for her general nastiness to everyone at the school.

'I think your story's brilliant,' says Ivy at last.

Elisabeth stares at Ivy. Nothing changes in her stony expression, except that there's a light behind her eyes.

'About your story, I want to know what's going to happen to Nigel/Nigella. You'll have to keep going, otherwise I'll go crazy wondering.'

'Huh. As if you aren't crazy enough already,' Elisabeth says. Her eyes glitter with less malevolence than usual. There is even the shadow of a smile. *Perhaps we'll be friends after all*, thinks Ivy.

'Let's go and find this stupid teacher, Miss – Miss Something.' The memory loss is kicking in again. 'I'm going to tell her I think your writing's great, and if she doesn't put it in the school magazine, she's an idiot. There's no appreciation of individual differences here.'

'That's this stupid college for you,' Elisabeth says, shrugging. 'We're the rejects, you and I, like everyone else at this morbid place. Me because I've had polio and look like a one-legged clown, and you because you look like a scarecrow.'

'Really? Well, you should've seen me before. I looked like a hairy monkey.'

'Well, whatever, we're both freaks. Forget talking to that bitch of a teacher – Miss McKenna's her name, just to remind you. Have you noticed how she's always scratching herself? Wonder if it's fleas, or crabs from sleeping around.'

It's getting late, and the light's fading. Soldiers in uniform, young adults in civvies, walk out of classrooms, talking loudly, some already lighting up cigarettes. Ivy and Elisabeth leave the study room, and walk down the corridor towards the Staff Room.

'See if the door's locked.' Elisabeth touches the shining brass doorknob tentatively. It turns, and in a moment they're inside. In the dim light shed by an overhead globe, Ivy sees someone at a desk at the very back of the Staff room. A body lies sprawled over the desk. The inkwell is knocked over, making a sinister navy blue stain on the blotter.

'It – it's Miss McKenna! I think she's dead!' Elisabeth screams. Ivy runs to the teacher's limp body, bent face down on the blotting pad, and gently turns Miss McKenna's head. A trickle of greenish vomit escapes from the teacher's mouth. It's then she sees the half-empty bottle on the floor underneath the teacher's desk.

'Erk, she's been sick,' Elisabeth whines. 'It stinks. Please let's go! If she's dead we'll be the chief suspects.'

From the corner of her eye, Ivy sees Elisabeth's face turn a sickly white. She slides to the floor beside the sink. *Underneath she's as scared of the world as I am*, thinks Ivy.

'Put your head between your knees,' Ivy orders Elisabeth, grabbing the black telephone squatting on the big desk. She frantically dials the number which by some miracle comes back to her.

'Aunt Sonia, quick! I need to speak to Uncle Sid!'

'At this hour? Where on earth are you? We're all waiting for you for tea. Are you all right? Are you sick? Sid just said the other day how you've been looking better, and…'

Ivy breaks in. 'Aunt Sonia, it's urgent. There's been an accident at school. A teacher's ill, and I don't know what to do. You have to get him for me, quick.'

'What a business! He's just coming out of surgery. I'll get him, you hang on.'

Ivy's hand holding the black receiver feels clammy. She hears faint children's voices echoing down the line. When Uncle Sid's gruff voice sounds in her ear, she almost laughs with relief.

'What is it, Ivy? Are you all right?'

'I'm fine, but it's our English teacher. She's collapsed, and she needs help straight away. I'm scared she'll die.'

'Slow down now. Where exactly are you?'

'At school. Elisabeth and I tried to …'

'Listen to me. Check if the teacher's breathing. Turn her on her side if you can. That might help to clear her airways. I'm on my way.'

*

Headlights shine through the window of the office.

Using the wall to guide her way, Ivy manages in the near dark to unlock the door to the entrance hall. Uncle Sid gets out of the car, his tie undone, his hair awry. Ivy almost weeps with relief when she sees his brown leather doctor's bag.

'She's in here. I checked she's breathing. I've tried to clear her airways. Uncle Sid – I think she's drunk. There's a half empty whisky bottle under her desk.'

Uncle Sid doesn't answer. He almost runs into the Staff Room.

*

'Worst case of alcoholic poisoning I've seen in a while,' says Uncle Sid to Ivy in the car on the way home. 'I must say I'm proud of you, Ivy. You showed great presence of mind by not calling an ambulance, once you saw the whisky bottle.'

'I smelled it on her as well, and I knew she'd be in trouble with the police, maybe even lose her job. Miss McKenna's not that great a teacher, mind, but she does like my writing. I poured all the whiskey down the sink and chucked the bottle in the outside bin.'

'Well, you've not only helped to save Lydia's life, you've saved her reputation as well. And we know it's not the first time you've come to the rescue. I like to think I've taught you some useful skills, and you're a quick learner.'

Ivy can't help feeling proud. 'Lydia? Is that her name? Doesn't suit her at all. Wait till I tell Elisabeth, she'll laugh her head off.'

'Really, Ivy, you should learn about patient confidentiality –although I just broke it myself. The poor woman's a patient of mine. You can tell your friend Elisabeth, but no one else. Understand?'

Ivy nods. She feels a small thrill at the words 'your friend'. *Will we be friends now, or is she going to avoid me, now that I know she's not so brave after all?*

*

Ivy needn't have worried. Not only is Elisabeth her best friend at school, she insists on inviting Ivy to study with her at weekends, at her parents' house. It is in a far more salubrious suburb than Clareville or Hightown. The streets are wide and clean, and Elisabeth's front garden has a well-manicured lawn, and bushes of the native Geraldton wax, whose tiny pink flowers delight Ivy. She helps Elisabeth with grammar and English, while Elisabeth coaches her in Maths, which Ivy hasn't studied since third year. It is, Ivy says, a symbiotic arrangement. Elisabeth adds the word to her growing vocabulary notebook.

Both girls swear never to breathe a word about Lydia McKenna's ignominious escape from death. In return, Miss McKenna makes sure both girls get extension work in English, as befitting 'emerging authors.' Other students treat Ivy with a new respect, both for her writing and her easy relationship with Elisabeth. They move to make space for her now at lunchtimes.

Over the months, Ivy's body is filling out, making her look younger and prettier than before. She is frightened at first by the changes, as if her old self has been stolen. Although she is still very thin, she sees a fat girl when she dares to look in the full length mirror behind the door of Aunt Sonia's wardrobe. The Voice is always there in the background, tempting her back into her old ways, telling her that only starvation will save her. She hears Dr B's words then, and uses the knowledge she's gained from their sessions to quell The Voice.

With the clear goal of University in front of her, Ivy works diligently at her studies, determined to matriculate by the end of the year. Thoughts of what might await her back home distract her. Will Joel still want to be her friend, and perhaps more than a friend? Her feelings for him have not changed over the years, and she holds close to the dream of sharing her life with him.

24. LETTERS HOME

Dear Sis,

Can I call you that? It's what sisters call each other in America. I know, cos Mum lets me buy this magazine called Seventeen. Every time I look at the cover I think of you, of course. Can't believe you're seventeen already. That's really old!

We all loved that photo of you going to Schule, with that cute hat and lacy gloves. Where did you get the wedgies? They make you look quite tall, and they're the latest fashion here. Mum won't let me wear anything on my feet but flatties.

Guess what? I measure five foot eight inches, and still growing! Bet that's why Mum won't buy me heels or wedgies, even though lots of other girls in Third Year have them. It's boring to be the tallest in the class. I'm scared I won't stop growing. Mum says it's not good for a girl to be too tall.

You look really pretty in the photo. Did Alex take it? I like your hair shorter, it really suits you. Just wish we could get photos in colour so I can see if your hair's still as red as ever, and if you're wearing lipstick. Are you?

Is it true you might be coming home after your exams? Hope so – I can't wait to have a sister again. Good luck with the Leaving. (I bet you'll come top in everything, so you'll hardly need luck.)

Some news: Uncle Oscar and Aunt Lena are moving to Castleton! Their house is just round the corner. And most exciting of all, they have a new baby, a little boy called Ira. He's super cute! I guess he's named for

Irina, that poor girl who fell off her horse years ago. Mum says never to mention it in front of Aunt Lena, but I reckon she might like people to talk about Irina. Otherwise it's like she never existed.

Well, I better close now, though I could go on forever. I've got heaps of homework which I'm s'posed to be doing instead of writing this letter.

Before I forget, Joel was home for the Uni holidays. He said to tell you he likes your photo too. Mum let me go to the movies with him last Saturday, just for the matinée of course. I'm planning to ask him to be my date for the School Dance, because he'll be back home for the Term break. Joel is such a dish!

Please write back soon, and send more photos,

Your loving sister,

Laura.

Ivy stares at the fine airmail paper covered with the blue loops of Laura's writing. She senses Irina looking down at her, smiling. Ivy hasn't thought of Irina for ages. The last time was when she told Dr B the whole story, how when Irina died something in Ivy died too.

The bit in Laura's letter about Joel makes Ivy smile – *how like him to be looking after my little sister.* She hasn't had a reply to her latest letter to him, all in German. There's a niggling, uneasy sensation in her chest when she thinks of Joel sitting next to Laura at the matinée. And he's much too old to take Laura to the end of term dance. Ivy smiles to herself. *Am I being jealous of my little sister? How silly, Laura's still only a baby.*

*

'There's someone on the phone for you,' Aunt Sonia says as Ivy's clearing the dinner table. There's a sly smile on her aunt's lips.

'Who is it?' Ivy hopes it might be a trunk call from Daddy, to wish her luck in the final exams.

'You'll see,' Aunt Sonia says. *Was that a wink?* Ivy thinks with alarm.

'Hurry up, lass, phone calls cost money, you know.' She holds the receiver out from the mouthpiece on the kitchen wall. Ivy takes it warily, as if it might bite her.

'Hi, is that Ivy?' She recognises Simon's voice. It has a slight lisp which she once found endearing, and now finds irritating.

'Hello Simon,' she says in a flat voice. Once she would have thrilled at his call. Now she can only think of Joel, wishing it were him ringing her.

'Um,' says Simon, 'would you – I don't s'pose you – er – you'd like to come to that show?'

'What show?' Ivy's impatient, and is already thinking of an excuse.

'It's the PJY Review. Jasmine's playing Queen Esther, and Rachel's one of the handmaids.'

Bet Mrs Levy put him up to this, she's such a busybody.

'Thanks for asking, Simon, but I've got such a heap of work to get through before the exams. My folks won't let me go out at night any more, at least, not till they're over.'

'Aw, c'mon, Ive. Anyway, my Mum's talked to Mrs Bronsky, and she said you can go. And it's not at night, it's next Sunday afternoon. How about it?'

Damn. Thanks, Aunt Sonia. 'Oh, then I s'pose – I mean well then, I guess I can come as long as I get home early.'

'Great. It's a date then, OK?'

Ivy pulls a face at the word 'date'. 'Sure,' she says. 'See you then.' She hangs up quickly before she says what she's really thinking: that she's not interested in 'dates' or having a boyfriend.

'*Nu?*' Aunt Sonia's been eavesdropping while pretending to polish the silver. 'What did the boy say?'

'Really, Aunt Sonia, it's none of your business. You know very well what he said, or else you can guess.'

'That's enough rudeness from you, young lady.'

Ivy knows these are face-saving words, without the venom that used to accompany them.

'You should count yourself lucky such a nice boy wants to go out with you. I know Esmé will be pleased. He's a good catch, you know. A rabbi's son, no less.'

'Don't be ridiculous, it's not like that at all. I'm only filling in for Jasmine, seeing she's in the play and she can't be his date.'

'Hah! That's what you think. A little bird told me Simon Levy's keen on you. Heaven knows why.' Ivy snaps a tea towel at Aunt Sonia, who dodges out of reach. 'Go and fetch Debbie from the cubby and get her in the bath. Dinner's almost ready. And mind you don't fill her head with more of those stories of yours.'

Debbie holds her soft chubby arms up to Ivy, who swoops her up from the play mat, which serves as a makeshift floor for the cubby house Alex is getting too big to play in. To be able to hold Debbie in her arms is to Ivy like a gift. She could never have held her before, in her weakened state.

At six Debbie's still babyish, with wisps of blonde curls around her apple cheeked face. Ivy would like to draw her, if she'd sit still long enough. In the bath Debbie lies on her tummy making swimming movements with her arms.

'Look, I'm a mermaid! Will you tell me that story again about how you once saw a real fairy?'

'Of course, but you've got to promise to keep it a secret from everyone else.'

'I promise,' Debbie says solemnly, looking up at Ivy with trusting brown eyes.

How will I ever be able to leave this little golden girl? Ivy thinks, as she soaps Debbie's back, making rhythmical movements in time with the words of her story.

*

When Sunday comes Ivy makes a minimum effort at dressing up, choosing a simple skirt and blouse with a button-up collar and puffed sleeves. She tucks the blouse into the skirt where it threatens to escape, and cinches a wide belt around her waist. It's a new experience to have an actual waist, and her breasts are budding into life, although she still doesn't need a brassiere. Her only jewellery is the little wrist watch she's had since she arrived in Perth. A quick flick with a comb through unruly auburn curls, and she's ready.

Simon's waiting in the lounge room, chatting to Alex about his new meccano set. Their heads are close together examining where to put the wheels on the army truck Alex is constructing. When Alex sees Ivy he jumps up, pulling her by the hand.

'Come and see what I'm making! Can you help work out where the steering wheel goes?'

Ivy squats down to Alex, as Simon gets to his feet. She focuses on the half-made toy, ignoring Simon. He coughs nervously.

'Um – g'day Ive, I guess we better get going.' Ivy hates it when anyone but Rachel calls her *Ive*. Simon's voice has dropped a few octaves lower since she's last seen him. She can still hear him saying 'You *have* improved' that day after Schule.

'Don't go yet, you have to help me finish the truck,' Alex says, disappointment clouding his eyes.

'I will when I come back, love.' Ivy's glad of a reason to get home early, and hopes Simon is taking note. 'We won't be late, will we?' She looks up at Simon and is surprised to see his face red and shiny.

'I bought you this,' he says, holding out a small box. 'You can wear it this afternoon if you like.'

Ivy takes the box gingerly, as if it might be dangerous. Inside is a silver chain, and on it a Star of David. She stares at it, then looks up at Simon.

'I can't possibly, this is much too good. It's not even my birthday.'

'I know, but I want you to have it. The other girls nearly all have a *mogen dovid*, so I thought you should have one too.'

Ivy slowly lifts the chain from its satin lining. 'It's beautiful,' she says, feeling an immediate sense of warning. She doesn't want this gift that feels like a claim on her.

'Let me put it on for you.' Ivy feels Simon's hands shake as he clasps the chain around her neck. A shiver runs down her spine.

At the Schule hall, Ivy's surrounded by Sharon, Audrey, David and Barry. Adam, limping a little, gives Ivy a warm hug. They're all talking at once: who's going out with whom, how many weeks till the Leaving, when's next year's excursion. When Ivy gets a word in and tells them she most likely won't be here next year, there are cries of 'You can't leave!' and 'We need you in case there's another accident!' Ivy shushes them glancing at Adam. They fall silent, abashed.

It's funny seeing Jasmine decked out in a purple satin robe with a gilt crown on her honey-brown tresses, to signify her royal status as Queen Esther. Legend has it that Queen Esther saved the Jews from the evil Haman, played by Simon's best friend Sam. At interval the Council of Jewish women serve *hamentaschen*, traditional fare representing the ears of Haman. Ivy refuses Simon's offer of a plate. It is not The Voice that stops her eating, but a big lump in her throat. Overwhelmed by the welcome from those who'd once shunned her, she wants to cry and laugh at the same time.

Sitting close to Ivy during the show, Simon tries to hold Ivy's hand. Instinctively she pulls it away. His hand moves to encircle her wrist. 'Look,' he whispers, 'how tiny your wrist is.' His long fingers overlap, and he caresses the bones of her arm. Ivy shivers again, and gently extricates her hand from his.

*

Dear Joel,

It seems ages since I've heard from you. I guess you must be busy with Uni. How's it going? I can't wait to get there, that's if I get enough marks in the Leaving to matriculate.

Last time you wrote you said Medicine was boring. Surely it can't be that bad? I'm not sure what I want to do next year, only that I want to study English Literature and Philosophy. That's if I get enough marks to matriculate. Keep your fingers crossed for me!

Guess what – I got a story published in the Women's Weekly! It's all thanks to my English teacher, Miss McKenna. Her first name's Lydia, but don't tell anyone. Only my friend Elisabeth and I know. We helped her out of a (literally) sticky situation, and now we're her favourites. Anyway she kept telling me to send off some of my stories to magazines, and finally one was accepted. It'll be published in next month's issue – not that I'm suggesting you read it there (think how you'd get teased for being a sissy if anyone caught you reading a women's magazine). I can send you a copy with my next letter – if you're interested, that is.

Last weekend I went to a revue put on by the Jewish Youth Group here. It was abysmally amateur, but I had to go because Aunt Sonia organised me to go with Simon, the rabbi's son. Don't worry, he's not my boyfriend, just a friend. Ever since that day I helped get the ambulance for poor Adam, the Group's been really friendly to me. Remember how I wrote you that he got attacked by a shark and nearly died? The best thing about the whole event last Sunday was seeing Adam alive and well.

Sorry to rave on – I wish we could talk in person. Not long now! If my exams go OK I'm planning to be home by Christmas. I'm counting the days.

Laura wrote me that you went with her to the pictures when you were home for the semester break. Thanks for looking after my little sister! I miss her more than I can say. She said you liked the photo I sent home. I'm enclosing another one, but this one's just for you,

Ich liebe dich

Ivy.

Ivy dreams of a life with Joel when she finally returns to Castleton. *At least he's Jewish, so there's no reason I wouldn't be allowed to marry him.* She remembers the time when Daddy had screamed at her and Laura, *If either of you marry out, I'll swing for you!* At first Ivy didn't know what he meant, only that he was furious at the thought of his daughters marrying out of the faith. Later she realised he meant that he'd hang, either by his own hand or as the legal penalty for murder. It was an old English saying, *I'll swing for you*, four words loaded with hatred and menace. She tries to wipe the memory away but it sticks, lurking in her Unconscious from where it erupts to frighten her.

25. RECLAIMING THE SELF

As Ivy's body strengthens and fills out, so does her mind. More and more memories are resurfacing. They are scattered, some from the distant past, others from before the shock treatment. Some are like glimpses of sunshine, others plunge her into darkness.

Ivy knows her analysis must end soon. In these final sessions, she wants to give her newly recovered memories to Dr B as a parting gift.

*

'I remember waking to birds calling when I was very little, and thinking they were speaking to me. The "caw" of the crows sounded exactly like a human voice. I strained to understand the words coming from the birds' throats.

On Sundays Laura and I would each hold one of Daddy's hands, and walk down the gravel road. "Tie their bonnets on," Mum called from the front porch. When Daddy bent to tie the loose ribbons under my chin, I could smell his smoky breath and see tiny black whiskers sprouting on his cheeks. We walked down the gravel road, under the shade of spindly gum trees. It seemed an age before we reached the gate of the magic house. There was always a moment of suspense. I would lean over the iron gate, and close my eyes for a moment to savour the suspense. I opened them, and there it was. The Coloured Path was still there. There were squares of bright blue, green, pink, and purple. The last square was as golden as the yolk in Daddy's breakfast egg. It was a wonder.'

*

'This is not the first time I've been to Perth,' Ivy says to the silent Sphinx behind her head. 'I was here with my mother and sister many years ago.

I remember waiting all alone outside a strange school, with hot wee running down my leg. I was around seven, and Mum had sent me to school in Perth so I wouldn't get behind. Anyway, this was my first time at the new school. My cousin Neal, Sally's brother, was a big boy of ten. He was supposed to pick me up and double me home on his bike. Only he never turned up, at least not for ages. Not until I'd wet myself, and was crying. Even the teachers had gone home; the last one to leave – I can't remember her name asked if she could ring someone to come and get me, but I didn't know any phone numbers.

The teacher left me there, standing in the street outside the wire fence surrounding the school. Finally Neal rode up, and without a word told me to hop on the back of his bike. He never said he was sorry. When we got back to his house, my mother and his were having afternoon tea, like two ladies at a tea-party. I ran to my mother and flung myself onto her.

"I waited and waited, and no one came!" I sobbed, wetting her blouse. I clearly remember the pearl buttons on it sticking into my cheek. She pulled me off her – I must have smelled of wee – and said something like "Never mind, you're here now." I expected her to be angry on my behalf, worried about me waiting all alone, not having tea out of a dainty cup as if nothing in the world was wrong. But she gave a nervous laugh and said, "now be a good girl, wipe your eyes and give Aunty Rosa a kiss." To her credit, Aunty Rosa seemed embarrassed, and apologised on her son's behalf, saying Neal had been held up at sport or some such lame excuse. I suspect the poor lad's forgotten.'

*

'That memory came back the other day, when I was waiting for Rachel to turn up to the picture theatre. I felt a wash of panic when she was only five minutes late. It was exactly like the panic I'd had that day outside the school. Ever since, I try to be on time, but never early, so's I won't have to wait all alone like I did that day.'

Dr B speaks at last. 'It must have been very frightening for you. It's probably a memory you'd rather forget, but now that we've uncovered your deepest fears, these experiences will return to you, almost like answers to a puzzle. This one could be related to your fear of losing control.'

'How do you mean?' Ivy asks. She was hoping for more sympathy.

'As you and I know, The Voice you imagined hearing was really yourself, projecting a very strict and cruel Superego, and allowing it to control if and what you ate. To relinquish that control takes enormous strength and determination, both of which you've shown in these sessions. It seems you internalised this controlling Voice around the time your friend died.'

Ivy's mind skitters away from memories of Irina. 'Actually it started even before Irina was killed. As a child I felt distaste, and still do, for the fuss over food at religious festivals, and the insistence on eating such disgusting things as boiled gefilte fish.'

'We were talking about Irina, and when you first heard The Voice.'

'Yes, I remember it warned me not to eat "at a time like this", and anyway I was too shocked to face food. But The Voice planted itself inside me before that night. Remember I told you how my father showed me pictures of dead people, including children, in the concentration camps? It was then that I felt some punishment was in store for me too.' Nothing more came to Ivy's mind except the hot shame she'd felt at being alive when others were dead. At last gentle words floated over Ivy's head from the high-backed chair behind her.

'It's called survivor guilt when someone close to you loses their life, and you are left unharmed. Perhaps, Ivy, you were a scapegoat for your family's survivor guilt after the horrors of the Holocaust. As you've told me, the Holocaust took the lives of many of your mother's relatives in Europe. Yet your parents were safe and sound in a country so distant from the horrors of that war, they could have been on the moon. Your family escaped being murdered by the Nazis simply by virtue of geography. Perhaps, deep down, your mystery illness may have seemed to them like the punishment they deserved.'

Something stirs in Ivy, a recognition, a signal. 'You mean they wanted me to get ill and die?'

'Never in their conscious minds. But the Unconscious is capable of such extreme and shocking thoughts – consider our nightmares, for example. Those unwelcome thoughts and dreams, even if censored by our conscious mind, can still control our everyday lives. Unconsciously you, as a vulnerable child, may have absorbed their helplessness, even their own guilt for surviving such massive tragedy.'

Ivy feels as if a great burden she'd been carrying all her life has been lifted. To think that her parents, unknown to themselves, might carry some responsibility for her near-fatal illness! 'Once, when I was extremely thin, my father called me "A Belsen horror". I often have nightmares of him calling me that. It hurt terribly at the time, but now I'm beginning to understand where that cruel comment came from.'

The room fills with a silence that seems charged with a soothing peace. Ivy's aware of the clock telling her there are still twenty minutes left of her session.

'Speaking of nightmares, I have been having this one more than once since we last met.'

*

'I'm looking for a lost object, deep in the forest. A party of friends and family are helping me to search. We find a dead baby buried deep in the ground. It's a baby girl, complete and perfect, dressed in a white nightgown and a frilled bonnet. Her skin and clothes are fresh and clean in spite of having been covered in soil. I touch her tiny hands. They are cold but soft. I love her and beg to keep her. But the men around me say that is forbidden; the laws of our people say the child must go back under the ground because she is dead. I wake up weeping.'

'I suppose the baby could be me, come back from the dead, yet not truly forgiven by my family for having worried them so much. Or it represents all the years I've lost being in thrall to this relentless disease, years I'll never get back.'

*

'And yet here you are, Ivy, alive and well, full of ideas for your future. I am immensely proud of you, and the way you've gained insights, which should sustain you in your life to come.'

'I've often wished I could give you something in return for all you've given me,' Ivy says.

'Ah no, the courage and strength you've shown in this room is more than enough. But I do have a favour to ask. The Australian Institute of Psychoanalysis has asked me to write a paper on the work you and I have done together. I would of course not name you or your family, and will show it to you before submitting it for publication. You see, the medical profession still doesn't know how to treat anorexia nervosa, and our story could help others with this insidious illness.'

'Really?' Ivy is so excited at the thought of being a subject of a scientific paper, that she sits up and almost jumps off the couch. 'You would tell others how you've helped me fight The Voice? How you took me to the depths of myself, to unearth secrets hidden there?'

'Well put, Ivy. It is only by confronting our deepest fears and finding truth behind them, that we can be set free of sicknesses of the mind. You have been a willing and able pupil, and it is your own work I would be documenting in this article.' There is a pause, which makes Ivy feel uneasy.

'The time is coming when our sessions must come to an end. You will soon be returning to your family, and now that you are so much better physically, I believe you will be able to continue the work we have started here on your own. The mind and body are intricately connected, and strength in one will lend itself to the other. We will work together over the next few sessions to give you tools which should sustain you after you leave here.'

With these words, Dr B stands up from her chair. To Ivy's shock and delight, the doctor embraces her warmly. 'My brave girl,' whispers Dr B.

Ivy will always remember her words. *Will I ever be able to survive without the wisdom and guidance she gives me?*

*

Shaking all over, Ivy waits for the exam results to be posted up on the courtyard wall of Hightown Tech. Elisabeth is clutching Ivy's arm as much for comfort as for balance. The other students, mostly grown men and women, are filling the courtyard. The early summer air shimmers with heat and anxiety.

A shout goes up as the Vice Principal, Mr Kingsway, emerges from the building with a sheaf of papers. He pins two sheets up. The crowd surges forward. Elisabeth is almost knocked over. Ivy steadies her.

'It's Maths and Science,' she hears people shout.

'Stay here,' she says to Elisabeth. 'I'll go and look for us both.'

The writing on the wall in front of her shimmers and shakes, black letters running into each other. At last she sees Elisabeth's name before her own, then realises the names are not in order of merit but of the alphabet. There's a D next to Elisabeth Coleman for Maths. It doesn't mean Dunce, but Distinction. Ivy's so excited she forgets to look further down the list for her own name.

Nearly knocking Elisabeth over, Ivy races up to her. 'You've got a Distinction for Maths!' she says, jumping up and down.

'Don't believe you,' Elisabeth says, although her eyes are shining. 'Let me see for myself.' She limps through the crowds and stands in front of the notice board.

All around her, fellow students are laughing or crying. Some have slunk away, shoulders drooping. Something holds Ivy back from looking at her own results. She hears Elisabeth panting as she returns. Her face is grave.

'What's wrong? Didn't you see the Maths list? I'm sure it said…'

'Ivy, I'm sorry. There's an F next to your name.'

Ivy feels nothing for a moment. 'You sure? But – but it's a compulsory subject. I can't fail or I won't matriculate!'

Elisabeth bursts out laughing. 'You duffer. Course you didn't fail. It's a C, not an F. You got a Credit.'

Ivy wants to slap Elisabeth but controls herself. 'Very funny, I don't think.'

A girl from their lunch group rushes up to them. 'Hey, Ivy Morgenstern, Mr Kingsway's calling your name. You deaf or something?'

I'm in trouble now, Ivy thinks. She's surprised when the crowd parts to make way for her. Faces are staring.

'Congratulations, Miss Morgenstern. You've done our College proud. Top of the State in English and German, and a Distinction in French and Biology. It's the highest result we've had at Hightown Tech since before the war. We are all extremely proud of you.'

Ivy feels blood flood her face then drain away. A girl behind her says, 'She's white as a sheet. Get ready to catch her, she might faint.' Ivy looks at the staring faces, and recovers herself. No way will she add to their entertainment by collapsing. Instead she says calmly, 'Thank you, I'm truly grateful to you, and to all the teachers here who've helped me this year.'

Ivy shakes Mr Kingsway's proffered hand, turns, and shoulders her way back, the sound of clapping in her ears. She feels numb, then everything becomes unreal. Perhaps she's dreaming. She feels Elisabeth's arms around her.

'Well done, you swot. Didn't I say I knew you had it in you?' Ivy returns the hug, her heart full of love for her friend.

'No, you actually said the exact opposite, remember? But I've forgiven you.' She laughs, but realises those words *Never knew she had it in her* still rankle. 'Now tell me, how did you go in your other subjects?'

'OK. Biggest surprise is English, my worst subject. I got a Distinction, believe it or not. And it's thanks to you.' Elisabeth stares straight into Ivy's eyes as she says this, without any rancour for once.

'Don't forget Lydia and those extra lessons she gave you, not that you really needed them,' Ivy reminds Elisabeth.

'Nah, you helped me the most, right from the moment you read my short story. You're the one who's the best of us. Guess this means you'll be leaving us to go to that posh university over East. You'd better write to me, or I'll never speak to you again.'

*

When Ivy tells Uncle Sid her results, he sweeps her up in his arms and plants a big kiss dangerously near her mouth. Aunt Sonia stands stock still with her mouth open, gasping in shock.

'Sid, what d'you think you're doing? That's your niece you're kissing, your own flesh and blood! And me standing here watching it all.'

Ivy breaks away from her uncle at once, embarrassed but secretly pleased. She knows why uncle Sid has embraced her. It's for all the years of witnessing her struggles, and the miracle of her survival.

Sonia, eyes flashing, says 'Good marks aren't everything in a girl's life. They won't get you a husband, that's for sure. You only have to say the word, and Simon Levy's yours. Anyone can see he's head over heels.'

'Don't be silly, Aunt Sonia. I'm going home to University, as you well know. There's no way I can have a boyfriend here now.'

'Well, you'll break his heart, and Esmé's too. You silly girl. Men don't grow on trees, you know. Especially nice Jewish boys like Simon. You'd be best to stay here with us till you two get married.'

Ivy can't stop laughing. 'As if I'd even think of getting married at my age! Thanks for your advice, but the very thought's outrageous.' Ivy's moved that Aunt Sonia would want her to stay, after years of wanting the opposite. She gives her aunt a quick peck on the cheek. Aunt Sonia's hand drifts up to her face, touching the spot where Ivy's lips have been.

She straightens, and says, 'Well, I'll be inviting the Levys to your party, so you better behave yourself.'

'What party?'

Aunt Sonia glances at Uncle Sid, who nods. 'Your farewell party, of course. Think we'd let you leave here without one?'

Ivy is about to protest, when Alex rushes into the kitchen. 'Look what I found under my pillow,' he says, holding a bright red bead. He has stayed in Ivy's old room, preferring to be close to the action of kitchen and garden.

'Give it to me,' Ivy says, snatching the bead from Alex's hand. 'It's something I was looking for.' She hides her wrist with its bead bracelet behind her back. It would take too long to explain.

'What d'you mean?' says Alex. 'It wasn't there this morning, so where'd it come from?'

'I'll tell you one day, I promise. Only right now I have to go for a walk, to burn off some of this excitement.'

'Can I come?' Debbie calls, clinging to Ivy's skirt.

'Not this time, love. I need to be on my own. But I promise I'll tell you a made-up story in bed tonight.'

Before Debbie can protest, Ivy grabs her sunhat and runs out the back door.

PART 3. SHADOWS AND LIGHT

1958 to 1960

I have a self to recover, a Queen.

–Sylvia Plath, "Stings" (*Ariel*, Faber and Faber, 1965)

26. WELCOME HOME

Flying across the desert through a sky so blue it hurts her eyes, Ivy sees clouds suspended like magic in the air, as they had on that first flight five years ago. She is a different person now, no longer the sick skinny child clinging to her father, but a young woman, proud of her new body. Ivy can tell she's changed by the way people at the airport no longer look away. Their stares are admiring now, rather than pitying.

So much has changed. The plane is smaller and its engines make less noise. The air hostess is called a stewardess, her uniform a pale blue straight skirt and matching jacket. This young woman has her hair fashionably short in the new pixie cut, and her lipstick is pale, almost flesh coloured. Ivy remembers the stewardess on that first flight, with her hair in a French roll, and her bright red lipsticked mouth smiling at Daddy. She returns her attention to her book, one from the reading list for Uni. It's *Crime and Punishment* by Fyodor Dostoevsky, and she thrills to the vivid language, the gripping plot. She's so engrossed that she doesn't hear the stewardess at first.

'Miss Morgenstern, we'll be serving luncheon in half an hour.' Ivy tears her eyes away from the page and looks up at a smiling face. 'Would you like the Chicken Maryland or the Salmon Fricassee?'

'Um – is there anything – plainer?' Ivy's never heard of these exotic dishes. Aunt Sonia always cooked simple fare, meat and three veg, or tomatoes on toast.

'Well, I guess I could ask the chef to prepare you a salad,' the stewardess's smile fades slightly, 'if you prefer.'

'Yes thank you, that would be perfect.' Ignoring The Voice muttering in the background, (*Who do you think you are, asking for special favours?*

Better to refuse lunch all together) she smiles at the stewardess in genuine relief.

'We have two desserts to choose from: Bombe Alaska and Pavlova. Which would you like, Miss Morgenstern?'

Impressed that the stewardess remembers her name from the passenger list, Ivy struggles to silence The Voice urging her to say she's not hungry, wants nothing. 'I'll have the pavlova,' she says brightly. She's seen glossy illustrations of this dessert in a *Women's Weekly*, one of the dog-eared magazines in Uncle Sid's waiting room, but has never tasted it. Apparently the pavlova is becoming a national favourite, like lamingtons and melting moments. The pictures in the magazine showed a snowy white concoction, resembling one huge meringue, decorated with strawberries or passionfruit, and lashings of whipped cream.

On that long ago flight with Daddy sitting next to her, the clouds had reminded her of the meringues her mother used to make. The Voice had forbidden her to taste them when she'd been ill. Now she's liberated at last, a pavlova poses no threat. Her mouth waters, imagining fluffy clouds of sweetness melting on her tongue.

*

Ivy has a moment of panic when the plane lands at Sydney Airport. Will her family recognise her as the sickly child who left them five years ago? Will she recognise them, or will they be transformed, like her, into different versions of themselves? She breathes deeply to still the tremor in her chest as she follows other passengers across the tarmac, which is blistering in the sun. It's a relief to get inside the airport where the air is cooler. Ivy rushes into the ladies' toilet the minute she sees one, fearing she might vomit, or faint, as her head starts to spin. At the washbasin she splashes her forehead with cold water, allowing some to drizzle into her eyes and mouth. Her stomach settles slowly, and her hands stop shaking.

In the mirror above the basin Ivy sees a pale face with a few freckles scattered across the nose and cheeks, like tiny flecks of gold dust. Her hazel eyes, are wide-set, their dark lashes still wet. She runs her fingers through rebellious reddish brown curls, pinches her cheeks to bring back some colour, and shakes the creases from her dress. She's chosen it especially so she'll look her best. It is made of calico in the latest pink and white checks, and has a skirt that stands out stiffly, aided by a rope petticoat. *I am a butterfly released from a cocoon of misshapen misery,* Ivy says to herself, already embellishing words in what she hopes is a writerly fashion.

She sees her father first. He looks the same, but seems smaller than when she last saw him on that dreadful day in Perth, before he'd disappeared without a word. He's wearing a charcoal grey suit, beautifully cut by the same workshop Daddy uses for The Business, which proclaims its suits are "made to measure." There are touches of grey at his temples too, but his moustache is as red as ever.

'Ivylie!' he calls across the barrier as Ivy walks towards her family. All at once they're all over her, touching her, hugging her. She can hardly breathe. Daddy's arms are around her, and she sees his eyes are wet behind his horn-rimmed glasses. Ivy's own eyes stay dry. She picks up the scent of roses, and knows her mother is near. In an instant she sees Mum has changed; she's thinner, and her beautiful black hair is a strange light blue colour.

'Mum! What's happened to your hair?' Ivy blurts, a child again. It's Mum's turn to hug her now. Ivy feels the slightness of Mum's body like a blow to her heart. *My fault, they'll all say it's my fault. Mum's got sick and her hair's gone blue, all because of me.*

'It's the latest fashion, darling. They call it a blue rinse, and you can have pink or purple too. I tried dyeing it black again but it turned out I was allergic to the dye.' Mum is smiling, holding Ivy at arm's length, looking her daughter over from head to toe. 'I knew that dress would suit you. It fits you perfectly, now that you have such a lovely little figure.'

It's a relief to talk about hair and clothes and everyday things, and Ivy doesn't mind her mother's words. At least she doesn't say 'you've put on weight'; those words send a shudder through Ivy, and wake The Voice, always waiting for an opportunity to strike. Ivy smiles back at Mum, and turning her head sees a tall slim girl, her dark shiny hair in a high pony tail, standing back shyly.

Ivy catches her breath with the shock of seeing the once chubby little girl transformed into a tall, leggy adolescent. Laura is barely recognisable as the curly-haired, dimpled sister Ivy left behind. 'Laura! Is it really you? I can't believe it – you look all grown up! Bet you're heaps taller than me – let's see.' Ivy stands back to back with Laura, who does indeed tower over her. 'Are you really only fourteen?'

'I'll be fifteen in five weeks and three days,' Laura says, turning around to enfold Ivy in her thin brown arms. 'I'm so excited you'll be here for my party!'

Ivy's eyes search the crowd for a tall boy with curly brown hair. She knows it's ridiculous to expect Joel to turn up at an airport one hundred miles from Castleton, but can't help a stab of disappointment. *Wait, he'll be there at the station,* she reassures herself. Ivy's last few letters to Joel have gone unanswered, and the very omission of his name from the family is like a deafening silence. Instinctively she doesn't ask where he is, fearing a crack in the careful veneer of pretence that all is well with the world.

Daddy's standing back, beaming at his daughters. 'Let's go and collect your luggage, Ivy. Wait here, Lily and Laura,' he says, linking arms with Ivy. She feels the rough serge of his jacket against her skin again, and inhales the sweet smell of tobacco and spicy cologne. Now it's a distant sensation, the craving for his touch long gone.

'I'm proud of you. You don't know what this means to me, and to all of us, to have you back at last. Look at you! A young woman, pretty enough to turn heads, wait and see.'

Ivy doesn't answer. Something in her father's tone worries her. No mention of the illness she's beaten by sheer will, or of her triumph in the Leaving Certificate, both far more important to her than her looks.

'I've booked us a table for lunch at the Royal Hotel, so we can relax before we catch the train to Castleton this afternoon. Ah, I recognise that suitcase, but not the huge one alongside it. Full of female frippery, I'll wager, eh?'

'Not really, it's mostly my books and notes for Uni,' Ivy says. 'Clothes aren't that important to me.'

*

Over lunch, the family's conversation is stilted, cautious. Ivy wants to ask about Joel, but dares not. It is too soon. First she must be regaled with tales of who's got married, who's died, and who's had babies in the small community of Castleton. The biggest news is Laura winning the State-wide swimming competition. Next most thrilling is that Mum's first cousin twice removed married a famous singer in New York, which by association makes their whole family famous.

Laura is extra quiet, maybe because her mouth is always full. Their meal is good country fare, crumbed lamb cutlets with roast vegetables, or sausages and mash. There's a plate of sliced white bread on the table, along with jars of tomato and Worcestershire sauce. Ivy's stomach clenches. She hates the taste of meat. She orders a plate of vegetables on their own. Mum and Daddy looked at each other.

'Didn't I tell you? I'm a vegetarian, have been for a whole year,' Ivy lied. 'Can't bear the thought of eating a cow or a little lamb that was once free to graze and live out its life.'

'What's this nonsense?' Daddy says, keeping his voice low. 'You're not a rabbit, you know, living on lettuce leaves and the like.' He's smiling, in a forced way.

Laura laughs. 'Rabbits are cute! I want to be a veterinarian too!' she pipes up, a forkful of beef sausage halfway to her mouth.

'It's vegetarian, not veterinarian,' Ivy says quietly, while Mum says 'Nonsense, darling. You're a growing girl. You need to eat lots of meat at your age.'

'I don't want to grow any more!' Laura says at the top of her voice. 'I'm too tall already!'

'Shush,' says Daddy. 'Everyone's looking at us. Stop making a spectacle of yourself, Laura. And Ivy, I'm disappointed in you. We thought you'd got over all that rubbish.'

Ivy feels her gorge rise. *Will it never end, the naming and shaming, and mostly the blaming?* 'This has nothing to do with anyone else. It's my choice. And as you can see, I'm doing very well on my meatless diet. It's a matter of principle. You can all do as you like, and allow me the same right.'

Daddy's lips lose their smile. 'Still the philosopher, I see, Ivy. No harm in that, but perhaps you should keep your principles to yourself.'

'All right, I will,' Ivy says, grabbing a glass of water and swallowing down the ball of anger rising to her throat.

They all fall silent. Laura shrugs, and shovels a last mouthful of mashed potato into her mouth. Ivy desperately tries to change the subject.'

'Tell me more about Oscar and Lena's new baby. I can't wait to see him.'

'Oh, he's gorgeous!' enthuses Laura. 'I was allowed to babysit the other night, and all he wanted to do was play with me when I was s'posed to get him to sleep. He's got the most stunning blue eyes, and heaps of thick black hair, so unusual for a baby. Hey Ivy, you can come with me to babysit next time!'

'I'd love that,' Ivy says. All the time Laura's been talking, her parents' eyes have been fixed on Ivy's plate of peas, pumpkin and roast potato. She can almost hear them thinking, *At least Ivy's actually eating. She'll soon stop this silly fad.*

*

At the train station in Castleton, Ivy is met by a reception committee. There's a contingent of teenagers who'd been primary school kids when she'd left. They all crowd around her, staring. A consortium of cousins, aunts, and her parents' best friends stand by, all wanting to have a good look. What did these people know of her struggles, her fight to survive after years of exile, as they stare at a pretty, apparently healthy young girl, returning their stares with a hesitant smile?

A boy with a pimply face steps forward, and presents Ivy with a huge bunch of flowers, red and white peonies, gold hyacinths, and ugly blue hydrangeas. Ivy feels her face grow hot. Her heart beats so strongly that she's scared people can see it pulsing through her thin summer dress. Now she wishes she'd worn an old dress, maybe that shabby blue one which hangs limply, and which no one would remark upon.

If only they'd all stop staring, looking for what had taken her away from Castleton as a troublesome teenager. She knows they'll find no sign of the ravaging disease that had emaciated her body. Instead they see a normal seventeen-year old girl, slight but not skinny. Her auburn hair is piled high in a chignon, and she wears the tiny gold earrings Uncle Sid had given her as a parting gift, after he'd pierced her ears with a sterile needle in his surgery. She misses Uncle Sid now, his quiet acceptance of her, and the sprawling house with his surgery at the front.

She feels eyes boring into her, calculating how much flesh was on her, how much she weighs. Her own eyes scan the crowd, for the face she longs to see above all others.

*

Ivy's bedroom has been redecorated in her absence; gone is the old single bed with its chenille spread and patterned eiderdown. The three-quarter bed is covered with an elegant silk bedspread in duck-egg blue. There are curtains to match, hanging in graceful pleats on either side of the window, the very same window through which Ivy had seen the oleander come to life long ago. On the bedroom floor is a royal blue carpet, soft and thick under Ivy's bare feet when she gets up in the morning.

'Laura told us blue is your favourite colour,' Mum says, the day they get back from the station. 'I hope you like it.' Laura looks on, expectantly.

'It's beautiful! I love my Blue Room,' Ivy replies in genuine pleasure, hugging Mum to her, feeling again the slightness where her mother had been plump before. Laura jumps up and down. 'She likes it! She likes it! I knew she would, see, I was right!'

Ivy sees her desk, expertly crafted in golden blonde wood by one of her father's Hungarian friends. He was a refugee from the Terrors, bringing with him nothing but his skills. Dad rescued him from the migrant camp, as he had done for many others, and gave him work in his field, instead of in the box factory.

Ivy loves her desk. It can turn into a dressing table by lifting its hinged surface, to reveal a large mirrored underside. It represents a pretty and privileged life. *Only I can never be pretty, thanks to The Voice almost killing me. Will I ever be 'normal'?*

Dad hauls Ivy's suitcases onto the bed, puffing and panting theatrically. 'What've you got in here, the crown jewels?' he jokes. 'You women with your frocks and unmentionables don't exactly travel light, eh?'

'I told you, it's mostly books,' Ivy says to her father, irritated.

'Off you go,' Mum says with a new asperity. 'This is women's business.' She busies herself with the smaller suitcase, unclicking its worn clasps. 'But what's this rag doing in your luggage?'

She holds up a frayed off-white square of material, worn almost transparent in the middle. Its original pale blue shade is faded after years of wearing and washing. Ivy grabs it from her, holding it to her chest.

'It's precious,' she tells Mum, her eyes filling. 'Dr de Berg gave it to me, and it kept me safe all those years when I thought I'd die.'

'Don't talk like that! Sid would never have let you die. We were right to trust you to him, and to send you away. I don't know how we can ever repay him for saving your life.'

Ivy smiles at Mum and Laura while she folds the once-blue scarf and puts it away in the top drawer of her new dresser. *It's Dr B and Sigmund Freud who truly saved my life.*

27. A PARTY

Ivy doesn't quite know her place in the family any more. She feels a little like a celebrity or an explorer who's miraculously found her way home. More than anything she feels like a visitor, a celebrated one to be sure, but also a temporary one.

In the long summer break, days full of sun and surf, Ivy lies on her blue beach towel soaking up the warmth of the sand beneath her, inviting the rays of light above to caress every inch of her new body, with its soft curves, its cushioned bones, its secret moisture. She's wearing a new two-piece costume, with a little pink top scarcely covering her new breasts, and matching bottoms, which show her belly button to the world.

Ignoring the eyes around her, she lies on her tummy with a book open before her. Propped on her elbows she reads with a hunger for all she's missed, and all that is to come. The reading list for English 1 becomes her world. Fielding, Melville, Woolf, Joyce –Ivy devours their words, not understanding all of them, yet is carried away by the music of language that seemed to speak to her alone.

Droplets of icy water land on the bare skin of her back, like cool kisses. Laura runs out of the surf, laughing as she shakes her long wet hair over Ivy, and flops down beside her. With Laura, Ivy feels a distance. They are still shy with each other, not yet with the true closeness of blood with blood. So much stays unsaid between them, the past resolutely silenced, the future a mirage.

'The water's divine,' Laura murmurs. 'When are you coming in? Always with your head in a book, when you could be catching waves with me.'

'Laura,' Ivy asks, making her voice casual, 'have you heard from Joel lately?'

Instantly there's a heaviness in the air. Ivy glances up, and sees her sister's face go pale beneath its tan. Laura's eyes brim over.

'Laura darling! Whatever's wrong?'

'I'm not allowed to talk about him, same as I wasn't allowed to talk about *you*, all the time you were away from us.' Laura's voice breaks, and she hides her tears behind her hands. 'Joel did a bad thing,' she whispers.

Ivy sits up, wrapping Laura in her arms. 'Shush, it's OK. I'm sorry. We don't have to talk about him, love.'

'I've been wanting to tell you for so long,' Laura stutters between sobs. 'He said he wanted to be my boyfriend. In the hols we used to meet after he finished work. It was our secret. I told Mum I was going to study with Linda from school, but instead I got on my bike and waited outside the fruit shop. Joel had a part-time job there during the Uni holidays. I can't help it, Ivy! I love him so much, and he loves me back, I know he does!'

Ivy feels her world turn upside down and inside out. Her mind goes blank for a moment, and in spite of the hot sun her whole body freezes. *It's me he loves, this can't be true*, she says to herself.

'H-how do you know?' she barely manages to squeeze out the words. There's a snigger in her head: *Why would anyone love you?* It's The Voice, surfacing whenever Ivy's cast down. She closes her eyes, as if that will stop her hearing more poison.

'One afternoon he took me to his friend's place,' Laura replies, oblivious to the hurt and shock on Ivy's face. 'He kissed me, not an ordinary kiss, and it made me go all twiggly in my tummy. You've no idea, Ivy, how magic it was, feeling his lips and then his tongue inside my mouth …'

'Stop it! I don't want to hear!' Ivy jumps up from her towel and runs into the surf, letting the waves pound her as she sinks beneath them. The water roils in her ears. She catches wave after wave, her nose and mouth filling with the sting of salt water, as she's dumped on the sand like a rag doll, again and again. She wishes the sea would keep swallowing her up and spitting her out.

*

At the party for Laura's fifteenth and Daddy's fiftieth birthdays, Ivy has to force herself to join in the merriment. It's also a welcome home party for Ivy, so she must try to look happy. Whenever she thinks of Joel with Laura her heart feels like a stone in her chest. It's a huge effort to smile and be polite to the guests.

A boy she used to know, Barry from the Castleton Drama Group, keeps asking her to dance. He has clammy hands and bad breath. It's all she can do not to throw up.

'Gee you've changed,' Barry says, his mouth too close to her ear. 'I'd never recognise you from before. What was it they said was wrong with you?'

'I had consumption, the disease that killed great poets and musicians like Chopin and John Keats,' Ivy lies. 'Oh, and the wonderful Emily Brontë. Have you read *Wuthering Heights*?' Ivy can see that she's boring the boy, which is her intention. He ignores her question.

'Wow, must've been real serious. We're lucky you lived to tell the tale, eh?' Barry squeezes her hand with his sweaty one. 'I reckon you're prettier than any of the girls round here. Wanna come to the pictures some time?'

'Oh, I'm not allowed in enclosed spaces, it's too risky for my lungs,' she lies again, enjoying the fabrications. 'Excuse me, I have to go help Mum in the kitchen.' She extricates herself, surreptitiously wiping her hands on the back of her skirt.

Daddy dances with her too. 'I'm truly proud of you, my Ivy,' he whispers into her ear, his breath warm and familiar. He's holding her too close. Ivy feels uncomfortable, and pulls away a little. 'I have something for you,' Daddy says. 'Let me show you.'

Ivy's relieved when he releases her, and they move towards the new mushroom-coloured settee, one of the many changes at the Wave Street house over the last five years. Its curved shape is the latest in décor, inviting sociable conversation, and the brocade upholstery has a luxurious velvety feel. Daddy pats the space beside him, motioning Ivy to sit. He reaches into the inside pocket of his jacket and extracts a narrow black box tied with a silver ribbon.

'I never gave you a proper gift for your birthday.' He hands her the box. 'Open it.'

Ivy takes the box with fingers suddenly cold as ice. She fumbles with the ribbon, slowly unties it, and opens the box. It's lined with cream satin. Nestling in its folds lies a circle of silver, round as the sun and as radiant.

'Turn it over,' Daddy says.

Ivy lifts the bracelet from its satin bed. On its underside there are words engraved in cursive script: *Love always, Daddy.* The words are shaped like Daddy's elaborate handwriting. Ivy almost drops the heavy jewellery. She feels suddenly overwhelmed. *What have I done to deserve such love? What must I do to keep it?*

'Oh,' says Ivy when she finds her voice, 'Thank you. It's beautiful.'

'Now you can take that cheap bauble off your wrist, and wear this instead,' Daddy says, taking her right hand in his and stroking it. His hand inches towards Ivy's bead bracelet.

Ivy pulls her hand away. 'No, this bracelet means a lot to me. I'd like to wear your present on my left wrist, if that's all right.' Ivy slips her wrist through the bangle where it dangles dangerously. It's far too big for her bird-like bones. She pushes it up to her forearm where it clasps her flesh like a manacle.

'I'd forgotten how tiny you are,' Daddy says, letting go her hand. 'I can see this is far too big for a dainty little thing like you. Let me take it back, get it made smaller. I'll take it into Lou the jeweller next door; he owes me a favour.'

'It's OK Dad,' Ivy says. 'Can I call you that? I'm too old to call you "Daddy".'

'Might as well call me Abe and be done with it,' Daddy chuckles. 'You know, Ivy, it's the delicate ones like you that the boys find attractive.

I hope you know how to look after yourself, now that you've become a young woman. Know what I mean?'

Ivy doesn't really know what he means, only that it makes her uncomfortable. She decides to ignore the question. 'Don't be silly, Dad. I'm not the least interested in boys. Anyway, I'll wear this beautiful bracelet on special occasions, like tonight.'

'No fear, Ivylie. I want you to wear it every day. I insist on getting this trinket to fit perfectly. It cost a pretty penny, but nothing's too good for my eldest daughter.'

It's a relief to hand the box and its costly content back to Dad. Ivy hopes she might never see it again. *Ungrateful girl, you don't deserve such expensive presents. Now you've hurt his feelings. When will you learn to hide your own?*

Ivy and her father move to the buffet. Laid out on the dining room table are glistening bowls of potato salad, freshly fried fish fillets decorated with lemon and parsley, and Dad's favourite sliced pickled herring floating in pungent brine. Guests are loading up Mum's best china plates with delicacies of their choice. Ivy feels sick, as she often does when there's a mountain of food to choose from. She finds it easy to avoid the lavish spread while appearing to partake. Ivy mingles with the visitors, while she holds a plate with a serve of salad on it, which she manages not to eat. Dimly she senses The Voice is back, whispering its approval.

*

'There's mail for you, darling, all with stamps from WA,' Mum says next day, while Ivy and Laura are helping Mum with the big clean up after the party. A clutch of letters in various sizes sits on the sideboard. 'I love touching these envelopes,' Mum says in a dreamy voice. 'They make me feel closer to home. If only your grandparents were still alive, and you could have got to know them while you were in Perth. But I can see from all these letters that you made plenty of friends over there …'

While Mum's still talking, Ivy takes the pile of mail to the privacy of her new Blue Room. She feels oddly uncomfortable lying on this brand new bed, and wishes for her old one with its worn quilt. She flops down on her tummy with the letters spread out before her on the bed. She turns each one over to check the address, savouring the suspense. Ivy loves to delay her pleasures, just as she used to save a square of chocolate or an apple till last thing at night, when The Voice would finally go to sleep releasing its hold on her.

There are letters from Elisabeth, Rachel, and Simon, and one in round childish writing from Debbie, its envelope illustrated with flowers drawn in blue and green crayon. Rachel writes that she's going out with Adam, that she thinks she loves him, and it's "serious". Ivy smiles. *I knew it, they're made for each other.*

She sighs at the sight of Simon's letter, and decides not to open it until later, if at all. She adds it to a growing pile of unanswered letters from Simon. His letters are always the same: a detailed account of his social activities, and boring descriptions of car rallies or football games, in which Ivy hasn't the least interest. The ending is always the same: *Missing you and wish you were here. Don't do anything I wouldn't do! Love, Simon.*

Her eye falls on an envelope that's slipped underneath the others. This letter has been redirected; the address in Claredale Avenue WA is crossed out, and underneath it, in Aunt Sonia's strong black writing, is Ivy's forwarding address: *28 Wave Street, Castleton, NSW.* Ivy recognises Joel's scrawl. Her breath almost stops. She tears open the envelope.

3 Garden Avenue
North Melbourne

Hi Ivy,

Sorry I haven't written for a while. Been having a hard time lately. I failed the Finals, probably because I can't concentrate on studying. I won't go into the reasons here. Also, my parents have decided in their wisdom that I have to transfer to Melbourne Uni where my Dad went.

Melbourne's not so bad, except I really miss Caves Beach in Castleton. My Nan and Pop still live in Melbourne but they're getting old – Pop's nearly sixty, ancient.

It turns out my best mate, Jack Lewis, is related to you guys. I hang out with him and his sisters a lot. His Mum found out I used to live in Castleton and kept on quizzing me till she worked out I used to live nextdoor to you lot., and then she tells me she's your Dad's sister. Also my Dad and Mr Lewis know each other from when they both went to the same Jewish school. Weird, huh? Anyway Mrs Lewis – I guess she's your aunt – has invited me to stay with them for a while, just till I can get a part-time job to pay board in a share house.

So I guess I won't be seeing you at Sydney Uni after all. I'll sure miss living next door to you folk, especially the lovely Laura. It's like I've had two sisters for most of my life.

Well, I better close off now,

See ya,

Joel.

Ivy reads the letter again and again. It doesn't sound like the Joel she remembers. Where is the affectionate camaradie of his letters a few months ago? *He must be having a breakdown – why else would he fail the exams? Maybe his mother made him write that letter – she never did like me.* Ugly doubts keep surfacing. Ivy tries to shove them away. She needs to know if Joel still loves her, and she needs to hear the answer from his own lips.

*

In the lounge room, Laura, Dad and Mum are crowded around a small box with tiny black and white figures moving around on the screen. Ivy joins them, watching them staring at the tiny box. Abe was one of the first in Castleton to buy this miracle of modern technology.

People in town are saying the novelty called "television" is a modern miracle. 'It won't last,' the townsfolk say, 'and no one can afford to buy one except those rich Jews like Abe Morgenstern' some think, and others utter. Ivy's overheard them down in the main street, where people gather around a large television in a shop window, showing the ABC news. *Do they know I'm Abe's daughter? I should tell them my Dad was so poor there was never enough food to go round in their falling down tenement house back in England, and my Uncle Sid had to work in a fruit shop to pay his way through Medicine.*

Every now and then Dad gives a huge guffaw at the woman with frizzy hair prancing about on the screen. They are watching a show called *I Love Lucy,* which Ivy thinks is too silly for words. The snarling American accent grates on her ears. Bored, she waits till the show's over to make her request. At last a fuzzy advertisement for Holden cars flashes onto the box, heralding the closing scene of the ludicrous Lucy. Dad gets up from his easy chair and presses a button on the box to switch it off.

'That's all for tonight, folks,' Dad says, aping Lucy's accent.

'Dad, there's something I'd like to do before Uni starts.' Ivy sees only a slim chance of getting her way. She knows Dad is in a good mood, judging from his bout of merriment, and that he needs to laugh to justify squandering the equivalent of an airfare on this latest fad. *And I'm about to ask him for a real airfare.*

'What is it now, Ivy? More books? Or maybe a new outfit to impress all those swanky students at the big University?'

'No, Dad. I really want to see Aunty Annie and my cousins down in Melbourne. I won't get another chance once Uni starts, and I've never met my cousins.'

Dad's smile fades. 'Well, well. I didn't think you were fond of my sister and her brood.'

'Of course I am, they're my family,' Ivy lied. 'Besides, I've spent five years with Mum's relations, so it's about time I visit yours, isn't it?'

'I want to go to Melbourne too!' Laura jumps up from the sofa, excited. 'Me and Ivy can go together!'

No! Ivy begs silently. *Laura mustn't come anywhere near Joel.*

'Slow down a minute, both of you,' Dad says, his jollity fast waning. 'First of all, what makes you think I can afford two air fares to Melbourne?'

'But Dad, I'm saving you heaps of money on Uni fees,' Ivy says, playing her cards cautiously. 'Remember I got a scholarship? It'll save you a fortune.'

Laura pipes up, 'And besides, you've bought a brand new television, so surely you can afford to send your daughters on a family visit.' Her big brown eyes are shining as she sidles up to her father. 'Please, please, pretty please,' she intones, beaming into Abe's eyes with all her adolescent charm.

Dad's face has completely lost its smile. 'Ivy, we've only just got you back. Why would you want to leave us again so soon?'

'It's not that I want to leave, not at all. More that I'd like to meet my Melbourne cousins. I never got a chance before I got ill, and … '

Dad cuts her off. 'We don't talk about your – er – illness, for want of a better word. Your homecoming is a new start for the whole family, and we must put the past behind us. Besides, do you really think you're well enough to go travelling to a strange city all by yourself?'

'Of course I am, Dad. I was all by myself in Perth, wasn't I?' Ivy can't quite keep the bitterness out of her voice. 'And I won't get another chance to travel for ages once Uni starts. Can't I go? Please?'

Dad's eyes are moist. 'We don't want to lose you again, Ivylie. You can't imagine what we've been through, not knowing whether you would live or die.'

Ivy feels a part of her is being rejected. She needs to feel her family loves all of her, not only this new, palatable model.

'Well, I didn't die, in fact I'm very much alive, and I want to make the most of it. I promise I'll be careful, nothing bad will happen to me, if only you let me go.'

'Listen to me, Ivy. Legally you're not an adult until you turn twenty-one, as you very well know. But I suppose it could work, as long as you don't slip back – or relapse, to use the technical term – when you're away from us. I'll talk to my sister to make sure she'll look after you.'

'Dad, I don't need looking after! I've learned how to do very well over the last five years. All I need is an airfare and your blessing.' Ivy knows she's asking a lot, but her longing to see Joel is stronger than her guilty conscience.

The next few days are a flurry of shopping sprees with her mother, while Ivy reassures her parents she's ready to be independent. Dad measures her up himself for a shapely suit, cut from his best-selling cinnamon gaberdine, 'Now you'll look like a city girl, down in the Big Smoke,' he'd said, at her final fitting in Morgan Bros' Tailors.

At the last moment Dad agrees Laura can come, but only after she's thrown the tantrum of all tantrums. The surly phrase, "It's not fair!" rings through the house in Laura's shrill voice, until Dad, worn down, relents.

'If you don't let me go I'll run away, and you'll never see me again!' Laura screams. Mum presses her lips together and shakes her head.

Ivy's irritated. The last thing she wants is Laura tagging along when she tracks down Joel. 'Two fares cost twice as much as one,' she says firmly. 'I'll be fine on my own, really Dad.'

'Either you both go, or no one goes,' Dad says. Laura claps her hands. Ivy groans inwardly. *But at least I can go to Melbourne. It's the only way I'll find out the truth.*

28. COUSINS

Ivy and Laura walk down the metal steps of the plane, and across the tarmac. Ivy disengages her hand from Laura's sweaty one. She holds herself straight, fixes a smile on her face lest her nervousness shows. Before landing she checked her face in the small pocket mirror Mum gave her, along with a new lipstick in a discrete light pink, and a sanitary pad and belt "in case it starts, Ivy dear." She hasn't had a period since the first one when she was thirteen.

They step out into blazing heat. Ivy worries the cinnamon-coloured suit with its peplum at the waist, and straight knee-length skirt, is unsuitable for a summer holiday. She's finished her outfit with a green crepe scarf at her neck, and a matching green pillbox hat perched on her unruly hair, which she tries to contain in a low chignon.

Everyone's told her Melbourne would be cold, but the sultry heat hits her as she and Laura wait outside the airport for their aunt to pick them up. They look around for Aunty Annie. She isn't hard to spot. Coming towards them, with her arms outstretched, is a tall, heavy-set woman, with their father's face. Fuller and softer, but still Dad's face.

'Darlings!' Aunty Annie crows, hugging them both at once to her warm squishy bosom. She holds each of them at arm's length, first Ivy, then Laura.

'My word, don't you both look smart. I must say your photos don't do you justice. I've wished for ages to meet my nieces, and now here you are! You wouldn't believe the weather, crazy for Melbourne. One of those freak heat waves. Wait, it'll be freezing tomorrow. You know what they say about this town, four seasons in one day.'

Their aunt stops to take a breath, then pulls Ivy close to her again, breathing in as if to inhale her niece's aura. 'A little bit of Abe. How is the dear boy?'

When Ivy hears the words "the dear boy" she feels a pang of jealousy. 'Abe's my favourite brother. You know, I miss him every day. You are very like him, my dear, even after all you've been through. But where does your gorgeous red hair come from?'

'It's from Daddy's moustache,' blurts Laura, 'and it's not red, it's auburn, like in *Anne of Green Gables*.'

Aunty Annie throws her head back and laughs, showing a set of perfect teeth. *Too perfect*, Ivy thinks, *most likely false, like Dad's.*

'You little monkey,' Aunty Annie says, holding Laura close to her, 'you most definitely take after your mother, with those glorious dark curls of yours. But you've got Abe's sense of humour all right.' Her voice has the Cockney lilt of Dad's, but more pronounced. Ivy warms to Aunty Annie more and more, although the words "after all you've been through" sound a jolt of warning.

'Now, I've got the car right outside. Let's go and meet your cousins. Oh, and we have a visitor, someone you'll know from up in Castleton. Joel Hammerstein, you might remember him. He's staying with us for the moment, until Uni starts. He's been having a hard time lately…'

*

When they enter the front room of Aunty Annie's house, Ivy is overwhelmed by its splendour. Laura turns away, her eyes wide, exploring the books on the shelves in their aunt's lounge room. Ivy can tell the original paintings on the wall are by famous artists. All the furniture is plush, elegant, and exudes prosperity. Dad has told them that Uncle Sam, Annie's husband, has done very well in the rag trade, and owns five shops in Victoria. "They could buy and sell us twice over," he'd said, with his black look.

Ivy's heart leaps at the sight of a tall thin boy with dark hair sitting at a roll-top desk. She can't believe it's Joel. *Am I dreaming? How could*

I be so lucky? Joel sits with his broad back turned to them. He doesn't turn around.

'Hi, Joel!' Laura pouts her lips, rolling her eyes at the same time. *Trying to look sexy and failing,* Ivy thinks with mild disgust.

'Joel! remember your manners. Ivy and Laura have come all the way from Castleton.' Aunty Annie speaks to Joel as if he were one of her own children.

Joel doesn't answer. Ivy stands behind him, her heart in her mouth. *Maybe,* she thinks, *if I speak to him in German he'll answer me. After all his letters, and all the years behind us, how could he ever forget me?*

'*Hast du mich vergessen?*' she whispers.

Joel raises his head. She sees his eyes are dull, his full lips unsmiling. He doesn't speak, doesn't even shake his head. To Ivy it's as if she and Joel are the only people in the world at this moment, but she can tell by his eyes Joel's not here at all. She mustn't cry, not with Aunty Annie watching.

'What has happened to you?' Ivy blurts out. Even as she asks, she can feel his pain behind those vacant eyes. Her own heart swells with compassion. Joel doesn't move, or answer her.

Aunty Annie's watching, her face a mask of sympathy. 'Don't mind poor Joel, darlings. He's not quite himself lately. Come and meet your cousins, they're dying to see you both.'

Blindly, Ivy follows Aunty Annie upstairs. In the main bedroom Hannah and Sophie are trying on necklaces in front of their mother's dressing table.

'This is Hannah, and here's Sophie, our baby,' Aunty Annie says, encircling her youngest daughter by the waist and gently pushes her forward. Sophie cringes. 'Sophie darling, you and Laura are around the same age. You two will have lots to talk about. Hannah dear, this is Ivy; she's been rather – er – unwell. I'm relying on you to look after her.' Hannah hangs back, watching.

Ivy's cheeks burn. Even here, hundreds of miles from home, she is seen as the weird one. 'Unwell', she knows, is another word for 'mad and bad'.

'Actually, I'm quite well, Aunty Annie. I don't need any looking after, thanks all the same.'

Aunty Annie's eyes open wide. For once she seems to have nothing to say.

Ivy and Laura look shyly at their cousins. Ivy can instantly see a family resemblance between Sophie and Laura, except for the gap between Laura's front teeth. The cousins have wavy hair, almost black in colour, and lustrous eyes to match. Hannah looks as different from the Morgensterns as it's possible to be. She has honey blonde hair, as straight as a ruler, and very light blue eyes. Ivy feels a touch of envy. *Would being blonde and blue-eyed mean you wouldn't feel different, marked by your colouring? Has Hannah escaped the taunts and jibes?*

'Unfortunately Jack won't be back from his field trip till next weekend,' continues Aunty Annie. 'He's studying to be an archaeologist, you see. He'll be sorry he missed you – unless of course you two can stay longer? We'd love that, wouldn't we girls?'

'Yeah, but I reckon we'll have more fun without Jack. He's the classic bossy big brother,' Sophie says, with a conspiratorial wink at Hannah.

Aunty Annie laughs. 'You're probably right,' she says. 'Poor boy's obsessed with his studies at the moment. But surely you two can stay with us longer? To come all this way for three days is *meshugge*. I'll talk to Abe.'

'Thanks, but we can only stay the weekend. Laura's back to school on Monday, and I'm about to start Uni.' Ivy feels trapped by her aunt's overweening hospitality.

'We'll see,' says Aunty Annie. 'Now, girls, why don't you show your cousins through the house? And then you can all go out into the garden. It's lovely and shady in the summer house.' Aunty Annie bustles about putting things to right on her dressing table. 'For heaven's sake girls, stop fiddling with my jewellery, you'll get it all mixed up. Ivy dear, you might like to change out of your charming outfit. Did you bring anything cooler? Or I'm sure Hannah can lend you a sundress.' She leaves the room still talking, although no one's listening.

Laura fills the awkward silence. 'I'm fifteen,' she says to Sophie. 'How old are you?'

'Fourteen. Only scraped through the stupid Intermediate. I want to leave school like my friend Betty, but Dad won't let me. I can't wait to leave school.'

'I'm doing the Leaving next year, even though I'm only sixteen. Being the youngest in the class is a pain,' Laura says.

'Have you got a boyfriend?' Ivy hears Sophie ask Laura, as they ascend the stairs to the girls' bedrooms. Sophie has a slight lisp, and a dimple when she smiles.

Laura giggles, shakes her head. 'Course not. I hate boys. A boy tried to kiss me once. It was revolting.'

Then what was all that about Joel kissing her? I knew Laura made it up, Ivy smiles to herself. *Unless she's a little liar as well as a flirt.* Cold doubts are back again.

'You haven't kissed the right one yet,' answers Sophie airily. 'Let's go look at my room. You'll be sharing with me.' Ivy glimpses a messy teenager's room, as Sophie pulls Laura inside.

Reaching Hannah's bedroom, all pink frills and blonde wood furniture, Hannah and Ivy look at each other.

'I heard you're starting Uni?' Hannah says. 'What are you doing there?'

'I wanted to do Law, but my teachers said it's not for girls. I'd only get boring work so it's better not to even try. I thought about journalism, but same thing: girls will get the boring jobs like social pages, if you're lucky, otherwise shipping news. I settled for Arts, and I'm majoring in English lit. What about you?'

'I'm going to Business College,' Hannah says. 'Dad says it's a waste of time educating girls. He reckons I'll only get married, and have to stop studying because I'll be so busy keeping house and so on. It's annoying, especially because I got enough marks in the Leaving to matriculate.

But Dad's probably right, and anyway I'm nearly engaged. His name's Robert, and he's training to be a doctor. We've been going out for six months. How about you? Have you got a boyfriend?'

Ivy stares at her cousin. She's certainly pretty, in a bland sort of way. She notices her eyes have turned a light green, and her cheeks are flushed pink.

'Not really, but there is someone I like.'

'I guess I wouldn't know him. What's he like?'

'Can we talk about this later? 'Ivy says, feeling she is in dangerous waters.

'Sure. We'll be sharing this room, so we'll have heaps of time.'

*

Gravel crunches outside as a car pulls into the driveway.

'At last, here's your father,' says Aunty Annie, as she re-arranges silver cutlery on the *shabbat* table. The unlit candles stand in their silver sticks. Cherry-coloured wine sparkles in its crystal decanter, reflecting tiny lights from the lamps in the dining room.

Sam Lewis turns his key in the lock, bursts in the front door calling out 'Good Shabbos everyone!' He is small and stocky, a checked waistcoat straining over his rotund stomach. He kisses both his daughters with a smacking sound then pecks Aunty Annie on the cheek. She helps him out of his jacket and hurries to the kitchen without a word. Sam's eyes fall on Ivy and Laura, standing behind their cousins.

'Ah. The visitors have arrived. And these are Abe's girls, eh? Which of you is the one who's been – er – not quite yourself, eh?' Uncle Sam ignores Aunty Annie's warning look, staring hard at Ivy.

'I'm Ivy. This is Laura,' Ivy says, deciding to ignore his question. She holds out her hand in greeting. Uncle Sam ignores it. A hug is out of the question.

'Ivy, is it? So you're the one who led your poor parents a merry dance, eh?'

Laura's dark eyes flash with anger. 'Don't say that about my sister. It's mean. And my Mum and Dad never dance.' Ivy silently squeezes Laura's hand.

'Got a sharp tongue there, young lady. Well, I suppose it must have been hard on you too. Let's start again, and respect the sabbath by not arguing. Anne! The candles?'

Aunty Annie's transformed from the bubbling fountain of energy she's been all day. She appears cowed as she comes back from the kitchen, wiping her hands on a frilly apron which she discards over the back of her chair. The family stands in silence while she lights first one, then the second candle. As soon as their flames flicker upwards, she waves her hands over them intoning the familiar Hebrew blessing. She hides her eyes behind her hands, humble before the majesty of the shabbat lights. Uncle Sam pours a little wine into a silver goblet and passes it around the table. Everyone takes a sip, echoing Uncle Sam's blessing. The coiled challah is pulled apart next. Ivy takes a piece, and passes the gold-rimmed plate to Laura.

'You sit beside Hannah, Ivy, and Laura next to Sophie.' Uncle Sam sits down at the head of the table. He loosens his collar and turns up his spotless white cuffs. Ivy sees his chair has arms, unlike all the others.

'Where's the boy?' he says, frowning.

'He'll be here soon, dear. You know how it is, we can't put pressure on him, Jack says.'

'Rubbish. That boy needs a good kick in the pants. He's a bad influence on our Jack.'

Aunty Annie pretends not to hear. 'Now, everyone, help yourselves to the entrées,' she beams, passing a platter around the table. It contains olives, herrings and sliced onion in brine, and pickled cucumbers.

Ivy shudders. Memories of other shabbat meals with her own family come back to her. She can't bear the thought of food. She takes an olive and passes the plate along.

Joel lopes up to the table in time to distract Uncle Sam's eyes from her plate.

'Ah, here you are boy. Took your time, eh? Why don't you tell us how you plan to entertain our guests?' Uncle Sam's voice has an edge to it, a bitterness that overshadows his bonhomie.

Joel doesn't answer, merely shrugs his shoulders in an attitude of dismissal. Ivy tries to catch his eye. He's the reason she's here, yet he seems to have no interest in her. She must confront Joel while she has this golden opportunity. But how, without attracting attention?

'Joel,' says Aunty Annie brightly, 'did you remember you and Jack were invited to Mark's twenty-first tomorrow night? Jack won't be back in time, but a thought came to me – why not take Ivy? She's here to meet some nice Jewish boys, aren't you dear?'

Ivy feels her face flush. She bites her lip to hold back a furious response.

'No thanks, I'd rather not go. Actually I've no interest in boys, not even nice Jewish ones.' Ivy avoids Joel's eyes. She bottles up her anger, but can't keep the sarcasm out of her voice.

Joel looks up. Ivy's eyes meet his dark brown ones at last. She sees a flicker of recognition before he shrugs again.

'OK, whatever,' Joel mutters. He gets up and leaves the table without another word.

'But Joel – your dinner!' Aunty Annie calls after him.

*

When Joel presents himself before her, holding out a fresh carnation formed into a small corsage, Ivy's resolve falters. She hates parties, the small talk, the choreographed flirting, the pretence of intimacy with people she'll never see again. She's ready to tell Joel to go away. But seeing his long rangy body in front of her, his face with its broad nose and full lips, like an African mask, undoes her resolve. She can never resist him no matter what he does or says.

'Oh, I almost forgot,' she says, heart fluttering. 'Let me go and change ' She hurriedly chooses the pink shantung dress and jacket Mum had made her pack "in case there's a formal occasion." Like her other clothes, it had been made for her. It fits her perfectly, showing her tiny waist and narrow hips, and hiding her still scrawny shoulders and arms with the jacket.

'Mrs Lewis is letting me take their other car, the one Jack drives when he's here,' Joel says. They drive in silence through the lit Melbourne streets. Ivy feels small and fragile with Joel beside her. The city seems to her a benign presence, enclosing the two of them in their secret bubble. She wonders if Joel is as nervous as she is.

Stopping outside a brightly lit terrace house, Joel pulls on the handbrake with a squeak. 'It's a bit of an old rattler, not up to the Lewis's usual standard.' Ivy expects he's making a feeble joke, but he's not smiling, not even with his mouth.

The party is in a room crammed with over made-up girls and smartly-dressed boys who look as if they were on the hunt. Joel asks if she'd like a drink. When she shakes her head, he gives that maddening shrug, walks off and leaves her to her own devices. She knows nobody in this rowdy drunken crowd. A short boy with glasses asks Ivy to dance.

'How does it feel to be perfect?' the boy says, squeezing her waist a little too tightly. A well-rehearsed line, Ivy suspects. She has to swallow bile, the bewilderment with Joel shoving all polite conversation out of her head. She pulls away from the boy's sweaty grasp.

'Excuse me, I need to go to the bathroom.' Ignoring the chagrin on her dance partner's face, she walks quickly from the party room down a dark hallway. There's a thin beam of light shining from under a door off the hall. Ivy stops outside and listens. Someone is crying.

Pushing the door open, she sees Joel with his head in his hands, sobbing. He's sitting on the edge of an unmade bed. Ivy doesn't wait to see if there's anyone else in the bed. Covering her mouth she tries not to retch. She closes the door softly, making her way to the bathroom where she sits on the lid of the toilet with her head between her legs.

I don't understand. Where has the Joel I knew so well gone? He must surely be ill. And it's up to me to help him, no matter how rude he's been.

29. THE QUEEN COMPETITION

The new academic year brings with it a flurry of preparations: there are books to buy, accommodation in Sydney to arrange, a wardrobe to pack. The excitement of starting a new phase in her life drives most thoughts of Joel out of Ivy's head. She only knows that she still loves him, even more since she witnessed his pain in Melbourne. The feeling she has for Joel is a relentless pull, almost like The Voice, and as powerful. She realises such obsessive love could be harmful, yet she's powerless to stop it.

Starting Uni is challenging. Ivy's lucky to win a place at the all-women St Mary's College, where Daddy is sure she'll be safe from the dangers and temptations of the big city. She feels entirely different from the other girls, most of whom come from wealthy properties in the country. Although Sydney University is only one hundred miles from Castleton, Ivy feels she's travelled to a distant country.

Between lectures Ivy joins a group of Jewish students outside the great stone entrance to the library. The other girls are freshers like her, but mostly about a year younger. They speak to each other with the intimacy of people who've known each other all their lives. Most have gone to the same school, the only Jewish school in the city. They are cold to Ivy, leaving her out of their conversations, which mostly centre around each other's boyfriends. It seems to Ivy that her fellow students are more interested in finding a Jewish husband than discussing Psychology or Philosophy. Ivy feels like the country cousin, having nothing in common with these smart, confident young women.

She's happy when the Term break means she can go home for a few weeks. It's getting easier to find her place in the family, being the apple of her father's eye, sharing secrets with Laura and being cosseted by her mother.

There has been little fanfare on Ivy's eighteenth birthday, at her request. Ivy's gift to herself is her new mastery over The Voice: *Shut up, I know who you are, and you have no power over me any more.*

'I've got some exciting news for you, darling,' Mum says while she and Ivy are in the kitchen one Saturday morning. 'How would you like a whole new look, a visit to a hair salon so those untidy curls of yours won't frizz, a manicure, even a facial now your acne has cleared up?'

'I wouldn't like it. In fact I can't think of anything worse. Don't fuss over me, Mum. I don't deserve it. Anyway I can make up my own mind about how to look. I am eighteen, after all.'

'Exactly the right age to enter the Queen Competition! You're the prettiest Jewish girl in Castleton, as I'm sure everyone will agree. You'll meet young people from all over the country, and there'll be some nice Jewish boys amongst them.'

'Mum! How could you say that! You make this Queen thing sound like a meat market. I'm not the least bit interested in meeting nice Jewish boys. Why can't Laura go instead of me?'

'Because she's far too young, and you need to start thinking of your future, darling. We only want you to be happy.'

Ivy's speechless with rage. Do her parents really think that happiness is marriage to a nice Jewish boy? Is this competition a 'Coming Out' like in Jane Austen's day? What century are her mother and father living in? She's never going to get married, unless it's to Joel; more likely they'll elope and live in sin. The thought calms her enough to hear what her mother's saying.

'… and I bought the material yesterday, white broderie anglaise. I've made an appointment with my dressmaker, Matilda. She's frightfully expensive, but … '

'Mum! Stop! What are you talking about? I'm not going in any stupid competition! Anyway, I start back at Uni next month.'

'Now darling, don't excite yourself. It won't hurt you to have a little break from your studies. And this is such a wonderful opportunity!'

'For who?' Ivy's mouth is dry, her heart racing. 'Don't I get a say in this?'

Mum casts her eyes down in that way she has when she wants to hide fear, or anger. 'Of course dear. But you must see that you need to meet more people to make up for all the time you've lost. I was sure you'd be thrilled. Most young girls would love the chance to be a Queen for a day. Anyway, the Council of Jewish Women's already voted, and it was almost unanimous that you're the best one to represent us.'

Ivy's heart sinks. The thought of parading around and making a show of herself, all for a cause she doesn't really believe in, is anathema to her. But she's helpless in the face of Mum's eager determination, her benign blindness. *At least I owe them this much.*

'All right, I'll do it. But only if I can go back to Uni next month.'

*

Matilda, Mum's dressmaker, is a small nut-brown woman with bright beady eyes. 'Wouldn't we all like to have such a tiny waist,' she mumbles, with her mouth full of silver pins.

Ivy cringes, feeling the tape measure pinch underneath her ribs, in what she suspects is a deliberate effort to squeeze the breath from her lungs. 'It's a bit tight,' she says. 'I like my clothes looser.' Matilda sniffs, and lets the tape measure out an inch. Ivy smiles at her with gratitude.

'Nonsense, dear,' Mum says, eyeing the ice cream cake creation being moulded onto Ivy's body. 'You need to show off your lovely little figure. We want you to be the belle of the ball.' Matilda may as well not be in the room for all the attention Mum pays to her.

*

'Wait till you hear who's coming to visit next week,' Mum says to Ivy. 'I had a letter from Esmé Levy, the *Rebbetzin* in Perth. She's a good friend of Sonia's, you know. So kind Esmé was to my poor Mama, may her soul rest in peace. Anyway, her son, Simon …'

'Ouch!' Ivy says as a pin pricks her shoulder. Simon. She hasn't thought of him for months. The *mogen dovid* he'd given her was somewhere in her jewellery box, along with Dad's bracelet, which she only wore when she was home. She feels a touch of guilt remembering the pile of his unanswered letters at home.

'Sorry love,' says Matilda. 'Needs lifting in the shoulders or it'll be falling off you.'

'So this boy Simon,' Mum continues, 'he's studying Medicine, but they only go up to third year over there. That's why he's coming to your University in Sydney for his last three years. You'll be able to show him around, Ivy. Introduce him to the other Jewish students. And darling, a little bird told me – never you mind who – that this Simon Levy's keen on you.' Mum went rattling on, oblivious to Ivy's silence and her set mouth. 'The best thing is, he'll be here in time for the Ball! I've arranged with Esmé that he'll stay with us that weekend, and be the perfect partner for you in the Queen Competition. It's like fate, don't you think?'

*

The night before the Ball, Simon sits beside Ivy on the mushroom-coloured sofa in the Morgenstern's living room. She's aware of a slight trembling in him, a need. It makes her shrink into herself. His hand reaches out, encircles her wrist.

'My fingers don't meet around your wrist any more,' he says, disappointment in his voice. 'You're different. You were tiny and kind of delicate. Now you've got some flesh on you I can see how beautiful you are, Ivy.'

'Don't say things like that, Simon.' Ivy touches Lowanna's bracelet on her other wrist, calling on the courage it gives her. 'Let's get this Ball over with so life can get back to normal.'

Mum comes into the lounge room. She's all dolled up for a night out. 'Darling, we're taking Laura to the Information Night for Teacher's College so your Dad and I can check out if it's going to suit her next year. Lucky there's a branch in Castleton so we won't have to support two of you down at Sydney Uni. We'll leave you two alone, to catch up on old times. There's cheesecake in the fridge, Ivy, make sure to serve Simon supper.' Laura makes a strange face at Ivy, wiggling eyebrows with a strange expression of curiosity and amusement.

Ivy's throat constricts, both at the mention of food, and the prospect of being alone with Simon. Once she would have welcomed his attentions. Now he reminds her of the years of shame and pain she's trying to put behind her.

'When will you be back?' she asks Mum, a tremor of anxiety in her voice.

'Quite late, dear. We know you two have a lot to talk about.' Is that a wink from Mum to Simon, or is Ivy imagining it?

'No worries, Mrs Morgenstern,' Simon says gruffly. 'I'll look after her.'

The door closes behind Mum, Dad and Laura. Ivy turns to Simon.

'Just so you know, I don't need looking after, thanks all the same. Let's talk about you instead. Do you like Medicine?'

'Only because it's bringing me closer to you. Ivy' – he's reaching for her hand again – 'you must know how I feel by now.'

Ivy's confused. What's Simon talking about? 'Feel about what?' she says, eyes wide with alarm. She hopes he's not going to say the words she fears.

'About you, of course. Why do you think I've been writing to you all this time? I could have transferred to Melbourne Uni, but I chose to be close to you. Ivy, I've loved you from that moment on the beach when you saved Adam's life. Why didn't you answer my letters?'

Why does he think I didn't answer his letters? Surely silence was answer enough?

'What about Jasmine? I thought she was your girlfriend?' Ivy casts around for an escape from the trap closing around her.

'That was a game, I was never serious about her. Anyway she's gone off with David, and he won't be the last. It's you I want to be with. Ivy, will you marry me?'

'What?' Ivy's scared she'll laugh; this is all so ridiculous. 'You must be joking. I'm only eighteen, and anyway I'd make a terrible wife. Did you know I can't have children?'

'That doesn't matter to me,' Simon sounds urgent. He leans over to kiss her. She moves her mouth away from his, and his lips land on her cheek.

'I like you a lot, but as a friend, not in the way you think,' she says, standing up from the sofa, moving away from him. 'I'm never going to get married. There's too much living to do. All I want is to be a writer.'

'You've been leading me on all this time. Mrs Bronsky told my mother you were in love with me, but too shy to tell me.'

'For heaven's sake! Why don't these busybodies mind their own business! I can speak for myself.' Ivy feels herself go hot and cold. *Best to be definite, put an end to this.* 'The answer's No.'

Simon stands up, his face flushed and angry.

'Now I see what you're really like. Well, you'll never get another offer like this one. You don't deserve it, Ivy the drama queen, the sneak. A prick-teaser, that's what you are.' Tears in Simon's eyes belie the bitterness of his words.

'I'm sorry,' Ivy says, feeling genuine pity. 'Let's forget this conversation. Please stop this, let's have supper and talk about something else.'

'To hell with your supper. And find another poor sod to escort you to the Ball.' Simon throws something at her, turns around and is gone. Ivy hears the front door shut with an angry bang. Bending down to the floor, she picks up a small box. It's not wrapped. She opens it. Inside is a ring, its tiny diamond glinting in the soft light from the overhead lamp.

*

The Ball is a miserable affair. Ivy's escort is the pimply boy, Dennis, who'd tried to kiss her at her Dad's fiftieth birthday party. Poor Dennis was pulled in at the last minute by Ivy's frantic mother, who hasn't spoken to Ivy since the night she'd come home with Dad and Laura, to find Simon gone and Ivy sitting like a stone statue, holding a jewellery box.

There is no need for words. Mum goes into the main bedroom and slams the door.

Dad comes and sits beside her. 'What happened, Ivylie?' He puts his arm around her, holding her a minute too long in a cloying hug.

'What do you think happened? Simon asked me to marry him. I said No.'

'I for one am glad you did, but don't tell your mother. She has it in her head that you'll marry that nice Jewish boy, a rabbi's son, soon to be a doctor, no less. Don't blame her, she only wants the best for you. No good if you don't love him. I know you, my Ivy, better than anyone. You're worth more than an arranged marriage.'

30. JOEL

Ivy's spoken to Joel on the phone often over last few months. Like his letters, Joel's phone calls are usually all about him. He asks her to buy him some books which he can't find in Melbourne, rare journals about motor mechanics and horseracing. *I'll pay you back*, he says. Ivy combs the Sydney bookshops for the journals although she finds the topics boring, spending her study time pounding the city pavements. She can't wait to put the one journal she's unearthed into his hands herself.

He has a new job, he tells her, so can start paying board to the Lewis's. And he can afford the flight home from Melbourne to Castleton for the summer holidays. Ivy's heart leaps. In a few weeks Joel will be living next door again, just like Before.

Hannah and Sophie have been begging to visit their new-found cousins, sending letters weekly to Castleton. Abe wants to reciprocate his sister's hospitality to Ivy and Laura, and invites his nieces to stay at Wave Street for the holidays.

On Wave Beach, Ivy feels the sun caress her skin with its golden rays. She could melt in the comforting warmth. She's lying on her beach towel next to Hannah, whose long tawny hair is artfully arranged to look tousled. Hannah's skin is perfectly tanned except where the white flesh of her breasts pops out of her bikini top. Ivy's envious of her cousin's slim athletic body, its stomach flat above her rounded hips. In spite of her thin frame, Ivy's stomach is always swollen, the result, she suspects, of the assaults of extreme starvation. Comparing her body with Hannah's healthy one makes Ivy even more self-conscious.

Young Laura's spread her towel next to Sophie's. The two girls are so close together that their dark curls mingle. They giggle and whisper together, as if they've been friends all their lives.

The blissful heat and the rhythmic sound of crickets rubbing their little feet together lull Ivy into near-contentment. If it weren't for Joel, lying face down on a striped towel at a respectable distance from the four girls and ignoring them, Ivy might feel almost happy.

'Gosh you're lucky, Ivy. Tell me, what's your secret?' Hannah's staring at Ivy admiringly. Ivy is lying on her front, chin on cupped hands, her book propped in front of her.

'Huh? What are you talking about?' Ivy can't believe this golden girl, rich, engaged to be married, beloved by her family, could possibly think she, Ivy, was lucky. 'What secret?' She looks up, her finger between the pages of her book.

'Your diet, of course. How else can you stay so skinny? I know girls who'd give their right arm to be as thin as you.'

Ivy closes her book, turns over, sits up. 'Didn't your mother explain what happened to me?'

'Only that you'd had an illness. It wasn't polio, was it?' Hannah, sitting up now too, shifts almost imperceptibly away from Ivy.

'I'm not lucky, Hannah. It wasn't polio. I nearly died from this sickness called anorexia nervosa. It makes you stop eating. It's terrible because you can't control it, and you can't eat, no matter how hungry you get. If you think I'm thin now, you should have seen me before. I was a walking skeleton. Don't ever think it's good to be skinny.'

'But of course it is! All us girls want to be thin, so we can look good in our clothes. Look at the models in magazines! They're so elegant,' sighs Hannah.

'Those magazines are criminal. They make people try to stop eating. It's dangerous to give girls the idea that you have to be thin to look good. But I was only thirteen when it started, and it was nothing to do with fashion. I was already thin.'

'Really? So why – why did you do it?'

Ivy sighs. 'I didn't *do* it. The sickness invaded my mind, and told me to stop eating. It wanted to kill me. And it very nearly did.

'Ivy! I had no idea. What did you say the sickness is called?'

'Anorexia nervosa. It's from the Greek for 'no appetite'. Only you do have an appetite, a raging one. Your stomach twists with hunger while a voice tells you not to eat. As for dieting, I guess it might be OK if your mind is healthy, but the very thought of deliberately starving yourself horrifies me, now I know what it can lead to. When people talk about how to lose weight I want to scream at them.'

Hannah leans over, puts her arms around Ivy. 'We didn't know, or at least Sophie and I didn't. I promise we'll never talk about diets again.'

Why can't anyone understand I didn't choose the sickness, it chose me? Ivy's tired of trying to explain. 'It's OK,' she tells Hannah. 'I just wish people would stop thinking it's all my fault.'

'I'm sorry,' Hannah says, concern in her eyes. 'I didn't mean to upset you. It must've been awful for you.'

'It was. But I'm getting better every day. Anyway, why would you want to change a thing about yourself? You have such a perfect, healthy body.'

Sensing a movement behind her, Ivy turns her head to see Joel rolling over and supporting himself on one elbow. He's gazing in the same direction as Ivy, his eyes searching for someone or something. Ivy sees his eyes on her sister, and hears Laura calling 'Sophie, c'mon! Last one in the water has to kiss a boy!' The two girls scamper down to the water's edge.

Hannah stands up, her arms above her head. 'C'mon, let's go in too, please forget what I said.'

'Wait,' says Ivy. 'There's something else.' Now that she's broken the ice with Hannah, she feels safe to ask her the questions burning in her mind. 'Let's go for a walk along the sand first.' Tiny waves lap at their feet, as the two girls meander along the water's edge, jumping out of the way whenever a big wave threatens to swamp them.

'It's Joel,' Ivy says, swallowing a lump in her throat. 'He's hardly spoken to anyone since we got to the beach. He wasn't like this back in Castleton a few years ago. I can't work him out.'

'Well, I know why he's been invited to stay at our house,' Hannah says, an edge of bitterness in her voice. 'Joel's father did our Dad a huge favour once. When Dad arrived here with nothing after the war, no one would give him a job. But Arnold Hammerstein, Joel's father, did. Soon Dad was the foreman at the factory where Mr Hammerstein was manager, and he gave our Dad a start in Australia. When Joel got into trouble and had nowhere to live in Melbourne, Dad felt he had to take him in.'

'Trouble? What trouble?'

'Don't know the details, but I can tell you he tried it on with me once, even though he knows I'm engaged. I told him to get lost.'

Ivy's head reels. *How many other girls has Joel 'tried it on' with? And why has he never even tried to touch me?*

'Let's not talk about him,' Hannah says with a toss of her shining hair. 'He's leaving our place soon, thank goodness. C'mon, let's go in, I'm boiling.'

Ivy looks out to sea and watches her sister's graceful body cleaving through the water. *She might be a champion swimmer but I'm still responsible for her while we're here*, Ivy thinks, never taking her eyes off Laura.

Retracing their steps along the sand, Ivy lets a rogue wave knock her clean over. She shudders with the shock of cold water on her skin. Hannah bursts out laughing. 'You did it! Here I come!' She enters the water gracefully, diving under a wave, arms stretched straight in front of her.

Struggling for breath, Ivy tries to recover her dignity, but another wave swamps her. She tries to swim towards Laura, who's way out to sea. But Ivy's no match for her sister when it comes to negotiating the surf. With relief, she sees Laura swimming effortlessly on the crest of a wave, towards cousin Sophie teetering on the edge of a wave.

'Laura!' Ivy splutters. 'It's dangerous – stay close to shore!' Laura ignores her, or pretends not to hear.

Back on the sand, Ivy shivers. She's wearing her new bathers, a one-piece with thin shoulder straps and what she thinks is a becoming flounce at the hips. She hopes Joel will notice and approve. His words in Winchester Hospital, long forgotten, suddenly come back to her: *I for one, am glad you're a girl.*

Joel turns his head slowly towards her, looking her up and down. 'You'll never be a bathing beauty, not with those skinny legs of yours.' He's grinning as if he's made a clever joke.

His words crush her. 'Is that all you have to say to me, after what you did to my little sister?'

'What?' Joel looks genuinely amazed. 'Where'd you get that from? Are you crazy?'

Even Joel thinks I'm mad, insane, deranged. After all his smarmy words of being best friends, he's the same as all of them.

'And Laura? What about her?'

'I honestly don't know what you're talking about. I'd never put a finger on your sister. But I'd sure bash up any bloke who came near her. I've known Laura since she could barely talk. What's she been telling you?'

'That you kissed her, and worse.'

'For Christ's sake, Ivy, what sort of monster do you think I am? I love her like a brother, that's all. But it's different with you. I've always thought of you as beyond my reach. You're so dammed clever and feisty, I could never keep up with you. You're special to me, always have been. Can't we start again, be real friends?'

Ivy's spine tingles, and her head spins. 'I thought we were friends already. Maybe more than friends. You haven't even thanked me properly for the journal I walked all over town to get you.'

Joel leans over, lightly touches Ivy's hand. 'I did say thanks, what else do you want?'. Her skin tingles all the way up her arm. 'Let's go back to the house,' he says in a low voice. I want to make up for everything. And I didn't mean that about your legs and anyway, I like skinny girls.' He stands up, holding out his hand. She doesn't take it.

Again Ivy's powerless to resist him. As if she's mesmerised, she picks up her towel and her book and takes a step towards him.

*

In Wave Street's small sunroom facing the back garden, dappled light falls on Ivy's face. Joel lies on top of her, crushing her bones. Ivy ignores the pain, craving to absorb every inch of him. She breathes in a scent of spices and yeast, a special Joel smell. His face hovers over hers. It seems to her to be wreathed in rainbows, as if he were the Greek god Apollo, blessing her. Her body seems to melt, her breath catches and her eyes fill with tears. She's crying not from pain, but from the joy of feeling Joel's body merging with hers. She's been waiting for this moment for her whole life. Instinctively she raises her lips to his. He jerks his head away. *But he loves me. I don't understand. What have I done to make him angry?*

'I'm hurting you,' Joel whispers. 'I can feel your bones, they're sticking into me.' He's fumbling with the zip on Ivy's new capri pants. She pushes his hand away.

'What the hell did you do that for? Don't you want it?'

'Sorry,' Ivy says. 'It'll be better when I've put on some more weight.' Confusion blurs her words. *What does he mean? Want what?*

'Well, put it on, why don't you. We can't do this any more till you do.'

Ivy's aware of a figure in the doorway, the glass doors separating the living room from the sunroom pushed roughly aside.

'What – what's going on?' Mum's glaring down at them, her face as white as chalk.

Ivy pushes herself up on her elbows, suffused with shock and shame. Joel swings his long legs to the floor, his face mottled red, eyes not looking at Mum. She brushes away tears. The room comes back into focus.

'Just remember, Ivy, you've been ill. And as for you, Joel, I never expected this of you, not after all the trouble you've already caused.' Mum's voice shakes a little.

'It's OK, Mrs Morgenstern.' Joel's voice is gravelly, as if he's forgotten to clear phlegm from his throat. 'I wouldn't hurt Ivy for the world.' He stands up to his full six feet. Ivy sees Mum's eyes dart to his jeans, which are safely zipped up and belted. She checks Ivy's capri pants, still intact.

'Just make sure this never happens again. Now Ivy, go and wash your face and fix yourself up. Let's all forget what just happened, and I won't say a word to Abe, provided you behave yourself from now on, Joel.' Ivy can't believe her normally gentle mother could sound so fierce. 'I came in to tell you both that lunch is ready. It's hours since you've eaten, Ivy. You know you can't afford to skip meals.'

Ivy shrinks inside at the thought of food, and tries to silence The Voice, warning her to keep well away from the stuff. She remembers Joel's words, *Put it on, why don't you,* and follows him to the dining room. *What if Mum tells Dad about me and Joel? After what's just happened, aren't we practically engaged?*

A screen door bangs. Laura, Hannah and Sophie run inside, sand falling from their bodies like fairy dust.

'Girls, girls!' Mum's voice is still a little shaky. 'Go outside and hang those towels on the line. Laura, show Sophie where the outside shower is. No lunch till you're decent.'

The table is laid with platters of cold chicken, sliced tomatoes, pale green lettuce leaves, slices of white bread, and pickled cucumbers. Joel piles his plate with bread, chicken, tomato, and cucumbers and proceeds to make a towering sandwich.

'Look, Joel's made a Dagwood sandwich, like in the comics!' Laura looks at Joel adoringly and throws her smooth brown arms around his neck, knocking some contents of his overloaded sandwich to the floor. Joel laughs, and tickles Laura's armpit, making her giggle uncontrollably. Mum frowns and presses her lips together.

Sophie rolls her eyes. 'Don't be stupid, Laura. Anyway it's called a club sandwich.'

'It is not! I can show you the exact comic! You're the stupid one,' says Laura, without a hint of malice.

Ivy hides a slice of chicken under a large lettuce leaf and pushes the pile to the very side of her plate so it looked like she'd eaten some. She cuts half a slice of bread. There's no butter because it's not kosher to serve it with chicken. Ivy's grateful there's one less food to avoid.

*

'I have to tell you something, Ivy,' Joel says, settling on the grass of the back garden beside her, squinting into the sun, his long legs in their blue jeans stretched out in front of him

Ivy rolls over, touches Joel's arm. 'You can always tell me anything, we're soul mates, remember?'

Joel flinches, moves his arm a hair's breadth from her fingers. 'I'm not going back to Uni. I can't. I stuffed up, see. Haven't got your brains, that's for sure. Medicine's not for me.'

'But Joel, you can do anything you want! Now that we're together, I'll help you. We can study together, like we used to.' Something stops her reaching for his hand again.

'It's not Uni. Something else happened. I met this girl, see. She's not Jewish. We – we got together and one thing led to another. I don't have to spell it out for you. She's pregnant.'

Ivy's skin freezes in the hot sun. She sits as still as a statue. She can't think, can't speak. There's a bitter taste in her mouth.

Joel's looking away from her, his eyes blank again. 'Her folks hate me. They won't let me see her ever again. They're sending her way some place I'll never find her. It kills me, Ivy. The way I feel about her – love's too weak a word. I want to die sometimes, you know. Her parents won't let her marry a *Jew, turns out they're* rabidly anti-Semitic. And it's too late now for her to get rid of it, not that I'd want her to. It's my child too, hers and mine. It's all such a mess.' Joel's voice breaks. He's weeping, letting fat tears burst from his eyes.

Ivy struggles to find her voice, almost deafened by the beat of her heart in her ears. 'What – what about us?'

'There's no "us", Ivy, not like that. I don't think of you that way. You're my good friend, that's all.'

'But what about before? When you rescued me from Winchester? And just now, when you were on top of me?'

'Listen, I was trying to make you feel better about yourself. I'd never go all the way with you. I respect you too much.' Joel's grey-green eyes are steady, staring into space. 'You're like my sister. It'd be like committing incest.'

For the first time Ivy notices how small Joel's eyes are. Her heart's pounding, her breath broken. The strap of her one-piece is digging into her shoulder. She focusses on the pain. Joel continues. 'Ivy, you must know by now.'

'Know? Know what? I only know I want us to be together. Always.' She hates the sound of her voice, the pleading note in it. She catches her breath, preparing to hear the words she's always known she'd hear, the dread hurting her chest as her heart breaks.

Joel looks at her, finally, full in the face. 'Ivy, we'll always be friends. But your future and mine don't belong together.'

It is a flat, bald statement, hanging in the air like a bad smell. Ivy's heart slows almost to a stop. She knows beyond all doubt that this is the beginning of the end.

31. THE BLUE ROOM

Ivy lines up with her fellow students in the student canteen, balancing a metal tray on the shelf surrounding food on display. She reaches inside the servery and puts a bowl of cut fruit onto her tray. *I can pick out the banana rounds, and take my time chewing on the apple bits.* She's told the girls from College that she's allergic to banana, and quite a few other foods besides – potatoes, corn, the wheat in bread. As well, she's a declared vegetarian, which engenders a certain respect from her fellows, and saves her from the smelly contents of the *bain-maries*. Her stomach churns when she sees slimy chunks of meat swimming in a vomit-coloured sauce.

Ivy's learning to eat just enough to keep herself alive and well enough to sit through lectures and tutorials. It doesn't matter if she doesn't go on living, now that there's no future, as Joel had said. There's still a tiny flame of hope deep inside her, a faint vision of Joel taking her hand, telling her it was all a mistake, he'd made it up about the pregnant girl. She waits for a letter, a note, a voice on the other end of the phone. The flame's been getting dimmer and smaller with each week that passes without a word from him. Ivy knows that when the flame flickers and dies, so will her life. She tells no one that she intends to make it happen. She just has to work out how.

The hunger's back, not for food, but for anything that might take away the pain inside her. The Voice is her friend now, a secret support to her determination. Again it whispers *No need to eat any more, isn't that a relief? There are quicker ways to end it all, and starving will surely help.*

Joining the other girls at a round table in Franny's, the Women's Union canteen, Ivy sets down her bowl of fruit, and moves the tray onto an empty chair.

'Is that all you're having?' asks Sally, Ivy's college roommate. 'You hardly needed a tray for that.'

Ivy flushes. 'I know, I was going to get something else but there's no vegetables today. And my allergies, you know – I have to be careful.'

'What exactly happens when you eat something you're not s'posed to?' asks Caroline, another occupant of their dorm. A medical student, she's forever curious about bodily functions. To Ivy Caroline sounds suspicious. Can she see through her lies?

'Well, I swell up and break out in huge welts all over my body,' Ivy says brightly, looking directly at Sally and Caroline. She's starting to believe her own stories. 'My throat swells too, so's I can hardly breathe and it hurts to swallow.'

'Anaphylactic shock,' Caroline says. 'We did that in Chemistry 1, and it's true it can kill you. Scientists are working on an antidote, but so far the research shows it might be genetic, in which case you're stuck with it.'

'You're such a brain,' Sally says to Caroline. The other girls roll their eyes.

'Show off,' says one, grinning at Caroline.

'You poor thing – Ivy, isn't it? Stuck with such a ghastly allergy. No wonder you're so careful.' A new girl, Stephany, sounds slightly patronising.

*

In the lecture theatre, Ivy stares at the plaits of the girl sitting in front of her. They're wound around the girl's head, thick and treacle-coloured. Ivy starts to count, first every section of shiny braid, one, two and three. When she's finished counting these she starts on the strands in each braid, separating the golden-brown threads from each other, examining each one. She reaches three thousand two hundred and twenty five. The lecturer's voice, deep and sonorous, is reciting from Gerard Manley Hopkins, the Poet Priest. It soothes the pain in Ivy's head. There's no meaning in the words, but the rhythm of the poem, its beat, is like a chorus to her counting.

After the lecture Ivy goes to the red phone box in the corner of the Quad. She dials Joel's number, as she does every day. He'd gladly given it to her that day on the beach in Castleton. She'd scribbled it on her bookmark, needlessly, because it lodged in her brain. She can always remember it, when other things are forgotten. The phone rings and rings. Ivy waits patiently, counts to thirty rings, hangs up and puts more pennies in the slot. She'll keep trying forever if need be, for one more chance to hear Joel's voice. Perhaps he will tell her he loves her, after all, and always has.

Some friends from the lecture catch up with Ivy as she leaves the phone box. They are polite and curious in the way of fellow villagers.

'Ringing your folks in Castleton again?' asks Sally.

'Bet it's her boyfriend more like it,' says another girl who Ivy doesn't know. She's small and fair, with huge round glasses almost obscuring her tiny pretty face.

Ivy manages a laugh. 'As if.' It's the latest in the student idioms she's picked up.

'Coming to Franny's for lunch?' Sally asks.

Looks like she could do with a good feed, Ivy hears another girl snigger, loud enough for her to hear.

'Sure, I'll catch up with you there. Have to get this book back to the Library first.' Ivy leaves the group, her stomach hollow. She hoists her heavy book bag over one shoulder.

Ivy has a plan. The Chemistry Lab is unattended in the lunch hour, she's discovered from Caroline. She also knows there are toxic substances in the lab. Cyanide kills in seconds, so she believes. Even the Nazis who wanted to escape the death sentence could crunch a pill between their teeth, and magically expire. An easy, quick, apparently painless death. That's what Ivy craves now, more than anything.

Checking no one's behind her, Ivy pushes the Lab door open. Finding it empty – of people, that is – she sighs with relief. Gleaming jars and bottles line the shelves, some behind glass doors. Ivy's told Caroline she needs some scientific information for her Creative Writing assignment, a historical thriller. *As if.* She walks down row after row of shelves and cabinets holding what she's sure are lethal chemicals. Inside a cupboard door, half open, she spots it – a small glass bottle labelled *sodium tetraborate*, the chemical name for cyanide, as Caroline had told her. 'One grain would be enough to kill a human,' Caroline had added. 'Good luck with your story.'

Ivy seizes the bottle, feels it cold and hard in her hand. She wedges it into her jacket pocket, and almost runs out of the Lab into the Quad, her heart banging with triumph and fear. Why is everything so still and quiet in the quadrangle? Even the grass appears benign, unmoved. Leaves drift down from the jacaranda tree in the corner of the Quad, as if the tree is weeping purple tears. Ivy feels judgement in the autumn air, knows the silence is a harbinger of punishment. Had someone seen her running out of the lab? *Wonder what the penalty for stealing dangerous drugs is?* A surge of elation dampens her shame.

Downstairs in the Ladies', Ivy smells disinfectant and bleach mixed with the toilet smells not quite masked by cleaning fluids. She pushes open the door of an empty cubicle, her bag of books by her feet. On the closed lid of the lavatory, Ivy sits and unscrews the lid of her treasure. There's white powder inside the jar. It gives off a smell which reminds her of the *mandelbröt* her mother makes, thin pale biscuits studded with oval almond slices. Ivy stares at the powder. It'd be much easier to take a pill, like the prisoners did after the war. She wets her index finger and presses a grain of the powder onto it. Closing her eyes, she puts the finger to her mouth, touches it to the tip of her tongue. It has a bitter taste.

Ivy waits for the obliteration, the blackness she craves, hoping and waiting. She's not afraid. *Maybe I'll only nearly die, and Joel will be sorry, and then he'll change his mind and love me forever.* Nothing happens. She opens her eyes, looks at the open jar with its opaque white contents. *I'm not meant to die this way, G-d has other plans.* Even in extremis Ivy can't think or write the word *God*, omitting the middle letter as she'd been taught back in Hebrew school. *Whatever this stuff is, it's not working.*

Her hands holding the glass jar start to shake. Ivy stands up, lifts the lid of the toilet bowl, and pours the powder into its gaping maw. *I'll have to get rid of it before they find it on me. I'm a thief and a liar. The police will come for me.* When she pulls the chain there's a fizzing sound beneath the flushing water.

*

Back home for the Easter break, Ivy's resolve to end her life is faltering. Perhaps there'll be a letter from Joel. She has a faint hope that he might come home, to spend Easter with his family next door.

'Any mail for me?' she asks Mum as casually as she can. Mum shakes her head. Her blue rinse is wearing off, leaving a salt and pepper pattern in her hair. Ivy wishes for Mum's lustrous black curls to come back, so she needn't feel guilty.

'Ivylie, you've lost weight again,' says Mum, concern creasing her forehead. 'It must be that awful college food they give you down there. Some good home cooking will fix that. It's hot dishes tonight, cauliflower mornay, spaghetti bake, and your favourite, duchess potatoes. All vegetarian. I've been collecting recipes for weeks.'

'Mum, you don't have to do that. I can eat the salad, and the bread. I don't want you to go to all that trouble on my account.'

'Nonsense, darling. We're so pleased to have you back. Laura's been beside herself with excitement. Anyway *Pesach* starts next week; there'll be no bread or flour for eight days after that. Never mind, I have a lovely recipe for a cake made from almond meal.'

At the mention of almonds Ivy's heart skips a beat. Cyanide's supposed to smell like that. The last few weeks of term were filled with terror that her theft would be found out. More shame, more blame. Ivy's roommates were kind to her, but often stopped talking when Ivy entered the dorm, exchanging looks of concern. It is a relief to get away from the ever-present danger of discovery, and worse, pity. Caroline had tricked her, Ivy discovers, giving her the chemical name for a fairly harmless cleaning substance. *She's cleverer than I thought, must've guessed it wasn't a writing assignment I needed the cyanide for. Caroline will make a good doctor.*

The Morgensterns are hosting the family *Seder* this year. Ivy's stomach quakes during the reading of the *Haggadah*. The smell of the gefilte fish still nauseates her, as it had at Aunt Betsy's *Seder* when she was little. Mum's made it into fried patties, which don't smell as bad as the boiled balls in fish jelly. When it's her turn to read, Ivy changes the words in the ancient fables from *he* to *she*, from the *four sons* to the *four daughters*. Aunt Betsy frowns and tuts, but Dad gives her a conspiratorial smile. Laura laughs with delight, and follows suit when it's her turn to read.

All through the interminable service and the four course meal, The Voice in Ivy's head is relentless. *You know how not to eat without them knowing. I've schooled you well.* Ivy tells The Voice to shut up, but her strength to fight it all over again is waning. *I thought you wanted to die,* it murmurs. *Where's your courage now?*

Over dessert of stewed apple, meringues and Mum's special almond meal cake (it was indeed delicious – Ivy allows herself a tiny taste), Laura says, 'Has anyone else heard the news from next door?'

'The Hammerstein's, you mean?' Dad's leaning back in his chair, replete and expansive. 'I was talking to Arnold the other day. Seems his son's gone and got himself engaged.'

Ivy goes numb. Joel doesn't have a brother. *No, please no.*

'Isn't it tragic! He always said he was waiting for me to grow up,' Laura says, not looking at Ivy's white face.

'Who's the lucky – or should I say unlucky – girl?' Aunt Betsy asks. 'Not that *shikse* he got into trouble, is it?' Like all their friends in Castleton, she's enjoying the scandal of a member of the faith disgracing himself, and with a non-Jewish girl, heaven forbid.

'Apparently it's a lovely young Jewish girl he met when he was doing Medicine,' Dad says. 'She's eighteen to his twenty-two, a good age difference. Anyway, the Hammersteins are delighted, and rightly so, I say. Just as well my sister Annie helped the boy out of that scrape he got himself into. A lucky escape for us all, I say.'

Ivy stands up, starts clearing the table. She moves like an automaton.

'If either of my daughters marries out, they'll be as good as dead to me and Lily. You know that, don't you girls?' Dad's smile is slipping as he fixes Laura and Ivy with his sternest gaze.

'Leave the dishes, Ivy dear. Some of us haven't finished,' Mum says, flustered as always whenever she's entertaining.

Ivy doesn't hear her, moves slowly and steadily between the dining room and kitchen. *If I go on as normal, it'll mean this hasn't happened.* Her hands start to shake. She drops a pile of dirty plates in the hallway. There's a huge crash.

'*Oy vey,*' Mum calls out. 'What was that?'

Dad gets up from the table, goes towards the kitchen. 'Ivylie! What's wrong? You're shaking like a leaf,' he says, holding her by her shoulders. 'It's all right Lily,' he calls back to the dining room. 'A small accident, that's all. Only one plate broken.'

Ivy stares at the two jagged halves of the gold-rimmed plate, one of the set Mum keeps for Pesach. Her lips move to say 'I'm sorry,' but no sound comes out.

'You're white as a sheet,' Dad says. 'Don't upset yourself Ivylie, it's only a plate after all. Pull yourself together and come back to the table. Don't let this spoil our Seder.'

'Dad, I need to lie down for a few minutes. Please. *Not long now and you can stop your life. That's if you have the courage.* The Voice is whispering its snide demands, and again Ivy is powerless against it. She knows where Mum keeps the pills she takes for her nerves, high up in the bathroom cabinet to hide from little fingers. There are no little fingers any more, only Ivy's shaking, seeking ones.

*

Ivy waits for an opportunity when she will be alone. At home a week later, Mum is out shopping, Dad at work, Laura at school. Normal people are always out at work or school, living their lives without question. What does she have to live for now that Joel is engaged, has shown he doesn't want her and has said so in some unwell chosen words? *Your future and mine don't belong together.*

There is only a blue bedroom, a single bed, her empty body, and a full bottle of her mother's 'nerve' pills. *Keep out of reach of children*, the label says. But she's not a child any more, is she? With a blank mind and a steady hand, Ivy swallows the round white tablets, handful by handful, until the bottle is empty. It is easy.

Immediately she panics. *I don't want to die*, she says to Thanatos grinning at her, winning at last. Who can help her fight him? She runs out of the house to where Oscar and Lena live, a few doors down the street. She sees Oscar's small blue Triumph in the driveway.

'Uncle Oscar, uncle Oscar,' Ivy screams at the front door, banging on it with failing strength. She will beg him to put his finger down her throat and force her to vomit up the pills. But the house is totally empty and ominously silent.

Ivy turns around for home shaking with every step. In the pink bathroom she leans over the square sink and sticks her finger down her throat. It is a feeble attempt. Nothing comes up and nothing comes out. She's always hated vomiting, the sound of it, the smell of it, the taste of it. It has never been part of her sickness. She clings to the cold hard washbasin. Everything goes black and her knees buckle.

*

She lies on a hard rubber slab. It is as cold as the grave. Something hard is being forced down her throat. A liquid is gushing into her from the rubber tube reaching down into her stomach. Pain sears her chest. She convulses as copious brown fluids are ejected from her nose and mouth.

The stiff white garment clothing her body scratches wherever it touches her skin. She feels herself dropping in and out of consciousness. In an interval of waking, she hears a man's voice.

'She's done a good job of it,' the man says. 'Stupid girl. She'll never have children from what I can see. Impossible to have functioning ovaries in this obviously starved body. What a waste.'

Ivy closes her eyes and waits to die.

*

All is eerily silent when Ivy wakes up. Where is she? She dares not open her eyes. Her throat is sore, rasping. With a shudder she remembers. She's supposed to be dead. Some time in the past she's killed herself. The whole bottle of Mum's nerve tablets must have done it.

Somewhere outside Ivy hears a screech of brakes. There's the sound of a bus stopping before resuming its stately way, lumbering with its load of passengers. *Are they dead too? Am I in Heaven or Hell?*

Another bus rolls past, its gentle roar somehow comforting. Ivy wishes she were on it. *Where are they going, these poor souls, gifted with the innocence of normality? They belong to a world from which I am forever banished.* The rumbling of the bus is like a great beating heart. She imagines it is the heart of her mother, pumping life into her, as she lies coiled inside her womb.

Cautiously Ivy opens her eyes, first one, then the other. Is this what it's like to be dead? Still, quiet and peaceful? She's in her new room, the one with blue carpet. She imagines her bed is a boat, floating on the carpet as blue as the ocean.

Ivy becomes aware that she's not alone in the room. Swivelling her eyes, slowly and painfully, she sees the seated figure of Aunt Betsy. A mirage, surely, or a horrid hallucination. *Perhaps this is all a dream, and this is me looking down at my body. Do the dead dream, I wonder? I can float away on the boat of my bed. I'll be safe here where no one can reach me.*

Ivy must have spoken her thoughts aloud, for Aunt Betsy, her plump knees jutting from beneath her sensible serge skirt, leans forward and says,

'You're at home dear, safe and sound. I'll get your Mum for you.' She creeps out of Ivy's Blue Room. Ivy can sense her Aunt Betsy's excited disapproval as an icy wind, making her skin prickle, and the hairs on her neck stand up in the still, silent air.

'She's awake,' Ivy hears Aunt Betsy call, as she disappears down the hall. Ivy shuts her eyes again. She does not want to see her mother, hear her admonitions. 'Ivy, how could you do this to your father and me?' Mum will say. 'After all we've been through, all we've done for you?'

But here's Mum now, bright and breezy, as if it's just another day, and her eldest daughter hasn't tried to do away with herself.

'Darling, thank goodness! You do look a little peaky, nothing a good strong cup of tea won't fix. I've made those shortbread biscuits you love, you can have one or two of those with your tea.'

'Aren't you going to say anything? About what happened?'

'Nothing's happened, dear. You've had a little setback, that's all. We don't need to talk about it to anybody, do we? Betsy's promised not to utter a word, although she thinks the Rabbi ought to know.'

'Mum, she'll tell! Aunt Betsy's the biggest gossip alive,' Ivy says, stumbling a little on her last word.

'Now Ivy, Betsy's been a wonderful support to me over the last few days. I'm sure she'll be the soul of discretion. Your father and I have made sure news of our troubles will go no further. Fortunately the nice constable who came around happens to be a good customer of Abe's. We might be seeing Inspector Wright in a new suit before Christmas.'

Aunt Betsy comes bustling in with a tray of teas and shortbread, which she sets down carefully on Ivy's desk. She's in time to catch Mum's last few words.

'Lily, that's disgraceful! You don't mean …'

'Let's put this unfortunate business behind us, as I said, Betsy. It's best for everyone. Thanks for making the tea. Don't you have to get back to Myer? He'll be wanting his dinner, and you've been wearing yourself out for us.'

Ivy hears Aunt Betsy mutter, none too softly, 'But after all she's put you through! You don't deserve this treatment, Lily. I've a good mind to …'

'Now, Betsy dear, remember our agreement. You needn't worry about us; Abe and I have been through worse with her, as you know. Now we have to hold our heads up, and be examples to the rest of the community.'

Ivy feels a rising anger. After the banishment, the rejection, how can Mum talk blithely about her, as if her illness has never happened? Is this the beginning of years of covering-up, of denial that she's ever been anything other than a brain and a pretty face? She hears the front door close amidst her mother's effusive thank-yous and hugs. Mum comes back into the Blue Room.

'Ivy dear, you haven't touched your tea that Betsy kindly made. Come on, sit up and give yourself a little shake. Everything's going to be all right.'

Gingerly Ivy stretches her aching legs, wipes gunk out of her eyes. She lets shame flood her, and anger at herself. Where is Dr B now, when she needs her more than ever? Who will help Ivy fight The Voice that wants to kill her, one way or another?

She hears Dr B's voice, pure and strong, her words *My brave, brave, girl.*

Mum comes back with a face cloth, and a basin of warm soapy water smelling of lemons. 'Now, let's get you cleaned up. We'll have you back to your pretty self in no time.'

32. AVIVA

Months in hospital follow the day of the blue room. It is not like Winchester, forbidding and torturous; instead it is a private convalescent home with light-filled rooms and flowers sending their scents from a sunny garden through large uncurtained windows. *A home from home,* Ivy thinks with bitter irony. She is fed three small meals a day, which she eats automatically. The Voice has been silent since its failure to kill her.

Ivy uses the time to write to Dr B.

Dear Dr de Berg,

I hope you are well. I can't tell you how much I miss you.

Last year Thanatos got the better of me, so to speak. I've spent almost twelve months now in hospital where they forced me to eat. I knew I was getting ill again, but without your voice behind my head, I couldn't fight The Voice. It seemed easier to give in to it, to stop eating and hurry death along. Believe me, I tried to think of all the words that have passed between us, words which brought me back to life. But your voice was drowned out, and I succumbed.

Remember the boy I told you about, who lived next door to my family, and who wrote me so many letters when I was living with my uncle? I thought he loved me, and we would be together after I got better. Turned out he did love me, but only as a sister. Or maybe not even as a sister – I think now he never loved me at all. I had romantic notions that Joel and I would elope if we had to.

Well, it wasn't to be. I'd pinned my hopes on a future with Joel and when those hopes were dashed I forgot all you'd taught me about calling on Eros. The Voice was urging me to die. First I took poison, but it didn't work. (Actually it wasn't real poison but I didn't know that.) When I heard about Joel being engaged I took a whole bottle of Mum's nerve pills. It was the lowest time of my life, except for the shock treatment.

I've had to drop out of Uni, even though I loved it. All the money for my education is going into keeping me in hospital till I put on weight and 'pull myself together' as the nurses often say. I have a vision of myself in pieces floating off into the universe, while the sane part of me reaches out to pull the pieces together into a whole new me.

I wonder if Mum could ever love me again. How could I be flesh of Lily Morgenstern? Was I ever so intimately enclosed inside her deepest self? My Mum will be forever disappointed, disgusted by the corrupted body of her first-born.

I often wished that you were my mother, because you understood me and never judged me. I am looking for the strength you saw within my soul, and would give anything for some words from you. If you could write back to me, I'll be forever grateful.

Your ever affectionate

Ivy

A doctor comes in as Ivy's sealing the blue aerogramme. He's young and rather handsome, with tanned skin and fine smooth fingers. He puts them lightly on Ivy's wrist and listens silently to her pulse, and shines a little torch into her eyes.

'Well, how are we today? Ready to go home?'

'Home? Really? No, I'd rather stay here.'

'Well, my dear, we can't keep you here forever. Now that you've put on enough weight, there's nothing more we can do for you. I'll be prescribing some medicine to help with those moods of yours. You'll need to get plenty of rest meanwhile, and of course keep to a nutritious meal plan.

'Can I go back to Uni?'

'I don't see why not. They're on a long Term break now, aren't they? We'll see how you are when term starts.'

*

The first thing Ivy does when she gets home is change the colour of her curtains and bedspread to green, the colour of living plants and wild seas. She cannot bear the reminder of that terrible day in her blue bedroom. Only the blue carpet remains, and she doesn't have to look at that.

The second thing she does is to adopt her middle name, Aviva, as her first name. *A new name, a new life*, Ivy thinks. She announces this at the shabbos table on the first Friday after arriving home.

'I'd like you to call me Aviva from now on,' she says in a firm voice, after her mother, father and Laura take their seats after the blessings. They all stare at her.

'Don't be silly, dear,' Mum says, exchanging a slightly panicked look with Daddy. 'Your name's Ivy, it's a lovely name, and we can't call you anything else.'

'I will! I'll call you Aviva!' exclaims Laura, her eyes shining. 'Can I be Elisheva from now on too?'

'Now see what you've done, putting your silly ideas into Laura's head. No. You both have perfectly good English names, to keep you safe from prejudice, and worse.' Dad's voice has an edge to it.

'I'm proud of my Hebrew name. It suits me much more than Ivy does. And anyway, you gave it to me. You can call me what you like, but I'll only answer to Aviva.'

Mum serves the soup with her lips pressed together. Ivy thinks she detects a smile.

*

Dear Dr de Berg

Thanks for your letter. It came at the right time to buoy my spirits. It was as if you were speaking to me again. I'm grateful you explained there will always be some residual depression, which is normal after all I've been through.

First I need to tell you that I've changed my name to Aviva. It's actually my Hebrew name so it's not like I'm actually changing it, rather I'm reverting to my true nature. Ivy never did suit me, and I will always associate it with the nightmare years of my illness. I would be very happy if you'd call me Aviva from now on.

I've had many months of struggling against this illness, The Voice that wants me to die. By replacing it with your voice I managed to pull myself out of the pit of despair. When I hear your words 'My brave, brave girl', they drown out the ugly clamour of that Voice. Your belief in me, and mine in the strength of my own Ego, lifted me up at a time when it seemed Thanatos would win.

It took a supreme effort of will to get back to my healthy self, the part of me that wants to live above all else. I set myself a goal to eat at least twice a day, and to listen to my body instead of the unhealthy part of my mind. Call it The Voice, call it the Superego, call it Thanatos, I accept it is part of my psyche, and I must be vigilant against it.

I've been reading Freud's paper, the Ego and the Id again, as well as the Melanie Klein book you recommended. It's like being able to speak a secret language, one powerful enough to go where others fear to tread (a cliché, I know, but seemed appropriate for now).

My good news is that I've had a story published in the University magazine, Veritas. It's based on my experience with ECT, and aims to dispel the ignorance about anorexia and other mental illnesses. I'm not afraid of people knowing the truth about my life. There is no shame in confronting people's prejudices.

I'm back at Uni, studying Anthropology and Philosophy. Much to the surprise of my friends, I got a High Distinction in Moral Philosophy. One girl said she thought it must be a fluke! I'm immune to such slights now; the years of teasing and shaming have thickened my skin. I'm proud of who I am, or who I've become, thanks in no small part to you.

I've decided not to follow up your referral to the other analyst, partly because I won't put a further financial burden on my family. But the main reason is that my experience in analysis with you was overwhelmingly positive. I fear any other therapist might obscure the light of your belief in me.

I must close now, dear Dr B (did you know I used to call you that, to myself and in my diary?) I almost forgot: of course you have my permission to publish a paper about our work together. I am proud to be the subject of your article, and hope it will help others who have suffered a similar illness to mine. It will show people that it's possible to survive, even when the odds are against it, given the strength and insights which will always be there.

Thank you for saving my life.

Affectionately yours,

Aviva.

A Dangerous Daughter: the Poem

She wakes with a jolt,
Already late.
Morning tea break.
Her limbs all ache.

She swings legs to the edge,
Mere bones like twigs
Skin stretched over,
Dry as sedge.

She moves from the bed,
Slow and painful.
Everything hurts,
Her heart and her head.

Smells hot buttered toast,
Craves just a taste.
The tiniest crumb
Will seal her fate.

Pulls on a skirt
Her gaunt frame bent.
To hide her shame,
A top like a tent.

She could be ninety,
But is only fifteen.
Her shrivelled body
Mustn't be seen.

You've blighted our lives
Daughter once dear.
The devil's got you
We're the victims here.

They send her away
Out of their sight
So they can forget
Their shame and fright.

Exiled from her kin,
Across the land,
Girl hides her sin
As best she can.

Aunt's teagown strains.
Over ample breasts.
"Just look at the state of you,
It's wicked," she says.

"Going out like that?
In the ground I will sink.
You'll frighten the neighbours.
What will they think?"

Girl shakes her head
Runs a comb through her hair.
A quick flick, no more
And she's out the door.

She has a disease
It has no name.
It brings her shame.

Only she's to blame.
She's nearly dead,
Has months to live
When a doctor, an angel
Sorts out her head.

At last a name
For what's possessed her.
An actual disease!
Anorexia Nervosa.

What's it mean?
They say, contemptuous.
A fancy name
Meant to impress us.

It's all the rage,
They say, overseas.
Needless to say
It's the slimmer's disease.

It seems she can't help it.
Should've believed her.
Now there's a label,
It's all so much easier.

© Dina Davis 2019

AUTHOR'S NOTE

Out of your vulnerabilities will come your strength.

–Sigmund Freud

- *'My anorexia patient whom I was glad to discuss with you is returning to her family. From a weight of four stone three ounces (27k) when she came two years ago, she now weighs eight stone (51k). She is quite transformed as far as her psychological development is concerned, has carried on normal school work for over a year, hopes to have a university education and to develop a very good talent she has shown in writing. I am extremely proud of her, and grateful for the encouragement you gave me early on when the issue seemed to me such a doubtful one.'*
- (Extract from a letter to Dr Clara Geroe from Dr Ivy Bennett, November 1956. Copy courtesy Christine Vickers, La Trobe University, 27 July 2019).

*

In 2019 I received an email from a historian, Dr Christine Vickers of La Trobe University, Victoria. She was researching the history of psychoanalysis in Australia, and had unearthed a letter from a psychoanalyst, Dr Ivy Bennett, to fellow analyst Dr Clara Geroe. In the letter, Dr Bennett describes treating an anorexic girl who'd been sent to Western Australia in a desperate bid to save the girl's life. Was this child the same as the one Ms Brett Vickers had read about on my website, where I'd referred to my own early struggles with anorexia, and subsequent treatment?

As soon as I saw the facsimile of the analyst's letter I knew the girl described there was indeed myself. Not only did the dates fit, but also there was reference to my family and the town I'd been exiled from in New South Wales. More convincing than any of these facts was my analyst's voice in her written words, resonating with me after more than sixty years.

At first I was shocked by this revelation, not wanting to remember those terrible years when I was terminally ill, yet blamed for my illness. After my world came back together, something stirred in me when I realised anorexic children are still stigmatised, although the available treatment has improved dramatically. There are still many people, young and old, dying from this disease. I needed to reach out to them and tell my story, in the hopes it would help others.

*

A Dangerous Daughter came about through a series of synchronistic events. In 2015 I was selected to take part in an international study on eating disorders, ANGI (Anorexia Nervosa Genetics Initiative). In order to be accepted into the study I supplied blood and saliva samples as well as completing an extensive questionnaire. The results of that research were ground breaking: scientists found eight genetic markers for anorexia nervosa. No longer a mysterious aberration, the markers for anorexia can be present from birth.

We now know that anorexia is a largely genetic, partly metabolic and partly psychological condition. For me and other survivors, this discovery marked an end to the feelings of guilt and responsibility for the years during which my family and I suffered because of the disease. To be able to say, and believe, 'It was not my fault' was supremely liberating.

In late 2019, I was approached by ABC/TV to give an interview about my experience as a survivor of anorexia nervosa. This I did, with some trepidation. The segment was aired on 22 January as part of the ABC/7.30 report. It felt scary to bare my soul, knowing most of my peers knew nothing of the childhood illness that had almost killed me.

But in doing this, I felt I had 'come out' to an unsuspecting world. I also hoped to give hope and courage to patients and their families battling with anorexia. I wanted to show that the sufferer has almost no control over this eating disorder. Rather, it is as if he or she is taken over by a relentless force, which I call "The Voice" in this novel.

Today a child displaying symptoms such as my protagonist, Ivy, did in the mid-1950s, is highly unlikely to be removed from his or her family, as I was. Instead the whole family takes part in treatment, in recognition of the crucial role of the family in the patient's recovery. Professor Erin C Accurso, Clinical Director of the University of California Eating Disorder Program, states: *anorexia nervosa is a complex condition with the highest mortality rate of any psychiatric disorder. Families are the most important resource in recovery, which is why family-based treatment is the gold standard for adolescent anorexia nervosa.*

Statistics from the National Eating Disorder Association for 2020 show that the prevalence of eating disorders in the overall population is sixteen per cent and rising. According to recent estimates, mortality is five times higher in individuals with anorexia nervosa than in the general population.

Throughout this novel, my purpose is to reach out to other sufferers of this insidious disease, and to show readers that anorexia nervosa is an affliction rather than a life choice. The popular view of this condition, as promulgated in the media, is that it is a decision by a (usually) young girl or boy to stop or restrict eating in order to become fashionably thin. In true anorexia nervosa, nothing is further from the truth.

A combination of many factors, particularly the discovery of my analyst's letter, as well as a growing urge to tell my story while there was still time, gave me the courage to write *A Dangerous Daughter.* Was it synchronicity or serendipity that led me to reach out to people who are suffering the same illness that had me in its thrall? I am not a follower of Carl Jung, being a committed Freudian, but Jung's definition of synchronicity as "messages from the soul" appears apt.

A Dangerous Daughter is a fictionalised version of my own story. It is intended to support and inform others suffering from anorexia nervosa, and to show that compassion, not criticism, is the way to healing. Blame and shame have no part in the treatment of the anorexic child or adult.

"Dr B" in the novel is based on my psychoanalyst Dr Ivy Bennett, a highly trained analyst in Freudian psychotherapy specialising in children. I owe my life to the work of Sigmund Freud, and especially to the late Dr Ivy Bennett. I have given her name, Ivy, to my main character.

ACKNOWLEDGEMENTS

This book owes its existence to many who are unaware of the part they have played in its inception. To Dr Christine Brett Vickers, who reached out to me on a hunch during her research into psychoanalysis, goes my gratitude for prompting me to write this book. To Dr June Alexander, my thanks for your encouragement and understanding of the struggle we share.

To my early readers, Dr Joanne Walsh, Richard Davis, Justine Davis and Christopher Edwards, I say thank you for your patience, insights and advice on the early drafts of this novel. You have all played a part in shaping the final product.

I thank my mentor and editor, Laurel Cohn, for your intelligent editing and guidance. You helped to bring coherence and structure to my manuscript, and your deadlines spurred me on when I found the task too daunting.

My sincere thanks to Cilento Publishing, particularly to Leone Sperling for her careful proofreading and warm response to my book, and to my publisher Evan Shapiro for his legendary patience, goodwill, and acute insights. Thank you for taking a chance on *A Dangerous Daughter*, and for bringing her into the world. Thanks to Evan Shapiro of Green Avenue Design for the beautiful cover design.

Thanks to Kaye Aldenhoven and Sandra Thibodeaux from Darwin who have given me feedback on early drafts of this book over the years. Workshops with Randwick Writers' Group and Waverley Writers Group have given me valuable comments on individual chapters. I particularly thank Gabrielle Lord and Marie Manidis, for their encouragement with draft chapters of this book .

Thanks to the organisers of the NT Writers' Festival 2020 for giving me the opportunity to read an excerpt from *A Dangerous Daughter* in the opening addresses of the Festival.

To my extended family who may look for themselves in this book: there may be a whisper of you here and there, but I have carefully crafted this story as fiction to ensure you will not find yourself in these pages. All the characters herein are my own invention, fed by my imagination and the faintest of memories.

As always I am grateful to my children, Justine Davis, Josh Davis and Anna Davis, for whom this book is written. I give thanks for the miracle of your existence. Your love, curiosity and faith in me are the catalysts that continue to inspire me.

Last but not least, my love and thanks to my partner Christopher (Kit) Edwards for his unstinting support and encouragement. It would have been a long lonely road without you.

REFERENCES

262

https://www.qimrberghofer.edu.au/media-releases/australian-researchers-help-identify-first-genes-linked-to-anorexia-nervosa/

https://eatingdisorders.ucsf.edu

https://dinadavisauthor.com/adangerousdaughter

https://thediaryhealer.com

https://freudinoceania.com

https://facebook.com/thebutterflyfoundation

Professor Erin C. Accurso, Nature Genetics Vol 51, UCSF Eating Disorders Program

Fiona Wright, *This Woman is Hysterical*, Meanjin, Winter 2019

GLOSSARY OF YIDDISH WORDS

Note: Spelling of Yiddish words is phonetic, thus can vary in English.

Bar Mitzvah	Boy's coming of age
Bat Mitzvah	Girl's coming of age
Baruch Ata	Blessed art thou (blessings over food, wine, etc.)
Buba	Grandmother
Bubele	Baby
Challah	Plaited bread served on the sabbath
Chutzpa	Daring, giving cheek
Davening	Praying
Gefilte fish	Dish of minced fish balls
Goy	A gentile, non-Jew
Haggadah	Story of the Exodus read at Passover
Ivylie	diminutive of 'Ivy'
Kosher	Ritually cleansed, permitted (of food)
Kugel	Pudding
Kugelhöpf	A round cake laced with chocolate
Matzo	Unleavened bread eaten at Passover
Mazeltov	Congratulations (lit. good fortune)
Meshuggene	Crazy person
Momsa	Bastard (derogative.)
Nebbish	A nobody, a loser
Nu?	Well? So?
Oy Gevalt	Lit. 'woe is me'
Oy Vey	Oh dear, bother, what a shame, etc.
Pesach	Passover
Qvetching	Complaining
Rebbitzin	Rabbi's wife

Schlepped	Hauled, carried
Schule	Synagogue
Schönele	Beautiful one (dimin.)
Seder	Order of service (religious)
Shabbos	Sabbath
Shema	Hear me; evening prayer
Shmutters	Rags
Siddur	Prayer book
Verstinkene	Stinking
Würst	Continental sausage
Yalmuka	Skull cap
Yom Tov	Holy Day

ABOUT THE AUTHOR

Dina Davis is an Australian Author. Her debut novel, *Capriccio*, was shortlisted for the NT Chief Minister's Fiction Award in 2020. Her short stories, articles and poems have appeared in the literary journal *Borderlands* and several anthologies. She has twice been shortlisted for the NT Literary Awards. In 2019 Dina co-authored and edited a non-fiction guide for writers, *Sharing Writing Skills*, published by Ginninderra Press. She is married and has three children.

www.dinadavisauthor.com